WHAT SHE SAW

MARK ROBERTS was born and raised in Liverpool and was educated at St. Francis Xavier's College. He was a teacher for twenty years and for the last ten years has worked as a special-school teacher. He received a *Manchester Evening News* Theatre Award for Best New Play. This is the second novel in the DCI Rosen series after the acclaimed debut, *The Sixth Soul*. Discover more at www.markrobertscrimewriter.com.

Also by Mark Roberts

THE SIXTH SOUL

WHAT SHE SAW

MARK ROBERTS

CORVUS

First published in trade paperback in Great Britain in 2014 by Corvus, an imprint of Atlantic Books Ltd.

10 9 8 7 6 5 4 3 2 1

A CIP catalogue record for this book is available from the British Library.

Trade paperback ISBN: 978 0 85789 832 6
E-book ISBN: 978 0 85789 833 3

Printed in Italy by 🦌 Grafica Veneta SpA

Corvus
An imprint of Atlantic Books Ltd
Ormond House
26–27 Boswell Street
London
WC1N 3JZ

www.corvus-books.co.uk

For my daughter, Eleanor

For thy sweet love remembered such wealth brings
That then I scorn to change my state with kings.

Shakespeare

ACKNOWLEDGEMENTS

I'd like to thank Dr. Chris Grocock, Veronica Stallwood, Sara O'Keeffe and all at Corvus, Peter, Rosie and Jessica Buckman, Linda and Eleanor Roberts.

PROLOGUE

9.22 P.M.

Macy Conner knew it wasn't good for young girls to walk alone on dark nights.

As she reached the corner of her tenement block, Claude House, she saw light flickering on the surfaces of car windows in the street and felt compelled to turn.

There was a car on fire in Bannerman Square. Next to it two figures, silhouettes, moved swiftly from the flames in her direction.

If I can see them. . . She turned the corner and ran. *They've seen me.*

She ran as quickly as she could, panic mounting inside her with each stride. She could hear the echo of their footsteps as they followed her around the corner.

Macy lengthened her stride, gripping the £10 note she was clutching in her damp fist. But they were like lightning, striking closer with each step. She could smell them.

Macy tried to scream but her voice was trapped.

She stumbled, lost her rhythm but kept on her feet.

She could hear their mingled panting on the edge of the breeze.

No one around. Just her. A ten-year-old girl on her own. And them.

And now they were right behind her.

She could feel their anger as they caught up with her. She could smell the petrol as they surrounded her in a cage of flesh.

One behind her. One in front, massive and oozing menace.

In the distance, back on Bannerman Square, she heard the sound of a child screaming.

She looked up into a face wreathed in darkness. His hood was up. And, when she turned back, the other was the same.

She stared down at her feet and the shaking started.

On Bannerman Square, there was an explosion.

A pair of hands dug into her shoulders, each finger pressing into her, enjoying her pain.

A whisper in her ear, sour breath drifting inside her.

'Did you really think you could out-run us, little bitch?'

DAY ONE

28 April

1

10.19 P.M.

Two places. One time. An impossible choice.

As Detective Chief Inspector David Rosen ran towards the brightly lit entrance of Lewisham Hospital, he saw himself reflected in the darkened surface of the glass doors. Late forties, thick-set body, dark eyes and dense black hair plastered to his head by rain, he wished he was as fit and lean as he'd been in his twenties so he could have made it faster from the car.

His reflection vanished as the automatic door slid back and he was inside, searching the direction board for A & E. The paramedic he'd spoken to on the phone had said Thomas Glass had suffered horrific burns but was still conscious and talking.

The kid was an eyewitness. The brutal truth was that his evidence was crucial. That was why Rosen, leader of the murder investigation team, was there and not at the scene of the crime at Bannerman Square.

'David!'

Rosen turned his eyes to a voice he recognized, Detective Sergeant Carol Bellwood. 'This way!' she called.

Rosen caught up with his deputy on a windowless corridor, illuminated by fluorescent strip lights. DS Bellwood, a tall black woman with braided hair drawn tightly into a band at the back of her head, walked ahead of him.

Rosen noticed Bellwood wore a sweat-stained T-shirt, jogging bottoms and trainers beneath her raincoat. She'd been working out in the gym when he'd put through the action stations call.

'Are his mum and dad here?' asked Rosen. He dreaded what awaited them and was filled with sadness and fear for them. Their shared life as parents was irreparably and horrifically changed.

'Not yet.' Rosen and Bellwood exchanged a glance of recognition. In a living nightmare, it was their job to orchestrate order from chaos as quickly as they could.

'You want me to go to the scene now that you've arrived?' asked Bellwood, to the point and as businesslike as ever.

'Gold and Corrigan are already there. Feldman's in charge.'

She nodded. Good. The three core members of Rosen's MIT.

Rosen felt short of breath and his chest was tight. Twenty-three minutes earlier, he'd been in the kitchen of his home in Islington, bottle-feeding his sleep-resisting son; now, he rushed towards nine-year-old Thomas Glass, who'd been missing from his home for eight days.

'What's the word from Bannerman Square?' asked Bellwood.

Rosen thought he heard footsteps following them but when he looked over his shoulder there was no one there. His voice dropped a notch.

'Corrigan's working with Scientific Support. Stevie Jensen's in Gold's car; Gold's talking to him.'

Corrigan, great with finding and handling evidence; Gold, a people person, taking care of the witness.

'Stevie Jensen?' asked Bellwood.

'The teenager who called the paramedics. The Prof's orchestrating the rest of the troops.'

Bellwood had nicknamed DS Feldman 'the Prof' because of his ability to concentrate for hours and retain information photographically. The nickname had stuck and Feldman liked it.

At the ITU they met a female nurse, a beefy blonde in a bottle green NHS uniform. To Rosen, she looked like the bouncer at the door of a low-rent nightclub.

'I'm DCI Rosen and this is DS Carol Bellwood. We're—'

'You're here about Thomas Glass?' interrupted the nurse, whose ID badge read STEPHANIE JONES, and whose picture whispered time had been tough on her.

'Is he still able to speak?' Rosen asked.

'He's fully bandaged and under heavy sedation.'

'Stephanie,' Bellwood said softly, and the nurse turned to look her way. 'Did Thomas say anything when he was brought into the unit?'

'No. He was ventilated.'

Rosen saw Bellwood's shoulders sink and felt the dead weight of her disappointment.

'Can I see him?' asked Rosen. 'Please.'

She looked hard at him.

'You can see him through the glass partition. Follow me.'

They arrived at a window in the resuscitation unit.

Lying on the bed, ventilated and bandaged, was the missing boy. On either side of him, a ward sister and doctor were involved in calm but focused discussion.

Rosen took a deep breath and scraped the barrel of his inner grit. 'Stephanie, did the paramedics tell you what happened when they arrived at Bannerman Square?'

'It was straight into ATLS scenario,' she replied.

'ATLS scenario?' asked Bellwood.

'Advanced trauma life support. Checked his airway, red raw. Got him on the spinal board, into the ambulance. They ventilated him. They got what was left of his clothes off him and saw he had sixty per cent full thickness burns. The boy's fluid balance was wrecked so they hydrated him with a line into his left arm and wrapped him in cling film to stop him leaking to death. Then it was morphine and back here. He's got a thirty per cent chance of living. Not good.'

With rising sorrow, Rosen looked through the glass. The probability was that Thomas's mother and father were about to face the most profound fear of all parents. And it was a fear that Rosen knew first-hand. The memory of his daughter's cot death, eight years earlier, was made fresh by the sight of the young boy. For a moment, he was frozen by terror, sorrow and devastating loss. His mind turned to his wife Sarah, on that terrible night, and the indelible image in his mind, the look in her eyes as she held Hannah in her arms, the moment she said, 'She's dead.'

Rosen forced himself into the present.

'OK, Carol. We need to beat it back fast to Bannerman Square. I need to catch up personally with this kid, Stevie.' Rosen turned to the nurse, one more thing on his mind. 'Tell your head of security. I'm putting an armed guard on the door here.'

Bellwood's phone was out and she pressed speed dial. 'I'll get onto CO19, David.'

'CO19?' asked the nurse.

'Central firearms control,' explained Bellwood.

'And we want all your CCTV footage, interior and exterior, Thomas's journey into this hospital – everything you've got,' insisted Rosen.

'An armed guard?' asked the nurse.

'Whoever did this wants him dead. They've had him over a week. If you'd done this to him, would you want him alive and talking?'

2

10.32 P.M.

At the wheel of his BMW, before firing up the engine, Rosen made a call on his iPhone. HOME.

After the third ring, he heard his wife Sarah's voice, tired but relaxed. 'Hi, David. You OK?'

He struggled to speak. 'Well. . .'

'David?' Her voice was laced with concern.

'How's Joe,' he asked. 'Is he OK?'

'He's fine,' she reassured him. 'Fast asleep in bed.'

'Go and check him for me. Please.'

'OK.' He heard her footsteps ascending the stairs. 'Thomas Glass?' she asked.

'It's looking bad.' Rosen wondered if Thomas's parents had arrived yet, if they'd seen their son.

He recognized the familiar creak of Joe's bedroom door opening.

'I'm in his room. The night-light's on. He's doing that thing when he wrinkles his nose when he's content. I'll lower the phone.'

Rosen listened to the sound of his baby son breathing and felt a dead weight of anxiety vanish from him.

'OK now, David?'

'Thanks, Sarah. I'm sorry—'

'I can only imagine what you've seen tonight. I'd be exactly the same if I was in your shoes.'

He turned on the ignition. Parental anxiety calmed, time took over as his tormentor-in-chief.

'Get going, matey,' said Sarah. 'Go!'

She hung up and, seconds later, Rosen was in fourth gear at sixty miles per hour.

3

10.47 P.M.

When Rosen arrived at Bannerman Square, he made a mental snapshot of the rain-soaked scene. Officers, plainclothes and uniformed, outnumbered the handful of curious stragglers hanging around the scene-of-crime tape.

Claude House, the building overlooking the square, was illuminated on each floor, and Rosen was reminded how dark it could be on a wet night in the Walthamstow tenement where he grew up.

Gold – a tall, bulky Welshman, an ex-rugby player with a shaven head and sharp blue eyes – raised a hand in salute and pointed to his unmarked car. He was as tough as he looked, but equally friendly.

As he joined him, Rosen looked over at the teenage boy shifting uncomfortably in the back of Gold's car

'Stevie Jensen.' Gold's melodic voice seemed to threaten to break out into song on each syllable.

'What's happening with him?'

'Local hero, he is. Two separate witnesses from the flats stepped forward to stand up for him, thinking we were pulling him in as a suspect. Saved Thomas Glass from that.' He nodded in the direction of a burned-out Renault Megane.

As Gold opened the back door of his car, Rosen thought he could hear Gold's tightly fitting shirt and trousers squeaking against the density of his body.

Rosen gave the kid a brief, avuncular smile as he slid into the back seat beside him.

'I'm DCI Rosen.'

He pulled the door shut as Gold took the driver's seat directly in front of the boy.

Stevie was good-looking, with platinum-dyed hair peeping out from the bottom of his baseball cap. He had light bandaging on both hands. He looked pale and nervous, like he wanted to go somewhere quiet and cry himself to sleep. There was a smell of petrol and smoke around him.

'Thank you for what you've done this evening,' Rosen said, gently. 'Are your hands OK? How are the burns?'

'I just want to go home now. Can I? Please.'

'We won't keep you much longer.'

'He took my phone offa me.' Stevie indicated Gold. 'Can I have it back?'

'I told him to, Stevie. I couldn't be here myself because I was over at the hospital where the little boy is, so I ordered all phones to be confiscated and I'll tell you why.'

Rosen reached up and switched on the car's interior light so he could look into the boy's eyes and have a shot at bridge building. His first impression of Stevie was clear. He was part of south London's unsung majority, a downright decent kid.

'First off,' said Rosen. 'I don't know what's going to happen to Thomas, but I do know he's still alive and that's down to you. You gave him a chance.'

He paused and looked away, letting the silence do its trick. Outside, DS Bellwood's attention was nailed to something to the right of the blackened Megane, and Rosen's curiosity was piqued. She was looking at a low wall and the light from her torch picked out an eye painted onto the bricks. He looked back at Stevie.

'Well,' said Stevie, nervously, nodding at the shaven dome of Gold's head. 'Yeah, so why'd he pocket my phone?'

Rosen remained silent until Stevie looked directly into his eyes.

'You're a witness at a serious crime scene. You could be the key to catching whoever's done this. You sit in the car, waiting, texting, talking, you pass information out there, and within an hour it's all over Facebook, and whoever's done this knows what you know. Whereas we'd like to keep it to ourselves.'

'I didn't think of it like that.'

Rosen let the significance settle in his head.

'My mum,' said Stevie. 'She's a worrier. She'll be pulling her hair out.'

Gold turned his head and looked at Stevie. 'Honestly now, I called your mum and told her everything was OK.'

Stevie looked mournfully at Claude House, and Rosen lay a hand gently on the boy's sleeve. Seeing the pleading look in the boy's eyes, as Stevie turned to look at him again, Rosen knew he'd be better off talking to him in his comfort zone.

'I need to talk to you, Stevie. How about we do it in your flat, with your mum there?'

'Yes please, Mr Rosen,' said the boy without hesitation.

'DC Gold,' said Rosen.

Gold turned his head. 'Yes, boss?'

'Give Stevie his phone back. We're just nipping over to his place.'

4

10.51 P.M.

The door of Stevie's ground-floor flat flew open as soon as the boy rang the bell.

His mother gasped, looked him up and down, and threw her arms around him.

He wriggled in her embrace and protested gently, 'Mum, there's a copper behind me.'

Rosen stifled the smile on his face into deadpan as he caught the woman's eye. Without a trace of make-up, she was a small, bottle-black-haired woman with sad green eyes that seemed too big for her thin, oval face. She reminded Rosen very much of his own mother.

'You can be proud of your son, Ms Jensen.'

She nodded. Of course she was proud of him. She let him out of her arms and looked with some horror at his bandaged hands.

'Oh my God!'

'I'm all right, Mum.'

Rosen felt the intensity of Stevie's awkwardness and steered the moment away.

'Can we all go inside, Ms Jensen?'

'I'm going to the loo,' said Stevie, heading off to the bathroom.

His mother went into the kitchen to switch on the kettle, leaving

Rosen alone in the small living room at the front of the flat. He looked around the walls and read the dynamic of the family. There were framed pictures of Stevie at all stages of his life and in most of them he was dressed in a running kit. Stevie, aged nine, holding up a gold medal at a track event; Stevie, aged thirteen, first across the line. . . On the mantelpiece, there were gold-plated trophies and, at the little table near the window, GCSE Chemistry and Biology books were stacked neatly alongside blank revision cards and a stationery set.

The door opened and Rosen turned as Stevie's mother came back into the room. Rosen extended his hand and said, 'I'm DCI David Rosen.'

As they shook, her hand felt small and fragile inside his.

'Marie Jensen,' she responded. 'Some neighbours told me he carried that kid away from the burning car.'

'Yes,' said Rosen. 'It was a brave and selfless act.' In the background, the water in the kettle began to boil, and the toilet flushed.

'His dad died in a traffic accident when he was five. I think he must've thought about his dad when he saw the kid. He's a very feeling boy, my Stevie.'

Stevie drifted into the room, his eyes red with the tears he'd shed in the privacy of the bathroom. Rosen looked away and pointed to a small sofa.

'You want to sit down, Stevie?'

His mother walked out of the room. 'I'll fetch in some tea.'

Rosen sat on an armchair adjacent to Stevie and said, 'I'm well impressed with your athletics trophies.'

Stevie looked directly at him, suddenly animated, distracted from the trauma of recent hours. 'That's what I want to do. My coach said I could compete in the nationals.' The boy suddenly winced and stretched his fingers, dissipating the shudder of pain in his palms. A siren rose and fell in the far distance.

'GCSEs next month?' prompted Rosen, nodding towards the window and the table of books.

'Yeah. Working like a dog, me.'

'What do you want to do, Stevie?'

'Go to uni and be a success. Make Mum proud of me. Take care of her, like.'

'You looking to join the police then?'

'No way, man.' Stevie laughed briefly.

'That's a shame,' said Rosen. 'For us.'

Stevie looked questioningly at Rosen as he took out his phone.

'You OK if I tape our conversation?'

'No probs.'

Rosen pressed 'record' and Stevie stared into space, as if reliving the memory in the thin air around him.

'Just tell me what happened – everything, OK?' Rosen sat back, feigned relaxed-for-a-fireside-chat.

'I was sitting at that table and, like, revising like crazy for me GCSE Chemistry, wasn't I? I look outta the window. There's a burning car on the square. So I went out. Next thing, the car door swings open and. . . It was a little kid and all I thought was, *That car's gonna blow, man; I've gotta help him!* When I got to him, he'd crawled himself into this big puddle on the ground, the stink of petrol and burning was, like, rank. But I grabs him by the coat and trousers, he was screaming, crying, I couldn't look at him, then, boom! The car went up but by then we were, like, safe and I lay him down on the ground and that's when I heard him say it.'

'What did he say, Stevie?'

'He said, "They're gonna do it again!"'

Rosen held the boy's gaze. 'He said "they"? He definitely said "they"?'

'Definitely. They. Not he, not she. They, definitely they.'

'You're one hundred per cent sure?'

'My adrenaline was pumping, for a second or two, my senses were all, like, super sharp. I could've heard a flea sneeze down Oxford Street.'

'Did he say anything else?'

'No. But I've got something to show.' Stevie looked nervously at the door, then he took out his phone and indicated to the space next to him on the sofa.

As Rosen joined him, Stevie's mother entered the room with two teas. Stevie paused in his scrolling.

'I'm sorry, Mum. Not now. Please. OK?'

Without a word, she left.

'I don't want my mum to see this. It's too. . . upsetting. Soon as I'd called the ambulance, I did this on me phone. You ready?'

Rosen nodded. 'I'm ready, Stevie.'

Stevie pressed 'play'.

On the screen in front of him, Rosen saw Thomas Glass on the pavement in Bannerman Square, his body wet, steaming and shaking, his face a blackened mask.

Rosen felt something clutching at his scalp, something sharp and metallic as his mind spiralled back for a moment to a time when he'd seen his first murder victim, a young woman with her head almost completely hacked off. Rosen clenched his fists at his sides, then focused on the screen again.

'I asked him questions. I wanted to get whatever evidence I could.'

'Good thinking, Stevie.'

Stevie had zoomed in on Thomas's face. His voice came through clearly: 'Can you hear me? Nod if you can, OK.'

Thomas had nodded, sodium streetlight picking out his charred face. He had no eyelids, just red raw whites, one blacked at the centre.

'Is your name Thomas Glass?' The boy nodded. 'Were you snatched?' A pause and then Thomas nodded again. 'Do you know who abducted you?' This time the boy had nodded as if he wanted to shout *Yes!* 'Was it a woman what snatched you?' He shook his head slowly. 'A man snatched you?' The sound of an approaching siren, an ambulance, grew louder and louder. 'Was it a man?' Stevie pushed and, distressed, Thomas nodded again. Then he had begun to scream and the film had stopped.

'I couldn't take any more. I had to turn my back,' said Stevie. 'I feel bad, like, turning away from him.'

'Don't. You've been brilliant.'

Stevie looked at Rosen, uncertain.

'I mean it, Stevie. You've been brave and shown presence of mind under duress. Your mother has every reason to be proud of you.'

Stevie nodded, digested Rosen's words.

'Send it to my phone, Stevie.' Rosen gave him his number and, within a few moments, received the sequence on his iPhone.

'You want me to delete it, Mr Rosen?'

When Rosen saw that the film had arrived safely to his phone, he said, 'Yes, please. When you came onto the square, you didn't see anyone near the car, or running away from the car?'

'Not a soul. I got back from a run around half seven, the Renault wasn't there then. Half eightish, I was revising, no car. About an hour later, there it was. On fire.'

'Anything else, Stevie?' asked Rosen, gently.

Stevie shook his head and Rosen knew that, had he spoken, the boy would have dissolved into tears. Quickly, Stevie stood up and left the room.

His mother came back in, carrying the tea.

'I have a son, Ms Jensen, a baby. I hope he grows up to be as decent as your boy,' said Rosen.

She beamed with pride. 'Thank you, Mr Rosen.'

'I apologize. I can't stay for tea.' Rosen smiled and left in a hurry.

5

11.01 P.M.

On Bannerman Square, the burned-out wreck of the Renault Megane rose into the air, lifted by a claw attached to the back of a large Ford pick-up. It was the start of its journey for forensic examination at Clerkwell Road Garage. Rosen reckoned it could still yield useful evidence.

Bellwood was staring at the wall next to which the car had burned.

Rosen approached on her blind side, asking, 'What is it, Carol?'

'I'm not sure.'

She pointed a beam of torchlight at the wall. It showed a piece of graffiti that, at first glance, looked like the scrawl on the nearby DLR station.

Rosen crouched for a better view.

It was the painted eye he'd glimpsed from the back of Gold's car. The low wall on which the eye had been painted was all that remained of a 1960s flowerbed. The quality of the artwork was impressive.

He broke it down into its component parts. The oval outline, top and bottom, was a thick band of black. Within the outline, the white of the eye was dappled with dark pinpoints that created a cast of grey within the white, a shadow effect that suggested the passage of light and made the eye seem alive.

'Well?' said Bellwood.

Rosen glanced up at her.

'I *think* it's good,' he said, 'but you're the art buff. What do you think?'

Off duty, Bellwood spent a lot of time in London's galleries, and had strong opinions that were focused and knowledgeable. Rosen seized on her enthusiasm.

'Graffiti art,' she said. 'It grabbed me as I was passing it by.'

He turned his attention back to the eye and listened.

'It's full of shadows. And they're well executed. You get this kind of detail, this kind of play of light in the work of top-drawer artists. This isn't just some snot-nosed kid looking for their fifteen minutes of fame in the neighbourhood. This work shows an understanding of technique and perspective.'

Rosen counted. From the iris to the oval outline there were fifteen lines that created the effect of the spokes of a wheel, narrow at the pupil and thickening as they progressed to the outline. She was right. In each line, the perspective was perfect.

Rosen heard Bellwood shiver on an in-breath and he wondered if it was because of the cold night and her damp gym clothes, or the image on the wall. She stooped beside him and gathered her coat together at her throat.

'Look at the centre of the white – there's a perfect circle, the pupil with a dash of white dead centre, the suggestion of light caught amidst the passing shadows.'

Rosen took his iPhone from his pocket and started snapping the eye. In spite of his ingrained dislike of anything linked to graffiti, he said, 'You're right, Carol, this is quality work.'

'It's going to be an uphill slog with the locals,' said Bellwood. 'I've heard there were over a hundred people at the tape at one point, and nobody saw the car being driven onto the square, nobody saw the driver get away from the vehicle, nobody saw the car being torched. Several people saw the car burning – the same people who saw Stevie carrying Thomas to safety.'

Rosen looked at Claude House and did a quick calculation. 'There must be a hundred-plus potential witnesses in there. Eight in the morning, we start door-to-dooring.'

'David!' The sound of a no-nonsense Liverpudlian accent drew Rosen's attention to DS Corrigan, who was approaching quickly.

'What's up?'

Corrigan, the rock at the heart of Rosen's murder investigation team, was agitated. Dark blond and with a hardened face that matched his track record in hand-to-hand violent confrontations, he stopped in front of Rosen with a look like he wanted to kill.

'Fucking bad news. Check it out, David.' Corrigan pointed at a wall behind him, a wall overlooking the scene. 'Premeditated. Bastards. That's what's up.'

6

11.11 P.M.

A long plume of vapour streamed from Corrigan's nostrils. He was calming slowly but was still livid. Rosen gazed at the source of his trusted colleague's anger and immediately shared in his frustration.

On the back wall of a warehouse yard was a rectangular metal cage. Inside was a CCTV camera positioned to look directly over Bannerman Square. The cage and camera were mangled. Rosen felt his heart begin to race.

'I just phoned CCTV central control,' said Corrigan, sourly. 'The camera went down this afternoon. Nice timing eh, David?'

Deep down, Rosen smiled for the briefest moment. It never failed to amaze or amuse him how Corrigan, a detective with twenty years on the darkest streets of Liverpool and London, still took every criminal's spoilers so personally. As Bellwood was to calm, Corrigan was to passion; it was a good combination.

'You're right,' said Rosen, shrugging, drawing in Corrigan. 'It's no coincidence. Come and have a look at this.'

Rosen led Corrigan to the painted eye and flicked on a light.

'We're going to have to get Tracey Leung from the Gangs Unit on board,' said Rosen.

'How come?' asked Bellwood.

'Yeah,' said Corrigan. 'Why?'

'She knows the streets. Vandalized CCTV. Graffiti. We need to know who could've spray-painted this masterpiece,' said Rosen. 'I'll call her now.'

Rosen took out his phone, seeing the turning wheels of Bellwood's mind expressed on her face.

'Tracey Leung?' Bellwood pressed him. Rosen found her on speed dial.

'I heard a story she got her arm tattooed on an undercover op,' said Corrigan.

'Yeah, I heard that,' replied Bellwood. 'I reckon it's just a story.'

Rosen was through to Tracey Leung's voicemail.

'You've reached Tracey Leung. Leave a message. I'll get back to you.'

After the beep, he said, 'Tracey, it's David Rosen. Ring me as soon as you pick up this message. I need your help.'

Rosen observed Corrigan and Bellwood examining the eye like a couple in a gallery.

'This is bad shit and I don't like it,' said Corrigan, as he glanced back at the trashed CCTV.

'Like you say, bad shit,' responded Bellwood. 'But all the same, very well made.'

DAY TWO

29 April

7

2.28 A.M.

For a moment, Rosen stayed at the window, observing the scene in the resuscitation unit. John and Emily Glass sat side by side, their backs to the door, gazing at their bandaged son as horrific reality dawned fast.

On the other side of the bed, a tall, grey-haired man, with a patrician air, spoke to them. Emily collapsed into tears. Rosen considered backing off but remembered the words Thomas had said to Stevie Jensen: 'They're going to do it again.' And he had known his abductor.

They were a well-dressed couple, good-looking and wealthy. Rosen knew his company was a successful one: Glass Equity, lending money to people who saw his adverts in the commercial breaks on daytime TV.

With no ransom demand and the recent turn of events on Bannerman Square, a financial motive to the kidnapping was dead in the water.

John Glass glanced over his shoulder and his eyes met Rosen's. The tempest of competing emotions on his face consolidated into hard-boiled antagonism, and Rosen knew that he was the cause of this reaction. The relationship between senior investigating officer and father of the missing boy – now victim – had been bad from the word go, and with each passing day of Thomas's disappearance, John

Glass had grown more entrenched in the personal blame he laid at Rosen's feet.

Glass mouthed something and turned his face away.

Rosen nodded at the sombre-looking CO19 officer at the door, his Heckler & Koch in both hands held diagonally across his bulletproofed torso.

As the tall man came out of the resuscitation unit, Rosen clocked his name badge. MR CAMPBELL, PLASTICS CONSULTANT.

He shut the door and asked Rosen, 'Who are you?', his voice like an old-fashioned TV newsreader.

Rosen showed Mr Campbell his warrant card and went for a second opinion. 'How do you think he'll do, Mr Campbell?'

'The odds are stacked against him. The initial assessment was flawed. He's got seventy per cent burns, a twenty per cent chance of living. That's what I've just had to tell his parents.' The specialist nodded to him and walked away.

Emily Glass's forehead was on her knees, her hands linked around the back of her skull. Her husband put a hand on her shoulder. She lifted her hand and threw him off sharply.

In the eye of the crisis, Rosen observed to himself, *an unhappily married couple.*

He knocked on the door and John Glass stood up.

As Glass moved from his son's bedside, Rosen recalled how, after Thomas had been absent from home for two days, the case of a missing child had converted into a potential murder enquiry, and the ball had passed to him.

Glass closed the door and eyeballed Rosen. 'Happy now?'

'Whatever do you mean, Mr Glass?'

'At least he's turned up. That's progressed your investigation, hasn't it?'

'No, Mr Glass. At this moment in time, I'm feeling many things, and happy certainly isn't one of them.'

'You in charge, DCI Rosen?' His name and rank spoken like an obscenity. 'You see, I'm in charge of over a thousand-plus people and when I issue an order that order is followed; when I issue an instruction it gets followed and results happen fast. So, you're either not issuing the right orders to the *handful* of coppers in your team, which makes you incompetent; or the people beneath you either aren't listening to you or aren't capable of doing their jobs—'

'Mr Glass!'

'I haven't finished. The end result being' – Glass pointed at his son – 'and I blame you.'

Rosen waited, watched Glass breathing hard.

'Market forces don't apply to criminal investigations,' Rosen answered. 'I wish I could, but I can't control human—'

'Nature. Yes, I know. You've told me time and time again.'

Yes and you're the Wizard of Oz, thought Rosen. *Great and mighty.*

'There's been an informational development and we need to talk,' he said now, steering Glass away from the recurring argument.

Emily returned her hand to her head and her tears fell faster, her sobbing louder. Inside Rosen's head, stress and pressure rocketed.

He suppressed the words *loan shark,* the memory of his childhood neighbours in Walthamstow crucified by versions of John Glass, and silently recited a simple mantra: *Victim's father, victim's father, victim's father. . .*

'Go on, Rosen, hit me with your big development.'

The expression on Glass's face told Rosen there was no room for sorrow or sympathy.

'Mr Glass, the list you supplied of people who know Thomas and who Thomas knows. Is it definitive?'

'Yes, it's definitive.'

The first thing Rosen had asked John Glass for was a list of names of people who knew Thomas, and he had supplied twenty-three. All of them had been able to provide cast-iron alibis.

'I need you to do something for me, as soon as you can, please,' said Rosen, holding Glass's hostile gaze. 'I need you to go through all your contact details and see if there are any names you've missed out.'

'It's a definitive list.'

It isn't, thought Rosen. *It can't be.*

'Mr Glass, I'd like you to supply me with the contact details of everyone you know, both business and personal.'

'Everyone?'

'Everyone.'

'There are people on that list in Glasgow, people who've never been within miles of Thomas!'

'We need to catch whoever's done this—'

'It's too late for my son!'

At the sound of his raised voice, Emily Glass lifted her head and turned her face towards her husband.

He took a deep breath and spoke more softly, 'You're useless, Rosen, worse than useless, actually.'

Rosen focused on Emily Glass, weeping at her child's side.

'Thomas indicated to the boy who helped him that he knew his abductor and that that person was male.'

As the information sank in, Glass said, 'I have databases. I'll ask Julian Parker, my PA, to email them to you.'

'Thank you.'

'No one I know would do such a thing as this.'

'You've never been surprised, shocked even, by the action of any individual who you know?'

'Not to this degree. It's unthinkable, Rosen.'

'Mr Glass, unthinkable as it is, it's happened. Someone's responsible. I need your help. I've got to nail them. Fast.'

Emily Glass sat up and reached out a hand to touch her son's arm. Her hand hovered over his bandaged skin and then fell back into her lap.

Both men watched the tender moment and Glass looked at Rosen, mystified.

'She wants to touch him,' explained Rosen. 'But she's terrified of hurting him.'

In the silence, something shifted in Glass's expression.

'Why do you make me feel like this is somehow my fault?' Anger welled up in Glass's eyes.

Rosen was amazed by the question and took a moment to get the measure of his tone right.

'If I've done or said anything to make you feel like that, I assure you it was never my intention. And I'm deeply sorry you feel like that.'

Glass took out his mobile and turned his back on Rosen. Within seconds, he was connected to his PA.

'Julian,' said Glass. 'Not good, not good at all. Now, listen, I've been told I've got to submit all our databases to the police – every contact, business and private, right?' He turned and looked at Rosen, his PA's raised voice leaking from the phone.

'Everything, Julian. Every single contact.' He turned his attention away from the phone. 'You've got DCI Rosen's email address. Get onto it!'

Glass closed the call down and turned to Rosen. 'Happy now?'

'I'm going back to work, Mr Glass.'

'That's very good of you, Rosen. Thank you, all my cares just lifted away.'

As Rosen walked away, he felt his phone vibrate in his pocket. The display read: Clerkwell Road Garage. He picked up.

'DCI Rosen, I've got some news for you.' It was Alan Carter, civilian forensic expert on burned-out vehicles. 'The entire search isn't over, but we've got some initial findings to present to you on the Renault Megane from Bannerman Square.'

8

2.54 A.M.

In the hospital car park, just as Rosen took out his phone to call Bellwood and see where she was, he heard her voice approaching from the darkness behind him.

'David, I went back and spoke to Stephanie, the nurse on ITU.'

'Oh, yes?' He recalled the nurse's folded arms, the bulk of her physique, the pugnacious cast of her face.

'What are you smiling at?' asked Bellwood, perplexed, as they got into Rosen's car.

'When I was a kid I was a keen amateur boxer – Red Triangle Boxing Club, Walthamstow. My absolute boyhood hero was a British heavyweight, Joe Bugner. Stephanie looks like him.'

Bellwood laughed. 'I'm glad you didn't tell her.'

'Yeah, me too. I'd be in A and E myself now. How'd you get on, Carol?'

'Stephanie had a Damascus moment after you left to speak to Thomas's parents. I asked about the journey from the ambulance to the resuscitation unit. She said he made quite a few noises but nothing they could pin down as speech. After all, how could he be understood? He was hooked up to a ventilator.'

'But—?' Rosen scented significance in Bellwood's manner but didn't know whether it was just wishful thinking. If there was a god to which he could have prayed for a crumb of information, he'd have raised his arms and talked in tongues.

'She said the boy's mood altered on the way to the resus. It was like he'd seen or heard something that spooked him. She thought he was going into heart failure.'

'Did Stephanie see anything that could have affected Thomas?'

'She thinks she saw the door to A and E reception close. So there could have been someone else on the corridor, David.'

Bellwood had a gift for making silence comfortable, particularly around witnesses. In every case they worked, she had yielded details that otherwise would have been lost through sieves of memory. The bitterness in Rosen's mouth, left over from the conversation with John Glass, eased off.

'Do they have CCTV on that corridor?'

'No, but they've got it at the front in A and E reception.'

A grim possibility formed in Rosen's mind.

'Then we need to see that CCTV footage and we need twenty-four-hour surveillance in A and E holding and reception. Order the footage; I'll speak to Baxter, ask him to release a couple of DCs. When they're assigned, you fill them in and they can cover the surveillance, twenty-four-seven: four hours on, four hours off. I bet you the perpetrators have already got their beady little eyes on A and E. Let's be waiting for them.'

9

3.24 A.M.

There was something about the space between the bare concrete walls of Clerkwell Road Garage that turned the air bitterly cold. The gas heaters, dotted around the barn-like space, did nothing to touch the chill. Rosen clutched at the collar of his white protective suit and Bellwood's breath formed a gentle mist.

'Come this way,' said Alan Carter, footsteps echoing.

Dead centre of the garage, the burned-out Megane looked tiny. Its charred frame looked like a surreal sculpture, devoid of any of the interior features except the roasted remains of half a steering wheel and a dashboard.

'They're absolute idiots, you know,' said Carter.

Rosen had noticed before the way Carter poured unwanted attention at Bellwood, and he smiled now at the way she made his admiring gaze drift past her. He guessed it was a skill she'd developed in her teens.

'Who?' asked Bellwood. 'Who are absolute idiots?' She guided Carter's attention towards Rosen.

'Anyone who thinks they can destroy all the forensic evidence in a car simply by burning it out.' Carter, a skinny man with heavily pockmarked cheeks, emphasized his point by jabbing his finger at his temple and then at the car.

A door opened on the adjacent wall and a particularly tall woman in her mid-thirties emerged, white-suited, platinum-blonde hair with a navy-blue parting. Her immaculately applied make-up made her seem strangely at odds with the oil-tainted space.

However, thought Rosen, *you walk the space like you were born in a garage.*

'Meryl Southall.' Carter introduced the woman. The name rang a bell but Rosen could make no definitive connection.

'Hi, Meryl,' said Bellwood.

Southall nodded at Bellwood in dour recognition.

To the left of the Megane there was a long metal table on which sat aluminium bowls full of blackened dust, and a range of sieves with different-sized meshes.

'We've been through everything that was left of the upholstery, front seats and back, and all we came up with was dust.'

Meryl Southall joined them, her bright red fingernails visible beneath latex gloves.

'Who is she?' Rosen whispered to Bellwood, uneasy about information being exchanged under the nose of a woman he couldn't place.

'Meryl's a telecommunications technician from Satellite Forensic Services,' explained Bellwood. 'Big Spurs fan, like you, David.'

I didn't know we needed her help, thought Rosen. *And I certainly didn't ask for it.*

As if reading Rosen's mind, Carter said, 'Mr Baxter, your boss, was down here earlier, seeing how things were progressing. He gave the all clear to bring Meryl on board when we showed him what we'd found.'

Baxter was the duty chief superintendent. In the decades he'd known him, Rosen had never seen the budget-orientated tightwad be open-handed with his own money, or the money he managed for the Met. *The development with Thomas,* thought Rosen, *must've rattled Baxter's cage for him to have given the go-ahead to employ the services of a pricey outfit like Satellite Forensic Services.*

Rosen's irritation over his intervention and the lack of communication around it was counterbalanced by the prospect of something significant having surfaced in the Megane.

'What have you got for me, Alan?'

'Two letters on the chassis – M and C – didn't get blitzed off the metal when the car went up.'

'Carol, Stolen Vehicles. . .'

She was already on her mobile, finding space away from the group to make the call.

'So, what's come up from the car?' he pressed.

'The fire was started inside the vehicle,' said Carter. 'From the back seat. It wasn't doused on the outside. Whoever did this wasn't taking any chances. He, they, wanted this kid dead. They were careful about where they started the fire, but not so careful about sealing it as they got away – they left the rear door ajar and unlocked. If you notice the pattern of the charring on the rear frame of the car, the densest flames were there. This is where the worst damage was done.'

Rosen looked through the empty windows at the way the metal was twisted in the lower half of the rear of the car, how the structure was blackened but slightly less damaged as it touched the roof.

'It was lucky the thing blew before the fire fighters got there,' observed Carter.

'Go on,' encouraged Rosen.

'Because of this.'

Rosen turned as Meryl Southall spoke. She held out a small metal bowl inside which sat a lump of shrivelled plastic and buckled metal. It was the remains of a mobile phone. 'If the fire fighters had sprayed the car with their aqueous film-forming foam, it could've got through the crack in this little baby and ruined the electrical circuit inside.'

She picked the phone up with tweezers and turned it round. There was a gap in the plastic, where the casing for the battery and SIM card had buckled away from the main body of the phone.

'The casing's useless,' said Southall, 'but I may be able to do something with the SIM card. I'm not promising, but I've seen worse than this and pulled info from the SIM.'

Rosen was silenced by wild hope.

'Well, say something,' said Southall.

'It's a Nokia C2-01, manufactured in early 2010 and on the market that autumn.'

'How do you know that?' Southall sounded impressed.

'It's one of the phones Thomas Glass took with him when he walked out of his family home. It's the cheapest of the three phones, the one that mattered least if it got lost because it didn't cost as much as his iPhone and BlackBerry.'

If they wanted him to burn to death in the back of a car, why did they leave him with his mobile phone? Rosen asked himself. *He could have called for help.*

Bellwood came back, pocketing her phone.

'Anything?' asked Rosen.

'Three Meganes reported taken without the owner's permission from the day before Thomas Glass went missing, one of them with the licence plate MC561 KAD. The other two are still missing.'

'Where from?'

'Forest Ridge Drive, off Croydon Road, just on the edge of outer London.'

Rosen nodded. 'That puts the stolen car within five miles of the Glasses' house.' He turned to Southall. 'How long do you think you'll be with the SIM?'

'Depends,' she said. 'Be as quick as I can, but it mightn't be good news.'

'Thanks, Meryl,' said Rosen. 'The sooner the better.'

She nodded. Rosen and Bellwood walked away. Then, Rosen

stopped and turned. 'Meryl, do me a favour?' he said. 'Drop every-thing, do that phone and nothing else? Please?'

'It's a king-sized pain in the arse. But all right.'

'Thanks, Meryl, you're a star.'

10

5.30 A.M.

At five-thirty in the morning, Rosen arrived home with the intention of grabbing a few hours' sleep. When he entered the hall, he heard the sound of the television playing in the living room and caught sight of his own reflection in the mirror. Just over nine hours earlier, he'd left the house looking reasonably dressed; now, he looked like he'd been on a drinking binge: his shirt was out on the left, top three buttons undone, tie skewed to the right and knotted way below his collarbone. When he'd become a policeman, it was the first chance he'd had to afford or wear decent clothes. But he had the knack of making the smartest threads look like charity shop rejects.

His wife, Sarah, walked out from the kitchen. 'David?'

'Hi, Sarah.'

She kissed him on the cheek and turned on the wall light. The smile crashed from her face. He had worked for eighteen of the previous twenty-four hours and it showed.

'You look exhausted. Here.'

She took the small Tupperware box from him, the one she'd sent him out with the previous morning. Rice salad, the fourth week of the diet she'd insisted he go on.

'How's the baby?' he asked, his hope that Joe would be awake disappearing fast.

Sarah pushed him gently into the living room, where he flopped onto the nearest armchair. There wasn't a piece of him that didn't ache.

'He had a *slightly* high temperature last night—' started Sarah.

'He's got a temperature?' Rosen sat up, anxious, his instinct to go to his son sharp.

'Just before eleven last night, he woke up crying. I had to strip him off and sponge him down. . .'

'Meningitis?'

Sarah laughed, 'God, you're so dramatic, David. No, it's teething. You know, those little white things we chew with?'

'OK, OK, I take your point.' Rosen felt himself smiling, relieved after the flash of parental panic.

'I've just fed him. He's asleep, he's great.'

In the corner of the room, Bannerman Square came onto the BBC News 24 channel. Rosen's attention locked on to the TV. A series of now all-too-familiar images played out as the reporter narrated the background story. Pictures of Thomas in school uniform, the school he attended, the palatial house he lived in, his parents, his father's TV adverts, replicas of the clothes he'd worn and the phones he'd taken on the day he went missing, came up one by one on screen.

'The disappearance of Thomas Glass,' said the reporter, 'was initially thought to be a kidnap for ransom plot. When no ransom demand came, his multi-millionaire father's connections with the Conservative Party provoked speculation that the abduction was politically motivated and that terrorists were responsible.'

Library footage played of a press conference in which Emily Glass wept and pleaded: 'Please, he's the only child we have, we'll ever have. We went through IVF.' John Glass, at her side, had looked uncomfortable at the release of such personal information.

Rosen sighed and turned off the television with the remote. He had hardly seen Sarah for days, and could have kicked himself for being hooked to the TV now.

'It's been all over the news about Thomas,' said Sarah.

'What's the media making of it?'

'A big deal. You remember the scene near the end of *Frankenstein*?'

David sighed. 'The torch-wielding mob?'

'That's the one, love. I heard a phone-in on Capital Radio. People are demanding the return of the death penalty. The consensus is it's a paedophile gang.'

'Well,' said David. 'They're not going to get the death penalty, and the consensus is wrong. Whoever's done this has just broken every protocol in the paedophile handbook: do not leave the body in a public place; do not do anything to attract attention; if not inclined to kill within twenty-four hours, do not give the child a chance of surviving. . . I could go on.'

'Have you seen his parents?'

'It was terrible. I told his father Thomas knew the person who took him.'

The painted eye flashed through his mind.

'How's his mother?' asked Sarah.

'Distraught.' He recalled how she'd thrown her husband's hand away.

'David, you're in the room but you're miles away. What's up?'

'I'm dead tired.' *They're going to do it again.* The idea rolled around his mind and his eyes closed. Darkness invaded his senses. Sarah tapped him on the shoulder and his eyes flew open.

'Have you eaten?'

'I've got no appetite.' For once in his life it was true. 'I'm just exhausted.'

'Well, come on then, David, bed.'

He walked up the stairs with Sarah right behind him.

'What time's the alarm clock set for?' he asked.

'Eight.'

He stopped at Joe's bedroom door and went straight to the Moses basket where his son slept. A soft glow from his night-light played on his skin and his little mouth pouted and smacked in the contentment of sleep. Love rose up inside David and, with that love, renewed determination. He kissed his son's forehead. The touch and the smell of a happy, healthy baby soothed the jaggedness inside him. Quietly, he said, 'I'm sorry I didn't see you awake yesterday. Or the day before.' He hadn't had waking contact with his son since Tuesday. It was now Thursday.

'I've missed you, little one,' said David. He felt the weight of Sarah's hand on his back.

As Rosen undressed, he pictured the sinister eye on the wall and was moved once again by the need for urgency. He picked up the clock at his bedside and reset the alarm clock for seven thirty.

11

6.45 A.M.

Sarah Rosen was woken by the absence of her husband. She rolled into the space where he should have been sleeping and the sheets were cold. Stepping out of bed quietly, she knew where he would be.

The door to Joe's room was half-open. Rising daylight filtered in through sky-blue curtains, and David stood motionless over his sleeping son.

'How long have you been here?' she asked.

'I'm not sure. I fell asleep straight away, woke up, nodded back off, then was wide awake.'

She was at his back now, her arms around his waist.

'This diet doesn't seem to be working.' She squeezed his stomach with her forearms. When she looked properly at him, she saw a rawness around his eyes that could have been caused by lack of sleep or a bout of tears. 'You OK?'

'Yeah.' He sounded fine but he was good at disguising his emotions.

'It's me you're talking to now.'

He sat on the chair next to Joe's basket and Sarah sat on his knee.

'I thought about Hannah a few times today.'

Silence.

'When?'

'When I saw Thomas in the hospital.'

He looked at Joe and felt the moment in all its painful intensity, the memory powerful and alive inside him.

'And how are you now?' she asked.

'Scared. Scared that something bad's going to happen to him.'

'That's natural. But don't trust those feelings and try not to hang on to them. Look at his hands.' Joe's fingers clenched and unclenched. 'He's waking up.'

'Can we move his basket into our room?'

'No. We're next door. We have an intercom. We have a smoke alarm. We have a burglar alarm. The windows are double-glazed. The walls are solid. This is his room. He's fine and he'll be fine.'

'You can't guarantee that, Sarah.'

'No, but I can guarantee that if you don't come back to bed and grab half an hour's sleep, your day's going to be ten times harder than it'll be if you stay up worrying.'

She slid off his knee and held out a hand. He took it and followed her back to bed.

Within a minute, David Rosen was asleep and Sarah was wide awake, worrying about her husband and their son.

12

8.30 A.M.

When Rosen walked into the open-plan office at Isaac Street Police Station that was doubling up as the Thomas Glass incident room, heads turned and tired faces looked quizzically at their SIO.

He placed a grease-smeared cardboard box down on his desk and looked around. All present. He gestured the officers towards him. As he did so, the door of Chief Superintendant Baxter's office opened.

Tom Baxter stood watching, leaning against the doorframe, and Rosen wondered was it psychic ability or an extra keen sense of smell that had drawn him out of his office?

Rosen met Baxter's eyes and read his face: *What are you up to now, David?*

'So, David.' It was Corrigan's pronounced Scouse accent that broke the silence. 'I can smell food.' Corrigan's hardened features softened with a smile.

'How many people here got four hours sleep or more?' No one made a sound. 'How many got three or less?' He heard the nodding and affirmative noises of consensus. 'I thought as much. How many people skipped breakfast because they wanted ten extra minutes in bed?'

'I didn't,' said the prematurely white-haired Prof Feldman. The group focused on the Prof. 'Two eggs with toast soldiers.' His deadpan face drew silence and puzzled looks and then laughter rolled round the room.

Rosen and Feldman caught each other's eye. *They think you're joking*, thought Rosen, who knew more about Feldman's background and home life than anyone else present.

'I've got some footage to show you. I'll transfer it from my phone to the laptop and show it on the SmartBoard in the next hour. But for now, I've been to McDonalds,' said Rosen. He opened the box. 'I know what you all order so here it is. Tea and porridge, Carol Bellwood.'

'Thanks, David.'

He took out a coffee and an egg McMuffin.

'The rest of you cave dwellers, sausage and egg McMuffins and coffee. Dive into the box. The cola's for you, Professor Feldman.'

Coffee and egg McMuffin in hand, Rosen wandered over to Baxter.

'I didn't forget you, Tom.' He handed the food and drink over to his senior.

'What are you having?'

'Sarah's got me on a diet.'

Baxter glanced at Rosen's stomach.

'She's got a good point.' Never one to give away a compliment easily, Baxter unwrapped the food skilfully with one hand and picked his words. 'That was. . . erm. . . decent of you, David.'

With a nod, Baxter indicated the shared breakfast in the incident room.

'They're going to be doing eighteen- to twenty-hour days for the foreseeable. It's the very least I can do.'

Baxter looked at the fast food as if was something new to him, but Rosen wasn't fooled. Despite his occasional tales of his wife's dinner parties and fine dining, Baxter was a fast foodie through and through.

'What's the footage of?' asked Baxter.

'Eat your breakfast first and then come and watch.'

'Why not show it now?'

'I need to set it up, but I also need time to test out an idea in my head – see if I think it's strong enough to throw into the mix.'

Baxter raised the muffin to his mouth but then stopped and said, 'They're banging the war drums at New Scotland Yard.'

'Because?'

'Not sure, David. But it's to do with your current case. I've been summoned this morning by ACCs Telfer and Cotton. Thanks for the breakfast. I'll eat in the office. Wish me well.'

As Baxter shut the door, Rosen wandered back to his desk wondering what the morning ahead had in store. At his desk, there was one sausage McMuffin left and a medium Coke.

He picked out DC Feldman from the crowd and said, 'Hey, Mike Feldman.'

Shyly, Feldman walked across and Rosen handed him the box. 'Breakfast is served.'

'But I've already eaten.'

'Yes, I know you have.' *Because your mother's a tyrant*, thought Rosen. 'Do *me* a favour, Prof.' *Blend in for once,* he thought.

Feldman said, 'Thank you, boss.' On the way back to his desk, Feldman took a noisy slurp of cola with the finesse of an eleven-year-old boy.

Rosen sat at his desk and fired up his laptop. He opened his emails, and one jumped right out at him. Looking around the room, he saw Bellwood and called, 'Carol, over here please, quickly.'

13

8.35 A.M.

An email had arrived on Rosen's computer, timed 8.32. Contacts sent to yr email.

At his desk, he opened the email sent by John Glass's PA. Bellwood was at his shoulder. Rosen looked across the room where Feldman and Gold, eating, were hunched over footage taken from Bannerman Square's CCTV camera before it was trashed.

He pointed to the email from Glass's PA.

DCI Rosen,
As requested, please find enclosed by two attachments, contact details from John Glass's personal and business databases.
Julian Parker

'I'll send it to you. Make a start please, Carol. Do you want support?'

'I'll see how I get on by myself to begin with.' And she was away, alert and energized by the challenge ahead.

Carol sat at her desk and opened the attachment containing personal contacts. Scrolling down quickly, she made an initial estimate and then looked to Rosen's desk, but he was on the other side of the incident room, his phone pressed to his ear, getting the low-down from Feldman on the CCTV footage.

'There are over a hundred contacts in the personal list,' she called to Rosen.

Feldman stared at his screen with absolute concentration, his hands supporting the sides of his face and the tips of his index fingers pressing down on the flesh of his ears to block off his hearing. Gold fidgeted, his face animated as he watched the screen.

Bellwood fixed her attention on the screen in front of her, clapped her hands together and thought, *Let's smoke you out, you vicious bastard.* The memory of Thomas Glass on a hospital bed had caused her to cry herself to sleep in the early hours of that morning but now she felt something different beneath her calm exterior. She was raw with anger.

Rosen summoned the attention of everyone in the room. 'Early warning. All present and correct here around nine thirty. Film to watch on the SmartBoard.'

14

8.37 A.M.

Emily Glass didn't turn or acknowledge her husband's return to Thomas's hospital bed. Instead, she carried on doing what she'd done since shortly before midnight: she talked to Thomas, her voice slowed by sedation.

'Thomas, I want to talk to you about your bedroom.'

Behind her back, John Glass concealed a sigh at the futility of his wife's endless chatter.

'Thomas, I'm opening the door of your bedroom at home. Thomas, look, look at the wonderful painted murals on all four walls. Space, outer space, your favourite subject. Look at the wall by your bed. Look at the Apollo moon rocket racing through the. . . star-spangled night, flames pouring from its tail. Look at the wall behind your bed. Look at the solar system and how all the planets turn around the sun. Look at the Milky Way. What a fabulous artist. All your. . . ideas, mind. Look at. . . the last. . . wall. Look at the purple. . . cloud. . . the birth. . . of. . . a. . . star.' She yawned, a long, slow, exhausted sound. 'Thomas, I might have to go to sleep soon. I'm finding it hard. . . to keep my eyes open. I want you to know, I'm still here, even if you can't hear my voice, I'm right. . .' She fell asleep but woke in a beat. 'I'm right here. . . and when I wake up, I'll tell you. . . about. . .'

John Glass put his hand on his wife's shoulder and she stiffened.

'How long are you going to keep this up? Emily? This not talking to me? Emily, we've got to talk.'

'Are you deaf?' At her words, he lifted his hand away. 'I need to sleep. Talk to him. Let him know you're here. God knows you weren't around him much up until. . . this!'

John Glass decided to humour his wife. 'Hello, Thomas. Hello, son.' And wondered what to say next. 'It's me. It's your dad.' Football. His son watched football on TV, kicked a ball around the expanse of walled garden around their house.

'Remember when I bought you that Arsenal shirt, signed by all the players? Hey? Remember that?'

Emily sank back in her chair, her breathing slowing and, within a minute, a woman who had slept for only twelve hours in the previous eight days was out.

Her husband fell silent. He stared at the bandages around his son's face and head and wondered if he could pay for plastic surgery to minimize the damage. He could pay for the best doctor. Then he wondered if his son was going to survive.

Looking at the bandages, he tried to picture the pitch darkness and complete silence that reigned in Thomas's brain.

15

8.38 A.M.

His dad's voice gurgled like he was talking into a tube with one end beneath the water in a fish bowl. And then it went quiet. The darkness surrounding Thomas Glass was as absolute as the silence.

Something in Thomas's mind shifted. He remembered where he was and what he must do to avoid punishment.

The wind blew outside and rattled the door, and the metallic din filled him with horror. It felt as if a fist was curled inside his skull, squeezing his brain like a lump of dough. Even so, he managed to swallow the gasp that rose inside him, because he had been ordered to stay utterly silent.

He was in a lock-up garage, with a roller-door just like the ones at home. And behind that, far away, a siren receded into the distance, thickening the darkness with tension.

Thomas heard a noise, an out-breath, and hoped with all his heart that he hadn't made that sound.

And then he hoped it wasn't someone else, that it wasn't one of *them*.

A rasp and the flaring of a single match. He shut his eyes against the sudden, unbearable brightness and smelled the smoke of a cigarette. After a moment he opened his eyes, blinking until he could make out the glowing tip of a cigarette.

I want to go home now. I want my mum, he thought, and as soon as the thought crossed his mind, he bit his tongue, knowing that it was dangerous.

They could read his mind and see in the dark.

The red tip of the cigarette came slowly towards him through the darkness in the direction of his left eyeball.

'No blinking.' It was the one called Ash. Thomas opened his eyelids and felt the heat of the burning cigarette near his eyeball. The tip moved right towards his other eye and drew a tight little circle in the air, round and round the pupil.

A small clump of warm cigarette ash landed on his hand. 'Ouch!' Thomas's voice was tiny and lost. He fought down the urge to weep. Sound was crime, and crime received immediate punishment.

A thin drawing in of breath and the tip of the cigarette receded. Another thick, hot, out-breath. 'We have reached our verdict.' It was the one called Oak.

A light came on, a brilliant white light that shone directly into his eyes. He twisted his head and closed his eyes. It was a light that was infinitely more hideous than the absolute dark that he had lived in for days – or was it weeks now? He had lost all sense of time.

'Thomas.' Ash, the old man – or was it a woman's voice? It was a voice that had confused him with its kind sound but nasty words. 'The prisoner has permission to speak. What do you want, Thomas?'

'I want to go back home; I want my mother.' The words poured out unbidden, and he was washed over with terror.

'There is only one Mother. Your mother is not your real Mother. There is only one Mother. Say it.' Ash's voice sounded almost sing-song.

'There is only one Mother. My mother is not my real Mother. There is only one Mother.'

'And that Mother, your real Mother, wants you here, where you are, right now.'

'But' – Thomas bottled up the thought *My mother is my mother* and tried the words they'd drilled into him over days and nights – 'the woman who fooled me into thinking she was my mother, she wants me to be with her.'

'Our Mother, the real Mother wants you here with us. And we have reached a verdict on her behalf,' said Oak, the other one, the one who craved blood. Thomas's heart rate increased and he sat up as straight as possible, tied to the hard-backed chair. He couldn't work out if Oak was old or young. Oak carried on: 'Emily Glass is a criminal, and you prefer her over your real Mother? You've been brainwashed and we have reached a verdict on Emily Glass. I know where she lives.'

'No.' Thomas mouthed the word.

Oak's voice grew louder, more angry. 'Jumping to defend her,' he mocked.

'Please.'

'Silence.' Ash. 'Hush now.' As kind as milk, as vicious as a snake. 'I'm sorry, Thomas, but Emily has been found guilty. I am sorry, but she's going to have to suffer for what she's done. Oak, pronounce sentence on Emily Glass.'

'By my red hand, Emily Glass is to be skinned alive from the neck to the belly and left in the woods where she played with Thomas Glass when he was a small child, in the place she brainwashed him, for the insects and the feral beasts to make of her what they will.'

Thomas tried not to make a sound but sobs of terror and despair escaped from his mouth.

'Hush now, hush,' said Ash.

'I . . . can't. . . help. . . it. . .'

'I'm not talking to you, Thomas. I'm trying to calm Oak's anger.'

Underneath his own crying, Thomas heard the sound of metal scraping against stone, back and forth.

'I don't want you to be in any doubt: Oak is sharpening his knife for Emily.'

'Please,' urged Thomas.

'Please what?' asked Ash.

'You're the leader. Make him stop!'

Rasp, rasp, rasp.

'I can make him stop. . . if you do what I say. . .'

'I'll do what you say, I'll do anything you say, leave her alone.'

Rasp, rasp, rasp.

'Oak, stop!'

Silence.

'Thomas?'

'Yes?'

'Give prayers of thanks to the one true Mother for the silence.'

'I'm praying.' He shut his eyes against the light, the words *I'm praying* racing around his head.

Thomas felt the flat surface of cold metal pressing against his cheek. He stifled the sob that rose within him and held his breath as the metal blade was rolled slowly across his cheek, one sharp edge to the other. The flat of the blade was drawn down to his throat and then turned so the lethal sharpness of the weapon pressed directly across his windpipe. He understood fully what would happen to his mother.

The blade was drawn away from his throat and he released his stifled sobs as a series of panic-driven breaths. 'I'll do. . . anything. . . you say,' pleaded Thomas. 'But don't hurt her. Ash, please, stop him.'

'You'll do anything I say?' asked Ash.

'Anything.'

Thomas still felt the coldness of the blade on his cheek and imagined the blade slicing his mother's throat and a pair of rough hands pulling the skin away from her body.

'Anything you say, anything!'

'Then I think we have an understanding.'

If his heart beat any harder, Thomas felt it was going to explode.

'Open your mouth, please,' said Ash.

Thomas opened his mouth and felt a cloth being driven into the space behind his teeth. On that cloth was a long thin strand, a hair perhaps.

'Say thank you – don't forget your manners to Mother.'

'Thank you, Mother,' grunted Thomas, through the gag, his senses reeling from the stench of petrol on the fingers that had forced it in his mouth.

The white light went out.

'If you do anything I say, Thomas' – Ash's voice dropped to little more than a whisper, and he had the feeling Ash didn't want Oak to hear – 'I'll appeal to Mother for mercy on Emily Glass and make sure that Oak goes nowhere near that woman. If you don't do what I say, there will be no plea for mercy and I can't stop Oak. And nor would I want to.'

The glowing tip of the cigarette swung back and forth again, like a pendulum.

'She'll scream for me to put her out of her agony. But I would show no mercy.' Oak spoke with relish and energy.

The red ember stopped, a coal in the darkness.

'And that, Thomas, would be all your fault,' said Ash. 'What happens to Emily is entirely in your hands.'

Suddenly, at speed, the cigarette tip flew towards Thomas's face and directly into his left eyeball.

He screamed, but the sound was absorbed by the gag. A volt of agony ricocheted from his brain through his entire nervous system.

'You must look on the bright side, Thomas. When you wake up – because you're about to pass out – pray to Mother that you get to keep your good eye, the one you can still see with. Thank you, Thomas, and good night to you.'

As the roller-door rose up, a wave of white flooded Thomas's senses. As the door shut again, and consciousness left him, Thomas saw his mother, Emily, being marched into the woods at the back of their house. *All my fault*, he thought. And from the depths of his heart, a single word echoed, hopeless and forlorn.

Mummy!

*

EMILY WOKE SUDDENLY and saw John staring silently into space. Through sleepy eyes, she saw the ECG machine that Thomas was attached to going haywire. Jumping up, she threw open the door and screamed.

Sister Barker came running round the corner.

'His heart!' Emily cried.

Sister Barker stopped at the boy's bed. The ECG showed a raised but steadier pattern of activity. As moments passed, Thomas's heart rate settled. She waited. After a minute of what passed for normality, Sister Barker said, 'I'll come back and monitor him. Try and rest.' She closed the door after herself.

'I—' began John.

'You didn't notice because you weren't even looking at him. I can't even trust you so that I can close my eyes and sleep.' Emily turned her back on her husband and looked at her son, as if seeing what had been done to him for the first time.

'I'm sorry, Thomas,' she cried. 'I'm sorry.'

16

9.38 A.M.

Rosen concluded the grim summing up of events by playing the mobile phone footage from Bannerman Square.

Stevie Jensen's film of Thomas's agonized responses ended and Rosen watched the grim expressions of his team. No one said a word.

'He knew his abductor. His abductor was male. "They'll do it again,"' said Rosen.

He turned his attention to the back of the group, to Bellwood, who sat at her desk. He was surprised by the sheer volume of paper she had generated there so quickly.

'Carol, how's the trawl through Glass's contacts going?' asked Rosen.

She indicated the neatly stacked sets of paper and said, 'I'm only an hour into it.' She felt her head spin from sheer concentration. 'The personals? The only groupings in the personal list are families and married couples. My initial thought is that this list's a dead end.' She paused and rubbed her eyes. 'The business contacts? I've dipped into the business contacts, picking out all the small businesses in a twenty-mile radius, eliminating all the big corporations initially. I've picked out ten contacts within five miles of here. I've googled. I can't figure any obvious link, how Glass is connected to them. But they all appear to be *groups*.' She read from a list: 'AllKinds CDs, Outlaws, Pearsons Water Spa, C & C Tylers, Outlook, Huntleys, Pampers Health Shop, Fingertips, HomeBrands, D. Bannion Cured Meats. Anyone have any ideas?'

'Maybe he lends to small businesses?' suggested Corrigan.

'Businesses wouldn't borrow money at his rates,' replied Bellwood; '247.9 per cent APR.'

'Maybe he invests in other businesses,' said Rosen.

'Maybe, but I can't see a pattern here, not yet.' Bellwood put the paper down on her desk. 'OK, I need some help here.'

'Corrigan,' said Rosen.

'It'll be nice to spend quality time with you, Carol,' quipped Corrigan, as Rosen picked out three more members of the team to assist Bellwood.

'Before you all go back to your work,' said Rosen, 'I want to throw a possible motive in the mix. Revenge. Maybe John Glass has messed with someone and that someone's getting back at him through his son.' Rosen felt the collective desire for elaboration. 'Are any of these businesses related to artists' materials? Paint, aerosols?' he asked.

'I don't know,' replied Bellwood. 'You thinking about the eye on the wall?'

'Yes,' said Rosen. During his brief periods of sleep, the painted eye had crept into his dreams: it had been the last picture in his mind before falling asleep and the first there when he woke up. 'Yes, the eye,' he said, heading away to call the hospital for a progress report on Thomas Glass. 'OK,' said Rosen. 'Let's go!'

17

12.29 P.M.

By noon, the Portakabin that Rosen had requested, the mobile incident room at Bannerman Square, was fully operational. He sat at a desk to open a text from DS Riley on surveillance at Lewisham's A & E.

DCI Rosen: Every 1 thru the doors genuine reason to be here thomas still highly critical 3rd change of guard at his door from CO19 Riley

Rosen called a number on his speed dial and was connected seconds later.

'Lewisham Hospital, A and E reception.'

'DCI Rosen. I need a list of all people present at the time of Thomas Glass's admission last night at approximately 9.40 P.M. and all those admitted within a two-hour time window either side.'

'No problem. I have your contact details right here.'

Rosen thanked the receptionist, closed down the call and, noticing the empty Tupperware box on his desk, wished he hadn't eaten his three-bean salad at eleven o'clock.

It was twelve thirty. *They'll do it again.*

'If you come this way.'

Rosen was surprised to hear Bellwood's kindly voice beyond the closed door of the chilly MIR.

He polished off the dregs of a coffee. He'd lost count of how many he'd had since waking, and the grim rumbling in his chest told him to cut the caffeine and switch to water.

The door opened and Bellwood indicated to a short, white woman – her face lined from sun beds or cigarettes but relatively young and attractive – that she could enter.

She held back a moment, consumed with anxiety.

'Good afternoon, madam.' Rosen smiled at her and turned the piece of paper he had been writing on face-down on the table to hide his memo to self:

Who wants to screw up John Glass? = A living form of death

He flashed Bellwood a look. *What are you doing here?*

'Lunchtime,' she said. 'I needed a change of scenery.'

As the young woman climbed the metal steps into the Portakabin, a small girl, ten or eleven years of age, followed her. Beneath the girl's black padded coat, she wore a green cardigan and tie, a clean but well-worn school uniform. From one arm of her coat, her cardigan cuff poked out, the edge unravelling.

The girl's face was bruised, her lip bearing a fresh cut, both her eyes purple and swollen. She hovered at the entrance, fear playing out beneath the wounds.

Rosen smothered the deep concern the girl's face provoked in him and smiled. 'Come in and sit down.'

The woman grabbed the girl by the hand and said, 'Don't keep the police officer waiting, Macy. Tell him what you saw last night, what happened.'

'You're Macy's mum?' asked Rosen.

She nodded and said, 'Ms Conner.'

Macy came in and sat on the chair Rosen set out for her. She sat on her hands, looking around the Portakabin, glancing at Rosen.

Rosen looked directly at her and said, 'My name's David Rosen, what's—'

'Her name's Macy Conner and this is what two big brave men did to her for the sake of a tenner.' The woman had a Scottish accent; Rosen placed it as Glaswegian.

'Hello, Macy,' said Rosen, stooping to be at eye level with her.

'Hello, Mr Rosen. I'm going to be late for school.' On each syllable, her voice dithered with fear. Her accent was pure south London and his first impression was strong: she was a good kid.

As he sat facing her, Macy settled her gaze on Rosen's smiling face.

'What happened to your face, Macy?' Sympathy flooded from him.

'I slept in this morning because I didn't get to sleep 'till five o'clock 'cause of what they did to me.' Her voice was soft, fragile and new to being broken by the world. She smiled but her eyes dipped like birds pressed down by a storm. *She is learning about suffering*. The thought saddened Rosen. She looked directly at him and said, 'I've never had a day off school in all my life. And I've never been late and it's spoiled it all now. And it ain't my fault. Afternoon register's one o'clock in school.' His heart was captivated

'Which school would that be?'

'Bream Street Primary.'

'Don't worry. If you've got something to tell me, I'll phone the school and explain that I made you late.'

Rosen glanced at Bellwood and took in the mother in the same moment. He knew that Bellwood would intervene to distract the mother if she interfered with her daughter's testimony.

'I'd very much like to hear what happened last night, Macy,' said Rosen. 'Just you.'

'I was on my way to the Mini Mart, on the high street. . .' Tears welled up in her swollen eyes. 'I went to buy a card for the meter 'cause the electric'd run out.'

Silent tears rolled down her cheeks. She wiped her cheeks with the back of her hand. Rosen noticed the length and fine shape of her fingers – the hands of a pianist or a surgeon. But he guessed neither occupation would be an option for her.

'Macy.' Rosen smiled. 'OK with you if I record our chat?'

The girl glanced down at Rosen's feet, frowned and looked up.

'OK, Mr Rosen.' Her expression was heavy. Rosen pressed 'record' on his phone. 'I saw. . . the burning car. . . I saw two men running away.' Her brown eyes locked onto Rosen's. 'It was like the fire in the car had only just started and they'd turned the corner off the square. I thought, *They're baddies*. I seen them and they seen me. So then I started running, to the high street, off of Bannerman Square.'

Rosen looked through the open door at the front elevation of Claude House. It was entirely possible that Stevie hadn't seen anyone if the perpetrators had run off the square in the early moments of the fire.

Macy took five shallow breaths through her nose and covered her lower face with her hand. Bellwood crouched to Macy's eye level and she offered her a tissue.

Macy took it and looked directly at Bellwood as she dabbed her face.

'My name's Carol. I'm a policewoman. I got punched on the street by two men when I was a constable. It was horrible then. But I'm all right now.'

'Yeah?'

Bellwood nodded. 'Macy?' She pressed gently. 'You know you said you saw the two men running away from the burning car. Did you see them actually *at* the car?'

Macy considered the question.

'One on, like, each side of the car. Yeah.'

'Did you see them set the car on fire?' asked Bellwood.

Rosen stood up and Bellwood sat directly in front of Macy.

'No. I didn't see them set the car on fire. The car was burning. I ran away. They run after me.' Macy blew her nose into the tissue and screwed it into a tight ball. 'They caught me, and surrounded me and then. . .'

'Take your time,' said Bellwood, leaning back in her seat to give Macy that extra crumb of physical space.

'It was dead rude.' Macy's voice dropped to a whisper and her eyes closed.

Rosen felt his stomach turn, a mixture of horror and anger at what was about to come.

'He used a swear word. I don't swear.'

Rosen sighed inwardly with relief.

'In this instance, it's OK to swear,' said Bellwood, looking up at Macy's mother.

'It's OK,' confirmed her mother. 'Tell 'em what they said to you, Mace.'

'OK. He said, "Did you think you could out-run us, little. . . *bitch*."' She mouthed the last word, and looked completely uncomfortable. 'One of them grabbed my hands and took the tenner and. . . then. . . one of them . . . I just felt his fist going *bam bam bam* in my face and then there were flashing lights in my head and then it was like they were in a real big hurry to get away and they were, like, angry with me because I'd seen them and they were trying to scare me into saying nothing.'

The mother caught Rosen's eye. 'I didn't want to send her out at that hour. I had a migraine. She wanted to go.'

'I didn't mind going,' said Macy. 'You were really sick, Mum, in bed with your head banging.'

'What did they look like?' Bellwood steered the interview back.

'I didn't see their faces. Their hoods were all pulled up. Hiding their faces, like.'

'Sure they were both men?'

'They moved like men. The one who spoke was a man.' She considered briefly but with concentration. 'Both were men.'

'What about their clothes? Any distinguishing marks?'

'You mean like a logo?'

'Yeah?'

'They were all plain, plain tops, tracksuit bottoms, dark trainers. I went sick when they robbed the money. Sorry, Mum.'

'It's not your fault, Mace, I've told you.'

'What happened when they ran off?' asked Bellwood. Macy looked puzzled. 'What did you do when they ran off?' she clarified.

'I stayed on the ground, listening as they ran away. When I couldn't hear them any more, I got up. My lip was bleeding a lot. I could taste blood in my mouth. My head was banging with pain. I thought I was going to faint. But I stood up anyway. I was crying me eyes out. But there was nobody about.' Macy suddenly dropped her head and sobbed loudly into the flats of her hands.

'Macy, you're a really brave girl,' encouraged Bellwood.

Over the space of a minute, Macy's tears subsided. Then she leaned forward and raised the hem of her long, black trousers up to the knee to reveal a saucer-sized bruise on her shin. She looked up and caught Rosen's eye.

'How did that happen, Macy?' asked Rosen.

She dropped her trouser leg. 'I banged my leg on the kerb as I fell. It's very sore but the doctor took an x-ray and said it's not broken, which is lucky, I guess.'

'What did the men sound like?' Bellwood probed.

'Only one of them spoke. He had an accent. Just before he ran away he said something about "coming back" and "burning me alive". He sounded like maybe he was from, say, Ireland.'

Macy's eyes were alert and intelligent.

'Macy,' said Rosen. 'Did they smell of anything?'

'What like?'

'Beer? Cigarettes? Aftershave?' Rosen shrugged. 'Anything?'

'Yeah,' she replied. 'Yeah, they did. But not the things you just said.'

'What did they smell of?'

'Petrol. You know that smell when you go past a garage, that petrol-pump smell. They smelled of that.' Macy looked at Rosen. 'Want to see a drawing of them?'

A bolt of energy screamed through him. 'Yes please, Macy.'

The girl reached into her pocket and pulled out a piece of white paper. She handed the paper to Rosen and he unfolded it to reveal a child-like cartoon of two hoodies, roughly drawn and crudely shaded with an HB pencil. Where the faces should have been, there was darker, deepening shadow, but no facial details.

'Good thinking, Macy. They *both* smelt of petrol?'

Macy's face scrunched up tight as she silently explored her memory.

'Both smelt of petrol, the truth?' said Macy.

Rosen nodded.

'It's a strong smell, petrol. I know definitely one of them did.'

'Which one, Macy?'

'The one who hit me. When his fist. . . hit me. . . I smelt petrol. If I had to swear on the Holy Bible, the hitter had petrol on his hands.' Her eyes looked sad, as if the awful truth about the world had descended like a foul night. 'But I couldn't swear the other one did.' Her face clouded over again and she leaned back in her seat, the memory of what had happened brought alive in her eyes by the mention of those words.

'Macy, can you read a street map?' asked Bellwood, retrieving a large white sheet from the nearby desk.

'I like Geography.'

Bellwood lay the map on the floor at Macy's feet and sat on the floor of the Portakabin. Macy slid off her seat and sat next to Bellwood, who indicated Bannerman Square on the map.

'Show me where you ran away from them, stop where they caught you.'

Macy traced her finger along Lydia Road, stopping not far from the start of the chase, about four hundred metres from where the road led directly to the high street.

'And how long did you listen before their footsteps were gone?' asked Rosen.

'It felt like a minute.' Macy looked up at Rosen. 'Is it true?'

'Is what true, Macy?'

'There was a boy in the car.'

'I'm sorry to say there was.'

'So they set him on fire?'

'We don't know—'

'They said they'd come back, that they'd burn me alive.' The blood had drained from Macy's face and it seemed that she was about to faint. Rosen took her by the hands, picked her up from the floor and settled her back on her chair. Bellwood was up and pouring water from a bottle as Rosen opened the door to let fresh air in.

She sipped the water, staring into the middle distance, a film of sweat forming on her brow. Rosen sat down again and leaned in gently.

'Why?' she said.

'Why what, Macy?' asked Rosen.

'Why's the world so. . . bad?'

'Do you know what, Macy,' Rosen replied, 'I've been a policeman for thirty years and I still ask myself that question every single day. I never get the whole answer, but I always come up with some of the answer. It's also a wonderful world with lovely people in it. Do you want to know who I met today who's a really good, good person?'

'Who?' She looked intrigued to the point of amazement.

Rosen leaned a little closer, dropped his voice. 'You.'

'Me?' Macy's face unfolded in a smile, a bud opening to the light. Then a shadow appeared. 'Are they going to come and get me, Mr Rosen?'

'I think. . . if they were going to get you, I mean make sure that you couldn't tell anyone what you'd seen. . .'

'Kill me?'

'They'd have done it last night when they had a chance. If they come back to Bannerman Square, it's a huge risk for them. There are going to be lots of policemen around here now.'

'Promise?'

'I can promise you lots of extra policemen.'

Macy looked at Bellwood for further reassurance.

'Macy, if you'd committed a serious crime, would you go back to where you'd done it if there were loads of coppers around?'

'No way.'

She drank the rest of her water and looked around for the bin. Rosen took the cup from her and felt the clammy heat from her hands on the plastic surface seep into his fingers. Macy still looked sick.

He looked at her mother.

'Why don't you keep her off school for the afternoon?'

'I want to go to school. Can I go now?' Macy insisted.

Rosen understood her sudden, urgent prompting to be in school, a place where she felt safe. He also reckoned that she had more information. But to detain her further at that moment would be cruel.

He took out his mobile phone and said, 'Macy, can I take a photograph of your face?'

'Yes, but why?'

'Evidence of your wounds. Don't smile, just look at me, that's a good girl.'

He took three almost identical pictures of her face.

'Macy, I'll call your school office and explain how you've helped us.'

As her mother walked ahead of her into a fresh shower of rain, Macy stopped at the door.

'There's something else. Something I can't get at.' She touched her skull. 'Why can't I quite think?'

'Sometimes,' said Rosen, 'the mind protects us from too much nastiness by going blank.'

'Oh,' she replied.

'Where do you live, Macy?'

'6F, Claude House.' She pointed. 'Over there.'

'Macy!' Her mother's voice cut in from outside the Portakabin.

'Can I ask you a question, Mr Rosen?'

'Go on.' He smiled.

Macy pointed at his feet. 'Why are you wearing one green sock and one red one?'

'The bedroom was dark. . . I hurried getting dressed. . .'

'Macy!' Her mother's voice again, this time sharper. And Macy was gone.

'Poor woman,' said Rosen. 'Did you see the coat, Carol?'

Bellwood nodded. 'Expensive shoes, though. Maybe she got lucky in a charity shop.'

'Carol, get onto CCTV. We need the footage from eight forty-five to ten o'clock, Lewisham High Street. There's a camera near the junction with Lydia Road. Seal off Lydia Road from Bannerman Square to the high street – we need Scientific Support there, quickly.'

Rosen's phone rang out. Mind spinning, he picked up the call: 'DCI David Rosen.'

'I need to talk to you, David.' It was Chief Superintendent Baxter.

Rosen, who was about to go back to Isaac Street to catch up on the CCTV, said, 'I'll be there in fifteen minutes.'

Baxter hung up.

Rosen took a deep breath and, heading towards his car in the thickening rain, saw Macy walk in one direction towards Bream Street Primary and her mother head back alone to Claude House.

18

1.35 P.M.

As Rosen entered the incident room, Gold and Feldman paused the CCTV footage. Feldman looked like he was soaking in a river of disappointment.

Gold, chewing gum and frustrated, was the first to catch Rosen's eye as he entered. 'You're never going to believe this, boss,' he said.

Rosen noticed that Gold was wearing the same shirt he'd had on the previous night when he was handling Stevie Jensen on Bannerman Square. He wondered if Gold had slept in the shirt and felt anxious for him.

'You know what, Goldie,' replied Rosen, approaching. 'Bet you I will.'

'CCTV on Bannerman Square,' said Gold. 'Word up from forensics. Someone's taken two gunshots at the camera. First one's buckled the cage, the second's screwed the side of the camera.'

'We've watched hours in the lead up to it,' said Feldman. 'Not one single frame of anyone casing the camera or doing damage to it.' He pointed to the screen. 'These are the moments leading up to the point where it was gunned. They're typical of the whole day.'

Gold pressed 'play'.

'So, what we've got is a really good view of Bannerman Square, round about three fifteen, specifically this. . .'

On screen, a young mother pushed a toddler in a buggy. The image shuddered and the mother carried on pushing her baby. As she disappeared off screen, the screen went blank.

'Got you,' said Rosen.

'Is she deaf?' asked Feldman.

'Freeze-frame the young mum,' said Rosen. 'Between the first and second bullet.'

Feldman froze an image of the woman. The quality of the picture was poor but there was no doubt that the woman didn't instinctively jump or turn her head to the sudden noise of a gunshot from just across the square. In the image, she just looked ahead, her head slightly dipped, talking to her child. She was heading for Claude House, the housing block where Macy Conner lived.

'She'd have looked if she'd heard it, so she's either used to guns going off and has nerves of steel,' said Rosen, 'or she's stone deaf.' He paused. 'Or they used a silencer on the gun. We need to find her, fast.' He focused on Feldman and was glad to have a team member with his level of inexhaustible patience.

'I'll go through the lists of tenants, narrow down women with small children in the Bannerman block,' said Feldman. 'It shouldn't take long.'

'I'll print off an image of her.' As Gold picked out a clearer image, Rosen said, 'Get it copied and I'll get the uniforms to door-to-door the flats again and find her.'

Feldman smiled enigmatically at Rosen.

'Go on, Mike, what's amusing you?'

'You're about to hit me with something. . . tricksy. Let me guess. CCTV footage of all the traffic incoming to the Bannerman Square vicinity?'

'We're looking for the stolen Renault Megane that Thomas got burned in,' said Rosen. 'It's got to be there somewhere on CCTV – they had to come in from one of five routes to Bannerman Square.

It's ordered – the footage'll be here in the next couple of hours.'

'I love making lists. I love looking at hours and hours of CCTV footage,' said Feldman, a small smile on his face, his voice deadpan.

Gold, however, did a poor job of masking his dismay.

'I don't take it for granted. From either of you.'

Rosen looked across at Superintendant Baxter's door and knew he had to crack on. He addressed both Gold and Feldman: 'I left a message on Tracey Leung's voicemail. She hasn't got back to me yet. We'll get the inside track from Tracey on who in the gangs especially likes playing with guns.'

'You think the gangs could be involved in this shit?' asked Gold, incredulous.

'If there's a gun involved on Bannerman Square, I want to check out what's what with the local gangs.' Possibilities raced around Rosen's mind. 'Yes, I understand your scepticism, as they don't usually go in for kidnapping small children, but it could be the case that whoever's abducted Thomas has paid a local bad boy to take out the CCTV camera. Let's see. Keep trying Tracey for me, OK?'

Baxter's door. ACCs. Rosen took a deep breath and knocked.

19

1.43 P.M.

There was no reply. Rosen opened the door. Baxter was at his desk, engrossed in his laptop, furiously typing.

Rosen took advantage of his superior officer's distraction and took stock of the room, particularly the wide-angled group photograph of the class that Rosen and Baxter had passed out from at Hendon just under thirty years earlier. Academically, Rosen had been mid-table, but tops in physical matters, street smarts and plain common sense. Baxter was an academic high-flyer, but beneath the middle in just about everything else.

Rosen knew that Baxter wasn't the Renaissance Man he liked to project. The two had a silent contract: whatever conflict passed between them, Baxter knew his former classmate would never talk about that other world they had shared when they were both young and raw.

Baxter stopped typing, looked at Rosen as if he was surprised to see him.

'David. Have you recruited your forensic psychologist yet?' He clicked the mouse to send an email. 'Henshaw, Welch or Simon? Take your pick or I'll pick for you.'

'Don't push me around, Tom.'

Baxter sighed. 'Close the door, David.'

'I've already closed it.'

On Baxter's desk there was a new family portrait: Baxter and his wife standing behind their seated children, now sixth-formers. It was taken only weeks after Baxter's mistress of three years had made it to sergeant and dumped him in favour of a higher-ranked commander.

'Henshaw's the best,' said Baxter.

'I agree, but why do *you* think so?'

'I had that meeting with the assistant commissioners this morning. They want a profiler on board—'

'Since when do the ACs run investigations on the ground?'

'Since Thomas Glass's father went to Capital Radio and said he apportioned a large degree of blame to the Metropolitan Police for what's happened to his son. Not acting fast enough, not doing everything possible, poor communicators. . . It's a long list, vague and unsubstantiated, but juicy enough for a damning phone-in debate this morning.'

Rosen imagined the scene. Baxter, political doggie, doing sit, stand and heel to the ACs because that was the way it worked. Baxter did it to those beneath as those above did it to him.

'I've done everything humanly possible.'

'Except pick a profiler. ACs Cotton and Telfer don't understand why you're not using a profiler.'

'So you reminded them about Peter Cale, *Doctor* Peter Cale, early days of the Herod case. . .'

Baxter looked battered.

'Cale had us all convinced that Herod was a woman. . . half the team spent a week on HOLMES, the rest went tracking down females with any form for abducting children or attacking pregnant women.'

'David, I remember it well.'

'Remember how Cale then did a sudden about-face and declared it may not be a woman after all? Same day, Alison Todd was abducted, victim number two.'

'OK, David, listen. John Glass is going to the IPCC. I've been told to start a damage limitation programme on the conduct of the case so far. Make sure no stone is left unturned. Profiler!'

Rosen watched the colour red rising from Baxter's collar line carry on upwards.

'I'm happy to argue the case for selective use of resources.'

'It was a lecture,' snapped Baxter. He composed himself. 'Not a debate.'

Silence.

'Who do you want, David? Name your man.'

There was something different about Baxter: he looked worn down, and, in that moment, Rosen amazed himself by feeling sorry for his boss.

'OK. At half past nine last night,' said Rosen, 'all we had was a missing child. Now we've other information, we could use a profiler and I'd like James Henshaw on board.'

Baxter said, 'Thank you. And thanks for not reminding me that I insisted Doctor Cale be made central to the MIT chasing Paul Dwyer, also known as Herod.' He exhaled, loudly. 'I'll call Henshaw personally. OK, David, I know you're busy. You can go now.'

Rosen stopped at the door when Baxter suddenly asked, 'Why do *you* think Henshaw's the right man for this case?'

Rosen smiled. Baxter was cribbing notes for his next run-in with the ACs. He fixed his face, turned and, looking at Baxter, saw a man who was down to the last of his energy.

'The perpetrators aren't paedophiles but there are at least two of them involved, possibly more. What binds them? Abnormality. Off the scale. Henshaw's our man. He's got a great track record on cases of collective insanity. Send him to me, Tom, ASAP, Bannerman Square.'

20

3.55 P.M.

As the late afternoon rain stopped, Rosen arrived back at the mobile incident room in Bannerman Square. He asked the PC manning the Portakabin if there had been any visitors, but had predicted correctly: not one.

He scrunched up a greasy brown McDonald's bag, the large fries and cheeseburger packaging still inside it, and dropped it in the bin by the desk. He felt a shiver of guilt at the thought of the hard work that Sarah put in to making calorie-controlled lunches but with his stomach full, his mind, he told himself, could focus.

His phone rang.

'DCI David Rosen.'

'Hi, David, DC Riley.'

'Problem at A and E?'

'No. I've just emailed you the list of people who attended A and E last night.'

'Copy the whole team in on it. Thanks, Barry.'

Rosen opened his laptop and turned it on, but his attention was drawn away by something he saw on Bannerman Square through the open door of the MIR.

He stopped what he was about to do and watched.

Stevie Jensen, on his way home from school, had acknowledged a younger girl who was tying something to the scene-of-crime tape that cordoned off the place where Thomas Glass had burned in a Renault Megane.

The girl made the sign of the cross and fell into a prayerful mode.

It was Macy Conner, eyes shut, face composed peacefully.

Rosen left the Portakabin and, walking quietly, stood behind Macy. The carnations looked just about fit for the bin, and the price drop label read '60p'. A poor little girl's offering for another unfortunate child.

She opened her eyes, turned and said, 'Mr Rosen?'

'Hello, Macy.'

'How's Thomas?' she asked.

'He's not very well.'

'Is he still alive?'

'Yes.'

'I'm leaving flowers because I want him to know I'm thinking about him.'

'That's very thoughtful of you.'

'Can you tell him I'm praying for him?'

'Next time I see him, I will,' said Rosen.

The cut on her lip was vivid and looked set to tear and pour blood. *Even after your own trauma*, thought Rosen, *you're mindful of the suffering of others.*

'Do you know his mum and dad?'

'Yes.'

'It must be terrible for them.'

Rosen glanced at the small card sellotaped to the plastic bag holding the virtually dead carnations.

To Thomas
Get well soon
Macy

The handwriting was immaculate linked print, and displayed a maturity beyond her years. The message was, Rosen guessed, the well-intentioned but naïve sentiment of a ten year old.

'Mr Rosen?'

He smiled, encouraging her, hopeful she'd come up with some other detail but not wishing to push her too hard.

'I've got something to tell you.'

'Go on.'

'We weren't totally honest with you when we called in over there.' She indicated the Portakabin with a nod of her head and a look of shame.

'OK?'

'Mum did have a bad head last night and that's partly why she couldn't go to the shop for the electricity card. But there was another reason why I had to go and Mum couldn't.' She touched the swelling on her lip. 'My grandma lives with us. She's that sick she's mostly in bed. Mum doesn't let her be on her own in the flat. In case she dies of the cancer. I've heard Mum talk to the nurses. She can't talk to me. I've tried to talk about things but she just clams up. She told the nurses she was terrified of her mother dying. And scared of her dying all on her own. When we came to see you this morning, my big brother, Paul, he was in the flat with Grandma, but Paul wasn't around for some of last night and so Mum let me go to the shop for the electricity card.'

'I'm very sad to hear about your grandma.'

Macy looked at Rosen directly, openly. 'So am I. I'm so close to her. Mr Rosen, I was on my way over to your cabin to tell you because I've been worried sick all afternoon.'

'What's been worrying you, Macy?'

He felt the warm stirring of a bond forming with the little girl before him.

'Because we didn't tell you the whole truth. About why it was me who had to go to the shop. I couldn't say anything when I was with

Mum. I'm sorry. It's wrong to lie and it's really bad to lie to the police.'

'You've nothing to be sorry to me for. I understand. You've been a wonderful help, a great witness and a brave girl. Don't think of it as lying, think of it as being tactful.'

'Tactful?'

'Mindful of the feelings of others, your mum's feelings.'

'You're not angry with me?'

'I'm pleased with you.'

Relief swept through her features and a moment of tenderness overwhelmed Rosen.

'"It's important to tell the truth at all times." That's what my grandma taught me. Truth.'

Rosen, who agreed in principle but not always in practice, smiled.

'Your grandma sounds like a very good woman.'

'She's the best. Because she's dying, I think that's why I feel so sorry for Thomas's mum and dad. Do you think he's going to die?'

'I'm not a doctor, Macy, I can't say, but I understand what you mean. Your situation has taught you to empathize with Mr and Mrs Glass, and that's a really good thing to do, it's very grown up.'

She held out a hand and Rosen shook with her. Her fingers were cold and he sat on his fatherly instinct and the words *Put your gloves on* because there was the possibility that she didn't own a pair.

'I've got to go to Lewisham Library, to pick up some books. Grandma likes me to read to her. I've got special permission from Mrs Dodson, who's head of the library, to get Gran's books from the grown-ups' section.'

He hadn't noticed the bag on her back.

'Macy?'

She looked at him, alert and eager to please.

'Remember when we were talking this morning, in the cabin? Did you remember that thing that you said you'd blocked out?'

'It's trapped.' She touched her head. 'In here. It's been bugging me all day. Soon as I remember, Mr Rosen, I'll come and see you, straight away, I promise.'

Rosen watched Macy walk away under the weight of a bag of books, strapped from right shoulder to left hip. He looked at her pitiful offering of carnations and the scorched tarmac where Thomas had been set alight.

He walked back across Bannerman Square to the graffiti-daubed wall, bracing himself to recreate the horror of Thomas Glass's experience in the back of a burning car.

21

4.03 P.M.

Rosen worked backwards from the point where Stevie had lain Thomas down.

He dipped under the scene-of-crime tape and crouched at the pothole where Thomas had fallen into a puddle. He looked up at the spray-painted aerosol eye.

The painted eye stared directly back at Rosen. As he moved his head a little to the left, the eye held his gaze.

He stood up and walked into the charred rectangle where the car had burned, aligned the front and back of the vehicle, and positioned himself in the space next to the back left-hand door. He pictured the rising flames and imagined the complete claustrophobia Thomas must have felt, banging on the window maybe, staring out, desperation mounting.

Rosen dipped to the height of a child in the back of that car. Through the imaginary flames and rising smoke, he stared directly at the painted eye and the words, *The position of this car, this was no accident* sounded clearly inside his head.

Bang, bang, bang, a fist on the window. A door they'd failed to lock. A door that fell open under a watchful, sinister eye.

He rose to his full height and made his way slowly to the pothole where Thomas had fallen; imagined the mind-bending terror, his agony; pictured Stevie running towards that place through the sodium-tinted night.

And his focus came back to the eye on the wall, the complementary black and white, the black of the oval outline, the white inner eye that housed all the details, the sinister pupil with the life-like speck of white light and the spokes linking the circumference of the eye to the centre.

'DCI Rosen?'

Snapped from the moment by the sound of a man's voice, Rosen glanced over his shoulder. A well-dressed man in his thirties, tall, close to six foot four, who wouldn't have looked out of place in a line-up of rising political stars, was approaching.

He stayed on the other side of the scene-of-crime tape and said, 'DCI Rosen? I'm James Henshaw. Chief Superintendent Baxter told me you'd be here.'

Rosen recognized his face and remembered seeing Henshaw on a TV documentary about Fred and Rosemary West, giving his expert opinion on their psychology, their shared mission, their hand-in-glove marital murder unit. He had been a convincing and articulate pundit.

'I came as soon as I picked this up,' Henshaw said, handing Rosen his card, and a folded sheet of paper. Rosen opened it and saw it was an email from Baxter confirming that Rosen wanted Henshaw on the team.

Rosen lifted the scene-of-crime tape and Henshaw ducked under it. As he shook hands with Rosen, the profiler smiled but Rosen read a sadness in him that sparked something buried deeply in his memory. When he let go of Henshaw's hand, although unsure of the details, Rosen knew he was in the presence of a man who had suffered deep and personal tragedy.

'Thank you for coming so quickly, James. Your timing's impeccable. I think I've come to a time, place and concept that you could really help me with,' said Rosen. He pointed at the graffiti.

'This is the exact place where Thomas was set on fire?' asked Henshaw, putting on a pair of glasses to study the image. He stood quiet and still while Rosen waited, watching the intensity of his reaction. 'He or she's a very good artist,' said Henshaw, eventually. 'It's been painted under pressure, possibly in the dead of night with a spray can in one hand and a torch in the other.'

Taking a digital camera from his pocket, Henshaw asked, 'May I?'

At Rosen's nod, Henshaw took several photographs of the eye. Then the profiler stepped in closer and examined the eye narrowly, nearly scraping his nose on the bricks in the wall.

'What's your take on this graffiti?' asked Rosen.

'The cave paintings of our time.'

Rosen looked at the graffiti with fresh eyes, breaking it down into its component parts as Henshaw pressed 'record' on his phone and dictated: 'Black oval outline, white, dappled grey within the white, fifteen spokes outside to centre, perspective perfect, execution exquisite, mindset abnormal.'

Henshaw turned, pressed 'stop' and pocketed his phone. For some reason, he reminded Rosen of a pilgrim standing before a holy icon. Henshaw looked at Rosen.

'"Mindset abnormal"?' asked Rosen.

'My instinct and my understanding are telling me that the combined content and quality' – Henshaw looked at the eye again, as if double-checking his judgement before delivering it – 'means this is the work of a damaged mind.'

'The thing is,' said Rosen. 'We had a trashed CCTV camera on that wall. . .' He pointed.

'Where's it now?'

'Scientific Support took it away.'

Henshaw's attention drifted back to the graffiti. 'Hollow scrawl or Holy Scripture?' He did a visual three-point turn: wall, scorched earth, eye.

'It's no accident he was brought here,' said Rosen. He moved in closer.

The wall had been covered on both sides with fingerprint dust, but so far nothing concrete had been uncovered from the dozen different, partial palm- and fingerprints picked up on the bricks.

He leaned over the wall and, dead tired, wondered if his eyes were playing tricks on him.

There were two horizontal lines of symbols scratched lightly with a sharp point on the surface of the bricks directly behind the eye on the other side of the wall.

He walked around the wall to get a full head-on view. For a moment, it appeared like an optical illusion created by the wear and tear of time on the brickwork but then, superficial as the marks were, the symbols were as real and vivid as the eye on the other side.

How come no one picked up on this? thought Rosen. *Me included?*

He felt the presence of Henshaw behind him.

Rosen squatted on his heels and stared at the symbols. From his pocket, he produced a torch and threw yellow light onto the marks on the brickwork. He looked at the top line and made out five sets with four spaces. Down to the second line. Again. Five sets. Four spaces.

He looked at the first set, top line, and compared it to the first set, bottom line. The symbols correlated. The second set, top line, matched the symbols below. Third top and bottom, the same. Fourth top and bottom, matched. Finally, he looked at the fifth set.

He stood up and took out his notebook and pen. At a fevered rate, Rosen drew lines on a blank page.

'What's this?' Henshaw crouched down.

Rosen counted the dashes.

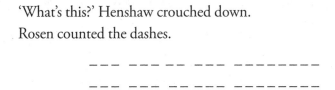

'Let's call these marks words,' said Rosen. 'The first four words top and bottom are identical. The last word, top and bottom, has the same number of letters and final two letters the same.'

Rosen lay down on his stomach and traced torchlight across the symbols again. An ill-defined but absolute sense of horror passed through him. He recalled Corrigan's gut reaction to the eye: *This is bad shit and I don't like it.*

He photographed the symbols carefully, making sure he got the two lines together, separately and each word on its own, in multiple copies.

'It's like the signature on a painting only instead of signing the front of the canvas, the artist's signed the back,' said Henshaw.

Rosen was up on his feet again, scrolling through the pictures, deleting the poor and saving the good images.

'He – we'll call him "he" for the sake of argument – has used covert language to counterpoint the sinister detail of his artwork.' Henshaw's face had changed like a chameleon: one moment actor-handsome, the next analytical academic.

In his notebook, Rosen drew the symbols in bold pen lines.

'Ever come across anything like this before?' asked Henshaw.

'I've seen things written in the victim's blood at murder scenes. But nothing as. . . artistic as this.'

'This isn't the work of an individual, is it?' said Henshaw.

'Did Baxter tell you?'

'No, Baxter just told me where to find you.'

'Then how do you know this involves more than one person?' asked Rosen. 'We didn't know this until late last night.'

'There's too much work involved for just one individual, unless

85

that individual's Superman. An abduction. . .' Henshaw threw out a thumb, bullet-pointing his response by counting with his fingers, a trait Rosen had noticed when he'd seen him on TV. He'd thought it was an affectation, but in real life it looked much less mannered than on the box. '. . . the concealment of a child for over a week. The precisely timed vandalism of a CCTV camera. The delivery of the child to this spot. This' – he indicated the eye – 'this labour of love. I just don't think one person alone could do all that. Too many skill sets and too much to do. I might be wrong.'

'Well, you're not wrong,' said Rosen, tapping in Henshaw's mobile number to his iPhone from the card he'd handed him when they met. 'I'll send the symbols to your phone, James. When you get back to UCL, approach your linguistics department. Don't contextualize it. Get someone to identify the alphabet these symbols come from. Though it may well be that the symbols are the group's own code, a self-generated secret language,' said Rosen.

'That's what I think,' said Henshaw.

Rosen looked at the symbols in his notebook, obscure configurations that mocked, *Crack me*.

'If it is a cult of some sort,' said Rosen, 'it's as vicious as it's strange, and I've no idea where it's coming from or what it's about.'

'I'll be back to you as soon as I hear anything.' Henshaw glanced at his watch. 'I'm going back to UCL right now.' He shook Rosen's hand. 'I'm available twenty-four-seven. No detail too trivial.'

'Likewise,' replied Rosen. 'Anything comes across your radar, I'm available any time of the day or night.'

'Just so you know, David, I'm on board as a volunteer. I'm not on the payroll.'

'That's decent of you,' replied Rosen.

Henshaw smiled. 'I've got an ulterior motive. I'm looking for the inside track on a big case so I can really make a name for myself and leave UCL.'

Rosen asked, 'You dislike teaching that much?'

'Not at all. I love it, but I really need to go freelance. I have a little boy. I need to spend more time with him.'

'What if this isn't the big break?' asked Rosen. 'It may or may not be.'

'That's the chance I have to take, David.'

Henshaw indicated the place where they'd attempted to burn Thomas alive.

'There's a big problem here for the perpetrators,' said Henshaw.

'Fire away.'

'If this was their first outing, then it rates as a disaster. They've messed up. The kid's alive. They'll have to strike back quick and make a better job of it, make sure next time they get it right. Whatever we call them, whatever they are, the peer pressure's going to be sky high.'

22

5 P.M.

Grandma's bedroom was Macy's favourite room in the world, although it no longer smelled of cinnamon, the scent she associated with the old woman propped up in the single bed. Macy sat on the bed, recalling the smell of her earliest memory of Grandma when she was a very small girl and the old lady had been fit and healthy.

Macy's earliest memory of being alive: Grandma, large and fat, cinnamon through and through, a memory suffused with the heat and light of the summer sun which Grandma blocked out with her generous shoulders as she stooped to kiss and cuddle her little granddaughter, and tell her how very much she loved her.

And how much did she love her grandma back? She'd hunted in books for a word but there was no word to convey the size and depth of that love.

The room now smelled of old age and the scented Glade candle burning in the corner, placed there by Macy to help lift the atmosphere in the old lady's room. Macy turned the box of matches next to the candle and stared, unblinking, at her grandma, at the light that played on her gaunt face and neck, drinking her in with her eyes in the knowledge that before too long she would exist only in memories.

In a family owning neither mobile phone nor camera, Macy tried to take photographs of Grandma's face with her mind's eye and, in closing her eyes, sealed the image of the old woman in her brain. Opening her eyes, she leaned in a little closer: the flickering shadows cast by the single tongue of fire made Grandma look something other than her usual self.

Slowly, the old woman opened her eyes from a shallow doze and said, 'Macy?'

'Yes, Grandma?'

'Come a little closer, Macy. Let me see you.' Macy obeyed and turned her face to the light.

'You didn't fall down any stairs,' announced Grandma, struggling to push herself from the pillow. 'Don't protect my feelings. Tell me the truth, Macy. Tell me the truth now. You know what I've told you about telling the truth.'

'Don't upset yourself, Grandma. I'll tell you the truth. I always tell the truth, you know that – that's what you taught me.' Macy paused. 'I was caught by two men on the street. One of them hit me. They stole my money. I'm OK. It's OK now. I was being tactful.'

'It's not OK, Macy.' Her grandma sank back on her pillows, emotional effort sapping her strength. 'Did you tell the police?'

'Yes, I told a detective called Mr Rosen; he was very kind to me. He looked sad when I told him what happened, like he was really sorry for me. I was lucky.'

'How can you say that, Macy?' Grandma's voice was so soft now that Macy had to scrutinize her lips to make sure of the words.

'The two men, they did something much worse. To a little boy called Thomas Glass.'

'The little boy who was abducted?'

'Do you want me to read to you, Grandma?' Macy changed the subject. Grandma appeared to have fallen asleep but then opened her eyes. 'How about I read from my school reading book? It's stories. I

89

don't like stories, I don't like made-up things, I've told my teacher, Miss Harvey, I prefer real things, I prefer the truth.' A thought occurred to Macy and she asked her grandma, 'What's the point of stories?'

'You like my stories about when I was a little girl growing up.'

'But those stories are real, they really happened, didn't they?' Macy explored Grandma's face and concluded, 'Am I making you tired?'

'I suppose I am a little tired, Macy.'

'Sorry, Grandma.'

The old woman's breathing was growing thicker.

'Don't. . . be. . . Don't forget. . . you and me. . . the bond eternal. . .'

Peace and stillness wreathed the old lady's face.

A terrible thought occurred to Macy and sickness overwhelmed her. She leaned in, pressed her ear to Grandma's lips and felt hugely relieved to hear her breathing in and out.

Macy got up from the bed, carefully so as not to jolt Grandma awake, and went over to the bedroom window overlooking Bannerman Square. She looked down. Last night, Grandma had told her, she had seen yellow light from the burning car dancing on her bedroom walls, had heard the explosion when the car's fuel engine blew up. She had even managed, on her way back from the bathroom, to stand at the window for a moment, watching the arrival of the fire engines, the ambulances and the police cars, but had been too ill to watch the spectacle below for long.

Macy pinpointed the Portakabin where she'd spoken to Mr Rosen, the policeman with the tired, kind eyes, and Bellwood, the black policewoman with the smiley face.

Grandma let out a very light snore and Macy knew this was a sign that she would probably sleep through till morning. She went to blow out the candle but, on second thoughts, left it burning because she didn't want to leave Grandma alone in the dark.

She closed the bedroom door behind her and, as she did so, the front door of the flat opened. She knew by the slow, heavy footsteps that it was her brother, Paul.

Macy wandered into the living room as Paul crossed towards the kitchen.

'Hello, Paul.' He ignored her and disappeared into the kitchen. In a room adjoining the living room, her mother's hairdryer created a small windstorm. She followed him to the kitchen door and stood in the doorway. 'Hello, Paul?'

He was at the sink, filling a mug with cold water, his back turned to her.

'Aren't you talking to me?' She spoke from the depths of her hurt.

He drank the mug of cold water without pause, his sleeve rising, three old scars on his forearm visible.

'Are you very thirsty, Paul? What you been doing?'

She switched on the kitchen light and he half turned, the profile of his seventeen-year-old face somehow much older in the bare light of the small kitchen.

'Paul, I don't like your new hairstyle. Why'd you get your head shaved? You've got lovely hair. Did you do it to raise money for charity? Or did you sell it to a hairdresser so she could make extensions?'

'Who are you?' he asked.

'I'm your little sister, Paul. You ought to talk to me.'

He filled his hands with water and splashed his face.

'That's not hygienic.' He span around, his mouth like a long healed wound. 'I'm joking, Paul, I'm trying to make you laugh! You always used to laugh at me. Remember?'

He turned his back on her and it felt like her heart had stopped beating.

'Oh,' she said. 'I . . . see. . .'

She switched off the light and went back into the living room. Staring at the blank TV – it was not to go on until *EastEnders* began on account of the electricity situation in the home – from the corner of her eye she saw Paul head back to the front door.

'Goodbye, Paul,' she whispered. 'I still love you, even if you don't love me any more.'

He almost threw the front door open.

'And I always will.'

But he closed it with infinite care.

'Thank you for not slamming the door. Grandma's just gone off to sleep. I'm glad you still care about *her*.'

She listened to Mum's hairdryer and stared at the blank TV screen. Mum was so selfish with her hairdryer.

Macy recalled how Paul used to talk to her but had stopped and wouldn't say why. They were alike in so many ways but the growing distance between them was crippling her inside.

The thought of what would happen after Grandma died filled Macy with a fear that made her want to be sick but, when these feelings assaulted her and she'd tried being sick, she could never manage it – she could never lose the awful feeling.

She took a deep breath, sat still and did the one thing the prospect of losing Grandma always made her do.

Alone, she cried in the shadows.

23

6.18 P.M.

From the doorway of the MIR, reality assumed a dream-like quality. Rosen looked out on a peaceful Bannerman Square. It was as if, twenty-one hours earlier, a bizarre and horrific crime hadn't been committed within touching distance of Claude House.

He bit into the ploughman's triple-decker sandwich he'd bought from Gino's, a deli on Lewisham High Street. As he did so, he heard in his pocket the reassuring crinkle of a mega bag of Walker's cheese-and-onion crisps.

At the desk, he opened his email and went directly to Riley's posting with the attachment marked A & E Lewisham list of outpatients and others attending. He opened it and scanned the names using his finger as a ruler. They were listed by the times they registered at reception, and there were approximately sixty names on the list, from 8.30 P.M. until midnight.

Finger and eyes arrived at 9 A.M. and down the list he went. Twenty past nine. Twenty to ten, the emergency admission of Thomas Glass with paramedics. At sixteen minutes to ten, the next arrival, Macy Conner and Paul Conner. She'd mentioned the x-ray on her bruised leg that lunchtime.

He called Riley.

'Hi, Riley, it's Rosen, where are you?'

'Changing over with DC Smith.'

'Thanks for the list.'

'Anything on it?'

'I'm not sure yet. I really need to see the CCTV footage from last night.'

'I've asked the head of security.'

'Ask again. Stress it's a matter of life or death. . .' Rosen sighed.

'I'll ask again.'

A cold, late April wind blew across the square and with it a sequence of traffic noises were carried from the high street. Rosen looked to the source of the sounds and at the place where the Megane had burned out and wondered, *Is that where you came from? The high street?*

And still, nobody except one little girl and one teenage boy had seen a thing.

Agitated, Rosen walked from the MIR to the epicentre of the crime scene.

A lone figure emerged from Claude House. Rosen saw it from the corner of his eye as a manifestation of speed, confidence and athleticism, and turned to see more.

It was Stevie Jensen, jogging powerfully in black Adidas jogging bottoms with three parallel silver stripes running from hip down to the ankle. He wore a royal blue Nike top with a black flash from the collar to the base of the arm and, on his feet, a pair of red Nike running shoes with an intricate silver pattern of parallel lines. But the thing that struck Rosen most was the manner in which Stevie ran; a young man with his life in front of him, striding the pavement as if he owned every paving stone, running as if towards his future life itself.

Their eyes met as Stevie hotfooted across Bannerman Square.

'Hello, Stevie!' said Rosen, his agitation relieved for a moment.

'Hello, Mr Rosen!' the boy responded, not breaking his step, running hard past Rosen and on his way out of Bannerman Square. *Keep running, Stevie,* thought Rosen. *Keep running as fast as you can from here. Don't stop for anything or anyone.*

As Stevie turned the corner away from Bannerman Square, Rosen heard a young child crying. For a moment, it sounded like his son.

As the crying came closer, he turned and saw a woman in her early twenties pushing a toddler in a buggy with one hand, a phone pressed to her ear with the other.

An attractive brunette, she walked very slowly, her mouth moving as she spoke into the phone. Across the bare space, her eyes connected with Rosen and then she looked away.

What do you want? thought Rosen. *And who are you talking to?*

She was heading towards him. Slowly.

Coldness crept through Rosen as he wondered if this young mother was a cult member, a scout sent out to tell the others when he was alone. He turned to see if there were people advancing silently towards him, but Bannerman Square was empty save for him and the mother, whose child raised his arms and yawned.

'Well, I never. . .' Rosen said to himself as she came closer.

It was the young mother from the Bannerman Square CCTV footage. He contained his excitement, stayed right where he was, did and said nothing.

She glanced at Rosen and said, 'Listen!' and looked away.

She carried on walking, directing her attention into the phone and then said, 'I want to talk to you, Mr Rosen, but I'm not walking into your Portakabin, know what I mean? I live at 4E, fourth floor, Claude House.'

She was past him now, heading home. Rosen looked at his watch. Six twenty-three.

'Leave it an hour at least, Mr Rosen.'

With mounting excitement, he headed back to the MIR, hurrying the last ten metres as the phone on his desk was ringing loudly.

'David.' It was Bellwood. 'Good news. Meryl Southall's with me at Isaac Street. She's got news on Thomas Glass's SIM card.'

24

6.25 P.M.

He walked towards the railway arches with the confidence of a man wearing the perfect disguise.

He looked ahead, saw a cluster of women advancing towards him and drank in their blank faces. It was as if he was invisible to them. Except to the small blonde nearest to him.

The briefest moment.

Her shoulder had brushed against his arm.

He didn't like being touched.

Her eyes met his and she said, 'Sorry.' His arm still at her shoulder, he breathed softly in the direction of her ear, and in that breath he encoded an ancient curse upon her.

Off she went, laughing, while above an aeroplane left a vapour trail, two blood-red scratches in the sky.

The black bag containing his tools weighed heavy on his left shoulder and he held onto the strap with his right hand, turning his head forty-five degrees to the right to gaze into the harshly lit interior of a double-decker London bus, its packed lower deck full of commuters. They may as well have all been blind, deaf and dumb.

The gathering momentum of a train, on an overhead bridge in the near distance.

In the bag on his back, the slosh of petrol in a can and the head of a hammer pressing into his flesh.

His thoughts turned to Mother and a smile broke out on his face.

Mother. He asked her silently, respectfully and lovingly, to inform his Other that if he wasn't already in the meeting place then to hurry there and not be late, because their sacrifice was soon and had to be as brief as it was bold. He had no need to communicate by phone or text or any of the other detritus of the modern world. His means of communication was ancient and perfect and never failed to reach the ears of his partner in holy worship. For Mother spoke directly to those who heard her.

Nearly there now. The arches. A garage door shuttered over for the end of the day, a mechanic with his back turned to him as he entered the shadow of the arches.

He turned left and walked directly towards the alleyway, around the corner and out of sight.

He pictured the face of Detective Chief Inspector Rosen, in the near future, when he saw the remains of their sacrifice, the fruit of their labour of love for Mother. *Rosen?* It was an insult that the best the London Metropolitan Police could put up against them was Rosen. *Rosen?* That tired and ever-sorrowful specimen had no chance.

Behind his back, he sensed the arrival of his partner and raised his hand in greeting as he turned the corner into the hidden alley, only metres from the broad and busy pavement, towards which the next sacrifice was heading at speed.

He paused to savour the squealing of brakes on the nearby street and the screams that followed it. His senses were alert, his ears keen enough to hear the wing beat of a fly.

Who was Rosen?

He slipped the bag from his back, opened it and took out the petrol can and the hammer. He rattled a box of matches in his hand and breathed in the holy aroma of petrol, the fuel created from the bones of prehistoric beasts, Mother's handiwork.

97

He heard his partner's voice inside his head. *'The small blonde bitch who touched you. . .'*

'. . . *Yes* . . .'

Their voices harmonized. *'Crushed. Car. Mounted. Pavement. Dead.'*

Who was Rosen against such power? *Who* was Rosen?

After tonight, Rosen was the next sacrifice. That's who Rosen was.

25

6.40 P.M.

In the incident room at Isaac Street Police Station, Bellwood noticed freelance telecommunications expert Meryl Southall eyeing up Gold and Feldman as they stared at CCTV footage.

'Not exactly spoiled for choice, are you?' said Southall.

'I'd never mix work with relationships,' replied Bellwood, agreeing with Southall, but not wishing to be disloyal or dismissive of her colleagues. She liked both men too much for that, and they always treated her with courtesy and respect.

Rosen hurried through the door, weighed the room up and said, 'Come on!' to Gold and Feldman. Immediately, they followed him to his desk as Rosen waved to Corrigan across the room.

Bellwood was especially pleased to see Rosen because Southall had been annoyingly reticent about 'the big deal' she'd picked up from Thomas's phone.

Meryl Southall had worked for fourteen hours on the SIM. She looked jaded and sorely out of patience. Rosen wondered for a moment if she was going to attack him with her vividly painted fingernails.

She handed Rosen a small plastic bag. Inside was a dark and fire-damaged SIM card. Next, she placed a blown-up photograph on his desk.

'This is an optical micrograph of that SIM card, the card in Thomas's phone.' It was an enlarged image, showing a metallic surface with double-digit numbers running parallel down the surface and linked by little lines, much like a ruler. On the surface of the image there were unblown metallic blisters.

Looking at the SIM card in the bag and the optical micrograph, the hope Rosen had incubated between Bannerman Square and Isaac Street withered.

He went for neutral: 'So, what did you find, Meryl?'

'When a phone's been subject to fire, data can be maintained in a SIM card's memory up to temperatures of 450 degrees Celsius. The temperature graph in a car fire such as this will curve off into four figures, so we're looking at 1000 degrees-plus Celsius at the hottest points in the fire where the fire burns most fiercely. Which part of the Renault was the least torched?'

'Back seat,' said Rosen.

'Left-hand side,' Bellwood recalled.

'Well, the phone in which this SIM was the brains either slipped or was pushed down the back seat, left-hand side, where the damage amounted to approximately 400–440 degrees Celsius; unlike the front seats of the car, the wheel and the engine, where the damage registered around 1100 degrees at the top of its curve. So, the data on the EEPROM wasn't necessarily affected.'

'The EEPROM?' Rosen asked.

'Erasable electrically programmable read-only memory. It's stored on the floating gate at the dead centre of the SIM.'

'What information was retained?' Rosen wondered how long or short the straw would be.

'The mobile phone was purchased directly from Virgin Media,' said Meryl Southall. 'The last active call made on it was from Thomas's home to a public phone box on Croydon Road on the day he disappeared. The last call received was last night at approximately ten past nine. The call lasted three minutes and came from an iPhone. I've already checked the number with DS Corrigan.'

She nodded at him and Corrigan said, 'It's the iPhone Thomas walked out of his house with.'

'The last call to Thomas's phone was made from the Bannerman Square area. I can tell when calls are made, not what was said though. Sorry.'

Meryl Southall reached in her bag and took out a pen drive, which she placed on Rosen's desk.

'It's all in my report and all the technical detail the Crown Prosecution Service will need is in there, too. I'm shattered. I've been awake since three o'clock this morning. Like I say, Rosen, this has been a king-sized pain in the arse.'

'And you, Meryl, are my brand-new friend.'

'No. No. . .' Swinging her bag over her shoulder, she handed Bellwood an envelope. 'There's the bill. It's not at all friendly. Not a bit of it.'

After she had gone, Rosen wondered if it was one man or two who'd driven Thomas to Bannerman Square. He gazed into space and imagined the confinement in the back of the car.

'David?' He looked up at Bellwood's voice. 'He had his phone with him. Why didn't Thomas call for help?'

Rosen remembered the case of a teenage boy, surrounded by a gang. The gang member wielding the knife had dropped the weapon. The teenager had picked it up and handed it back. Within a minute, the boy had bled to death on the pavement.

'They had him in a complete state of terror,' said Rosen. 'It's possible they ordered him by phone to set the car on fire, to set himself alight. That last phone call, ten past nine from Bannerman Square, it could have been the death sentence. It's possible that Thomas Glass set himself on fire.'

There was a hideous silence as the theory sank in. Bellwood looked at Feldman, who shook his head. Gold stared at the floor. Rosen leaned his weight against his desk, clutching the edges as his knuckles turned white.

'Jesus,' said Corrigan, softly, looking up but not looking directly at anyone.

'He must've thought' – Rosen found it hard to come to terms with the idea, but pressed on – 'that setting himself on fire was better than another option.'

'But what about the two men Macy Conner saw?' asked Gold, his round face red, a film of sweat forming on his forehead.

'The order came by mobile phone,' said Rosen, the logic of it unravelling in his head and making him feel sick. 'They came out of the shadows and descended on the car. They were the physical menace that ensured the order of the voice was carried out. They were the enforcers.'

The long, ugly silence was broken when Feldman said, 'CCTV.' And went back to his desk. He turned and spoke to Gold with an irritation in his voice that none had heard before: 'So am I going to do this by myself, Gold?'

Rosen gave Gold a subtle nod of the head and he followed.

'Christ,' said Corrigan. Rosen suspected he wasn't blaspheming but instead was praying beneath his breath.

'What did they do to his head during his captivity?' asked Bellwood.

'Stuck a head worm into his ear, let it gnaw into the centre of his brain. They made him believe burning to death was the lesser of two punishments.'

Rosen headed for the door at speed.

'Where are you going, David?'

'Bannerman Square!'

26

7.30 P.M.

The door of 4E Claude House was ajar, the opening music of *EastEnders* leaking into the corridor outside. Rosen knocked slowly, firmly, three times and the theme music died as the TV was turned off.

'OK.' The woman's voice came from inside the flat. He closed the door behind him and followed the sound of her voice.

The living room was immaculately decorated, tastefully laid out with a black leather three-piece suite and a print on the wall that Rosen recognized as a Monet. A toddler sat in a high chair as the young woman cut up food for him on his plate. On the floor, a large protective sheet covered the carpet.

In the hour since they'd spoken on Bannerman Square, the young woman had put on far too much make-up: her pleasant features had become a caricature. Rosen wondered, *Why? Where are you going tonight?*

Without looking up, she said, 'He won't eat in any other room, will you, Luke?'

The baby picked up a forkful of meat and shovelled it into his mouth, assured in his action and approving with, 'Mmmnnn. . .' Rosen noticed the peas and broccoli on the boy's plate. She was bringing her child up with a good attitude towards healthy eating.

The woman radiated maternal love, lost in her son's every action.

'Sit down, Mr Rosen. I won't offer you a coffee because I've got to keep it brief. I'm off to work soon.'

He perched on the edge of an armchair and she positioned herself at the side of the high chair so she could see him.

'What's your name?' asked Rosen.

'Chelsea Booth.'

'Thanks for coming forward, Chelsea.'

'I ignored the knock on my door this morning because I wasn't sure I was going to say anything. But I can't stop thinking about that boy.' She looked at her own son.

Rosen glanced around for signs of a man, but it seemed the toddler was the only male presence in the flat.

'Yesterday, I was on Bannerman Square round twenty past three in the afternoon. We were coming back from a mother and toddler group.'

She wiped her son's face with a flannel.

'Were you the only people on Bannerman Square?' asked Rosen.

'At first we were,' she replied. 'It's always empty, more or less, round that time because the kids are still in school. Three to three thirty it's like a ghost town. Then I saw a hoody come around the corner from the back of the builder's yard, where the CCTV camera is mounted on that wall, right? You learn not to stare round here. I just carried on, turned the buggy so my back was to him. Then I heard a noise. It was like a pair of hands clapping twice.' She clapped twice to demonstrate. 'Then this double clank. When I got to the door of the block, I saw the hoody running back around the corner. End of.'

'How long between the sound of the double clap and clank and you getting to the door of Claude House?' asked Rosen.

'Fifteen, twenty seconds. The rain started hammering down again.'

So he had time, thought Rosen, *to pick up the shells and then the bloody rain co-operated by washing away the gunpowder residue.*

'Can you tell me anything at all about the hoody?'

'Like I said, I didn't stare. But he was head to foot in black.'

'What was your impression? Height? Age? Anything?'

She fed her child and wiped his face again.

'I'm sorry for that kid, for Thomas. Everyone's saying the CCTV was bashed by the ones who tried to kill him. But I'm scared for Luke, my kid. I'm scared they'll find out I came forward and they'll come and get Luke. You understand how cracked up the whole thing's making me feel?'

'I understand perfectly. You have my word, this is confidential.'

'All done?' She addressed Luke, lifting him out of the high chair and holding him to herself. 'OK, Mr Rosen, this is my impression of him. He moved like a bloke in his late teens, early twenties. There was an arrogant air about him, he didn't appear nervous, the kind who loves himself and no one else very much. I'd put him at five eleven. . .'

'All that from a glance?'

'I'm good at reading men, close up and from a distance.' She shrugged. 'Gang kid with a gun but Mummy still washes his clothes every night.'

There was a knock at her front door, insistent. It stopped and started again, louder, sharper, increasingly impatient.

Chelsea carried Luke out of the room and Rosen stood at the door, straining to hear the voice outside. But all he heard was Chelsea, saying, 'Yeah, not now. . . Later on, as usual, same time. . . I'm not ready to leave yet. . .' The inaudible voice outside spoke at length and finally Chelsea said, 'Don't worry about me, I'll be fine, won't we, Luke?'

The front door closed and Chelsea returned. 'Just a neighbour, nothing to worry about.'

Rosen reached for his phone and thought, *Call Tracey Leung again.* 'Thank you, Chelsea.'

He took in Luke's face, the blueness of his eyes, the clean, well-groomed mop of blond hair, the contentment of a much-loved and well-cared-for little boy.

As Chelsea's front door closed behind him, Rosen heard a door swing shut down the landing and, taking out his phone, walked quickly to that place. He opened the door onto a grey concrete staircase and stepped into the stairwell. Rosen looked up a floor where another door closed. As he dialled Tracey Leung, he felt the coldness of an inexplicable fear.

After three rings, she answered.

'Hi, Tracey, it's David Rosen.'

'David, sorry, I've been in Liverpool picking up a pair of fifteen-year-old dope-dealers. I've just got back.'

'How fast can you get to Isaac Street?'

'Thomas Glass?'

'You got it.'

'Now. What do you want me to bring?'

'Anything on gang members with access to a gun.'

'Loads. I'll be there as soon as poss.'

Reaching the top of the stairwell, he started the descent. As he did so, his phone registered an incoming text with two sharp notes.

BELLWOOD the screen said.

The ground-floor staircase door opened and he heard someone coming up as he was going down. He turned the corner and a good-looking, shaven-headed boy passed him on the stairs, brown eyes staring ahead.

'Got the time, mate?' asked Rosen, but the boy carried on in complete silence, up the stairs. His eyes reminded Rosen of someone recent in his memory but he couldn't make the connection.

In the fresh air outside, he opened Bellwood's text.

David, get back to Isaac Street. We think we've come up with something interesting in Glass's contact lists. Carol

106

27

8.03 P.M.

There were many officers still slogging away in the incident room at Isaac Street Police Station, but the only sound to be heard was the creaky air conditioning and the buzz of the overhead lights. Sheer graft showed in all their faces.

Gold looked up from the CCTV footage that he was sifting through with Feldman and half waved at Rosen. Feldman stayed glued to the images of last night's traffic coming into Lewisham as it flickered on their laptop screens.

On the other side of the room, Corrigan was weighing in with Bellwood, her desk flooded with paper. The rimless glasses on Corrigan's nose softened the toughness of his face.

'What's up?' asked Rosen. He took in the state of Bellwood's desk and acknowledged their labour with an appreciative nod of the head.

'Nothing out of the personal contacts. We've narrowed down a couple of oddities in the business list, and one that strikes painfully close to home if your home's called Lewisham,' replied Bellwood.

She handed Rosen a thin brown card file inside which were a handful of A4 sheets. Rosen sat on the edge of her desk and slid the papers into his hand.

'Give me the overall picture,' he said.

Corrigan began: 'John Glass borrows money from big financial institutions and lends that money to people who the big institutions wouldn't touch with a barge pole, because of county court judgements against them and the like. Scumbag.' Corrigan was becoming vexed, louder, and Gold and Feldman glanced over from the CCTV hunt. He took a deep breath and lowered his voice. 'He insures the loans with Lloyds of London but also secures them against the borrower's assets, their homes for example. It's win-win all the way for Mr Glass and pretty much bite-it-and-like-it for the borrowers.'

'Carol?' Rosen drew Bellwood in.

'Of the four-hundred-plus business contacts, twenty-seven are within the Greater London area. This includes Barclays and several other big institutions. The DCs' next job is going to be going behind the door of the banks and exploring the question: "Who knows John Glass well enough within these companies that they could have met his son?" OK, the two interesting finds are' – she indicated the papers in Rosen's hands and he looked at the top sheet – 'Fingertips Escort Agency.' Rosen hurried past a flier of a blonde in expensive lingerie. 'He could have a financial interest in the agency or it could just be where he gets his nasties off. Backburner that one for now.'

Rosen read the next sheet. 'Outlook. What's Outlook?'

Outlook
info@outlook.org
www.outlook.org
02085151115

'It's the only charity on his contact list. It was based in Deptford—'

'Was?' queried Rosen.

'Yes, was. . . within spitting distance of Lewisham. The idea was to train up and get young, unemployed kids off the scrapheap. The Prince's Trust, but without that clout. I got those details from the Charity

Commission office because Outlook's website's folded, as has Outlook itself. What do you reckon?' asked Bellwood.

'If you wanted to commit suicide, John Glass wouldn't give you a push off the bridge for free. So, what's he doing with a charity on his associates list? I don't get it,' said Rosen.

'Nor do we,' said Corrigan

'How far have you gone with this?' asked Rosen

'Outlook. Fingertips. We think they're linked, but we don't know how.'

The door of the incident room opened. Rosen looked across and he smiled. 'Boy, am I pleased to see you,' he said. 'Come in, Tracey.'

28

8.10 P.M.

Tracey Leung, long dark hair and mid-thirties, walked in briskly, casting around the room and making eye contact with Rosen. She was a good-looking Chinese woman, and had perfected a gloss that made her look like she'd just won an arm-wrestling match with Satan.

Rosen waved Gold and Feldman over to his desk. As they gathered around it, he noticed the green tip of a serpent's tail, a tattoo on Leung's left forearm, peeping out from the edge of her sleeve. It appeared the story was true: when she'd been working deep undercover infiltrating the Wo 51 C Triad, she'd had the gang's totemic logo tattooed onto her skin to foster trust.

'So how're the gangs of south London treating you, Tracey?' asked Rosen.

'The death threats are becoming less courteous, but I guess that's a sign of the times.' DS Leung cut to the main business. 'Gang members with access to guns? I've got some names and faces to share with you,' she said. 'The Bannerman Square gun incident, right?' Leung sat down on Rosen's seat and asked, 'What's your take on it, David?'

Rosen met all present eye to eye. 'It's possible Thomas was taken by a cult of some sort.'

Leung let out a low, thin whistle.

Rosen flicked open his notebook and showed the symbols from Bannerman Square. 'I found these on the wall behind that painted eye. Any ideas?'

Silence from Gold and Feldman, and a short head shake from Corrigan.

'We missed them?' Bellwood was vexed.

'Could be that what happened to Thomas was some sort of public human sacrifice. I'm guessing,' said Rosen.

'And where do my parishioners fit in on that scenario?' asked Leung.

'I've got a description of the gunman from the mum with the buggy, the one we saw on CCTV. Head to foot a street-gang member. Probably. So the person who took out the CCTV camera was a gun for hire.'

'That figures, totally,' said Leung.

She took out a lean folder and passed it to Rosen. 'There are seven names in here. These are people who have access to guns. Four of them are locked up. The other three are within a one-mile radius of Bannerman Square: Patrick Ruskin, Jay Trent, Oliver Jones. Ruskin and Jones are Brockley Tribe – they're still a unit, but it's embarrassing for them at their age, hanging with thirteen year olds. Trent's nineteen years old, the last member of the Stockton Squad, burned out and in a gang of one. His former buddies are either in YOIs or have split town to get away from him. Ruskin and Jones have only been convicted of minor offences; Trent, we've never been able to pin anything on. When his mates were being packed away by the courts, none of them said a word about him.'

'How'd he manage that, Tracey?'

'Terror and a twisted cult of personality. When Trent was fourteen, he and another Squad member were cornered by three older rivals from another gang. They were armed with chains and metal bars. Trent's mate did a runner.'

'How badly did he get mauled?' asked Rosen.

'He didn't. He hospitalized the three of them, got their weapons from them and laid into them. When he caught up with the runner, he put him in a coma and went straight to the top of the heap. His capacity for vengeance is matched by his skill in close up and personal violence. They were all scared to death of him. Look at their pictures. Do they ring any bells?'

Rosen pointed at the middle of three mug shots that Leung had spread out on the desk. The youth had cropped black hair with carefully shaved parallel zigzag patterns on the side of his head. He looked directly at the camera as if he wanted to kill the photographer but, beneath his nose, he pouted like a petulant child.

'The lovely Jay Trent,' confirmed Leung. 'Eighteen months back,' she prompted, 'by the cricket ground on Hilly Fields. . .'

'I know,' said Gold. 'Hate crime – beat a gay teenager to within an inch of his life. This was on the front of the *Evening Standard* when he was charged.'

It came flooding back to Rosen. 'The victim pulled out of giving evidence the day before the trial, said he'd been mistaken in fingering Trent. Motive for this attack, Tracey?' he asked.

'Trent told his victim, whilst kicking him in the head and body forty-eight times, that he, quote' – Leung was reading from a file – '". . . fucking hates queers, I'd fucking round you all up, castrate the lot of yah, stick your stinking balls down your fucking throats, then I'd herd you into cattle wagons and send you to a concentration camp, starve yah and gas yah, you fucking perverts." Shall I go on?'

'I get the picture. Does he have Nazi sympathies?' asked Rosen.

'No political ideology whatsoever. Just a load of hate and aggression.'

'Who's employed him to use his gun in the past?'

'Loan sharks, drug dealers – the sight of a gun usually scares people into paying up or backing off. He hasn't got the capital or the infrastructure to loan shark himself, and he's too smart to deal drugs.' She looked at Rosen. 'What kind of gun was it? What kind of bullets were used on the CCTV camera?'

'Forensics haven't come back yet,' said Gold.

'Tracey, I'm going to call Superintendant Stephens and ask him to release you onto this MIT. Are you good with that?' asked Rosen.

'I'm better than good with that.'

A ripple of laughter passed around the group. Rosen noticed the way Feldman couldn't keep his eyes off Leung but that when she looked round, and her eyes met his, he instinctively looked away. In nearly thirty years, Feldman was the shyest officer Rosen had ever worked with.

'Tracey, what do you know about the guns the three stooges possess?' pushed Rosen.

'If the bullets used on Bannerman Square were 10.16 mm diameter, it was a Smith & Wesson and it belongs to Trent. Ruskin uses a Beretta 21A Bobcat and Jones has a third-generation Glock 17.'

Rosen looked at the pictures of Ruskin, Jones and Trent and saw a potential bridge to the people who set fire to Thomas Glass. But he guessed the gunman wouldn't know the full picture, or how deeply in the mire they'd dropped themselves.

'What's your hunch, Tracey?'

'Any one from three.'

'It started out as vandalism for cash,' said Rosen, 'and wound up as conspiracy to murder. One crime leads to another, and it's always an upgrade. Any questions?'

'About this cult idea?' asked Corrigan, his Liverpudlian drawl marbled with scepticism. 'What are the implications?'

Rosen considered.

'If it is a cult and we get into a stand-off, they're not going to take any prisoners, us or themselves included. Think Waco. I hope I'm wrong. My alarm bells are chiming.'

'I can't see any of the gang kids being directly involved in a cult,' said Leung.

'Why, Tracey?' asked Feldman, his voice almost a whisper.

'To them it'd just be completely uncool, and weird with it. If it's not rooted in the moment, concrete reality, instant gratification, they don't want to know.'

Rosen took her words on board. She knew the disaffected young men who scourged the streets better than anyone else in the Met.

'Thanks for that, Tracey,' said Rosen.

'No problem.' As she reached her hand to her head to smooth back her hair, her sleeve pulled back to reveal more of the intricate, thickening body of the tattooed serpent.

29

9.03 P.M.

In his car, Rosen called Lewisham Hospital's A & E and got through to Stephanie Jones, the nurse he'd encountered the night before.

'Hello. . .' He almost called her Bugner, but paused. 'Stephanie, how is Thomas?'

'Highly critical, but stable. He's still in the resuscitation unit.'

'I'd like to see him.'

There was dead silence and Rosen wondered if she'd heard him.

'Mr Glass says *you*'re not to visit Thomas.'

'Me, personally?'

'I'm afraid so.'

'Any particular reason?'

'He doesn't want to talk to you.'

Doesn't he? thought Rosen. *Why?*

'What does Mrs Glass say?'

'Nothing to anyone except Thomas.'

'Please tell Mrs Glass I called and asked after Thomas.'

Macy's withered flowers, her thoughts and prayers for the Glass family consumed Rosen for a moment, and he felt a deepening to the ever-present sorrow that the world caused him.

'Is that it?' asked Stephanie

'For now,' responded Rosen.

30

11.15 P.M.

Three women emerged from Claude House and walked briskly across Bannerman Square. At the front, a woman in her late thirties took a long drag on a cigarette, but it did nothing to steady her nerves. Thin and with bottle-black hair, her green eyes danced with agitation.

'Marie,' said her sister, clasping her hand.

'All day long there's a constable standing there. Where's he now, Jan?' asked Marie Jensen, frustrated, tearful.

'The tape's down, they must've got all they needed,' replied Jan. Dressed in loose, grey jogging bottoms and a black quilted coat against the cold, she was a little shorter than her sister and with blonde hair and a rounded face.

'There won't be anyone in there,' said Kaye, their friend. Red-haired and pale-skinned, she marched directly to the mobile incident room. Inside, a light was on but the door was closed. She turned the handle. Locked. The bluebird tattooed on the heel of her hand was a mistake she'd made in her teens and regretted every time she saw it.

Marie threw her cigarette on the ground and hammered on the door with the flat of her hand. 'Anybody there?' Anger and fear competed inside her.

Behind her back, Jan exchanged a look with Kaye.

'I want to report a missing person. A missing person! Are you in there, Mr Rosen?'

'Marie! This ain't gonna help none.'

She stopped banging the Portakabin door.

'Let's go to Isaac Street and report him missing there. There's someone there, twenty-four-seven.'

Marie took out her cigarettes and tried to spark up her disposable lighter, but her hands were shaking too hard. Jan wrapped an arm around her shoulders, and she fell into a fit of sobbing. Kaye took the lighter from her and said, 'Here.'

The friend ran her thumb over the wheel of the lighter and a flame shot up. She lit the cigarette but kept the flame alive, her attention captured by graffiti on the Portakabin door.

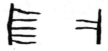

The sisters were already walking away.

'It didn't take 'em long. . .'

'Kaye, are you coming or what?'

She lifted her thumb and the flame died.

Some kids round here. . . thought Kaye, trying hard to distract herself from the thought of her friend's son who'd been missing for hours. *No respect for anyone, especially the police.*

DAY THREE

30 April

31

3.05 A.M.

After three hours' sleep, David Rosen took the bottle of formula from the bottle warmer and shook the excess water from its sides. Sarah sat up in bed with Joe in her arms, the room lit by a lamp in the corner, the darkness outside dense. The short walk across the room to the bed felt like an uphill march. Rosen up-ended the bottle and shook it again to test the temperature of the milk on the back of his hand. It was just right. He handed it to Sarah and, within moments, Joe's face was half-obscured as he drank enthusiastically, two bright blue eyes shining over the rim of the bottle.

Rosen looked into his son's eyes and his tiredness eased a little.

'Why don't you go in the spare room and try and sleep through?' asked Sarah.

'I'd rather be up all night with him than sleep in there. I don't see enough of either of you as it is.'

'Any progress?' Both Sarah and Joe had been asleep when he returned home, and Rosen had only spoken briefly to his wife mid-afternoon. Of all the day's developments, his mind went back to lunchtime and his conversation with Macy Conner.

'We've got an eye witness, says she saw two men running away from Bannerman Square. They knocked her to the ground, threatened to come back and burn her alive, stole her money. She's ten.'

'Poor kid.'

'They punched her in the face.' The memory made him angry, and something knotted in his gut.

'Did she give you a description?'

'It was dark and their hoods were up. So nothing facially. But she gave me the smell of petrol on one of them.'

'What's her name?' asked Sarah.

'Macy Conner.'

'How do you rate her as a witness?'

'Good. I need to know more about her. She could be crucial. Gold and Feldman are sifting CCTV, looking for the two of them exiting onto Lewisham High Street and the inward traffic coming towards Bannerman Square.'

'She sounds like a good kid, stepping forward like that.'

'She is. She's also a poor kid from a poor family,' said Rosen, looking at his son, grateful for the security he had with two working parents.

He recalled the way she'd been keen to get off to school that lunchtime and thought aloud: 'I'll phone her school first thing in the morning; get an appointment to talk to her teacher. Get a bit of background on her.'

'Good idea.'

Rosen recalled Macy's mental block, the piece of information she couldn't quite recall.

Sarah removed the teat from Joe's mouth and a sucking noise drifted across the softly lit bedroom.

'Here.' Rosen held his arms out and Sarah placed their son in his hands. Sitting on the edge of their bed, he lifted the baby to his chest and started gently patting his back.

In his mind, Rosen watched Macy head off for the library, weighed down with her grandmother's borrowed books. He was stabbed by sadness at a sudden thought, a connection of two ideas. He looked at his wife closely and something tender shifted in her face.

'What's wrong, love?' she asked.

'Macy's the same age Hannah would've been if she was still alive.'

Nearly nine years had passed since she'd died, and there wasn't an hour that passed by in which he didn't wonder what she'd be like had she lived. He knew it was the same for Sarah: very often, when they were out together – shopping, visiting a cinema or in a restaurant – he caught his wife looking at girls of the age she would have been, and the pain in her eyes always showed behind the smile she cast at these children and their incredibly blessed parents.

There were still times – her birthday, usually, but other days as well – when alone in the bath or behind some closed door, Rosen would weep for their loss and wish he could hold her just one more time.

Rosen held on to his son, looked down protectively at the crown of his head.

'He'll be just fine,' said Sarah. 'We've so much to be grateful for now. This little boy needs us and we need him. He needs us to be upbeat. He's our future.'

He cradled Joe in his arms and, watching his eyes closing, Rosen felt the full force of his unconditional love but, with it, an undertow of fear.

It was a dangerous and violent world for children and he asked himself, *Would anyone save Joe if I wasn't there?*

'He'll probably sleep through for the rest of the night now.' He stood up and walked Joe up and down the room. The motion did the trick of sending him into a deepening slumber.

He took him back to his room and lay the baby down in his Moses basket.

As he settled back into bed, Rosen said, 'One day, I'll come home and Joe'll be five years old. He'll look at me and say, "Who are you?"'

'He's a baby but he knows you're his dad, and he always will.'

Rosen switched off the light. As he lay in the dark, trying to empty his mind and sink into sleep, the thought of Thomas Glass's father refused to leave.

Money. Outlook. Fingertips.
Cult. Gang. Gun. Fire.
Glass. Thomas. John.
'Who's hiding something?' asked Sarah.
'What?'
'You just muttered under your breath, "He's hiding something."'
'Oh, no one, nothing, love.'
John Glass, that's who, thought Rosen.

32

7.30 A.M.

On her way in to Isaac Street Police Station, Bellwood had received a call from Rosen telling her to make a diversion to Bannerman Square and the mobile incident room.

As she crossed the square now, she noticed that the door of the Portakabin was wide open but there appeared to be no other signs of life.

As she got there, Rosen emerged from behind the back of the unit, black coffee in one hand, camera in the other. He looked very tired and rattled.

'Are you OK, David?' she asked.

He looked over his shoulder. He had made a call to James Henshaw as well, and the profiler was almost running to get across Bannerman Square.

'Have you met James Henshaw?' asked Rosen, indicating him.

'I've been to the lectures he gives at New Scotland Yard,' she replied, coyly.

'James, thank you for coming so promptly.'

Bellwood glanced over her shoulder and back again. Rosen noticed the flicker of a smile cross her face.

'James, this is Carol Bellwood, my deputy.'

Dressed in a black linen suit with a white, open-necked shirt and no tie, Henshaw looked like he'd just stepped out of a department store window display.

How different we are, thought Rosen, sipping his coffee and noticing the undertow of shyness with which Bellwood shook Henshaw's hand.

Bellwood turned to Rosen and asked, 'Why did you call us here?'

He reached for the edge of the Portakabin door and closed it over, exposing the fresh graffiti.

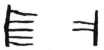

'They're right under our noses. This appeared some time between ten last night, when I locked up, and seven fifteen this morning, when I arrived here.'

Bellwood and Rosen turned to James Henshaw, who stared at the symbols.

Rosen noticed that now work was at the forefront, Bellwood's demeanour had changed: the glimmer of attraction she'd displayed moments earlier had been replaced by professional focus and self-discipline. And he dreaded the prospect of Bellwood ever leaving or being transferred.

Henshaw said, 'Yes, David, you're quite right – they're under our noses and operating in this neighbourhood. Not that that makes life any easier for us. On the contrary. What's your take on it, Carol?'

'We're looking for them but we don't know what they look like, who or where they are. So we're at a disadvantage because. . .' She recalled the lecture she'd attended where Henshaw had spoken about the significance of graffiti. 'They're marking this as their territory and letting us know that in their eyes we're interlopers. They're letting us know that even though we can't see them, they're watching us and that gives them a psychological advantage. In vandalizing our property with their symbols, they're claiming ownership of us.'

The academic analysis that had intrigued and stimulated her at Henshaw's lecture, when applied to the cold light of day, made Bellwood shudder inside.

'Anything to add, David?' asked Henshaw.

'I've checked the rest of the Portakabin, but there's nothing else there. I felt, I'll be honest, I felt quite afraid when I saw this.'

Henshaw stayed silent but Bellwood asked, with kindness, 'Why?'

'I felt like a marked man. I believe this is aimed at me because I'm in charge and I've been here most often.'

'You're right, David. I'm sorry, but you're quite right in my opinion,' said Henshaw.

'James, I called you here because I want to know the significance of its location. The door. . . why the door?'

Henshaw seemed to retreat back into himself, and Rosen instinctively knew that the profiler's take on his question wasn't going to be good news. He was clearly trying to frame his words carefully.

'It would help if I knew what the symbols *meant*.' Henshaw indicated the vast space around them, and the Portakabin. 'They could well be watching us now,' he said. 'This small structure represents your personal space, yours and your team. The door is the boundary. They're right on that boundary, they want you to know that.'

Rosen weighed it up. As the logic of Henshaw's point of view unfolded in his mind, his skin crawled, and he felt the weight of the breath entering his lungs.

'David.' Bellwood took a step closer to him, stood at his shoulder. 'You're not alone – this is aimed at all of us. *We* are *their* enemy because *we're* out to get *them*.'

Rosen nodded. 'If they're at the boundary, then there's really only one place they can go. That's over the boundary and into that personal space.'

On the wind, the noise of a moving train on the Docklands Light Railway.

He considered their weapon of choice.

There was little protection from fire.

And even though Rosen could feel his blood pressure rising, his face warm and red, he considered what it was to be turned into a human torch, knowing that the only options were disfigured agony or death.

Given an option, Rosen knew which one he'd take.

Death.

33

10.45 A.M.

At eight o'clock, through a phone call to Bream Street Primary's head teacher, Mrs Price, Rosen had arranged to meet Macy Conner's teacher, Miss Harvey, at eleven that morning. Less than three hours later, he travelled to the school as a passenger in Bellwood's car.

'The future belongs to those who are educated for it.' On a large board beside the gate, the mission statement and the name 'Bream Street Primary' stood out in white letters against a blue background over-arched with a rainbow.

At a quarter to eleven, the electronic gates of the school swung open and, window down, Bellwood steered slowly into the almost full car park.

The sound of the playground drifted from the other side of the building; the collective noise of spirited children, the clamour of play.

At the front of the building, Rosen rang the bell and the door swung open slowly. Entering, he focused himself on the task in hand. Information. Now.

At reception, a woman who looked as if she'd been born with a smile on her face glanced at their warrant cards and pushed a Child Protection Document and paper visitor badge at them, saying, 'Please read and sign the document. Sign and date the visitor badge, thank you.' She checked a Post-it note on the ledge in front of her. 'You're here to see Miss Harvey?'

An unpleasant electronic beeping suddenly sprang from within the building. Rosen glanced inside and saw an engineer on a ladder, working on the school's security alarm.

'Yes, we're here to see Miss Harvey,' Bellwood confirmed.

A plate-glass door swung open and Rosen and Bellwood made their way to the narrow two-seater sofa just inside reception.

The engineer continued with his screwdriver in the box on the wall and the sound died as suddenly as it had started.

At the foot of the ladder, the school's site manager looked on, a kindly looking man who seemed to be on the verge of anger. 'You said you'd fixed it last time! Twice in two nights I've been called out of my bed by the neighbours because it's gone off in the dead of night,' he said.

'Well, I'm sorry,' replied the engineer. But he didn't sound it.

Rosen smiled at the site manager, who offered Rosen a conspiratorial glance. On his boiler suit he wore an ID badge: MR ALEC FINN.

'This rotten burglar alarm system is going to be the death of me,' Finn observed to Rosen. The system beeped as the engineer examined the central control box. He turned the screwdriver and the system let out a horrible howl. Noise as a form of torture. He turned the screwdriver back and the howling stopped.

Rosen now focused on another noise: a sound coming from somewhere deeper inside the building. It was crying, interlaced with a babyish voice protesting a point. The swing door opened and a well-dressed woman emerged, one hand sealed around the hand of a boy of around ten years of age. Holding his other hand was a calm but fierce-looking classroom assistant.

'It weren't me!' The boy was genuinely distressed, his tears frantic, his indignation deep. 'I don't do that stuff any more, honest to God, Miss, I swear. . . The RSPCA got me head sorted, honest.'

'Chester, I don't want you to speak at the moment.' The well-dressed woman was firm but kind. She caught Rosen's eye as she opened a door, name-plated MRS PRICE HEAD TEACHER. He recognized her voice from the phone call that morning.

A bell above their heads clanged into sudden life. A clock on the wall read five to eleven – the end of playtime.

Behind the closed door, the boy's crying grew more hysterical.

'DCI Rosen?' A young woman approached. Her face was pale and drawn, her eyes red and wet with the residue of tears. Rosen shook her hand. It felt damp and chilled, like she'd been washing it under the cold tap.

'Miss Harvey?' Rosen checked. She nodded.

'I'm afraid we've had a rather unfortunate incident,' explained Miss Harvey, as the noise behind Mrs Price's door escalated. 'Come on, follow me.'

She walked away at speed. Rosen and Bellwood followed.

'I'm on non-contact time now. I'll make you a drink in the staffroom.'

As they reached the staffroom door, Rosen indicated the vinyl floor with a subtle gesture. Bellwood glanced down.

There was a single drop of blood on the tiles.

34

10.53 A.M.

As Miss Harvey made tea, Rosen drifted to a notice board, drawn there by a pool of pictures of young smiling faces. The title of the board read: MEDICAL NOTICES.

A seven-year-old girl with asthma, a nine-year-old girl with a nut allergy, an eight-year-old boy with diabetes and, at dead centre of the faces, Chester Adler, the ten-year-old boy who he'd just seen protesting his innocence to the head teacher.

Rosen looked at the picture of the boy, aware that Miss Harvey was snuffling quietly as she poured hot water onto tea bags.

Chester Adler, his face smiling and utterly gormless.

His condition: epilepsy. What to do if Chester fits?

1 Stay calm.
2 Allow him room.
3 Note time of fit starting and time the fit ends.
4 Dial 999.
5 Stay with Chester until the paramedics arrive.

Triggers: stress, strobe-effect lighting.
Please note: Before Chester goes into a fit, he will sit/stand rigidly, go pale, sweat, eyes will glaze.

Rosen joined Bellwood at the cluttered table that dominated the large and untidy staffroom. Miss Harvey brought three teas to the table and sat down with a sigh.

'I'm sorry, we appear to have arrived at a bad moment.'

'Chester. . . you probably saw and heard him at the front. He's just killed our class pet, our gerbil.' Miss Harvey clearly found it hard to believe the words coming from her own mouth.

'I'm sorry,' said Rosen. 'Are you OK telling us about Macy Conner?' He focused the moment, aware of time passing.

'One of the brightest girls I've ever taught.' The certainty was impressive but Rosen estimated, by her fresh complexion, that Miss Harvey could only have been a teacher for two or three years: it was a limited compliment. 'And Macy's as stubborn as a mule when she has an idea in her head.'

'What's her art work like?' asked Rosen, recalling the drawing of the two men who had assaulted her as she attempted to buy electricity for her home.

Miss Harvey smiled, 'Well, even clever children can't be good at everything. She's an absolute star, but she can't draw and she doesn't do *fiction* – that's the big thing in her head.'

'How do you mean?' Bellwood returned the ghost of a smile that crossed the young teacher's face. 'She doesn't *do* fiction?'

'Well, I asked her to write about someone or something she liked, and she did a report on "A Day In The Life Of Mr Finn". . .'

'Your school caretaker?

'Site manager. She came up with a detailed, articulate account of Mr Finn's day – how and why he's so important to the school, that sort of thing. You can get the smell of the school's boiler room out of it, but if I ask her to retell a fairy story, say "Red Riding Hood", she'll do three lines, and grudgingly at that. And if I ask her to read and explain from an encyclopaedia, brilliant; Harry Potter? She turns into this tongue-tied, almost near-robot. I've explained to her, you have to do fiction

– I've coaxed her, I've tried bribing her, I've begged her, but all she ever says – the same old thing, time and time again – "Miss Harvey, what's the point if it isn't true?"'

That's good news, thought Rosen, who then asked, 'What do you think it is with her?'

'She sees fiction as a form of lying. She's one of those rare human beings who'd rather drink poison than tell a lie. She lives with a very sick grandmother who's drummed the whole truth thing into her.'

'And she's consistent with the truth?'

'Absolutely.'

Rosen felt a shiver of pure happiness where he usually felt a worn-out antagonism at the duplicity of human nature.

'And she's bright, you say?'

'IQ of 157.'

'My sister's a teacher,' said Bellwood. 'She said to me there were a few children she couldn't stand, the vast majority she could bowl along with quite nicely, and the odd one she'd trust her house keys to. You know where she's coming from?'

'Yes, I do.'

'So where does Macy fit in on that spectrum?'

Without hesitation the young teacher said, 'I'd trust her with my house keys.'

Bellwood sat back, made a brief motion with her hand. *Tell me more.*

'She's on free school meals, you understand,' said Miss Harvey. 'But when she found a £10 note outside school, she brought it straight in to the office and handed it over.'

'When did this happen?' asked Bellwood.

'Yesterday. She just did the right thing. It was around the end of lunchtime – she'd been to the doctors.'

'What did the head teacher do with the money?'

'She handed it over to our community police officer. Macy's very kind to the. . . less able children. When she finishes her work, she wants to be the teaching assistant, she's quick to go and help the strugglers. I say, "Look, Macy, I have this extension activity for you," and she'll do that but then she'll be looking out for others who are still halfway through the thing she finished ten minutes earlier.'

'She's never been in trouble in school?' Rosen pitched the question into the pause.

'Never.'

'Mr Finn, your site manager? You mentioned a report. . .'

'Yes?'

'She relates to him?' asked Rosen.

'She worships him. On Friday afternoon we have Golden Time. The kids who've worked hard and been good all week can chose an activity: TV; computer; sit and chat. Every Friday, Macy gets Golden Time and she spends it shadowing Mr Finn, watching him do jobs, passing him a screwdriver, whatever.'

Rosen recalled there had been no mention of a father by Macy and asked Miss Harvey, 'Any dad at home?'

She shook her head.

Like a surrogate father then, thought Rosen.

The staffroom door suddenly opened and Mrs Price said, 'Excuse me!' glancing at Rosen and Bellwood. 'Jenny, I need you in the office now as I talk to the girls. I want to double-check the story Macy, Su Li and Lucy-Faye told you, before Chester's mother gets here.'

Miss Harvey stood and apologized to Rosen and Bellwood for leaving so abruptly.

'I'd like to come and listen to this,' said Rosen, standing and addressing the head teacher.

'Why?' she replied, defensively.

'As I said on the phone this morning, Macy Conner is our key witness in a very serious crime. It's entirely probable that she'll have to testify through the judicial system. I gather there's been an incident in school this morning?' Silence. 'I want to see how she copes in your office.'

The head teacher's face relayed the story: she was not in the habit of being told what to do by others.

'Follow me!'

35

11.01 A.M.

'Where's Chester now?' Rosen asked Mrs Price.

'In the library, dictating a statement to Mrs Judd, our Special Needs co-ordinator.'

The head teacher's office was the opposite of the staffroom. Here, every paper clip knew its place, just as every hair on her head appeared to sit correctly, according to the brush of its mistress's hand.

Macy and her friends appeared in the open doorway.

'Come in, girls.'

As Miss Harvey ushered the three girls into the office, they didn't seem to notice Rosen and Bellwood watching from the corner nearest the door.

'Are we in trouble?' asked the blonde one, her face lined with vague but deeply felt anxiety.

'Not at all, Lucy-Faye,' said the head teacher, shutting the door as Miss Harvey directed the girls to a trio of seats on the other side of Mrs Price's desk. The head teacher looked at Macy, who met her gaze directly, confidently.

Good girl, thought Rosen.

'Macy, would you like to tell me what happened this morning?'

Macy scanned the surface of the head teacher's desk.

'Is that Miss Harvey's camera?' Macy pointed to the small silver digital camera on the desk. Mrs Price nodded.

'What happened, Macy?'

'I left the hall because Miss Harvey'd forgotten some props for the class assembly rehearsal. It was about a minute after Chester left the hall to go to the toilet. I asked Miss Harvey if Su Li and Lucy-Faye could come with me because the props were heavy chairs. We were in the corridor and Chester was way past the boys' toilet on the left and was turning into our classroom. I went' – she held a finger to her lips – 'what's he up to? Lucy-Faye and Su Li were there.'

Mrs Price looked away from Macy's gaze and at solemn Lucy-Faye.

'Lucy-Faye, carry on.'

'We walked down the corridor, quietly. Macy was first to our classroom door. Macy said, "Don't make a sound!" It was just awful. . .' Lucy-Faye dissolved into tears.

'Macy?' Mrs Price prompted her.

'Chester didn't seem even aware we were there, he just stood there, the gerbil in one hand, with the compass in his other. . . stabbing it and laughing as he did it. I crept across the classroom to Miss Harvey's desk and picked up the camera and turned to video. The camera made this small sound. Chester seemed to wake up – it was like he was in a daydream but then he saw us all there and he dropped Mr Big on the ground. There was, like, a weird silence about the room and I filmed the lot on Miss's camera. Did you see the film, Miss?'

'Yes, I did see the video. That showed great presence of mind, Macy. Have you got anything to add to that account?'

'All this happened in the lesson before playtime. The truth is on the camera.'

'Thank you for your help, you can go back to class now. One thing, girls. You mustn't discuss this with anyone in school. Do you understand?'

'Yes, I promise,' said Lucy-Faye.

Su Li echoed, 'Promise?' and Rosen wondered how much English the Chinese girl spoke or understood.

Macy looked directly at Mrs Price and said, 'I swear on my grandmother's life, I won't discuss this with anyone in school. And I'll make sure these don't either.'

On their way out, Rosen made a mental note of the three little girls' faces: Su Li and Lucy-Faye serious and stone-like, with Macy in the middle, her eyes dancing with intelligence.

Mrs Price walked towards Rosen, having guessed his next request.

She gave him Miss Harvey's digital camera. Bellwood stood at an angle to Rosen, the better to watch the recording. 'Ready?'

'Yes.'

They watched the brief footage.

Chester retracted the point of the compass from the gerbil's body, laughing.

Rosen thought how a significant number of serial killers started their careers on vulnerable, available animals.

The boy turned his head, saw he was being filmed and dropped the impaled gerbil. Silence.

It was just as Macy had testified.

The sequence ended, and he handed the camera back to Mrs Price.

Rosen did a quick mental calculation – Chester at ten years, he at the gate of fifty – and worked out that when the boy got into his stride, he would be retired, leaving the aftermath to some other, younger officer.

And so Hell's merry circle would keep on turning.

'Can I have your mobile number?' said Rosen.

'All those empathy sessions with the RSPCA,' said Mrs Price, raising her hands briefly in mannered disbelief. 'It seems that was a waste of time.'

'A waste of time?' Rosen questioned. 'What's the alternative?'

'There is none. He was signed off by the child psychologist last month. He's had us all fooled.' She wrote down her mobile number and handed it to Rosen. 'For a kid with special needs, he put on quite a performance of innocence.'

36

11.20 A.M.

As Bellwood drove the car away from the front entrance of the school, Rosen suddenly said, 'Pull over, Carol!'

Through the railings, Rosen caught sight of the back view of a woman hurrying inside the building. As she entered the school, Miss Harvey walked out through the same door.

Rosen got out of the car and headed across the road.

Miss Harvey had a trowel in one hand and a small cloth package in the other. She crouched close to the ground at the circular plant bed near the front door to the school and dug in the soil with her trowel.

As he approached, Rosen noticed a blue plaque with white writing on the wall.

In memory of Denise Rainer aged 6, Jane Rainer aged 4, Gail Rainer aged 2

We will never forget

As he arrived at the railings, Miss Harvey stopped digging and looked up, over her shoulder.

'I didn't mean to disturb you,' said Rosen. 'I saw you coming out of the building as we were on our way from the school. Then I remembered.'

She stood up and approached the railings, the small cloth package almost entirely concealed by her hand.

'What did you remember?'

He offered her his card in between two railings. She placed the trowel on the flowerbed, took the card and slipped it inside her pocket. Rosen indicated the flowerbed.

'What are you doing?'

'Burying a gerbil. That's the first and last time I bring in a class pet.'

'Not every class has a Chester.'

'But they might do, they just might.'

Rosen felt saddened: disillusionment didn't sit well on her.

'You OK with me calling you Jenny?'

'The only ones who don't are the kids in my class.'

'I was wondering two things. If we need to talk in the future, let's meet someplace else. I'm not crazy about Mrs Price.' Her face softened into a conspiratorial smile. 'Do your kids keep a diary?'

'Ten minutes first thing each morning during register as the stragglers arrive.'

Henshaw crossed his mind. Rosen had a job for him. 'Can I borrow Macy's diary and Chester's diary?'

'It's Friday,' she thought out loud. 'Bannerman Square. Your Portakabin – Macy told me. I'll drop them off at lunchtime. Listen. We're not supposed to. . .' She glanced back at the main door.

'I'll make sure they're photocopied and back to you before the close of school.'

'No problem.'

'So, what's the drill for Chester now?'

'His mum's just arrived. She's going off the deep end. He'll be excluded for five days, the ed psych will call an emergency case conference, then he'll come back to school and face the hatred of every kid in the class – unless his mother manages to persuade some other school to take him on.' She sighed, then said, 'I'll sort the diaries for you.'

Through a gap in the railings, she shook hands with Rosen and, shoulders a little slumped, returned to the flowerbed.

Rosen watched her dig and then asked, 'Jenny?'

'Yes?' She didn't turn but carried on digging.

'Who were the three children that the flowerbed commemorates?'

'It was before my time. But if the eldest girl was still alive, she'd have been in my class now.'

She placed the cloth package in the hole in the ground and started scraping soil on top.

'How did they die?'

'Some sort of accident. No one ever discusses it. No one ever discusses the past here – we're all too busy sprinting to keep up with the present.'

She patted the earth down and placed a fist-sized stone on it.

'David!' Bellwood was out of the car, animated. 'David!'

He hurried back to the car. She was behind the wheel and into first gear as soon as Rosen's door was closed.

'Another burned body. Under the arches. Loampit Vale. Two minutes from the Lewisham Centre.'

'Dead or alive?'

'Dead. Young male, teenager.'

A hideous noise followed them as they sped off down Bream Street. It sounded like a banshee. It was the school's alarm.

37

11.35 A.M.

Life flowed past the scene-of-crime tape, with constables moving along interested passers-by. Buses, lorries and cars streamed in counter-flowing directions on the high street.

Scientific Support Officer DC Eleanor Willis waited at the entrance to the white tent she'd erected around the body. In silence, DCI Rosen and DS Bellwood dressed quickly in protective suits at the rear of Willis's Scientific Support van and went to join her.

'It looks like it happened late last night or in the early hours of this morning,' Willis informed them. Natural light was in short supply and deep shadows from the arches fell across the crime scene.

Petrol. Burned flesh. Coldness flooded Rosen as he flicked on his torch. He pulled back the flap of the tent and his beam picked up the victim's waist where the elasticated band of his running bottoms had burned into the skin and muscle of his lower torso. He trailed the light down the victim's legs. The tracksuit bottoms were smart, expensive. He flicked left and right to pick out the hands: it appeared the victim was holding a burned cloth in his blackened fingers.

Rosen paused, fearing the worst damage was to come.

The upper clothing was unrecognizable. On his chest, the charred clothes were indistinguishable from his torso. His face and upper body had been the primary targets. His teeth were visible to the gums and gave his visage a look between astonishment and agony. Rosen checked the skull and saw at least two clear depressions, indentations that looked like hammer blows.

Rosen tracked light back down the body to the trainers. A bell tolled inside his head and he hurried to get the light back to the face, to the eyes, but all he found were two burned-out pits. Back to the trainers. Red. Intricate silver pattern of parallel lines. Nike.

He crouched on his haunches next to the victim and played the light over his hands, on the material twining round his fingers and embedded in his palms.

They're going to do it again!

He felt a presence behind him and a bleak epiphany within.

'Carol?'

'Yes.'

'Where's Gold?' Rosen needed a second opinion from the officer who'd greeted him at Bannerman Square on the night Thomas Glass had crawled from the burning Renault.

'He's just arrived. Are you all right, David?'

He tried to stifle his feelings and fix the desperate sadness he knew was playing out on his face. He went for neutral but answered, 'No, I'm not all right.'

Rosen felt as if he'd just fallen from a cliff. His heart pumped, his head reeled.

'Carol, call James Henshaw for me.' As Bellwood left the tent, Gold arrived. 'Look at his feet,' said Rosen, flicking his light onto the trainers.

'Oh, shit!' The battle-weary cast of Gold's rotund face was softened by what he saw, and he looked child-like as his eyes widened and drilled into the murder victim. It was the same rare and vulnerable expression Gold always exhibited at murder scenes, but it was heightened because this time it was just too close to home.

Rosen stood up and composed himself.

He took the light to the boy's hands, to the remains of his bandages, considered the boy's overall shape and height. He recalled standing on Bannerman Square watching an athletic teenager at the start of his evening run; the same boy sitting in the back of Gold's car.

'It's Stevie Jensen,' observed Rosen. 'They couldn't get to Thomas, so they went for the next best thing, the eye witness. . .' He was consumed with the recent memory of a dutiful son who had asked his colleague to call his mother and let her know he wasn't in trouble. Stevie's life taken in his prime, his mother left behind to grieve until the moment she died, an emotional equation that could never be balanced. Rosen was silenced by sorrow, but then he focused and forced himself on.

'Yes,' Gold confirmed. 'He was respectful in the car. I liked that. I liked him.'

Gently, Gold lifted Stevie's arm with his paw-like hand and revealed a patch of blue on the teenager's running shirt that had been untouched by the fire.

'Nike. It's the blue Nike top I saw him in last night,' said Rosen. 'Someone watched the scene unfold, saw Stevie try to save Thomas.'

Bellwood re-entered, her calmness rattled. 'Henshaw's on his way.'

'Where's Feldman?' asked Rosen.

'I left him in the office at Isaac Street, still ploughing through CCTV,' replied Gold.

Rosen turned to Bellwood. She was almost dancing on the spot. *What's up?*

'David, this way.' They left the tent together.

A train roared overhead. Traffic pounded. It was like being in a sound storm. *A great place to commit a murder*, thought Rosen. *Timed correctly, with the trains and the traffic, no one could hear a victim scream, even if his head was on fire.*

Bellwood directed her torchlight at the blackened bricks of the lower arches. At first glance, it was almost impossible to tell them apart but, black marker on black brick, the human eye soon became accustomed to the graffiti eye.

This time the eye on the wall was smaller. And this time the medium was not aerosol.

'Who found this?'

'Me,' said Corrigan. 'As soon as I got here, I went looking for graffiti.'

'Well done. Good work, Corrigan.'

Rosen scrolled down the contacts on his phone.

'Gold, you spoke with Stevie's mother last night?' Gold looked miles away. 'Right?' pushed Rosen.

'Yeah.' He sounded distant but ready to kill.

'I need you to do something for me, for Stevie.'

'Go on,' said Gold.

'I need you to take a deep breath and put in a call to Stevie's mother. Ask when she last saw him.'

In an emotional corner, Gold was as tactful and sensitive with victims and their families as he was hard and scornful towards perpetrators.

'Carol,' said Rosen. 'Line up Victim Liaison.'

Rosen came to the number he was looking for: Stevie. He dialled, connected, but there was no sound of a phone ringing, just: 'Sorry, the person you're calling is currently unavailable.'

They took your life, thought Rosen. *Why not your phone as well?*

Willis held a torch up to the wall, and Rosen said, 'OK, Eleanor, we're looking for symbols – vertical lines with short horizontals coming off either to the right or left.'

He opened his notebook and gestured Willis forward. She stood next to Corrigan and they looked intently at Rosen's notes.

⫣⊣⧫ ⧫Υ⧫ ⧮⊨ ⧣⊣⧫ ⊢⧫⊢⧫⧫Ⅴ⧫⧥

⫣⊢⧫⧫Υ⧫ ⧮⊨ ⧣⊣⧫ ⫣⊨⧣⧫⧫Ⅴ⧫⧥

'I copied these from pictures I took. I found this scratched into the brickwork on the wall in Bannerman Square right behind the aerosoled eye.'

Willis looked sick with embarrassment.

'Eleanor, you were looking in the dark, it was raining, the marks are very superficial. It took me a dozen turns in the daylight to find them. You know what you're looking for?'

Uniformed and non-uniformed officers were arriving at the edge of the scene-of-crime tape. Rosen approached them.

'I'm DCI Rosen. We'll pass protective clothing over the tape. DS Bellwood will organize and take charge of the fingertip search.' He picked out a sergeant he knew from Isaac Street. 'Sergeant Cross will take care of the log book.'

Gold was at his shoulder, his phone to his ear.

'I'm still on the line to Stevie's mother,' warned Gold. Rosen knew. He could hear the hysterical crying filtering out of Gold's phone. 'Could you pass me over to your sister, please,' said Gold. He listened, then held the phone to his body. 'She reported him missing at midnight. He was four hours late. Left the house some time after six fifteen to go jogging, told his mother he'd be back by seven fifteen. His mother, her sister and a friend went walking the streets looking for him from nine at night until dawn.'

He returned the phone to his ear.

'Please listen to me, madam. In my view, right now, you need to be with your sister. OK. She needs you so much. On my honour, madam, I will phone you back shortly.' Gold closed the call down.

'What did you tell her?' asked Rosen.

'We heard about her visit to Isaac Street and were looking for him.'

Rosen returned to the tent, hoping against hope that another look at the body would rule out its similarity to Stevie. He stepped inside, looked long and hard and was bitterly disappointed.

This was your reward, thought Rosen, *for your decency, your courage.*

Rosen turned. 'Thank you for handling that, Gold.'

'I'll get on to Victim Liaison now and then back to Ms Jensen and her sister. You want me to go and see her with VL?'

Rosen was reminded of Gold's personal strength and was grateful he was on the team. The former rugby player never shied away from the painful encounters murder investigations always threw up.

'In an ideal world, yes. . .' said Rosen.

'But you want me to go back and CCTV-it with Feldman. You're right, boss, we've got a savage to catch.'

Rosen walked out of the tent and into the quiet, intent action of the murder scene, determined and inspired by Gold's parting words.

38

3.25 P.M.

D S Bellwood had two jobs to do in one journey to Bream Street Primary School.

To all intents and purposes, she was playing messenger girl and quietly returning Macy and Chester's diaries. She handed in a sealed brown envelope, marked FAO: MISS HARVEY PRIVATE AND CONFIDENTIAL to the receptionist and waited at the gate with the gathering groups of adults.

At two o'clock in the afternoon, Mrs Price had confirmed to Rosen that Macy, a girl on the verge of secondary school, very often walked home on her own.

Bellwood waited at the gate and looked through the railings at the memorial to three dead sisters where Miss Harvey had buried the class pet. Rosen had mentioned it briefly.

We will not forget. Bellwood made a mental note of the names and ages of the Rainer sisters: Denise six, Jane four, Gail two. Something deep stirred in Bellwood's memory and left her feeling like she was suspended in water, held in place by a huge weight as the sunlight played on the surface above.

Bellwood looked around at the waiting mothers, felt a surge of jealousy and wondered if they knew how lucky they were coming to school to pick up their children. She was thirty-four years of age and it seemed all the good men were now gone. She doubted that she would ever have a child, stand at the gate waiting for that look of recognition, mother to child, the deep hug that plugged the absence of a day spent apart.

An electronic bell rang inside. Soon, the main door opened and children filed out, bursting into life as they hit fresh air. Bellwood watched the tide of faces and spotted Macy in the flow, flanked by Lucy-Faye and Su Li. Macy frowned on making eye contact with Bellwood, but then smiled and raised her hand.

At the gate, Su Li burst out into a stream of Cantonese and hurtled to her mother. Lucy-Faye and her mother – a larger replica of the child – greeted each other with less enthusiasm.

And Macy said, 'Hello, what are you doing here?'

In the course of a frantic afternoon, which had included three bad-tempered phone calls to Superintendent Baxter, Rosen had organized covert protection for Macy in the form of a patrol car with an officer at the front of Claude House.

'I'm giving you a lift home, Macy. It's nothing to worry about. I need to speak with your mum, so I'll come up to your flat when I drop you off.'

'She's not in.' Macy showed the front door key in her hand. 'She's gone with Grandma in an ambulance for an appointment at St. Thomas's Hospital.'

'Who the fuck are you?' A voice came from behind Bellwood and she faced it head on.

Baseball cap over his shaven head, pale-skinned, gym physique, he was about seventeen or eighteen, with a tough guy persona that didn't quite come off. He pointed a finger at Bellwood and said, a little louder, 'Who . . . ?'

'I heard you.' She flashed her warrant card. 'DS Carol Bellwood, Metropolitan Police. And you are?'

His nails were bitten to the quick.

He folded his arms and leaned back, head tilted and looking at Bellwood as if she were behind bars in a zoo. She drank in the cheap body spray he'd doused himself with and guessed he wasn't easy with his own personal scent. She held on to the quiet and watched him, waiting for him to crack.

'That's my sister and I've come to walk her home from school.'

'Oh, you must be Paul,' said Bellwood.

'Yeah, Paul Conner.' His jaw twitched.

'Well, let me give you a lift home.'

He stared past Bellwood's head.

'I'm not arriving in Bannerman Square in the back of a police car.'

'It's not a marked police car, Paul.'

He unfolded his arms, hands dropping to his hips.

'I need to see your mother really, but I understand she's unavailable this afternoon.'

He made a noise. *That's right.*

'Come on, Macy, you can sit up front with me.'

As they walked to her car, with Paul metres ahead, Bellwood smiled at his affected street swagger. He was trying for tough and cool but looked like he was in desperate need of the toilet

'Has he?'

'This past couple of weeks, actually.' She drew a circle in the air near her temple and pointed at her big brother's back as they arrived at Bellwood's car.

'What kind of weird?' asked Bellwood, confidentially.

'He's been giving me the silent treatment.' Macy's voice was soft and lined with pain. 'I don't think he likes me any more. And that's kind of weird really.'

'I'm sure it's not your fault, Macy,' said Bellwood, kindly. 'Maybe there's something playing on his mind right now.'

Macy smiled at Bellwood but sadness remained in her eyes.

'Maybe there is,' said Macy. 'Maybe.'

39

3.33 P.M.

From Bream Street Primary to Lewisham High Street, not a word was spoken in Bellwood's car. Every few moments, she glanced in the rearview mirror. From the nose down, Paul's face was buried behind a fist, his eyes fixed beyond the window, his cap set low.

'How did the class assembly go?' asked Bellwood.

'OK. No one was really in the mood, though. Miss Bellwood?'

'Yes, Macy?'

'Can I ask you a question?'

'Go ahead.'

'Did you ever meet your father?'

'Shut up, Macy!' snapped Paul from the back seat. 'That's none of your frigging business.'

'It's OK,' said Bellwood.

'It's just I've never met mine,' said Macy.

'I met him when I was a teenager. Once. My parents divorced when I was a baby, so I don't remember him as such. He went back to Nigeria after the divorce, as it's where my parents came from originally.'

'We've got something in common,' said Macy, sounding more than a little pleased with the connection.

Bellwood slowed in the line of traffic as her car came close to the bridge. Rearview mirror. His fist had dropped and he shifted in his seat at the police presence under the arches.

'What happened?' asked Macy, pointing at the Scientific Support van.

'Ooh, I don't know,' said Bellwood.

'It wasn't like that this morning when I walked to school. Was it, Paul?'

He blanked his sister's question.

'I only came on duty an hour ago,' lied Bellwood. On the soc tape, she saw Corrigan and Rosen watching a gleaming black mortuary van pull away. Rearview mirror. Paul Conner mouthed the words, 'Fucking hell.'

'I'm not like most kids nowadays,' said Macy, brightly.

Bellwood hung back to allow the black van to enter the traffic directly ahead of her.

'How do you mean, Macy?' asked Bellwood.

'A lot of kids nowadays ride in cars all of the time, like. For me, it's dead unusual. This is really nice. Thanks, Miss Bellwood.'

'You're welcome.'

At a red light, they sat behind the black van.

'This is miles better than walking home from school.'

'Mmmn.' Bellwood considered the journey. 'Lots of busy roads to cross.'

'Seven to be precise. Quick 24.'

'"Quick 24"? What do you mean, Macy?' asked Bellwood.

Macy pointed at the licence plate of the mortuary van and read, 'K24 1CUQ. It's an anagram. We do them in school when it's wet play.'

In the back, Paul sighed bitterly.

The mortuary van pulled away and at the next junction turned left.

Rearview mirror. Paul Conner's eyes followed the mortuary van with a darting glance. His eyes came back to the rearview mirror where he met Bellwood's, smiling at him.

'All right in the back, Paul?'

She glanced back and this time, in a beat, made direct eye contact with Paul. His personae crumbled and, in that fragment of time, she saw Macy transformed into an older boy. Bellwood warmed to him.

'What the fuck,' snarled Paul, looking away.

'Oh, Paauul!' Macy's disappointment was jagged.

Two silent minutes elapsed.

When Bannerman Square was just around the corner, Paul sat up straight in the back. 'OK! You can drop us off here.'

Bellwood pulled up at the kerb. Paul tried to open the door.

'It's child-locked, or in my case, Paul, prisoner-locked,' said Bellwood.

'Obviously,' said Macy, glancing at her brother as she opened the front passenger door easily and stepped out. Bellwood opened the back door and Paul walked off straight away.

'Paul!' Bellwood put sufficient iron in her voice to make his shoulders sag and for him to come back, slowly, unwillingly.

Sullenly, Paul stopped in front of Bellwood, who turned to Macy and said, 'Go over there for a minute, Macy.'

When she was out of hearing range, Bellwood fixed her attention on the teenager.

'When will your mother be available, Paul?'

'I don't know. I'm not fucking talking to her and she isn't fucking talking to me.'

'Well, you've got to talk to her when she gets home.' She offered him a card, which he made no effort to take.

'We haven't got a landline or a mobile. Some people don't.'

'Give her a message from DCI Rosen, then, through me, DS Bellwood. Macy's a key witness in a particularly nasty crime. Do not allow Macy out of your sight. Either you or your mother should be with her at all times. She must not be allowed out on her own under any circumstances. If you notice an increased police presence in your immediate neighbourhood, you notice correctly.'

'What's going on, Bellwood?'

'Talk to your mother. Follow my instructions. Don't say or do anything to make Macy afraid at this time because that would really upset me.'

She stared him down.

'You going to look after your little sister?'

'Yeah, if you say so.'

'I'll be popping round to the flat. Not sure when, could be any time, to try and catch your mum. Tell her. Don't let Macy out of your sights.'

40

3.58 P.M.

'That's a wicked, wicked thing to do to a living creature.' Moved by the tale Macy told her about the day's cruelty, Grandma spoke firmly and clearly in spite of the cancer lodged in her spine.

Macy adjusted the pillows behind her to make her comfortable and sat on the edge of her grandmother's bed. Carefully, she raised a spoonful of Heinz tomato soup to the old woman's withered lips.

'Take your time, Grandma.'

It was a slow and cautious process, but Macy was well practised in the art of feeding the old lady. She wiped the merest trace of soup from beneath her grandma's lower lip.

'I don't want any more, sweetheart.'

'But, Grandma, you've only had eight spoonfuls.' Macy paused, thought about it. 'But that's one better than yesterday's seven.'

The old woman smiled and Macy questioned it with a perplexed glance.

'You should have been named Pollyanna, the little girl who always looked on the bright side of life,' said her grandma.

Next door, in Mum's room, Capital Radio news began its four o'clock broadcast. The words *second body* filtered through the wall, and then *found* and *horrific burns*. Mum turned the radio off.

Macy put the spoon down in the bowl and placed the tray on the floor.

'Want me to read to you, Grandma?'

'Not now, love, I'm a bit tired.'

'Well, would you like me to sit with you?'

'Haven't you got homework to do?'

'I'll go to the library later. Friday. It's open until six.'

'Then sit with me awhile.'

The old woman closed her eyes and Macy drank in her face. She opened her eyes and saw Macy staring at her.

'What is it, Macy?'

'I'm sorry.'

'What for?'

'Telling you about what happened in school today, you know, with the class pet. But I was upset and I needed to get it off my chest.' She leaned into the bed, confidentially. 'And Mum doesn't really want to listen, not like you, Grandma. I'm sorry if I've upset you with that bad news.'

'Worse things happen at sea.' The old woman pre-empted the child's question. 'Which is an old saying meaning, yes that was very bad what happened in school today but at sea – which means in the whole world – other, much more terrible things happen and we must keep all these things in context. Do you understand what I'm saying, child?'

'I understand perfectly.'

'That's because you're very clever, Macy. You only have to hear a thing once and you understand. . . good girl, clever girl. . .'

The energy was now drifting from the old woman's voice, and Macy watched as fragile sleep crept in.

'Take what happened' – her breathing grew denser and the dim candle light animated her tired features – 'to you. Macy. The terrible, terrible things. . .'

'Don't worry about me, Grandma.'

Silence. Macy waited until she was fast asleep and knelt beside the bed. She looked up at the window, at the heavy sky. *Please don't take her from me*, she prayed silently. *Please don't take her away from me. I couldn't stand it. I beg you, don't take her away from me.*

She picked herself up, lifted the tray, and left the room, closing the door quietly with her foot so as not to disturb Grandma.

As she made her way to the kitchen, Macy was stopped in her tracks by the sound of her mother's bedroom door opening. She carried on to the kitchen and placed the tray down on the small table.

Macy spooned soup to her lips. It had gone cold but she was hungry and even a cold spoonful was better than an empty one. She paused, spoon close to her mouth, as she heard the sound of a match striking and she smelled the familiar aroma of her mother's cigarettes.

She turned the corner into the kitchen and faced Macy.

'Did you see Paul?' asked Macy.

Her mum looked through Macy as if she wasn't there.

'I'm taking you to a solicitor Monday.' Macy opened her mouth to speak but Mum placed a finger to her lips. 'I can claim money for your face – criminal compensation – so when we go, you keep your fucking big mouth shut and I'll do the talking. Just nod if you understand because I don't wanna hear your fucking voice.'

Macy nodded and Mum went back the way she'd come. Across the edge of the doorway, a thin line of smoke cut through the air, and her mother's bedroom door closed.

Macy raised the bowl to her lips and in one hungry stream of sips drank the remains of the soup. Then she wiped her mouth with the back of her sleeve and drifted to the window of the living room.

Macy looked down at Bannerman Square and saw a woman, a stranger to her, carrying a baby in a carrier towards the mobile incident room. DCI Rosen stepped out of the Portakabin and walked towards the woman with the baby. Macy could tell Rosen was pleased and surprised.

She watched as Rosen and the woman met and he kissed her on the face. She raised the basket and Rosen took it from her, pressed his face closer to the baby inside and kissed it.

Rosen was a daddy. Longing and disappointment played inside her, and she headed for the front door of the flat, wishing she could slam it as she left because she felt so utterly sad.

41

4.09 P.M.

'I'm not staying long, David. I was driving through the neighbourhood, so I thought I'd come here on the off-chance.'

Inside the mobile incident room, Rosen cradled Joe in his arms and looked into his eyes, wide awake and content.

'This is a lovely surprise.'

'You said you didn't see enough of us, so I thought. . .'

'Where are you parked?' asked Rosen, wondering if he'd nodded off at his desk and was dreaming.

'Just round the corner from Bannerman Square.'

The surprise, the sight alone of Sarah and Joe, gave Rosen an energy boost. And the ever-rumbling guilt of his prolonged absences from his child disappeared in those moments.

Rosen's mobile phone rang and Sarah took Joe back.

'I know you're up to your eyes in it, so we'll get going,' said Sarah.

He picked up the phone from the desk.

'We're behind you all the way,' she continued.

He glanced at the display and felt sick.

'David, what's wrong?'

He sensed darkness crossing his face. Tension built behind his eyes.

The phone vibrated in his hand as it rang out again.

He double-checked the display.

He shut the door of the Portakabin. Sarah looked both quizzical and unsettled.

'Answer your call.'

It was as if each ring touched every edge of the enclosed space.

He connected the call to Stevie Jensen's mobile.

Silence.

'DCI Rosen.' He broke the silence and, as he did so, Joe let out a cry that made Rosen feel utterly afraid for his son. He held a finger to his lips.

Eyes pinned on her husband, Sarah shushed Joe, rocking him in her arms.

'Baby, baby, baby.' A voice, mechanical and cold, whispered in Rosen's ear.

Joe cried a little louder.

'It sounds like your baby's being tortured, Rosen.' It was neither male nor female.

'Why did you murder Stevie Jensen?' asked Rosen, matter of fact.

Sarah looked like an invisible hand had slapped her face. She held her child a little closer, smothering his cries in her coat.

'Rosen. You're dead! You're next!'

The caller hung up.

Duration of call: thirteen seconds.

Rosen stood with his back against the Portakabin door. He gripped the phone in his hand.

'Tell me, David,' said Sarah. Joe had stopped crying. 'Tell me the truth.'

'It was from the dead boy's phone. It was the killer. It was a death threat against me.'

'What are you going to do?' she asked.

'What can I do? I'm going to carry on.' The resolve in his tone was meant to reassure Sarah but, behind the facade, images of Stevie's

161

charred remains streamed through Rosen's mind and he pictured himself doused in petrol, agonized by fire, the smell of his own burning flesh in his nostrils.

He pressed speed dial. He needed Corrigan, the toughest team member, fast.

Corrigan connected at the other end. The background noise told Rosen he was in his car.

'David, what's up?'

'Where are you, Corrigan?'

'Driving to Bannerman Square from the new scene.'

'How close are you?'

'A minute.'

'I've got a job for you. Hurry, OK?'

'I can see Claude House.'

Rosen closed the call down.

'What's happening?' Sarah was agitated and afraid.

'Where did you say you parked?'

'Round the corner, Lydia Road.'

The place where Macy Conner was attacked.

Rosen estimated it was a sixty- to ninety-second walk.

'They know what I look like, but they won't know you. If I go with you to the car. . .'

There was a knock on the door. Rosen imagined opening it and receiving a face full of fuel and a freshly struck match.

'Who is it?' asked Rosen.

'Jeff Corrigan.'

It was good to hear Corrigan's voice. Rosen opened the door enough for Corrigan to get in and then shut the door as soon as he was inside.

'Hello,' said Corrigan, pleasantly surprised to see Sarah. And then to the baby, 'All right, kidda?'

'Jeff, I want you to walk Sarah and Joe back to her car.'

'No problem.' Corrigan smiled, but his brow creased.

'I'll explain later. You're not to leave them until the doors are locked and they're away from here. Call me as soon as they've gone. OK?'

He turned to Sarah.

'You don't want us to do this again.'

'I'm sorry. No.' The good their surprise visit had done him was gone. She kissed him on the cheek. 'Be careful, be extra careful.'

From the window, he watched Corrigan escort his wife and child across Bannerman Square. Then they turned the corner near Claude House and were out of sight.

He looked at his phone, silent in his hand, and willed it to ring, wanting nothing more in life than to hear Corrigan say, 'They're in the car. They're away.'

In his mind he ran through every corner in the neighbourhood, every blind spot, every dark hiding place, and he wondered which one they'd be lurking behind, waiting with petrol, waiting for him.

42

4.28 P.M.

'Sarah?' asked Corrigan, as they reached her car. 'Is the boss OK?'

Sarah was pleased to hear deeply felt concern for her husband from Corrigan, a man not given to public shows of tenderness.

'I think I'd better let him explain.'

Sarah placed the baby carrier down on the pavement next to the passenger door of her silver Citroën. Joe hiccupped softly as she opened the door and pushed the passenger seat down.

'Excuse me.'

She turned at the sound of a young girl's voice. Her face was bruised, her lip cut. From the sleeve of her black padded coat hung a thread of unravelling green material from the cuff of her cardigan. The girl smiled, and Sarah felt a rush of sympathy for her.

She looked at Corrigan and said sweetly, 'Hello.'

'All right, love,' said Corrigan. 'Macy Conner.' He'd seen her picture on Rosen's phone.

A light went on in Sarah's head. Macy Conner. Eye witness. Good kid.

The girl pointed at Joe and said, 'What a lovely baby you have.'

'Thank you,' said Sarah.

'You're welcome,' said the girl. She touched the cut on her lip. 'You don't live around here, do you?'

'No, Islington.'

'Ah, nice. I thought I hadn't seen you before.' She turned her attention to Joe, crouching on her heels to be closer to him. 'What's his name?'

'Joseph.'

The girl reached her hand into the baby carrier and stroked the fine hair on his head.

'We call him Joe.'

'Poor little thing's hiccupping like crazy.'

'Teething, hiccupping, that's babies for you.'

'I know a cure for hiccups. I learned it with the little boy I babysit for.'

The rain started.

'Here, let me have a go while you put the baby carrier into the back of the car.'

Sarah and Corrigan exchanged a glance.

'I guarantee I can cure those hiccups.'

'OK,' said Sarah, eyes pinned on the girl.

Corrigan took a step closer to Macy.

The girl had her hands carefully underneath Joe. She lifted him swiftly and skilfully from the baby carrier. 'I'm good with babies,' she said, then looked at Sarah. 'You keep looking at my cut and bruises. . .'

'What happened to you?' asked Sarah.

She held Joe close to her chest, one hand supporting the weight of his head, the other firmly against his spine.

'If you give him a little squeeze, not too much, just a little pressure, like this. . .'

Her hand relaxed a little from his spine and Joe chuckled. Several moments passed, and the hiccupping had stopped.

'That's very impressive,' said Sarah.

'Well done,' added Corrigan. 'You *are* good with babies.'

Macy held Sarah's gaze, turned her face as if showing her wounds to the sky and said, 'What happened to me. I was beaten up. Two men. I'll be OK, I guess.'

She turned her attention back to Joe, rocked him in her arms with great ease and smiled at him with absolute pleasure. Both children's faces lit up, delighted with each other's company.

Sarah turned her back, lifted the baby carrier onto the back seat but was then alerted by Corrigan's voice.

'Hey, Macy, hey, what do you think you're doing?'

Sarah stood up straight, turned back and her heartbeat quickened. Macy was five paces down the pavement and walking away, jogging Joe softly, her shoulders moving in maternal rhythm.

Corrigan was following. 'Macy?'

On she walked, her mouth was close to Joe's ear, whispering to him.

Then Corrigan was in front, blocking Macy.

Macy stopped and smiled at Corrigan. But the smile quickly dissolved from her face because he now looked cold and mean. She turned away from him.

'Yes?'

Sarah held out her hands. Her mouth was suddenly dry, and a prickly heat ran down her spine.

'Thank you. I'll take him now.'

Macy walked towards Sarah. She looked Joe in the face and spoke to him as if he was a child of her own age. 'Joe, some people have all the luck. Here's your mum now.'

Macy handed Joe to Sarah and, without another word, walked away.

'Thank you,' called Sarah. 'For helping with his hiccups.'

The rain shifted up a gear, hammered down, and Macy lifted the collar of her coat up over her head. She looked like a short, headless being.

Sarah strapped Joe in and, when she closed the passenger door, noticed that Macy had stopped at the corner. She caught Sarah's eye.

'I bet you can't wait to hear him talk, to hear his voice,' said Macy, with a sadness that released a tender glow inside Sarah.

'I can't wait for that,' replied Sarah.

'I'm so happy for him.' Macy turned the corner and was gone.

As Sarah drove away, Corrigan called Rosen's mobile and said, 'They're safe and sound. In the car and on their way back to Islington.'

'Thanks, Corrigan, much appreciated.'

43

5.59 P.M.

Just before the team briefing at Isaac Street Police Station, Rosen picked up a call on his landline and immediately recognized a fragile elderly voice.

'Mr Rosen?'

He looked across the room and picked out Feldman's snow-white head.

'Mrs Feldman?' said Rosen, to his colleague's mother.

'I'm worried about Michael,' she said. Rosen looked at his watch. People were waiting. 'Please don't let him do anything dangerous.'

'I'll take care of him, Mrs Feldman.' She was in and out of early dementia and Feldman had moved back home to take care of her. He was a dutiful son who didn't know his mother called his boss. Nor did anyone else. Rosen shielded Prof Feldman from the utter embarrassment of the calls that came in her periods of clarity.

'Did I tell you he was always a bit odd as a child?'

'There's nothing odd about Michael Feldman,' said Rosen. 'He's the brains in my team and I couldn't do without him, frankly.'

'Did I tell you he was tested for Asperger's Syndrome when he was a schoolboy? The educational psychologist said he had autistic tendencies.'

'Yes, you did and I'm aware he was given the all clear. It's been nice to talk, Mrs Feldman, but I'm going to ask you *again* to send any messages to me through Michael.'

'You didn't tell me that.'

He had done, every single time.

'I have to go now. I'm leading a meeting.'

'Make sure he doesn't go on any roofs chasing robbers. He hasn't got much of a head for heights. Thank you, Mr Rosen, and goodbye.'

He placed the receiver down.

'Everyone's here, boss,' said Feldman.

As Rosen positioned himself to speak, his phone vibrated twice in his pocket, signalling the arrival of a text. MORTUARY, the screen said.

He read the text and felt his heart sink at the inevitable news.

The room was silent.

'Fresh in, dental records confirm, today's victim is *definitely* Stevie Jensen, our witness from Bannerman Square. . .'

A wave of disappointment ran round the room.

Rosen let it roll out and called, 'OK, more thoughts on today's events at the conclusion. Let's start with the two suspects running from the Bannerman Square scene. Have you viewed all the footage?' Rosen asked Gold.

'With Feldman, we've been through every scrap of CCTV, all the junctions onto the main road, and there was no matching combination of two like suspects coming onto Lewisham High Street,' said Gold.

'Your view?' Rosen turned to Feldman.

Baxter's door opened and he drifted into the incident room, eyeing the presence of Henshaw and moving in Rosen's direction.

'They knew where all the cameras were on their point of exit onto the high street. They either split up and entered separately or they took off down a side road, such as Wales Close, and stayed out of the way of CCTV.'

'Any individuals on the high street who could've fitted Macy Conner's description of the men?'

'Yeah, we identified and printed them off. Paper copies on Rogues Gallery!' Feldman pointed to the sea of faces on the wall near Rosen's desk.

Baxter stopped close to Rosen and stood at an angle to him.

Rosen looked at the faces on the adjacent wall and asked, 'How many?'

'Twenty-six maybes in the five-minute time span you gave us. We're going through the CCTV that's come in for the Renault Megane. Nothing yet. Work in progress.'

Rosen thanked them and caught Henshaw's eye. The profiler stepped forward.

'I'd like to introduce you to James Henshaw. He's now the profiler attached to the case. He's based at UCL and he's the man who helped Avon and Somerset nail the South Coast Hammer Club, so he's well tuned in to what I believe this case revolves around. Over to you, James.'

Henshaw nodded at Rosen, and began to speak: 'Contradiction. The Bannerman Square crime scene screams *contradiction* over and over. We have the most brutal yet secretive crime – the burning alive of a young boy – and where is it performed?' Henshaw pointed the remote at the SmartBoard and brought up a picture of the burned-out car. 'Right in front of a residential housing block where hundreds of people have a clear view.'

He clicked and brought up another image, this time of the buckled CCTV camera in its battered cage.

'However, they go to the trouble of taking out the CCTV but have, probably, also gone to the trouble of. . .' *Click.* An image of the painted eye appeared. '. . . painting a symbolic, probably all-seeing eye on the wall directly in front of the car.' *Click.* The symbols from the rear of the wall appeared on screen. 'These symbols appear at the bottom rear of the wall. They could have hidden behind the common assumption that they were a paedophile ring, but they leave a symbolically coded message for us that screams out to me, *We are a cult.*'

'What's happening with the symbols? asked Baxter.

'On DCI Rosen's instruction, I've made copies and circulated them, de-contextualized, around the linguists at UCL. I'm waiting.' Henshaw handed Rosen the remote.

Click. The small, angular symbols from the wall blown up and magnified on the SmartBoard.

On the board, Rosen over-wrote the symbols with a red board marker.

'First two words. Anyone recognize these symbols?'

Silence.

Rosen pinpointed Corrigan. 'Jeff Corrigan found an eye marker-penned on the brickwork in the arches where Stevie's body was found. Did anything else come up, graffiti-wise?'

'Not yet, but I'm still badgering the scene with Scientific Support,' said Corrigan.

'OK.' Rosen hid his disappointment, but knew exactly where he was going when the meeting ended. 'So, how do the two incidents sit alongside each other?' he continued. He brought up Thomas Glass's school photo on screen. He was smiling, handsome, the world was his playhouse. He brought up an image of the burned car in relation to the eye and the gunned-down CCTV camera.

He then brought up a picture of Stevie's charred face. It was as if the room took a collective punch in the stomach.

He indicated the photo of Stevie Jensen. 'This was an improvization.' He brought up the burned-out car. 'This one, Thomas Glass, was carefully orchestrated. What happened today happened because Stevie went to help Thomas Glass. There are at least three people involved in this group' – Rosen made eye contact with Henshaw and Baxter – 'Let's go as far as calling it a cult. Two of them are men, aged eighteen to thirty. An eyewitness saw them running away from the scene. Someone else must've been on the square and seen Stevie help Thomas. That makes a third party. The strong possibility is a local freelancer was commissioned to attack the CCTV. I don't believe at this point, after talking to Tracey Leung, that any of the local gang members are involved in the core activity of attempted murder and murder. James, do you have anything to add?'

Henshaw shook his head.

'Based on evidence left on the SIM card from the Megane, I believe Thomas Glass set himself on fire.'

Rosen could feel the mixed weight of surprise, scepticism, disbelief even, and addressed it directly.

'He had the Nokia with him in the car. Why didn't he call for help? Because they told him if he did that, x would be the first consequence. If he didn't follow the instruction, y would be the next consequence. God knows what they did to his head in the days he was missing. But we do know Thomas said they'd do it again, and they did. And they'll do it again.' *Rosen! You're dead! You're next!* The words of the caller from Stevie's phone swam around his head, but Rosen said nothing about the death threat to him. 'Any questions?'

'What about the little girl, Macy Conner?'

'She's an intelligent and truthful child, and we've taken measures to keep her protected.' He turned to Baxter. 'Thank you for that, Tom.'

'If anything happens to her,' said Baxter, 'we're all going to look really bad.'

There were no more questions. Rosen closed the meeting as Baxter extended a folded copy of the *Evening Standard* towards him.

Rosen approached, took the newspaper from Baxter and unfolded it.

The front page. A photograph of John Glass. An image of

Bannerman Square and a headline: **INCOMPETENT.** Subheading:

Victim's father blasts police.

Rosen handed the paper back and said, 'There's a technical term for John Glass. Arsehole.'

Before he returned to the arches, Rosen had another place he had to visit. He looked at the clock on the wall and, at a pace that left him a little breathless, Rosen hurried out of the incident room.

44

6.40 P.M.

Sergeant Valerie McGuinness, of Victim Liaison, opened the door of the two-bedroom flat that was once Stevie's home. There was no need for Rosen to ask how things were: he could hear two women weeping bitterly somewhere inside the flat.

'His mother's with her sister, and WPC Jane Reid, in the bedroom. There's a family friend called Kaye Webb in the living room.'

'How's Kaye holding up?'

'Rattled as hell.'

'Any chance she'll talk?'

McGuinness considered and said, 'Maybe, yeah.'

'I need some daylight on Stevie's last movements.'

Rosen entered and McGuinness indicated the door to the living room. The layout was almost a replica of the flat he'd grown up in, back in Walthamstow. He glimpsed the compact kitchen at the end of the corridor. These were his people.

McGuinness opened the living room door and ushered Rosen inside. Kaye, elbows on knees, face in hands, looked up. She looked as if she'd been crying for weeks.

McGuinness sat next to her and said, 'This is DCI Rosen. Do you think you could answer a few questions?'

Kaye whispered through her tears and Rosen focused on the window that looked directly onto Bannerman Square. On the table by the window were Stevie's GCSE textbooks and exercise books, not touched since he'd last used them. Rosen wondered if they would ever be moved again.

'DCI Rosen? Kaye is willing to try a few questions.'

Rosen sat down opposite the women. Kaye held McGuinness's hand tightly.

'I was fortunate enough to meet Stevie the night before last,' Rosen started. 'He was an exceptional young man and I can't tell you how sorry I am.'

Kaye nodded. 'The sergeant at Isaac Street . . .' She took a cigarette from a packet on her lap and lit it with a disposable lighter. 'When Marie, Stevie's mum, called at midnight, the sergeant said he couldn't record Stevie as missing. But he was missing. Stevie's the most reliable kid you could meet. Regular as clockwork.'

As McGuinness explained missing persons procedures, Rosen once again took in the trophies in the room, and recalled Stevie's words. His coach had said he was good enough to try out for the nationals. A bitter taste filled Rosen's mouth.

'Kaye,' said Rosen, firmly but kindly. 'I know Stevie left the house after six-fifteen to go running. Did he do the same every night?'

'He didn't like the TV news and his mum does, so as soon as the news started, he'd get ready for his run, warm up in his room. Six-fifteen, six-twenty, he used to go for his ten-mile run. He used to do the same route every night because he promised his mum he'd stick to well-lit and busy main roads.' She took a deep drag on her cigarette. 'Lewisham to Catford, round the back of Blackheath, Shooter's Hill up to Deptford, Old Kent Road, New Cross back to Lewisham. Back by seven twenty, tops. We walked it three times last night into the dawn, me, his mum and Jan, his auntie, looking for him. Went past him at Loampit Vale three times, maybe fifteen, twenty metres away down that alley where . . . his body was.'

Rosen worked out the distance from Bannerman Square to Loampit Vale: a mile; and the speed at which Stevie ran, average time: six-minute miles.

'He never varied the route? Are you sure he wouldn't get bored and change the route, maybe go round the other way for variety?'

'If he was going to change, he'd have told his mum. He was very safety-conscious. It was a safe route, he knew the traffic, he knew the crossings – he wouldn't even wear an iPod. "My ears are for hearing traffic," he always said.'

Time of murder? Six minutes, seven or eight, even, to Loampit Vale. He was attacked before half past six.

'Kaye,' said Rosen. He waited until she focused on him, through a stream of cigarette smoke. 'To the best of your knowledge, does anyone round here know the route he took?'

'Yes. People used to ask him where do you go? They were impressed. Mostly. People who weren't sure of his name used to call him The Runner.'

She stubbed her cigarette out in an ashtray on the sofa's arm and started crying again, assailed once more by what had happened to Stevie.

Rosen stood up. 'Thank you, Kaye, I know how difficult this must be for you.'

'What about his poor mother? How will she live?'

One slow and agonizing moment at a time, thought Rosen, recalling Hannah, and the mind-warping grief her absence had caused him and Sarah.

'Kaye, I need to go and check something, based on what you've told me.'

Absently, she nodded and Rosen walked to the door.

'Thank you, Kaye.'

As he let himself out, Rosen was pierced by the forlorn words of Stevie's mother, drifting from the bedroom.

'Why wasn't. . . it. . . *me?*'

Because you didn't help Thomas, thought Rosen. *You didn't make yourself a target. Like Stevie.*

Once outside, he hurried towards his car.

A target. Like me.

45

6.58 P.M.

'DCI David Rosen, six fifty-eight pm,' he said to the constable now guarding the crime scene and running the log. He dipped under the tape and looked through the first of the three open arches, Silk Mills Path, at the pavement ahead, as far as Stevie went on his final run. With the possible exception of the killers, Rosen wondered if he was the last person Stevie had spoken to.

He looked to his left – two more open arches – and beyond that, the boarded-up arches that were the rear elevation of a car mechanic's workshop. Deeper in, the narrowing alleyway in which Stevie had been murdered.

'What got you,' asked Rosen, softly, 'from here to there?'

The same compulsion, he thought, *that made you help Thomas Glass.* He recalled the rising emotion in Stevie's voice, the way the experience had impacted on the boy.

Slowly, Rosen retraced Stevie's final journey from open pavement to the hidden alley.

Was it a scream? The word, 'Help', even? wondered Rosen, *that stopped you in your stride and lured you to your death?* He walked past the back of the mechanic's shop, the sharp turn into a dead end. Bang! The place where he was hit. The place he fell and was doused with petrol, the killers taking no chances this time.

Rosen stooped to look at the charred ground. He looked around the corner at the open arches. *They set fire to your eyes.* He felt a sudden dip in the temperature. Voices carried on the wind from the nearby street with its cafés and shops.

How neatly the abnormal and cruel tucked itself in next to the everyday humdrum.

His phone rang and he answered it.

'Hi, David, it's Jeff Corrigan. Doctor Sweeney's just about finished his autopsy. You'd better get to the mortuary ASAP. There's been a development.'

'Good or bad?' asked Rosen.

'Weird,' replied Corrigan.

As he walked swiftly to his car, Rosen made a call.

'James Henshaw,' replied the profiler.

'James, it's David Rosen. I'm going to the Dale Street mortuary, the second body—'

'I can be there in twenty minutes.'

46

7.15 P.M.

For the third time in the space of a minute, Bellwood knocked on the door of Macy Conner's flat. After the second time of knocking, she had heard movement inside, and had no intention of leaving with the door unanswered.

'Hello?' she announced, in a slightly raised voice. 'It's Detective Sergeant Carol Bellwood.' Then another knock, louder, signalling a louder voice to come.

A bolt slid back and the door opened a little, the chain still on. A gap between door and frame housed a band of darkness and into that place, half of Macy's face, her visible eye looking up at Bellwood.

'Hello, Macy.' Bellwood was heavily relieved to see her.

'Hi, Miss Bellwood, hello.' She sounded lost.

'Can I come in, Macy?'

Macy shook her head. 'This isn't a good time.' A single tear rolled down the girl's face.

'What's wrong, Macy?'

'My grandma, she's really sick. She went the hospital with Mum and...'

'Is your mum in?'

'Yes.'

'Could she come to the door for a little minute?'

'She's in a bad state.'

Macy's hand reached out from the darkness and touched the back of Bellwood's hand. Bellwood folded her fingers around Macy's for a moment, and then she let go. The little girl's tears fell fast and silent, her face wracked with sorrow.

'Please don't be angry with me, but I can't let you in.'

Having anticipated this possibility, or Macy's mother's absence from the flat, Bellwood reached into her bag and produced a sealed envelope inside which was a brief note outlining what she'd told Paul Conner earlier that day.

Macy glanced at the name on the envelope. *Ms Conner.*

'Could you give this to your mother, Macy? It's important she reads it.'

'Am I in trouble?'

'Of course not. DCI Rosen wants to make sure that *all* the children on the estate are safe. We just want to make your mother aware of that. Will you pass the letter on to her?'

Macy took the envelope. 'OK. I'll pass the letter on. Promise.' She looked down and slowly, without another word, shut the door.

Bellwood walked heavily towards the door to the stairs and, staying on the landing, opened the door and let it slam shut. Then she took off her shoes and crept back to the door of Macy's flat, listening for voices.

All she heard was the silence that wreathes a home awaiting death.

She waited a bit longer, and then walked back to the stairs. Putting on her shoes, she hurried past the community officers drafted in to patrol the stairway of Claude House.

47

7.21 P.M.

Macy sat on the edge of Grandma's bed. The old lady's eyes were closed but she was awake. She opened her eyes, her left eye nearly fully open, her right eyelid slipping down to cover all but a crescent of white.

'Who was at the door, Macy?'

'The policewoman I told you about, Miss Bellwood. She gave me a letter to give to. . .' She looked at the name on the envelope. 'It's addressed to you, Grandma. Ms Conner. Shall I read it to you, Grandma?'

On the pillow, she nodded. Macy tore open the envelope with eager fingers.

'"Dear Ms Conner, Given recent events in your neighbourhood. . ."'

Macy fell silent, read ahead to herself.

'Macy, read the letter to me.'

'"DCI Rosen and I strongly urge you to make sure that Macy is not left alone at any time. We have put extra police officers immediately in the vicinity of your home. We suggest that Macy is not to be allowed out on her own and is accompanied at all times by an adult. If you have any questions regarding this issue, please contact either myself or DCI Rosen on the numbers on the cards enclosed with this letter. Yours sincerely, DS Carol Bellwood."'

Macy saw that Bellwood had underlined the words 'Macy' and 'accompanied at all times by an adult' in red pen. She peeped inside the envelope and there were two small white contact cards, one for Bellwood, one for Rosen.

The letter was typed and was set on Metropolitan Police letter-headed paper. Her fingers trembled as she refolded the letter and placed it back inside the envelope. She heard the blood pumping in her ears and, welling up with tears, covered her face with her hands.

After painful moments behind this mask, she spread her fingers and, through a veil of tears, saw that Grandma was dozing, snoring.

She put the letter in her pocket and stood up carefully. As she left the candle-lit room, Mum's hairdryer sounded like a roaring beast and she, for whom feeling alone and afraid was almost a permanent state of being, felt the strength in her body sapped by the depth of just how alone and afraid she truly was.

They're coming to get me! They're coming to get me! The words span inside her brain. *They're coming. To get. Me.*

48

7.25 P.M.

Every time he visited the mortuary, it was somehow harder than the previous visit. Everything about the place alienated Rosen, made him want to turn on his heel, delegate, walk out and drink in the London air outside.

Instead, he stood his ground and breathed the chill, chemical air of the windowless room where Stevie Jensen's body lay beneath a white sheet on a metal trolley.

The whiteness of the cloth concealing the body sent Rosen hurtling back in time to the seventh day after Hannah's death, the morning of her funeral. He closed his eyes and turned his face away.

He saw again the paleness of Sarah's hand as it lay on Hannah's tiny white coffin. His own hand had rested next to Sarah's, and he had heard his wife say quietly, 'Don't go.'

The image blurred behind the tears that had welled up in his eyes, and he had heard his own voice say, 'Sarah, we have to leave now.'

He had wiped his eyes. Purple curtains parted as her coffin had begun to move. Rosen had leant down and placed his arms around Sarah as she had collapsed onto the rollers that had taken Hannah away for the last time.

'Cause of death, Stevie Jensen, confirmed.' Sweeney's matter-of-fact voice snapped Rosen back into the present, just as the pathologist turned back the sheet that covered what was left of the boy's face.

The top of his skull was missing, the brain removed from its shell.

'He was hit by a hammer. The first blow knocked him out. The second sent a long, thin splinter of bone into his brain. Do you want to see the evidence, DCI Rosen?'

Rosen shook his head.

'So, the good news is, he died more or less instantly before they set him alight.'

Sweeney turned the cloth down some more to reveal the ravages that petrol and fire caused to the fragile human body.

'It's clear to see that they only made a direct target of the head, face and chest. The sporadic, accidental damage to the shoulders, chest, back, abdomen and genitalia has been caused by what has splashed down, with a few minor, scattered burn marks on the upper thighs. . .'

Henshaw walked around the table, looking at Stevie's face from a few different angles. 'So they're fast learners,' he observed. All eyes turned to him. 'They tried to burn Thomas to death in a fire that was meant to obliterate the victim, and they failed. So far. So when they went for the second victim, they were much more economical, site specific. Who's going to survive an attack like that?'

'There's a reason why his lower half was untargeted,' said Corrigan.

'The bizarre thing you mentioned on the phone?' probed Rosen.

'They planted a clue.'

'Where?' asked Rosen

'Inside his sock,' replied Doctor Sweeney. 'I found the cap of a pen between the small and second toe of his left foot.'

Sweeney lifted the white sheet from Stevie's feet. There was a vivid red ring around the tip of the small toe, as if the killers had tried very hard to get the cap to fit on the toe itself. But the diameter of the toe had proved too wide for the pen cap to fit.

Henshaw wrote quickly in a notebook.

The nail was torn and coming away. The compression of the top of the toe had left the base swollen and bruised by the sheer force used.

'We keep this detail to ourselves,' Rosen said. 'We'll use it to weed out crank confessions. Where's the pen cap?'

Sweeney reached across to a trolley and produced an aluminium kidney bowl. He handed it to Rosen.

In the bowl, inside an evidence bag, was a bright florescent pen cap.

'As soon as I saw it, I thought about highlighter pens,' said Corrigan. 'That drew a blank. Then I had a blast from the past from when I was co-ordinating Metropolitan Police community work. It's from a UV marker to protect your property against thieves.'

'Do you know what make it is?'

'It's mass produced,' said Corrigan.

No symbols other than the eye, thought Rosen, *on the walls where Stevie was murdered. But no symbols.* A chilling possibility occurred to him.

'Can you bring me a fluorescent light?' Rosen asked Sweeney, who turned back to the trolley and opened a drawer in it.

Sweeney handed the fluorescent light to Rosen. He clicked the end of the slender tube with his thumb. A beam of blue light.

'Cut the lights!' said Rosen. A technician obliged and the mortuary was plunged into almost virtual darkness. He pointed the fluorescent light at Stevie and the beam hit the charred ruin of his face.

He stroked the neck with light and drew the blue glow down onto Stevie's collarbone, where pink flesh poked out between blackened patches. His left arm was less severely burned than his right, but the chest was devastated down to the centre of the rib cage, where most of the excess petrol had dripped, causing a pathway for the fire to fall.

His stomach was largely clear of damage, but when the light hit the boy's hands, Rosen felt his breath desert him briefly: the superficial marks caused when he'd tried to save Thomas were a tragic reminder of what had brought Stevie to this place.

Rosen now moved to the boy's feet, feeling his way down the

side of the trolley in the darkness, and using the light to guide him. He explored the toes of Stevie's left foot, starting on the inside and working out to the damaged digit at the end, circling, leaving no part unlit. He reached the damaged little toe. And stopped, stooping to make sure he wasn't mistaken. 'It's here.'

He moved then to the right foot, working the other way this time, starting on the little toe and examining each digit closely. He could hear the pulse within his ears when he arrived at the big toe. 'And it's here. Have you got a larger fluorescent light?'

Sweeney called to the technician and, within moments, a stronger light was delivered to Rosen.

Rosen looked at Corrigan and Henshaw through the sinister glow and said, 'They've marked the body this time. Look.' He shone the light on the left little toe and the right big one.

He turned to Sweeney. 'I need to see his legs.'

Sweeney lifted the sheet and Rosen used the florescent light to pick up invisible UV marks on the outside of Stevie's left leg.

The same style of symbols as Bannerman Square, but different.

Rosen picked out:

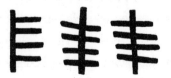

The symbols were drawn over the smooth curve of his calf. And above his knee, halfway up his thigh:

The writing narrower over cartilage, skin and muscle.

Rosen moved the light up and down from hip to ankle and saw that the message ran from Stevie's ankle to his hipbone.

The room was quiet as all the UV graffiti became clear to see: the entire message.

Rosen held the UV light as Corrigan photographed Stevie's vandalized toes.

In the pursuit of that which is sacred, thought Rosen, *the sanctity of others is nothing.*

'Done,' said Corrigan.

'Lights up!' The room stuttered into light. 'Copy the pictures onto my phone,' said Rosen.

As Corrigan did so, he looked agitated, angry and upset.

Henshaw's phone rang. He checked the display and said, 'God, yes, I'd better take this.'

Rosen looked at what remained of Stevie's naked body and reminded himself that a little over twenty-four hours earlier, he'd been alive, vibrant and with everything before him. *I'm sorry*, thought Rosen and, lifting one edge of the white sheet looked across at Corrigan, who took hold of the other side. Both men were of the same mind as they covered Stevie's body: to protect his dignity.

Rosen recalled the last glimpse of Hannah's white coffin as it sank away into the darkness, and the fire behind that. For a few moments, he felt dislocated from reality, his legs like water, the floor beneath him crumbling.

Corrigan was at his side and Rosen felt the weight of his hand pressed against his spine. 'It'll be OK, boss, whatever you're thinking about. It'll be OK.'

'Thanks, Jeff, I appreciate that.'

Henshaw turned and closed his phone. His face was animated with excitement.

'What is it?' asked Rosen.

'Great news. That was Dawn Coltraine, history professor at UCL. She knows exactly what the symbols mean and where they come from.'

49

8.03 P.M.

As Rosen escorted Dawn Coltraine into the incident room at Isaac Street, he could feel something almost electrical in the air as he passed Gold and Feldman at their laptops. Feldman was virtually dancing in his seat and Gold, catching Rosen's eye, was excited. Rosen kept walking, followed by Henshaw.

'We're on to something, David,' said Gold.

'Brilliant,' replied Rosen.

'Bellwood and Leung,' smiled Feldman. 'We've called them in.'

'Give me a minute, yeah?' Rosen pointed at Professor Coltraine's back. 'She can read the symbols.'

Gold gave Rosen a thumbs-up and turned back to the images he was pinpointing with Feldman. Feldman laughed, the high shrill laugh he gave when he'd cracked a problem.

'Thank you for stepping forward to help us out,' Rosen said now, to Professor Coltraine. She sat at Rosen's desk, Henshaw at her side.

At first glance, she looked elderly because of the shock of white hair that framed her face, but on closer inspection her face was youthful and alive with intelligence and kindness.

'It's perfectly all right, Mr Rosen.' She reached inside her bag and took out a brown folder. Placing it on the desk, she said, 'This is very straightforward.'

An overhead fluorescent light buzzed. She looked up and her face was suddenly pained. 'I'm sorry, can you do something about that light? The sound is like nails on a blackboard to me.'

Henshaw jumped up. 'I've got it, Dawn.'

Rosen turned on the desk light as Henshaw knocked off the fluorescent at the wall.

'Is that OK?' asked Rosen, kindly.

'Much better.'

She opened the folder and handed Rosen two pages of twenty separate symbols. They were the same symbols scratched onto the wall in Bannerman Square, the same as the UV marker on Stevie's leg.

Stave:	letter:	name:	Stave:	letter:	name:
⊢	B	Birch/Beth	⊣	H	Hawthorn/Huatha
⊨	L	Rowan/Luis	⫤	D	Oak/Duir
⊫	F	Alder/Fearn	⫢	T	Holly/Tinne
⊫	S	Willow/Saille	⫢	C	Hazel/Colle
⫦	N	Ash/Nuin	⫥	Q	Apple/Quert

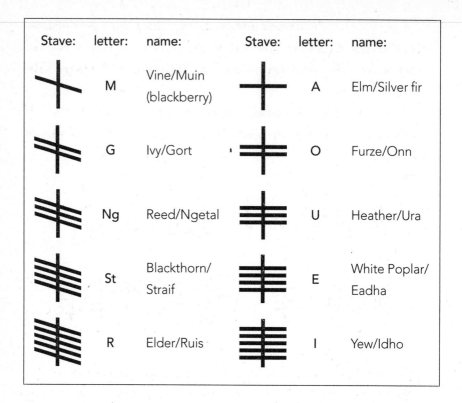

Stave:	letter:	name:	Stave:	letter:	name:
	M	Vine/Muin (blackberry)		A	Elm/Silver fir
	G	Ivy/Gort		O	Furze/Onn
	Ng	Reed/Ngetal		U	Heather/Ura
	St	Blackthorn/Straif		E	White Poplar/Eadha
	R	Elder/Ruis		I	Yew/Idho

'This is the Celtic oracular alphabet,' she said. 'The written form dates from the fourth century and was widely used to mark stones in Scotland and Ireland. But it's much, much older than that, and possibly predates the Roman invasion. It matches the English alphabet but only has twenty symbols including two phonic blends. There are no oracular matches for the English letters J, K, P, V, W, X, Y or Z.'

She moved the oracular alphabet aside. Beneath it was Henshaw's email with his own decontextualized imitation of the graffiti from Bannerman Square.

'Five words on the top line, five on the bottom. There's the alphabet,' said Professor Coltraine. 'The Vs and the Ys are modern English. The top line says, "The eye is the believer" while the bottom line says, "The eye is the deceiver."'

Rosen found the clearest shot that Corrigan had taken of the UV symbols on Stevie's leg, the whole message, and showed it to Professor Coltraine.

'See we is many. See I are one,' she said, without hesitation.

Rosen wrote the English translations on two separate pieces of paper and handed them to Henshaw. 'What do you think?'

'More contradiction? Give me a minute, David. Let me think.'

'What can you tell me about the alphabet?' Rosen asked Professor Coltraine.

'It's called Ogham, after the Ogmos, the Celtic god of knowledge and communication. The parallel god in Gaul was Ogmios and in Greece, Hermes. The shape of the symbols indicates it started out as a series of secret hand gestures – a secret sign language.'

Deftly, left hand acting as the vertical spine of the symbols and the digits of her right hand as the horizontal slashes, she signed *the*.

'The alphabet survived because the Druids started marking it on tombstones and road signs. It can be found as far away as Spain, Portugal. The Celts were a widespread people. Each letter relates to a tree that was sacred to the Druids. The B to the birch, the L to the rowan.'

Rosen showed her a picture on his phone, the two symbols on the Portakabin on Bannerman Square.

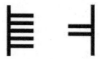

She looked up at Rosen and said, 'N and D. Ash and Oak.'

'Are they malevolent signs?' asked Rosen.

'Not as such.'

'You're aware, Professor Coltraine, of where this graffiti was discovered?'

'No.'

'How could this alphabet relate to fire?'

Within a breath, she said, 'Oh, no! The little boy. And the teenager.'

'Can you tell me how Ogham and Druidism might relate to the deaths of those two boys?'

'Certainly. There's a clear link. We know this thanks to the Roman invasion of Britain. Pliny and Caesar both wrote about Druidism. The Druids practised human sacrifice; burning their victims as a means of appeasing the gods and ensuring the rebirth of crops, new life.' She paused. 'It's strange. . .'

'What's strange?' asked Rosen.

'Modern druids abhor violence. They're peace-loving eccentrics.'

If only, thought Rosen, recalling the bitter tears shed by Stevie's mother.

Rosen saw Feldman and Gold looking over, smiling. Feldman made to stand up but Gold held him down in his seat with a hand on his shoulder. 'He's busy, Feldman,' Rosen lip-read Gold's words.

Turning back to the matter in front of him, Rosen showed Coltraine a photo of the graffiti eye on his phone.

She assessed it. 'The all-seeing eye: it's both a protective symbol looking out, and a conceptualization of the inward-looking eye, the human soul, a soul that can be born again into many bodies. Are you aware, Mr Rosen, of tomorrow's date?'

'May the first. Is it significant?'

'Highly,' replied Professor Coltraine. 'Tomorrow is the most significant night in the Druids' religious calendar. Tomorrow is Beltaine Night, the night of the Beltaine Fire. They used to use hostages from war and battle and if there were no hostages, criminals, burning them alive in huge cages of wicker, shaped into giants. It is the culmination, the night of multiple human sacrifice by fire.'

'Thomas and Stevie,' said Henshaw. 'They were preparations, a rehearsal. One ritual. One reprisal. Thomas was a hostage. Stevie a criminal, for going to the assistance of their hostage.'

'What's the window of time for Beltaine Night?' asked Rosen.

'Sunset to evening astronomical twilight,' replied Professor Coltraine. 'First of May, in London, that's 20. 24 to 22.55.'

'Two and a half hours, just before half-eight until five to eleven,' Rosen said. 'Evening astronomical twilight. What is that?'

'It's the point in time when the sun's relationship to the horizon is such that the sky turns completely dark.'

Henshaw showed Professor Coltraine a photograph of the UV spirals on Stevie's toes.

'The spirals predate the Ogham. They're symbols of life, death and rebirth,' explained Coltraine.

'What's their significance?' asked Rosen.

'Whoever's made these marks is claiming ownership of the victim's body and staking a claim to his soul in the afterlife.' An uncomfortable shadow fell across her face.

'What is it?' asked Rosen.

'If this. . . murderer. . . these murderers. . .' Professor Coltraine spoke hesitantly, as if thinking out loud. 'If they function like *ancient* druids. . . well. . .'

Rosen recalled the phone call from Stevie's mobile. The death threat rang in his ears.

'Go on, please tell me what you're thinking,' Rosen encouraged her.

'I hope it isn't the case but. . .'

He saw Tracey Leung enter, excited.

'From their religious point of view, they have no choice. They have to make human sacrifice.'

'I'd be grateful if you could keep this to yourself,' said Rosen.

'Of course,' she replied. 'Anything else?'

'No. Thank you for your help, Professor Coltraine.'

She stood up. 'I'll leave the symbols with you, in case. . .'

As Henshaw escorted Professor Coltraine out, Rosen joined Gold and Feldman.

Bellwood hurried in. 'What's going on?' she asked.

'There's going to be a blood bath tomorrow night,' said Rosen. 'A fire storm.'

50

8.15 P.M.

Rosen, Henshaw, Corrigan, Bellwood and Leung were around Feldman's laptop on the desk he shared with Gold. Gold's side of the desk: a jungle of stationery with memos to self on randomly placed Post-its; Feldman's side: pens set out in evenly spaced parallel lines around a neat and tidy ring-bound notebook.

'What have you got?' asked Rosen.

'A sequence of CCTV, a journey with a beginning, a middle and an end, with three clean shots of the green Renault Megane.'

'Show me.'

Feldman set up the sequence and asked, 'Ready?'

'Go on, Feldman.'

Tracey Leung was beside Rosen, her face a mask of anticipation and hope.

He pressed 'play' and a frozen image of an anonymous-looking road came to life as a light-coloured car sailed past the CCTV camera.

'Where's this?' asked Rosen.

'This is Blackheath Road. The Megane's travelling west to east towards Lewisham Road. The car's doing forty to forty-five like it's in a real hurry but it doesn't want to be pulled up for speeding. And he's camera savvy – he knows where each camera's fixed because each time he comes up to one, he accelerates to sixty or seventy mph. Here it is.'

The Megane nosed quickly into the frame and the film stopped on a full shot of the car in which Thomas Glass was soon to become a human torch.

Sitting quietly on the back seat, Thomas was in clear shot, his face just above the bottom of the window, one hand touching one eye. The time in the corner of the screen read 8.54.13.

'We've only just found it. We've called CC4U, video enhancement. We've emailed the footage, we mentioned Thomas Glass and they're working on it as we speak.'

'Great work. Any shots of the driver?' asked Rosen.

Feldman pressed 'play' again. 'Junction of Blackheath and Lewisham Roads, we get the Megane from the other side.' The brief sequence concluded with an indistinct image of a man at the wheel.

'Zoom in, Mike.'

Feldman optimized the image of the man and, as the picture got bigger, it lost clarity.

'Baseball cap, could be between the ages of fifteen and fifty. And where's his other hand?' asked Rosen.

'What do you mean, David?' said Corrigan.

'He's got one hand on the wheel, his left hand, and his right's suspended in mid-air.' Rosen considered the picture and, imitating the pose of the man at the wheel, the coin dropped. 'You're right, he is camera savvy, but he didn't get the timing dead on the beat.'

'Well?' said Corrigan. 'What was he doing with his right hand?'

Rosen lifted his hand from shoulder height to conceal the exposed profile of his face. 'Hiding behind it. What about the third shot?'

'Then we're onto Lewisham High Street, around about the station, where we should've had shots galore, but the traffic was so dense all we got on those different CCTV angles were double-decker buses, lorries – anything except the Megane.'

'So he played dodge 'em with the cameras, using traffic as a shield,' observed Rosen.

Feldman nodded. 'OK, this is where he comes into view, right now, the corner of Portnall Road and the high street. He has to slow to a stop and wait for a gap to cut across the oncoming traffic heading towards the station, and here he turns.'

The moving image froze to an image of the people in the car, the last working CCTV camera between that place and Bannerman Square. Thomas sat up almost straight, recognizable from the pictures supplied by his parents. The driver glanced to his right, his face turned for a moment and, using his left hand, pressed down on Thomas's head, his mouth open, talking.

'He's telling Thomas Glass to get down,' said Rosen.

'Zoom in,' said Leung.

'On the driver?' Feldman questioned.

'Yes, the driver,' she replied.

Feldman produced a whole-screen image of the driver's face, mid-flow in an outpouring of anger.

'I've been waiting for a chance like this for so long,' said Leung.

All eyes focused on her.

'You know who the driver is?'

'His baseball cap's not a common one. It's a Pittsburgh Pirates cap, dark-blue hat, yellow P against the hat and a matching yellow peak.' She shuffled through a folder and took out a photograph that she held up for all to see. It was a picture taken on a sunny day with a single individual photographed walking out of the north entrance of the Lewisham Centre. The cap looked the same as that worn by the driver of the Megane.

'This is a surveillance photograph taken last summer. It's Jay Trent.' She pointed at the image on-screen. 'That is Jay Trent.'

Rosen looked at the surveillance picture and the CCTV picture. It was a good likeness, but by no means unassailably so.

'When did CC4U say they'd have the enhancements back?' asked Rosen, his heartbeat rising.

'We pressed all the *time is short* buttons. Within hours, they promised.'

Rosen weighed it up. Trent could easily fit Chelsea Booth's description of the Bannerman Square gunman, but so could Ruskin or Jones.

'We'll pull in Trent, Ruskin and Jones purely on the pretext of questioning them about the CCTV camera on the square. It'll buy us time until the enhancements come back. Tracey, any angle we can use to our advantage?'

She smiled. 'Yeah, co-ordinate it so the three of them see each other being taken in for questioning. Is that possible?'

'That's no problem,' replied Rosen. 'Why, though?'

'They absolutely hate each other. It'll rattle them going into the interview.'

Rosen headed for the door. 'Come on, all hands. Tracey and I'll pick up Trent.'

Downstairs, Rosen placed Gold and Corrigan on the other two jobs, in case matters turned physical. 'Bellwood and Gold bring in Ruskin. Corrigan and Feldman, Jones.'

Tracey Leung clapped her hands as she chanted out their addresses, known by heart.

'Got you, Trent, after all this time,' said Leung. 'River Road, here we come.'

51

8.34 P.M.

As they approached River Road, Rosen asked, 'I take it Trent's not your favourite guy?'

'I don't know how he found out, but you know that restaurant on Shaftesbury Avenue, The Beijing Star?'

'Sure do.' It was the scene of many a joyful banquet for Rosen, and the very mention made him crave Chinese food.

'My mum and dad own it. Trent sent his mates round to try and intimidate my parents and the staff. When I say staff, I mean my brothers and sisters. The little bastard.'

'You the only cop in your family?' asked Rosen.

'I'm the only person in my family who doesn't work in the restaurant. I've been in the Met for fifteen years now. Mum still thinks I'm going through a phase, that I'll quit and come into the business.' She laughed but, as Rosen turned into River Road, her face set to professional severity.

The council houses in River Road were a combination of house-proud and couldn't-care-less. Jay Trent lived at number 16, the neat-and-tidy set: as Rosen and Leung arrived at the front door, he noted the small manicured lawn, the immaculate blue paintwork on the door that screamed 'respectable'.

Rosen pressed the bell.

'He lives with his mother and kid brother,' Leung explained.

'Hopefully, not for much longer.'

Within moments, the door opened wide and Trent stood there, staring impassively at Rosen and then at Leung.

Trent's brow creased as he looked at her.

'Yes?' he asked, smirking.

Leung didn't reply and Trent shifted his gaze to Rosen.

'What do you want?' asked Trent.

Rosen showed his warrant card. 'Jay Trent?' he said.

'Yes?' Trent leaned forward to examine Rosen's warrant card, making a show of the whole process. He looked at Leung, half shrugged, held out the palm of his hand.

She showed him her warrant card.

'If you want a coat, go and get it now. I'm taking you in for questioning to Isaac Street Police Station, regarding an act of vandalism to public property.'

'What's going on?' A woman's voice followed rapid footsteps coming down the stairs. The woman was middle-aged, wearing the uniform of a McDonald's manager. 'What's happening?' She directed the question at Rosen with menace.

Rosen stared at Trent and, as he did so, his confidence grew that this was the driver of the Megane.

Trent's mother stood shoulder to shoulder with him. The name on her badge read SYLVIA.

Trent sighed. 'It's OK, Mum. The police officers want to take me to Isaac Street to question me about some vandalism to public property.'

'What public property? What vandalism?' asked his mother. 'You can't do this.'

'Yes, we can,' said Rosen. 'Jay, coat. Quickly.'

'What's he meant to have done?' She jabbed a finger in the air between herself, Rosen and Leung.

Trent slid on a red-and-white baseball jacket. 'When are you people going to stop harassing me?' he asked, as if he was addressing two small, dull-witted children.

Rosen pointed at the car.

'See you later, Mum.' Trent glanced at what looked like a very expensive watch: thick gold, crystal. 'Say, ten thirtyish. Put MTV on the planner for me, nine o'clock onwards. Documentary. Eminem.'

Leung walked to the left and at the front of Trent, Rosen behind and to the right, in case Trent did a sudden runner between the front door and the car.

'You're a disgrace!' Sylvia Trent poured contempt from the doorstep.

Leung opened the back door. 'Mind your head, Jay,' she said, as he ducked onto the back seat.

Rosen climbed into the driver's seat. Sylvia Trent was already on her mobile, mouth motoring at a hundred miles an hour.

As Leung got into the passenger seat, Rosen checked his phone. One missed message from Bellwood. He checked the message, then showed it to Leung.

Ruskin and Jones on way back to IS. Start simultaneous interviews at 9.15 as per your plan?

Trent's eyes in the rearview mirror. *The eye is the believer*, thought Rosen. *The eye is the deceiver*.

As he texted back, the words, *See we is many. See I are one* rolled around his head.

He texted one word.

Perfect

52

8.37 P.M.

Macy could smell Chelsea's perfume from the other side of her neighbour's front door. It smelled expensive and came in a bottle that was green and gold and looked like it belonged in some fairy story. Although Chelsea lived only one floor down and one door away, her tall, pretty neighbour seemed to live in a completely different world to hers.

Macy knocked on the door softly because Chelsea had asked her nicely not to ring the bell as it may wake little Luke. Most nights, though, he'd be awake for at least an hour after his mother left for work, demanding that Macy play with him and his latest expensive toy.

She raised her knuckle to tap again but before she could, the door opened. Macy drew in a deep breath at Chelsea's face: she wore blood-red lipstick and her eyes were bright beneath the coal-black eyelids and long, curving eyelashes. Chelsea looked more beautiful than Macy had ever seen her. She felt something strange, a turning inside her, in her stomach, where butterflies flapped when she was nervous.

Chelsea smiled and asked, 'You all right, Mace?'

'I'm fine,' she replied.

'Come in, honey. He's fast asleep.' Chelsea turned and went back inside, leaving the door open for Macy to follow.

Shutting the door, Macy listened to the music of Chelsea's high heels on the laminate floor. By force of habit, she switched off the light and, remembering she wasn't at home, switched it straight back on again.

A fleeting thought about Luke's absent father crossed her mind.

Sparky, Luke's cat, walked over from his basket and started circling Macy, his soft side against her shins and around her calves. The cat looked directly up at her, and her eyes connected with the pale green of his.

Chelsea approached behind her, laughing.

'What's funny?' asked Macy.

'You're funny,' said Chelsea. 'OK, the usual drill. Help yourself to whatever's in the fridge, watch as much TV as you like but keep the volume down, and if there's a problem you're not sure of, knock next door for Prue.'

Chelsea produced a £10 note and offered it to Macy.

'Give the money straight to Mum. You know she insists.'

'I'll do that, Macy, but I'm giving this to you, for you.'

Macy took the money from Chelsea's hand. She folded her arms around Chelsea's waist and sank herself into her.

'Thank you,' whispered Macy. She pulled back a little and smiled up at Chelsea.

'What did you do with the last tenner I gave you, last Tuesday?' asked Chelsea, whispering confidentially.

'I put it somewhere safe,' replied Macy.

Chelsea laughed. 'So serious, and such a funny, deep voice for such a pretty little girl. Talking to the cat like it's human.'

'Is that what made you laugh? Was I talking to the cat?'

Outside, a car horn sounded.

'That'll be my cab.'

Chelsea kissed Macy on the cheek and focused briefly on the fading bruise on her face. Then she made swiftly for the bedroom door but stopped when Macy asked, 'Chelsea, is it OK with you if I have a friend over?'

'You haven't got a sly bone in your body, have you?'

'This is your home. I respect that.'

'This friend isn't noisy, wouldn't disturb Luke?'

'If they were like that I wouldn't let them in. I wouldn't let anyone do anything to disturb little Luke.'

'Night, night, sweetheart.' Macy heard Chelsea kiss her son and she pushed down a wave of jealousy. Grandma had been clear. It wasn't right to be jealous of a two-year-old boy.

After Chelsea had left, Macy drank in the last of the lingering traces of her perfume. Watching Sparky walking from kitchen to living room, she asked, 'Did I just speak to you, Sparky?'

She followed the cat and perched on the edge of the deep black leather armchair facing the 42-inch plasma TV. Not for the first time, Macy wondered how Chelsea could afford such expensive things when she worked as a barmaid in a West End pub? She'd looked up barmaids' wages on the internet in the library. They simply weren't that good.

Sparky made eye contact with Macy, and the pale green shine made her recall her absent-mindedly spoken words. Thinking of Luke's dad she whispered, 'He must've been mad to leave you, Chelsea. . .'

She made her way to the doorway of Luke's bedroom, lit up by a blue night-light. Inside the little boy's room, Macy stopped when she could see his profile: a puckered mouth and eyes closed, soft blond hair made turquoise by the cast of the light.

'He must've been mad to leave you.' Macy stretched out her left hand, her fingers drifting through the dreamy light towards Luke's face.

Tap, tap, tap.

She froze and withdrew her hand

A gentle rapping on the front door.

'If I was your father. . . She wouldn't have to go to work each night. . . If I was your father. . . If I. . . If. . . I. . .'

Sharper, louder, knocking on the door.

She turned away from the little boy, headed for the door and opened it.

'Come in if you're coming in, if not just go away.'

'It's cold, cold outside. I saw her leave in her cab. She looks like a model.'

Macy stood aside and felt the soft pressure of the cat against her legs again. She returned to the door of Luke's bedroom and watched his sleeping form, a bundle of warmth and comfort in a little boy's bed.

The front door closed.

'I'm starving.'

'Food's in the fridge,' she said, not taking her eyes off Luke. 'You can have two cheese triangles and two slices of bread from the bread bin, with one glass of milk. That is all.'

53

9.15 P.M.

Behind the door leading to the reception desk at Isaac Street Police Station there was a narrow, windowless corridor on which Interview Suites 1, 2 and 3 were situated.

At fourteen minutes past nine, three separate journeys began towards the interview suites. Bellwood and Gold escorted Ruskin; Rosen and Leung had Trent; and Corrigan and Feldman were in charge of Jones. Each suspect walked ahead of the duty solicitor they'd picked from the list.

At a quarter past nine, the three groups converged at the head of the narrow corridor.

Ruskin saw Trent and his face tightened as Trent stared coldly at him. Jones arrived. Ruskin threw a thumb jab in Trent's direction as Trent walked down the corridor. Jones called, 'Faggot!' Trent looked back, shook his head and calmly responded, 'Hear what he called you, Ruskin?'

'You are so fucking dead, Trent!' responded Ruskin.

'Maggot dick!' Jones heckled Trent.

Rosen closed the door of Interview Suite 1, insults still flying in Trent's direction through the fabric of the walls.

There was a glow on Trent's cheeks, a slight but distinct blush. Rosen gestured to the seats on one side of the table as he and Leung set up for battle on the other side.

Trent placed the flats of his hands on the surface of the table as Rosen formally opened the interview.

'What were you doing three days ago, on the afternoon of April the twenty-eighth?'

Trent tilted his head, looked doe-eyed at his solicitor, Mrs Cairns. She nodded.

'I'm still not sure what this is all about,' replied Trent, innocent, injured by suspicion. 'OK, what was I doing three days ago. . . in the afternoon. . .?' He rolled his eyes left and right, *recalling* for his audience. 'I got out of bed at two o'clock and had a shower. I got dressed and ate a bowl of Frosties in the kitchen. Then I went into the front room and put on a music channel called MTV and I played on my Nintendo DS. At a quarter to four or thereabouts, a taxi arrived dropping my little brother off from school.'

'OK,' said Rosen. 'Were you in or around Bannerman Square at all during the afternoon of Wednesday, twenty-eighth of April?'

'I don't go to Bannerman Square if I can help it, it's too rough.'

There was a knock at the door. Rosen walked across and opened it. In his hand, Corrigan had a brown envelope. His eyes shone and, behind the door, he pointed in Trent's direction and raised a thumb. In the corner of the envelope, the logo CC4U.

'Thanks for that, DS Corrigan,' said Rosen, evenly.

As he settled back next to Leung, Trent asked, 'Why? What happened in Bannerman Square, three days ago?'

Rosen blanked him as he carefully slid out the contents of the envelope.

There was a digital photograph and a covering note.

Keeping the blank side in Trent's direction, Rosen and Leung examined the enhanced CCTV image of the driver of the Megane. The picture was clear. Trent in the driver's seat; Thomas in the back with Trent's hand on his head. One of Thomas's eyes looked inflamed, and there was something in his hand.

They read the covering note from CC4U:

DCI Rosen – an initial digital forensic comparison of the faces of the driver of the Renault Megane and the mug shot show this is one and the same character. More-detailed report to follow, along with close-ups of driver and child in rear of vehicle.

Rosen and Leung looked at each other and then at Trent.

'Mr Trent,' said Rosen. 'Do you own a Pittsburgh Pirates baseball cap?'

'That's so last year, that's so not me.'

Rosen leaned into Leung and whispered, 'Duty magistrate, we need a search warrant, quick as can be issued.'

Leung left the room.

'What about the night of Wednesday, twenty-eighth of April?' asked Rosen.

'What about it?'

Slowly, Rosen turned the CCTV image towards Trent, watching his eyes as the picture became apparent. He stared dead-eyed at it, unflinching.

Rosen clocked the solicitor's face, the barely concealed surprise in her face.

'Do you know the little boy in the back seat?'

The solicitor scribbled a note, showed it to Trent.

'No comment,' said Trent.

'The little boy on whose head your left hand is resting?'

'No comment.'

'Do you recognize the driver?'

'No comment.'

Rosen leaned back, looked at the solicitor, then at Trent.

Mrs Cairns spoke up. 'I'd like to request a break, please, so I can advise Mr Trent.'

'Absolutely not,' said Rosen, sliding the note from CC4U across the table. As his solicitor read it, Trent looked away. She nodded and tried very hard not to look like a woman who'd walked into the opening blast of a fire-storm.

'This ain't the first time I've been maliciously harassed by police.' Trent spoke to the space between Rosen's eyes. Fear had kicked in hard, and its shadow, anger, was animating his features.

Rosen said nothing, just drilled his eyes into Trent's.

Trent turned to his solicitor. 'This is shit. They've paid to have this picture manufactured to set me up. Just like the celebrity magazines use computer software to make fat bitches look skinny.' Trent turned his head and smiled at Rosen.

'As in, *The eye is the believer. The eye is the deceiver?*' Rosen curved the question, but Trent looked completely baffled.

'What are you talking about, Rosen?'

'Thinking out loud.'

'Anyway! Anyway, I've got an alibi.'

'Go on.'

'Wednesday I was in all night, babysitting my little brother.'

'We'll talk to him then.'

'You do that,' said Trent, as if granting permission.

'I'm about to notify the custody sergeant that I'm suspending this interview and that you, our prime suspect, will shortly need to return to your cell. We'll talk to your brother, after we've searched your house.'

'Whatever.'

Rosen rang the desk. Silence. Neither Trent nor his solicitor looked in his direction.

A knock on the door. The custody sergeant entered, his face heavy. 'DCI Rosen? A word please.'

Rosen walked across and closed the door after himself. He looked at the sergeant and knew bad news was imminent.

'We've just had a call from Lewisham Hospital. Thomas Glass is dead.'

'Thank you for telling me.'

The blunt pain Rosen carried at all times sharpened into the most utter sorrow. He closed his eyes for a moment of respect. 'Poor little boy.' Rosen opened his eyes. 'Sergeant, release Ruskin and Jones immediately. Stick Trent in the cells.'

Walking to the car park, Rosen thought about the image of Thomas Glass in the envelope in his hand.

He was sure of one thing and certain about another.

In the enhanced picture, Thomas looked like he had a wounded eye. In his hand, he held his Nokia mobile phone. It was through this phone that Rosen was increasingly convinced his death sentence had been served.

The sound of a passing train drifted on the wind, its rhythm sparking off a chain of words inside Rosen's head. *See we is many. See I are one; See we is many. See I are one*. . . over and over.

54

9.38 P.M.

On the ground floor of Lewisham Hospital, Bellwood waited outside the Bereavement Office and noticed the absence of sound behind the closed door where John and Emily Glass were talking to a bereavement counsellor. She'd been told when she arrived ten minutes earlier that they'd been in with the counsellor for over an hour.

In all her time as a police officer, she had never got used to dealing with the parents of dead children. It didn't get easier and she hoped it never would.

She listened. A slow and rising tide of blurred and interchanging voices coming closer to the door indicated that the meeting was coming to a close. When the handle turned and the door opened, an elderly woman with a kind face smiled at Bellwood and asked, 'Yes?'

Bellwood showed her warrant card. She looked across the woman's shoulder and saw John and Emily Glass standing behind her, washed out, silent, not touching.

'Mr and Mrs Glass,' said Bellwood.

'I don't think they're up to questioning,' objected the counsellor.

'I've come to offer my condolences,' replied Bellwood, directly to Mrs Glass and, turning to her husband, 'and to give you an update.'

John Glass turned back and sat down on the nearest chair. The counsellor whispered in Emily's ear and she shook her head.

'I'm taking Emily with me for a coffee,' said the counsellor.

'Of course,' said Bellwood. 'Thank you.' She closed the door and faced John Glass.

'DCI Rosen apologizes for not coming in person, but we have a suspect in custody at present and he's conducting a search of the suspect's home.'

Glass was quick to respond. 'What's his name?'

'I can't tell you that. He's been questioned. He hasn't been charged. Yet.'

'How was he involved in what happened to my son?'

'That's what we're trying to find out.'

'Is he young, old, middle-aged?'

'He's a young unemployed man from south London. Thomas indicated to the boy who tried to help him that he knew his abductor. Do you know if Thomas knew any young unemployed men from south London?'

'As if.'

'Or if he knew of him through you?'

'What are you driving at, Bellwood?'

'I'm waiting on information from the Charity Commission office. We're pursuing a line of enquiry that our suspect was linked to a now-defunct charity.'

'What charity?'

'Outlook.'

'Outlook?' John Glass looked blank.

'The name Outlook doesn't ring any bells for you?' asked Bellwood.

He looked beyond her and gave the impression he was digging deep. 'Never heard of Outlook.'

Bellwood counted to five in silence. 'It was listed in your contacts details.'

'Well, I've never heard of it.'

'OK, but our suspect. . .'

'Why don't we cut the crap and you just tell me the name and I'll tell you whether I know him or not?'

'Our suspect entirely fits the bill for the remit of that failed charity. Outlook existed to help get young unemployed people from south London back into education or into a job.'

'Why would I support a charity like that?'

'I've no idea,' replied Bellwood.

'I don't do charity,' said Glass, contempt for such a pursuit marbled through his tone.

'That's absolutely your prerogative, Mr Glass.'

'Wait a minute.'

'Yes?'

'Do you know how many begging letters I receive every week? Hundreds. I get begging letters from individuals who think the world owes them a living and I get begging letters from people in charities acting like Jesus-on-a-stick. And they all come through my company. We have a policy that I imposed. Record all incoming mail and send the begging letters straight to the shredder. It's obvious what's happened here: there's been a clerical error. Some idiot's sent Outlook's details through to my database.'

'OK.'

'I'm out there to make money, plain and simple.'

Bellwood considered Fingertips, the escort agency on Glass's list.

'So, do you invest in other companies, other businesses?'

'Such as?'

'Restaurants? Leisure pursuits?'

'Too risky. I lend money. Money I know I'll get back one way or another. End of.'

So you're a client of Fingertips, thought Bellwood. *Or did that just slip accidentally from one database to another?*

215

Even through the rawness of his grief, there was a defensiveness about Glass that manifested itself as an aggressive veneer. He looked away from Bellwood's face and she was conflicted between sympathy for a grieving father, and cast-iron suspicion of a man she felt convinced was lying to her.

'I'm deeply sorry about your loss, Mr Glass. I'll leave you now. DCI Rosen asked me to tell you that he'll visit you personally at the earliest opportunity.'

'Tell him not to bother. Tell him to spend his time and energy catching the sick fuck who did this to my son. My son's dead now, so my dealings with you cowboys are over. Tell your boss. Tell him I don't want to see him ever again.'

Bellwood opened the door. Down the corridor, she could see Emily Glass sitting, head in hands, next to the counsellor, on a double seat screwed to the wall.

She realized that she didn't know whether John and Emily Glass had been in an information-free bubble since their son's admission to hospital. She tried one last appeal. 'Mr Glass, do you know what happened to the boy who tried to save your son?'

'Yes, my PA told me, and I'm sorry for him and his family.'

'As soon as we have anything concrete, we'll be in touch.'

Bellwood glanced back as she closed the door and was amazed by what she saw in that brief moment. As she was leaving the room, it seemed John Glass had been eyeing up her backside.

55

10.38 P.M.

'Make sure you get a full three-hundred-and-sixty degree sweep of the room, and when we get to lift the floorboards, I want a single tight shot of that action,' said Rosen to DC Blake, the officer responsible for filming the search of Jay Trent's bedroom.

Rosen folded back the duvet and, seeing the dried oval crust of a semen stain, lay it back down. He turned to the doorway, to Sylvia Trent, her arms folded tightly and narrow mouth clamped shut. She looked away from Rosen.

'When was the last time you did the bedding?' The stale, masculine odour in the room was rank. 'A week?' asked Rosen.

He beckoned Corrigan over and whispered, 'Bag the bedding and get it out of here, ASAP. I want a list of every substance that comes up from the fabric and a DNA check on the sperm stain. I want it in three days, not six weeks. They can do it. Insist.'

Naked to the waist down, pumped-up muscles decked in outsized jewellery, 50 Cent peered at Rosen from the wall directly facing Jay Trent's bed. The glossy poster was the centrepiece of a shrine to toughness and machismo: Tyson was there knocking six bells out of Michael Spinks; Jason Statham pointed a gun, his gaze fixed on the viewer. *Eyes*.

Rosen turned to the wall adjoining the bed. Girls galore. Pouting, puckering, bending over, looking directly at the viewer and blowing kisses into the void.

See we is many. See I are one. The words invaded Rosen's head and refused to budge, like bad music. *See we is many. See I are one.* There was something in these words that gripped Rosen, that made him wonder, *Is this the key?* Or was it just wishful thinking?

Sour-faced at the task, Corrigan had starting putting the duvet, sheets and pillows in large transparent bags.

Rosen opened the double doors of a built-in closet, crammed with quality street clothes: American Apparel, Urban Outfitters and top-quality trainers lined up in the large space at the bottom of the closet.

'Has he ever had paid employment, Mrs Trent?'

'Jobseeker's Allowance.'

'Take the clothes,' said Rosen. As he issued the instruction, his eyes fell on a dry cleaning ticket on the bottom of the closet: Speedy Clean, Lewisham High Street. He showed it to Trent's mother. 'I'll collect his clothes from the cleaners.'

'Move aside please.'

Rosen stepped away as Gold and Feldman lifted the bed away from the wall.

'This time I'm going to the Police Complaints Commission.' Trent's mother stared directly at Rosen as she spoke, her brown eyes on fire with anger, her lashes flecked with small clusters of stale mascara. She smelt of McDonald's and cigarettes.

'We need to talk to your younger son,' said Rosen. 'Jay told us he was babysitting him two nights ago.'

'Well, you'll have to go to his father's house to collect him. And that'll just be another point when I go to the IPCC. Harassing a little kid now, that's what this is.'

'Where does his father live?'

'Thirteen Woodstock Street.'

'Isle of Dogs, not far from here. When'd he go to stay at his father's house?'

'Today, when he came home from school.'

'And where was he the night before that?'

'I've told you, bonehead.'

'Tell me again.'

'He was here, with Jay looking after him.'

'And where were you?'

'The carpet in the corner, under the bed space, is really loose,' said Gold, kneeling down and turning the flap back. 'Like it's well used to being turned back.'

'I was in work, McDonald's, Bermondsey.'

'So you weren't physically present in this house from, say, six o'clock onwards?'

'I want my lawyer.'

'Thanks, Mrs Trent, that's all I needed to know.'

Blake settled into position with his camera.

'When you go to the IPCC, Mrs Trent, I wouldn't bother saying we planted evidence in your son's room because this is getting filmed as it happens.'

'I've been around the perimeter of the room,' said Gold. 'The rest of the carpet is tight, gripper-rodded into the skirting board.'

Rosen read the frustration in Gold's eyes. Since his wife had kicked him out, Gold had been forced to live in a shared house with five people he disliked and who disliked him. When Rosen had visited, with a house-warming gift of a bottle of Chivas Regal, he'd been disappointed at the state of the house.

Materially, Jay Trent, who'd never worked, had a better quality of everything than Gold, after his twenty years in the Met.

The remaining threads of Mrs Trent's composure snapped and she almost shrieked, 'You can't do this!'

Rosen showed her the search warrant for the fifth time in twelve minutes with, 'Yes, we can.'

Gold raised a loose board and propped it against the wall. He shone a torch into the darkness and moved aside to allow Blake to get a close-up.

'It's a Tesco carrier bag,' said Gold. 'I'm lifting it from beneath the boards. Inside it appears to be an envelope.'

He took a large brown envelope from the bag and showed it to Blake's camera.

Rosen clocked Mrs Trent. She looked genuinely perplexed.

Gold lifted the flap of the envelope and took out a collection of 10×7 photographs.

The top image showed a pleasant-looking teenage boy, dressed in a school uniform, standing in the sunshine against a brick wall. Gold handed the pictures to Rosen. He flicked through them, and his face darkened.

Rosen looked at Sylvia Trent and she stared back.

'What?' she spat.

The action in the room fell still and all eyes turned to Rosen

'Do you know this boy?' Rosen showed her the top picture.

'No.'

'Do you know why Jay has hidden these photographs?'

He opened the set mid-way and his heart fell hard and fast.

'What?' she screamed. 'What? What is it? What are the pictures of?'

56

10.42 P.M.

Rosen dealt the top photo – *snap* – to the bottom of the pile to reveal the next image. It was the same teenager again, taken at a different angle. He showed the third image. The same teenager again, this time sitting on grass with a cricket score board in the background.

'I wonder who this is?' said Rosen, examining the boy's face, feeling as if he'd breezed past the face quite recently.

The next picture showed the boy in a bedroom, dressed in his school uniform but seemingly unaware of the camera as he unknotted his tie, gazing at his own reflection in a full-length mirror on the wall. The pictures of the walls around were different to the ones in the bedroom in which they now stood.

Rosen showed the photo to Trent's mother and walked to the mirror screwed onto the wall of Trent's bedroom.

'Not the same mirror?' asked Rosen. 'Not the same room?'

He turned and turned, fourth, fifth, sixth, seventh, and said, 'The boy in the photographs is performing a striptease for the person holding the camera. The person holding the camera and taking the pictures is using a variety of angles.' Turn, turn, turn. Rosen paused on one image, noticed a crisscross pattern of old scar tissue on the boy's arms, the marks of a self-harmer. 'The boy is naked in this picture.' He showed the image to Sylvia Trent, who looked away. 'The interesting thing about this one is that the photographer's identity is revealed in the mirror. It's your son, Mrs Trent. That's why he hides them,' said Rosen. 'And I guess he took them. . .' Rosen looked around and saw an Olympus digital camera on a computer table next to a printer. 'He took them with that camera, and printed them using that printer.'

Rosen looked at the next image, his face darkened with sorrow and anger.

'It's not against the law,' said Mrs Trent.

'The legal definition of a child is anyone under the age of eighteen. If he's under sixteen, and it looks like he could be, he's a minor. Making images like this is very much against the law, Mrs Trent. Do you understand that? I bet you Jay does. Does he use the internet a lot?'

Trent's mother looked like she was in the early stages of trauma and Rosen knew that the photographs had shocked her.

'Gold, look through the rest of the pictures, see if there are any of Jay.' He turned to Mrs Trent. 'Are you sure you don't know who this young person is? I mean, all this did take place in Jay's room, under *your* roof.'

'Do you think I'd allow this?' She looked around the room but there was little support for her. 'My son is not a paedophile. My son is not a queer. He hates them.'

'Paedophiles or homosexuals?'

'Paedophiles. And queers.'

'He's a complicated human being, your son.' Rosen turned to the other officers in the room. 'We'll have his computer, camera, phone, anything that can make and distribute indecent images. We'll issue one of the clothed pictures and ask the model or anyone who knows him to step forward. . .'

'He's not a paedophile and he's not a queer, someone's set him up. . .' Her voice trailed away as she hurried downstairs.

Rosen turned to Corrigan. 'Trent's younger brother. Get the father's phone number. Check out her so-called alibi.'

Corrigan followed her.

'I'm going back to Isaac Street to see Trent. DC Gold, the pictures, please,' said Rosen.

As Rosen passed Mrs Trent at the bottom of the stairs, Corrigan asked her, 'The phone number of the place your son is?'

She pulled a face at Corrigan, an attempt at intimidation. Corrigan stared back contemptuously and she backed down immediately. She rattled off a string of numbers.

Corrigan dialled the number and asked, 'What's your son's name?'

At the front door, Rosen stopped, a gut feeling making him stay put.

She remained tight-lipped.

'He can give Jay an alibi,' said Rosen. 'If he does that, things may be a lot less serious for Jay.'

'Chester, his name's Chester!'

'Chester Adler?' asked Rosen.

Sylvia Trent looked astonished. 'How do you know? I said, how do you know him?' she asked.

'You were married to Jay's father, but not Chester's?' asked Rosen.

'Mind your own damned business.'

'Sure.'

After a few moments, the call connected and Corrigan introduced himself, then turned on the speakerphone. 'We need to talk to your son, Chester.'

'Chester? Why?' replied the boy's father.

'About Jay. . .'

'That fucking arsehole. What's the deadbeat been up to now?'

'We just need Chester to confirm Jay's alibi regarding his whereabouts the night before last.'

'He's not here.'

'He's not there?' Mrs Trent shrieked.

Corrigan ignored her. 'His mother said he's with you in your house.'

'He hasn't been here. Not for a week or so. If he was here, I'd put him on to you right now. But he ain't here.'

Corrigan thanked him and closed the call down.

A look of genuine distress overwhelmed Mrs Trent's hard-bitten face.

'But he should've been there four hours ago. He phoned me, said he was just getting off the bus by his dad's. He goes to his dad's on his own all the time.'

'I suggest you go to all the places where he may go. If you find him, call us, and we'll hear what he has to say. He's ten, isn't he?' said Rosen.

'How do you know him?'

'If you don't find him, call us and we'll issue a missing-child notification to all cars and stations on Chester Adler.'

'How *do* you know him?'

'This morning, we left his school as you were arriving,' said Rosen, walking out quickly into the rain. 'The class pet. Very sad.'

57

11.35 P.M.

As he prepared to interview Trent again, Rosen surveyed the pictures on his desk: two dozen images of a young man performing a plethora of auto-erotic acts, his arms riddled with scars from wrist to shoulder. Rosen wondered what sorrows had driven this young person to self-harm and sighed profoundly as he returned the images to the envelope.

'David!'

Rosen looked up at the sound of Henshaw's voice, urgent and hurried. Henshaw pulled up a chair.

'Had any insights on the meaning of the graffiti?' asked Rosen.

'See we is many, the eye – not as yet. But I've been through the photocopies of Macy Conner's school diary.' He produced a set of colour copies of her exercise book and lay the wad down on top of the pornography. 'It's quite a read.'

'Chester Adler's diary?'

'He can barely hold a pencil. He writes like a four year old. But *Macy*,' emphasized Henshaw, 'she worries me.'

Rosen looked at the top sheet, dated '3rd September' in blue Berol pen handwriting and underlined with a black pencil line. The writing was neat but unlinked.

Rosen was torn. He was eager to get down to Trent and, at that moment, Macy's school diary felt simply like an interesting distraction. And yet, he was drawn by Henshaw's unease.

He read quietly to himself.

In the summer my grandmother come down from Scotland to stay with me because she is an old woman and has a bad heart and a sore chest and a lump on her spine. She is not well. She has come to live with me because I will take care of her. And that is what I did all summer long. She was kind and thankful to me and told me she had loved me from the moment I was born and would love me until the day I die. We prayed every day for her recovery, sometimes for a long time, but she seems to be growing weaker and weaker. I am very scared of losing her.

Rosen's humanity was pricked. 'She's a good kid.'

'Look at this, David.' Henshaw lifted a set of top sheets and showed Rosen the diary entry for 30 September.

Rosen took a quick peep at his watch. The interview was due to start and his focus was shifting. 'That's great,' said Rosen, observing the vast improvement in handwriting in the space of less than a single calendar month. It was almost perfect linked print.

'Day by day,' observed Henshaw, 'the quality of the handwriting matures visibly. I called Miss Harvey, who only started with the class in the following January. I found a written comment, mid-September, from a supply teacher. "It is good to work hard and be determined but you must take time to play." Macy's comment back: "I'd rather improve my handwriting and I'll practise all playtimes and each night to do so." Check out the entry for September the thirtieth. I will sacrifice time.'

Yesterday, I received the alarming and tragic news that my beloved grandmother is terminally ill. The illness is called cancer and she is being treated by an oncologist from St Thomas's Hospital in central

London, overlooking and overlooked by the Houses of Parliament, the
seat of power in this hallowed Britain. This is how my grandmother
has described things. She has a Macmillan nurse who calls to our
humble flat to assist her. In the meantime, we have prayed together
for her recovery and I have sacrificed time to help her get better.

'Look at the difference in the language, David. It's like she's aged five
years in the space of four weeks.'

'And the supply teacher didn't pick up on this?'

'Miss Harvey told me they had supply teacher after supply teacher –
the class was full of disruptive children and people were walking after
half a day. No continuity, September through to December. Now get
this entry, January the fourth, Miss Harvey's first day. Guess which kid
stood out straight away?'

I did not give or receive Christmas presents as I do not believe in the
concept of a Christian Messiah, born to die for the sins of mankind.
On this matter, my grandmother and I are of the same mind. This
is a myth circulated in the Middle East two thousand years ago
and popularized by Rome for its own political ends. This can be
verified by the books I have borrowed on behalf of Grandmother from
Lewisham Library.

'What do you think, David?'

'Odd,' said Rosen. 'I saw her laying flowers in Bannerman Square
for Thomas Glass yesterday. She struck a standard hands-together, eyes-
closed, Christian-at-prayer pose.'

'She could've just been mimicking the kind of shallow piety she's
seen on TV, but it's an interesting contradiction. Or. . .?'

'Go on,' urged Rosen.

'Where were you positioned in relation to each other?'

Rosen considered.

'I was sitting in the mobile incident room, the door was open, she was fully in my sights and I was in hers.'

Henshaw performed a swift mental calculation.

'She was putting on an act for you, David. Drawing you out of your lair. Did you go out to her?'

'Yes.'

'Did she take you into her confidence?'

'She told me she hadn't been entirely truthful at lunchtime. She hadn't mentioned her grandmother, her grandmother who was dying.'

Rosen skimmed both pieces of writing.

'I think she spends an awful lot of time with her grandmother and she's parroting the old woman's hobby-horse. She's a stickler for facts and truth. She despises fiction. What's your take on it?' asked Rosen.

'I think she's protesting too loudly about this truth business. She doesn't add up to me. I don't believe she's a reliable witness. It wouldn't even surprise me if the "two bad men who beat me up" story was exactly that. A story. I wouldn't lean too heavily on her evidence.'

Rosen handed the photocopied sheets back to Henshaw. 'What do you suggest?' he asked.

'I'd like to observe her in the children's suite with one of your trained children's officers and a child psychologist.'

'We'll set that up. Her teacher thinks she's wonderful,' said Rosen.

'Her teacher's inexperienced and not as intelligent as Macy. I bet she can play people like a concert pianist.'

Rosen slid the enhanced CCTV picture of Trent into a separate envelope.

'I've been through the diary over and over and two things keep repeating. Every day Grandmother gets a little bit worse and every day they pray together that little bit harder for her recovery. She's a white kid from a UK family and she doesn't buy the myth of Jesus Christ. So what does she believe in? What has she been praying to?'

'She's a child. She'll pray to whatever the adults closest to her pray to, surely? Do you have the entry for the night she was attacked?' asked Rosen.

His desk phone rang. He picked it up.

'Do you want me to take Trent back to his cell?' asked the custody sergeant.

'I'll be down in two minutes. Keep him in number one.'

'David,' said Henshaw. 'This kind of rapid and sustained improvement in her writing – it's the reverse of the coin when a kid goes from A to U. This speaks to me of a massive underlying trauma. I think you need to dredge through every word she's said to you and pull them apart.'

As Rosen walked down the stairs to interview Trent, his footsteps echoed behind him. The sound unsettled him. He didn't know if Henshaw was on the money in everything he said, but of one thing Rosen was certain. For whatever reason, Macy had enticed him from the mobile incident room and he'd walked onto Bannerman Square like a two year old.

58

11.45 P.M.

Rosen and Leung faced Trent and his solicitor, Mrs Cairns, across the table of Interview Suite 1. Trent stared at the space between their heads, his arms folded tightly across his chest, just as his mother had done. *A genetic trait?* wondered Rosen.

He formally opened the interview. 'OK, Jay, I'm going to show you the enhanced CCTV image of you at the wheel of a Renault Megane.'

'No comment.'

As he slid the photo out of the envelope and passed it to Leung, Henshaw's words about Macy's diary danced around his mind: *I bet she can play people like a concert pianist.*

Leung showed Trent the picture, holding it in his eye line.

'Look at the time, Jay. 8.58.13. In the corner.'

'No comment.'

'Look at the driver, Jay.'

'No comment.'

'A lime-green Adidas jacket?'

Rosen placed the CCTV picture of Trent in front of his solicitor and showed Trent the dry cleaning ticket. 'Is this where you took that jacket? Because it isn't in your closet.'

'No comment.'

'CC4U are working on close-ups of your face, Jay.'

'No comment.'

'Why did you do this, Jay?' asked Rosen.

'No comment.'

'This isn't *you*, Jay. This is *weird shit*!' broke in Leung. 'I mean, come on, little kids?'

Rosen gave Trent a long, hard stare and modulated his voice to let him know more bad news was flying his way. 'Another issue's come to light, Jay.'

Rosen pushed the carrier bag with the envelope of pornography towards him.

'We found this under the floorboards beneath your bed. Do you recognize it?'

'No comment.'

Trent looked like he'd just been told he had five minutes left to live.

'Open it, Jay.'

He didn't move. Rosen looked at Mrs Cairns and then back at Trent, who looked away. Anywhere except at Rosen.

Rosen took the envelope from the bag and showed the first photo, of the schoolboy fully clothed, to Trent.

'It was a warm day, a good day to take pictures of a close, personal friend,' said Rosen.

'No. . . comment. . .'

'I understand, Jay. I understand perfectly.' He turned to Trent's solicitor. 'Have you engaged a barrister yet?'

'Not as yet.'

'Well, you need to,' said Rosen. 'Who is this boy, Jay?'

Silence.

'How old was he when you took the photographs of him taking off his school uniform?'

Silence.

'OK, we'll try again in the morning. But before I close this interview,

Jay, I've got a piece of family news for you. Your little brother's been missing for hours.' He looked closely at Trent. 'Given the people out there who are attacking young males, doesn't that give you cause for concern?'

'No comment.'

'You've got a name, names maybe. If you gave me a name, it could be the difference between life and death for Chester.'

'No comment.'

His solicitor leaned into his ear, made a wall with her hand, whispered quickly, her eyes alert. She sat back.

Trent looked at her and said, 'He's not my brother, really. We don't have the same father or the same surname. . .'

'Jay,' said Rosen, indicating the CCTV photograph. 'If we've got this all wrong, he's your alibi. Your mother's tearing her hair out. He left your house to go to his dad's and didn't show up.'

Trent laughed sourly. 'He's a retard. She shouldn't've let him travel on public transport. Go lay a guilt trip on her, not me.'

'Last chance, Jay?'

'No. . . fucking. . . comment!'

*

WHEN THE DUTY sergeant had escorted Trent and his solicitor from the interview room, Rosen looked at Leung and said, 'He couldn't look at me. I'm handing over interviewing Trent to you and Carol Bellwood for now.'

'Why?' asked Leung.

'Two big issues in his head. One, he's up to his neck in the abduction and murder of a child. Two, he's a closet homosexual. He'd rather be outed as a child murderer than a homosexual. His sexuality's causing him the most stress. As a man, I'm a stumbling block to cracking him. Nine o'clock in the morning, this room, you and Carol can fry Trent.'

59

11.55 P.M.

Just before midnight, as he sat at his desk reviewing in his mind the events of the day, Rosen's mobile went off. MORTUARY. He picked up the call.

'DCI Rosen speaking.'

'Hello, David.' It was Doctor Sweeney. 'I've got Thomas Glass's body here. I'm just about to examine him, but thought I'd give you a ring with an initial finding.'

Rosen knew Sweeney was teasing him with a pause.

'Go on.'

'I explored his mouth and found something stuck to the lower gums.'

'What was it?'

'A human hair: a long, single strand. Want me to send you a picture?'

'Send me a picture immediately.'

'No problem.' Doctor Sweeney paused. 'There's evidence of torture before the main incident.'

Rosen closed his eyes and felt a lightness overtake his being, the giddy stab of horror like a knife in the head.

'Are you there, Rosen?'

'Yes.'

'There's a single burn mark to the left eyeball. Probably with a lighted cigarette. I retrieved a fragment of ash. . .'

Rosen picked up the CCTV image of the Renault Megane, Thomas holding his hand up to his eye. *The eye is the believer. The eye is the deceiver.*

'Anything else?' asked Rosen. *See we is many. See I are one.*

'No. I'll send you the shot of the hair.'

Rosen replaced the receiver and felt tears welling up in his eyes, tears of sorrow and rage for the horrors inflicted on Thomas.

Bellwood approached him, her face filled with concern.

'You all right, David?'

He blinked, sat up straight and indicated the colour copy of Macy's school diary.

'What do you make of Macy Conner, Carol?'

'Nice kid. Poor as poor can be but *so* bright. When she was in the car. . .'

'Go on.'

'We got behind the black van taking Stevie's body away from the scene. She took all the digits from the number plate and scrambled them together. Quick 24. Clever, active mind. Nice kid.'

DAY FOUR

1 May

60

5.08 A.M.

The sound of a paramedic ambulance leaked through the edges of Macy's dream, the real world seeping into the moving images within her skull. In her dream, she sat in the A & E department of Lewisham Hospital, with DCI Rosen in the seat next to her. Grandma's bed was not in its usual place in her mum's flat, but in the space between the reception desk and the seats.

DCI Rosen examined the bruises and cuts on her face with great sadness in his eyes.

Grandma asked, 'Can you hear that? There's an ambulance on its way.'

'Who said that?' asked DCI Rosen.

'My grandma,' said Macy. 'I told you about her, Mr Rosen. Remember?'

'I remember.'

She slid her hand inside Rosen's and stood up. *I wish you were my dad*, she thought, and even though she didn't say it, it was as if Rosen heard her mind and his mind responded, *I'd take good care of you, Macy.* He smiled at her and she led him to her grandma's bed.

'This is my grandma,' she said.

Rosen looked at the pillow, the smile dissolving on his face as

Grandma said, 'Good evening, DCI Rosen. It's a disgraceful world, where two grown men can get away with hurting a young girl such as this.'

Rosen said nothing. He just looked down at the pillow.

The ambulance siren came closer, louder.

Macy squeezed his hand and folded herself into his side. He held her in place with his free hand.

'What's wrong, Daddy Rosen?' asked Macy.

'I can hear Grandma's voice but it's strange, I can't see her.'

'That's because you're a detective.' Grandma smiled up from the pillow. 'You have to look harder than most.'

'Well,' responded Rosen. 'It's a pleasure to hear you and I'll do my best to see you. I'll keep looking – no stone unturned and all that.'

The ambulance siren reached a peak and stopped.

A noise of friction, two metal surfaces colliding.

The doors of A & E burst open and a doctor and a nurse came running in with a stretcher bed pushed by two paramedics, only the paramedics weren't real paramedics in green uniforms: they were the two hoodies who'd beaten her as they ran away from Bannerman Square. Their faces were hidden by the darkness within their hoods.

'Look!' Macy pointed. 'DCI Rosen, they're the ones who hurt me.'

On the stretcher, Thomas Glass smoked and a smell of burning flesh pervaded the air. In the black and bloodied ruin of his face, his teeth shone, unnaturally white, and he sang in a nursery-rhyme voice:

'I don't know why, I don't know when,

'But those bad men, they'll do it again!'

Metal ground into metal.

Thomas screamed, 'Mummy!'

Silence.

And a key turning in a lock woke Macy up. She opened her eyes and reassured herself. She was in Chelsea's living room, asleep on the sofa under a duvet. Terror gripped her. What if it wasn't Chelsea coming into the flat? What if it was the two men, and they'd watched Chelsea coming home in the early hours of morning? What if they'd taken the key? What if they were coming to douse her with petrol and finish her off? She drew an unsteady breath. She wanted to scream but was well practised in hiding her emotions, and simply silently gripped the edges of the duvet.

The light went on in the hall and she recognized the *click-clack* of Chelsea's elegant high-heeled shoes, caught the edge of her expensive perfume.

Chelsea peered into the darkness of the living room.

'I'm awake, Chelsea,' said Macy, desperate to hear her voice.

'Hi, Macy. Everything OK?'

Macy could tell from her voice that Chelsea had been drinking wine, just a couple, like she usually did when the pub closed its doors.

'Fine and dandy, Chelsea.'

Macy got up from the sofa and crossed the room to be with her. As she came to Chelsea's side, Chelsea turned away and headed for Luke's bedroom.

'Did your little friend arrive?' asked Chelsea.

'Shortly after you left. Ate a cheese sandwich and had to go home.'

Chelsea opened Luke's bedroom door, wobbled a little. 'These heels're too high.'

Macy placed a steadying hand on her back and said, 'He's fast asleep, it's best not disturb him.'

In the corner of Luke's room, the night-light picked out the raised Fireman Sam duvet cover, the contours and shape of Luke's sleeping form.

Chelsea stepped inside, two paces.

'You look dead tired, Chelsea. Luke's going to be awake in a few hours, pulling you out of bed.' Chelsea stepped forward, but Macy continued: 'Go to bed and get what rest you can before little Luke wakes you up. He's a ball of energy.'

Chelsea's shoulders sank.

'You're an old woman, Macy. You're darn right. I'm going to bed.'

Chelsea turned and headed for her own room. She took her top off. Her bra black, intricate and lacy, a decoration that celebrated her body.

My mother, thought Macy, *could never carry that off.*

'Want to come in the bed with me, Macy?'

'He's asleep now,' said Macy.

Chelsea giggled, looked over her shoulder, turned. 'Eh? Who's asleep now?'

'Luke, he's asleep now, and you need your sleep. I guess I'll go home, look in on Grandma. School in the morning.'

'It's Saturday, isn't it?' questioned Chelsea.

'Oh, yeah,' said Macy. 'Silly me.'

Chelsea leaned forward and kissed Macy's forehead. 'You're a good kid. Thanks.'

'Gotta go,' said Macy, hurrying to the door.

'Thanks, babe.'

Macy turned off the light in the hall, closed the door of Chelsea's flat and walked towards the cold concrete stairway towards home.

61

5.30 A.M.

Dawn broke over east London and two red fingers of light crossed the sky over Bannerman Square.

When Macy entered her grandma's room, she felt sorrow as a physical pain that filled her and hollowed her out in one assault. She wanted to faint and scream in the same instant but, gazing at the old lady, in the semi-light of the candle that burned in the corner, she couldn't do either. She moved to the bed and felt as if she was floating.

The abysmal silence was only broken by the faintest sound of Grandma, barely breathing.

The sweet cinnamon aroma of the scented candle seemed to be overwhelmed by an invisible blanket, by something that had no name but was awful from beginning to end, down to its very core.

Slowly, she peeped at the old woman and realized that the awful thing did have a name: Death.

'Come here, Macy, and look at me properly.'

Macy drifted towards the bed, above the loose boards that usually creaked beneath the threadbare carpet.

Grandma *looked* at Macy from the pillow but didn't seem to *see*. Her eyelids flickered, her eyes rolled up behind the lids and all Macy could see were the bloodshot whites.

Macy's brow creased deeply with two thick lines: pain and anxiety. 'Grandma, can you hear me?' She knelt at her bedside and her hand travelled across the top blanket until her fingers found their goal, Grandma's hand. The old woman clasped her fingers tightly around Macy's but as soon as she gripped, the power in her fingers leaked away.

'I'm scared, Grandma.'

'Of?'

'Everything.'

'Don't be scared.'

'Grandma, is this it? Are you dying?'

'I've been waiting for you to come back, to be with me, so I died with my beautiful girl beside me. Now, I can die in peace.'

'If you can put off dying for a few hours so you can be with me, surely you can put off dying for another day, or a week, or a month?'

Her eyes shut. 'Macy, Death has already been patient with me and it's a sin to test the patience of anything for too long, especially Death. Death has waited for you to return because I asked. Death has listened to our prayers long enough. And Death has said, *Now*. And I have said, *Yes*.'

Grandma's head shifted slightly on the pillow and it was as if half her face disappeared into the fabric of the pillow slip. In dying, she was becoming invisible to Macy's tear-filled eyes, dissolving.

'Don't make a sound, Macy. You know what your mother will do if she hears you crying. She'll make you cry some more with the back of her hand and the flat of her foot.'

Finally, Grandma's fingers fell away from Macy's hand. The absence felt like a colossal loss, a loss that drew the breath out of Macy and made her wonder if she too was dying in the same dim light.

'Grandma, please ask Death to take me with you.'

'It's not your time, Macy. Death chooses the final time to take you, just as Life chooses to put the breath into all living things.' The effort of speech made her face crease. She moved her lips but made no sound.

242

Macy watched, and the silent words ran through her mind like a warm breeze through a verdant bush.

This is how it has been ordained. Now is the time for your life and when it's time for you to die, then you will die and it'll be time for me to come back and the whole circle will turn again, only next time, we'll leave your mother out of it, for her sins are heinous; she will stay in eternal darkness and we will come into the light of a new life and I will be your mother and you will be my daughter and I will love and cherish you as you have not been loved and cherished as you deserve. I will protect and love you, and your new life will not be blemished by beatings and privation and cruel tricks of the mind. And the beasts that haunt your head and heart will be destroyed. We will live with nature, with the animals and the trees and the spirits that dwell inside all that is natural and beautiful. But when I am gone, you will take my place as the High Priestess, and the rituals you perform will bring us back together in a brand-new life far away from here.'

The wind shook the bush and, inside Macy's head, it ignited with a small flame at the heart of its branches.

Grandma sighed and her eyes opened. Her face was whole again. Macy pressed her face close to Grandma's and touched her mouth to the old woman's lips, breathing a stream of air from deep inside herself into Grandma's mouth.

'I love you so much, Grandma, I don't think I can bear to. . . lose you.'

The light, the life, dissolved from Grandma's eyes. As Macy drew back, Grandma breathed out and the room was plunged into silence.

With the tips of her index fingers she closed Grandma's eyes.

The candle in the corner went out and the room darkened.

She smelt the wisp of smoke but soon even that disappeared.

Macy buried her face in the blanket, held on to Grandma's fragile body and, in profound silence, howled from the core of her being.

And, inside her head, the small flame inside the wind-soaked bush exploded into an inferno, a fire-storm: the final fire.

62

5.30 A.M.

After two hours of sleep, Rosen hurtled back into consciousness from a terrifying dream. In the dream, he'd opened the door of Joe's room and the walls were covered in Ogham symbols. Behind him Sarah whispered, 'See we is many. See I are one.'

Awake, panic-stricken, Rosen was out of bed and moving fast.

'Oh, God,' Sarah groaned. From the troubled margins of her own exhaustion, she'd watched him squirm and heard him mutter as he slept, and now he was on his feet lumbering through the darkness of their bedroom towards the door.

She followed.

'David, what's wrong?'

'Joe.'

Rosen pushed his son's door open and turned on the main light. He rushed to the Moses basket, fully expecting to see an empty space.

Joe, asleep, content, turned a little to the left.

Relief flooded Rosen, washed through every piece of him and assumed a physical sensation that was beyond pleasure. But his heart was banging against his ribs, his breath was shallow and short, and his pyjamas clung to him with perspiration.

'David.' Sarah spoke softly from the doorway. 'I'm turning the light off.'

After a short interval, he responded, 'Oh, OK.'

The room fell back into the blue semi-light of Joe's bedside lamp.

'I want you to come back to bed,' said Sarah.

'Yes, back to bed.' He reached out his hand to double-check his senses, to touch his son to make sure he was really there, completely safe, and that his presence was not a trick of the eye. But then he didn't want to wake him; in his mind, he was back outside the resuscitation room in Lewisham Hospital watching Emily Glass reach out to Thomas, her gesture withering away before contact. He withdrew his hand.

I'm terrified of anything hurting you, son, thought Rosen.

'He's fine, he's OK, he's sound asleep,' said Sarah, telepathically reading his thoughts.

He took a final lingering look at his son and wanted to go downstairs to double-check that all the doors and windows were locked, but his attention was seized by a sound in their bedroom, of his mobile phone vibrating twice against the surface of his bedside cabinet.

When Rosen picked it up, he became very cold and his scalp prickled.

1 new message
Stevie

He opened the message, his palm feeling clammy against the phone in his hand.

Where on earth is Macy Conner?

Rosen connected to Bellwood on speed dial on his mobile and she picked up on the second ring.

'Call Corrigan, Gold and Feldman. They're to call everyone to Bannerman Square now. Call the on-duty uniforms. I want the front entrance and back exit to Claude House covered. No one goes in, no one goes out. Meet me there as soon as you can.'

In under a minute, Rosen was dressed. At the front door, he heard the sound of Joe crying from his bedroom. He looked at Sarah and said, 'In the end, they couldn't get to Thomas so they went for the next best thing. Stevie.'

If they can't get to me for whatever reason, he thought, *they'll get to you and Joe.*

At the car, he looked back. Sarah in the doorway. Joe upstairs.

'Sarah, pack an overnight bag for you and Joe.'

'What?'

'Special Branch will be here soon. Please. Get inside. Lock the door.'

Rosen dialled Baxter and, as he sped away, he heard Baxter's voice, sleepy and irritable.

'What is it, David?'

'The safe house in Orpington. I want Sarah and Joe taken there immediately.'

Baxter sounded wide awake. 'OK. I'm on it.'

63

6.01 A.M.

When Rosen arrived at Bannerman Square, Bellwood and Henshaw were waiting at the main door of Claude House, watching morning unfold in the sky, where one plane ascended and another was on its way down to Heathrow.

Rosen addressed the constable at the front entrance.

'Is the back covered?'

'I checked. It is,' replied Bellwood. 'I called Social Services. Just in case. A social worker's on her way here now.'

He turned to Henshaw. 'Wait here for her, James!'

As Rosen and Bellwood hurried into the building, she asked, 'What is it, David?'

He showed her the text as they made their way up the concrete stairs.

'Shit,' said Bellwood, steaming ahead of Rosen.

When Rosen opened the door onto Macy's landing, Bellwood was hammering on the door of her flat. When he got there, she stopped and they could hear movement inside.

'Awright, awright, who is it?' Behind the front door of her flat, Macy's mother's voice was steeped in sleep and a smoker's husky rattle.

'Police. DCI Rosen. We met when you brought Macy to the mobile—'

'Yeah, yeah, yeah.'

She unbolted the door and, opening the door to the width of the chain's length, blinked herself into wakefulness.

'We've come to speak to Macy,' said Rosen.

'What?' She looked at him as if he was speaking an alien language. 'She's. . . what time is it? She'll be asleep in bed.'

'I won't wake her up, but I want to see her. Open the door, Ms Conner.'

She made no physical or verbal response.

'Open the bloody door, woman!' Rosen felt as if his head was going to explode.

'Did you get my letter, Ms Conner?' asked Bellwood.

She squinted at Bellwood, wiped her lips with the back of her hand and responded, 'Letter? What letter?'

'Open the door and let us in,' snapped Bellwood.

The door was shoved shut, the chain rattled and then the door opened sufficiently for Bellwood and Rosen to enter.

As they did, the stair door to the landing opened and two pairs of footsteps followed. Henshaw called, 'Social worker's here.'

'Fucking social worker?' Macy's mother suddenly sounded wide awake. 'What's going on here?'

In the narrow hallway of the flat, she made a physical gesture with her whole body, as if to block Rosen's path.

'Don't bother, Ms Conner!'

'You caught the two men who attacked her yet?'

'Show me where she is,' said Rosen. 'Show me where she's sleeping.'

'Why should I?'

A tall, thin woman stepped between Rosen and Macy's mother.

'I suggest you follow DCI Rosen's instruction,' said the social worker.

'And who the hell are you?' Macy's mother asked.

The social worker raised the ID badge hanging from her neck.

'Where is she?' asked Rosen.

He followed Macy's mother, noticing the whiff of expensive perfume drifting from her body, the good quality of her nightdress completely at odds with the squalor of the flat.

The living room was like a shell. A single sofa that looked like it belonged in the 1970s faced a primitive digital TV, which was standing on a worn carpet that didn't stretch to the skirting boards. The walls were grey; the window, overlooking Bannerman Square, had no curtains or blinds and the energy-efficient light bulb above their heads had no shade.

Rosen recalled how his mother had alleviated the bareness of their flat in Walthamstow with colourful paper flowers, could hear her voice, always cheerful: *It's not where you live, it's how you live that matters.*

Macy's mother knocked on a heavily dented door that looked as if someone had punched it hard, over and over.

'Macy, Rosen and Bellwood're here to see you.'

Silence.

Rosen looked beyond the open door of the kitchen. A two-burner cooker, a fridge, a table with three odd chairs and a sink full of unwashed dishes. A cockroach walked across the threshold.

Bellwood glanced at Rosen as Macy's mother banged harder on the door.

'Macy, wake up, the police're here!'

She opened the door, appeared a little surprised but not alarmed.

'Oh. She's not here.'

Panic seized Rosen.

'She's not here,' said Rosen, his voice rising with the mounting anxiety inside him, 'because she's been abducted.'

64

6.04 A.M.

'Abducted!' Macy's mother laughed. 'What time is it?' she asked.

'It's just gone six in the morning,' replied Rosen.

'She often wakes up with the birds and goes for a walk.'

Rosen looked around the flat. There was nothing for Macy to do, nothing to comfort her, and he understood why she would walk the streets at dawn.

Rosen held Macy's mother's gaze.

She appeared not to notice. 'She's usually down the library, filling her head with all kinds of shit. But the library's not open at this hour.' She paused, light dawning. 'I know where she'll be. She babysits for a neighbour, sleeps over some nights.'

'Name?'

'Chelsea.'

'Booth?'

'You know her?'

'4E, next floor down. Check it out, Carol.'

'Oh, you know her.' The woman mocked Rosen. 'You one of her clients?'

As Bellwood rushed from the living room to the front door, Rosen positioned himself to see the interior of Macy's room. A single bed, one pillow with a single blanket and a small stack of clothes on the floor. It was more like a monastic cell than a young girl's bedroom.

'What did you buy her for Christmas?' asked Rosen.

'Sorry?' replied Macy's mother.

'You heard.'

'OK, OK!' The social worker touched Rosen's arm.

'Open the doors of the other rooms.'

'Have you got a search warrant?'

'Your daughter's not in her bed, and it's just gone six on a Saturday morning. Open the other doors, Ms Conner.'

'She's not like other kids, she don't even like toys. I tried to get her into them, cuddly toys and dolls and the like, but all she said was, "They ain't real." So, no, I didn't buy her a Christmas present. I give her the money instead, all right!'

Rosen gazed into the poverty of Macy's room. He had seen brighter cells in Brixton Prison.

'Open that door!' Rosen pointed at a door adjacent to Macy's room.

'I gave her money and she bought sweets if you must know.'

'I said, open that door!'

Reluctantly, she pushed the door open.

The bathroom. Rosen's scalp tingled. A dripping tap on a corroded sink, a bath full of cold dirty water, the end of a bar of soap on the side, a solitary towel wet and bunched on the floor, a toilet with a broken seat.

Two more doors directly faced the cell that was Macy's room. Rosen was struck by an unbalanced equation: Paul. Mother. Grandmother.

'Open that door, Ms Conner.' Rosen pointed to the right-hand door opposite Macy's.

As she opened the door, Rosen was hit first by the smell of cheap cologne and then by the vivid artwork on the wall, each square centimetre of space painted lovingly with graffiti art. The name 'Macy' dominated each wall. Images of the girl – baby, toddler, infant, child – covered the walls.

Rosen stepped inside and made a slow three-hundred-and-sixty-degree turn, stopping mid-way when he saw an eye identical to the one aerosoled on the wall in Bannerman Square.

Rosen looked at Macy's mother and indicated the elaborate artwork on the walls.

She touched the side of her head and said contemptuously, 'Paul? He was obsessed with her from when she was a baby. I think he was seven or eight when she came along. He did everything for her. So I let him, the little crank. Saved me a job.'

'Where's Paul?' asked Rosen. 'Where is Macy's brother, Paul?'

'I don't know. He comes and goes.'

Rosen walked out and to the next door.

'I'm assuming this is your room. Open the door, Ms Conner.'

'Well, I know for a fact she ain't in there, because I've just come out of there when you woke me up at this hour. So I don't need to open that door, do I?'

'Open the door, Ms Conner – she may have gone into your room when you were opening the front door to let us in.'

'She's not in there; I'm telling you.' Rosen stared hard at her. 'It's private. It's my room and if you want to see my room, you'd better get a fucking search warrant.'

'Your daughter's missing—'

'She'll be with that slag, Chelsea—'

'And what if she's not?' asked Rosen.

'And what if she is?'

'Open the door!'

'Open it yer fucking self.'

He turned the handle and pushed the door wide open.

An elegant and tastefully decorated bedroom: an antique brass double bed, Laura Ashley wardrobes, a Brinton fitted carpet, a plasma

TV mounted on the wall facing the bed, a box of chocolates on the bedside, on the dressing table designer perfumes, a hairdryer and GHD straighteners, an open bottle of wine, an iPad.

Rosen turned to her. She looked back nonchalantly.

'Where does Macy's grandmother sleep?'

She appeared not to hear but then, quietly, said, 'Grandmother?'

'Macy said her grandma was seriously ill, that she was living here with you and couldn't be left alone.'

Her face became twisted and perplexed. 'Sorry?'

'Macy's grandmother?' questioned Rosen.

'She doesn't have a grandmother. I was taken away from my mother when I was born. So I don't even remember her. Macy's father walked out when I was seven months pregnant. His mother was dead according to him, the bastard. What's she been saying? What's she been saying about a sick grandmother?'

'That her grandmother was terminally ill and was here with you.'

Macy's mother laughed, a harsh, almost mechanical laugh that seemed to go on for ever.

'Calm down,' said Rosen.

'You're the one that needs to fucking calm down, Rosen.'

She lit a cigarette and let out a long, thin stream of smoke. 'She's been taking the piss out of you, Rosen. But that's Macy for you. She's a piss-taking little bitch. A liar. She gets these fantastic ideas in her head and spins a yarn like you wouldn't believe. Acts out these little plays in her bedroom, with all these funny voices. I wouldn't believe a word she says if I was you. I don't.'

'Such as the two men running away from Bannerman Square, the two men who hit her and stole her money?' asked Rosen.

'No! That happened,' she insisted. 'You saw the bruises. She had to go to Accident and Emergency with Paul.'

In the background, Rosen recognized Bellwood's footsteps, hurrying back towards the flat.

Rosen looked once more into the spartan space that was Macy's room and the self-indulgent elegance of her mother's room and caught the eyes of Bellwood and the social worker.

The social worker started dialling on her mobile.

'Who you calling?' asked Macy's mother.

Bellwood did a double-take at the contrast of luxury and poverty within the same living space. 'I spoke to Chelsea,' she said. 'Macy left there in the early hours to see to her grandmother.'

Macy's mother snorted with laughter. 'She is such a good liar. There you go, you've all been fucking had.'

'Have you any idea where Macy might be right now?' asked Rosen, resisting the urge to grab her by the shoulders and shake her until her teeth rattled.

'I've said already. Try the library when it opens. Maybe she's visiting her sick grandmother.' Macy's mother followed Rosen to the door. 'Don't be making any judgements about me. Don't be trying to make me feel bad, because I don't. She fucks off in the middle of the night, but she's old enough to know better. See what I mean?'

At the door, Rosen turned on her, the anger and volume in his voice stunning and sudden. 'Who hit her?'

'It wasn't me!'

'Who caused those bruises and cuts to her face?'

'If you believe her, it was two men with hoodies.'

'Who attacked her?'

She blew out a thin line of smoke.

'Have you got a photograph of Macy?'

Without hesitation, she said flatly, 'No.'

'I'll be back.'

And he rushed to the door of the stairs.

Corrigan was on his way up, his hardened features made heavy by lack of sleep. Rosen called down to him, 'We need it circulating to every station manager – we've got two missing children on the street. Macy

254

Conner, ten. Chester Adler, ten. They're connected. Classmates. I've got a picture of the girl on my phone. Get the boy's mother to supply an image. We need their faces on the street and on TV within the next half-hour. At this point, I believe they've been abducted by the people who took Thomas Glass and murdered Stevie Jensen.'

Rosen hit the fresh air and was filled with a disturbing certainty. Whoever was responsible for taking the children had insight into his head and heart.

He paused at his car, supporting his weight with his two hands pressed on the roof as the thought process came to its conclusion.

Children? My Achilles heel. The children are bait, thought Rosen, *but I am the real target. Tonight I will burn alive.*

65

6.15 A.M.

Trent's nine o'clock interview had been brought forward to six thirty, by which time digital images of Macy Conner and Chester Adler's faces had arrived at BBC News 24, ITN and the Sky news desks, with the urgent request to broadcast them as missing persons.

As the entire murder investigation team assembled in the incident room, Rosen refocused on the photograph of the hair found in Thomas Glass's mouth and made the futile wish that it didn't take two to three days working flat out for the DNA database to match the hair to any individual on their records.

Corrigan intercepted Bellwood and Leung as they approached Rosen, and handed them a plastic dry cleaners bag.

'They opened up shop in the early hours for us. It's a little present for Jay Trent. Do you know what it is?'

Bellwood and Leung looked inside the bag and smiled at each other. Bellwood said, 'Sure do.'

'Tell him not to worry about the bill,' said Corrigan. 'Cleaning bills are gonna be past tense for Trentie.'

They turned to Rosen and he handed each of them an envelope.

'Trent. Enhanced CCTV and pictures of the boyfriend.'

'I haven't seen these yet,' said Bellwood.

'Prepare yourself.' Rosen glanced at his watch. 'Not pleasant.'

She slid the photographs out of the envelope and flicked through them, with a face that was both depressed and disappointed.

After a few moments of silence, Leung asked Bellwood, 'What is it?'

'These were found under the floorboards of Trent's room?'

'Yes,' said Rosen.

'I know who the boy in the school uniform is,' said Bellwood. 'Come on, Tracey. Jay Trent – let's get him.'

66

6.41 A.M.

Just beneath the polished apathy of Jay Trent's face, there was a burgeoning uncertainty. As he'd entered Interview Suite 1, Leung had whispered to Bellwood, 'He hasn't slept a wink.'

Stone-faced, Trent's solicitor sat down next to him.

Looking directly at Trent, Bellwood formally opened the interview and placed the picture of him in the Renault Megane under his nose.

'Do you still maintain this isn't you, Jay?'

'Where's Rosen?'

'He's busy. Something else has cropped up.'

'So I'm not public enemy number one now. That's good.'

'Jay, your present situation is lots of things. Good isn't one of them.' Bellwood reality-checked him.

'Here you go, Jay,' said Leung. She placed the dry cleaners bag on the table. He made no effort to look at it or touch it.

Leung slid the lime-green Adidas jacket out of the bag and held it up for Trent and his solicitor to see.

'This is the jacket you're wearing in that photograph. We found the dry cleaning ticket when we searched your room.'

'No comment.'

Leung folded the jacket slowly, and carefully placed it back into the bag, which she left on the table.

'OK,' said Bellwood. 'We're still not sure about the age of the model in your indecent images because we don't know when they were taken. Maybe he's now seventeen or eighteen years of age, just, but it's not beyond the realms of possibility that the photographs were taken well over two years ago.'

She took the top photo: fully clothed, smiling, against a wall.

'His name's Paul Conner and he lives in Claude House on Bannerman Square.'

Trent glanced up from the pictures but didn't look at either Bellwood or Leung.

'How do you know that?

'He was in the back of my car, yesterday.'

'Bullshit. . .'

'The day Stevie's body was discovered. His little sister, Macy, was in the front with me.'

'Bull*shit*!'

'I was giving her a lift home from school. Paul had come to collect her. When we were on Lewisham High Street we were behind the mortuary van taking Stevie Jensen's body away from Loampit Vale. Are you currently in a relationship with Paul Conner?'

'No comment.' A muscle twitched in Trent's cheek. He drew in breath and blinked at the wall between Bellwood and Leung.

'Well, that is progress towards the truth,' observed Bellwood. 'You're not confirming but you're not denying any knowledge of a relationship with Paul Conner. Paul Conner's your boyfriend, isn't he, Jay? You'll feel better when you get it off your chest.'

'My client's sexuality isn't the issue here,' said his solicitor.

'Stop!' Leung held a hand in the air and leaned in the direction of Trent's solicitor. 'He's a prime suspect in the murder of one child, and that murder is very probably linked to another murder. He has a relationship with the brother of a key witness in this investigation. His own brother and that little girl have both gone missing. I suggest that his sexuality and the exact nature of his relationship with that little girl's older brother is very much the issue here. Do you understand that, Mrs Cairns?'

Bellwood stared at Trent across the table. In a matter of moments, he looked older and smaller.

'He's got lovely hair.' Bellwood took the photograph back, made a show of inspecting it, caught Trent watching her over the top of the picture, dipped her eyes back. 'I have to say, he's really good-looking. It's a shame he shaved his head.'

'When'd he get his head shaved?' asked Leung.

'The other day,' said Trent. His face wrinkled. 'I don't know.'

Between them, the women nurtured the silence and, in that quiet, Bellwood had a moment of inspiration.

'We're within a day or so of the result coming back from the DNA database, but we're fairly sure that one of Paul's hairs has turned up in Thomas Glass's mouth.'

Trent looked at Bellwood.

'His hair in the boy's mouth; you at the wheel of the Megane on CCTV. You're in this together, you and your friend, Paul Conner. I think the time to stop denying the truth is now.'

Bellwood threw him a lifeline of machismo. 'Let's go back a few steps, Jay. You gunned the CCTV on Bannerman Square, didn't you?' She faked grudging admiration. 'Broad daylight, that took some nerve.'

'Did you find a gun when you searched my place?'

'No, but as soon as we find Paul Conner – he's not like you, is he? – he's going to sing the whole song his way. If I were you, I'd want to get my version of things over before he does.'

Silence, long and dense. And out of that silence came words that were little more than the clearing of a congested throat.

Bellwood waited for Trent's eyes to rise from a scratch on the table.

'I'm sorry, Jay. I didn't quite catch that.'

'It was his idea.'

'Who?'

'Conner.'

'Paul?'

'Yes, Paul.'

'What was his idea?'

'The fucking photographs, all right, the fucking photographs! He loves himself, thinks he's got a great future as a model or something, I only did it for a laugh, like to humour him, all right!'

'So you are friends with Paul Conner?'

'Sort of.'

'Boyfriend, partner perhaps?'

'He's not my boyfriend. I just. . . have sex with him.' Trent looked astonished. 'That's not true! I don't know why I said that, you tricked me into saying it, yeah. . . that's it. . . You made, like – my sexuality's not the issue here. . . You made me say something false!'

'I'm interested in this, Jay.' Bellwood pointed at the CCTV photograph. 'We know this is you. We're waiting for a more detailed CGI analysis of your face and, nowadays, a face is as good as a fingerprint – better even.'

For a moment, Trent looked like he was going to start crying.

'I'm not gay,' he said. To whom, it was unclear.

'OK, let's try this. I'll give you a choice. We can talk about you and Paul Conner or we talk about you and Thomas Glass.'

He started beating the edge of the table with his fingertips, hammering out the rhythm of his speech as he said, 'In the afternoon, I gunned the CCTV camera on Bannerman Square. I had no idea what was behind it or what was to follow, I swear to God, I didn't.'

He stopped beating the table.

'Where did you pick Thomas Glass up from?'

'I didn't.'

'You've been caught on camera,' said Leung. 'Every piece of action you've been involved in, you've wriggled your way out of. Time's up, Jay. You're not getting out of this one.'

'Why did you gun the camera?'

His head sank and he looked completely ashamed.

'Did you do it for money?'

He shook his head.

'Who told you to do it?'

Silence.

'Did you do it for Paul, because you love him?'

'No. . . no. . . comment.'

'The cricket ground, Hilly Fields,' said Leung. '*I'd fucking round you all up, castrate the lot of yah, stick your stinking balls down your fucking throats.* Is that why you beat up that young homosexual male?' Leung threw a grenade. 'Was he cutting in on your action with Paul?'

'I fucking warned the pair of them—' He made a noise in his chest. 'Shut up your questions, you bitches!'

He whispered with his solicitor for close to half a minute.

'My client feels unable to speak any further as he finds himself becoming emotionally more and more distressed. He requests respectfully that you give him a pen and paper and he'll make a written account of his involvement in this case in his cell. He categorically denies all involvement in murder.'

'Pen and paper?' said Leung.

'No problem,' said Bellwood. 'But here's our condition. We have two missing children out there and no time to spare. You can write your account but you've got half an hour to do that. Do you understand me, Jay? Jay? I'm not closing the interview until you tell me you understand. Half an hour. Do you understand?'

He drew air through his nostrils and muttered, 'Yeah.'

'Thirty minutes. Get writing, I'm waiting.'

67

6.45 A.M.

After a sleepless night in what felt like endless purgatory, Emily Glass lay still on Thomas's bed, her head pounding, and wished she was dead. She looked around the walls at the space collage, the one he'd designed himself and the one she'd commissioned the artist to paint. She looked at the rocket spewing flames from its tail, the moon silver and ethereal on the opposite wall, the sun burning with nuclear explosions, the planets arranged around it in perfect position.

How happy Thomas had been as he'd watched the artist realize his vision; how he'd stayed and watched, a normally shy child asking question after question.

Emily heard the doorbell ring downstairs but didn't care who it was or what they wanted. She lifted her head from the pillow and the pain was fierce. Slowly, she raised the rest of herself from the bed and walked to her son's bedroom door, each step an agony. Grief was not abstract; it was physical and overwhelming.

In the bathroom, she emptied an entire bottle of co-codamol into the sink and poured a glass of water. She looked at herself in the mirror and decided in that moment to take her own life, to join her son in death. For this she would need privacy and space. She moved to the door to lock it, and heard her husband's voice downstairs, shouting behind a closed door.

The shouting grew louder: 'Did you check the fucking lists before you emailed them, dickhead?'

Astonishment crept into her haze of misery. How could he get so worked up and passionate about work at a time like this? She heard a muffled answer and recognized the voice as Julian Parker, her husband's PA.

'Yeah, well, I had the police asking me about that one. And dropping big hints.'

His voice dropped.

Without thinking or having intended to, Emily found herself halfway down the stairs.

'I go through the database every week to make sure we've updated what matters and delete what isn't relevant. Your instructions, John!' She heard Julian try to defend himself now.

'You're either lying or stupid.'

Her husband's ranting dropped in volume but grew more intense. She imagined he was poking his finger in Julian's face. Julian? She'd insisted on John employing a male PA given his track record with the others, the women PAs: women, woman, any woman.

Julian fought back. 'John, I'm telling you to stop this right now.' But it only stirred the hornets' nest.

Emily was at the door.

'I don't have to put up with this. I'll email you my resignation.'

Julian opened the door; looked into her eyes.

'Emily? Emily, I'm so sorry about Thomas. I – I have to go. I'm sorry.'

'Stay,' her voice was little more than a whisper. She looked at her husband. 'What have you been up to now?'

'Nothing.'

She pointed at the papers in her husband's hand.

'What's that?' she asked.

264

'John's databases,' replied Julian.

'Shut up!' said John.

'Give it to me,' demanded Emily.

'Look, this isn't the right time—'

'Give it to me!' she raged. 'Give it to me!' Her voice rose. '*Give it to me!*' She screamed at her husband.

In the silence that followed, she held out her hand but he replied, 'No.'

'OK,' she responded, quietly. 'OK.'

She followed Julian to the front door, opened it for him and followed him outside.

'Emily, get back in now!'

'I'd be grateful,' she said to Julian, 'if you would give me a lift into London. You are going into London, aren't you?'

She followed Julian to his car. He opened the passenger door.

'Get in here now, Emily! Get back here now!'

She got into the car, closed her eyes tightly and, as Julian pulled away, she stuck her fingers in her ears to block her husband's voice.

'Whereabouts in London do you want to go to?' asked Julian, the electronic gates of the walled-in Glass house opening.

As he pulled away, she opened her eyes, took her fingers from her ears and replied, 'Isaac Street. Isaac Street Police Station.'

68

6.50 A.M.

Chelsea Booth was woken up by thirst. She struggled to open her eyes and, when she managed it, wished she'd taken her make-up off before she'd gone to bed. The pillow slip was covered in mascara and looked like Luke had been scribbling on it.

Feet on the floor, she made her way towards the kitchen, the silence in her flat appeasing the throb in her head. As she turned the tap and poured herself a cup of cold water, she recalled the visit from a police officer in the early hours and wondered if she'd dreamt it. Just as she wondered if she'd imagined the drunken stag party from Glasgow throwing money at her as if they were allergic to it.

She drank the water in one take. No, both things were for real. Police officer asking for Macy. Drunken Scotsmen handing over £200 for a five-minute pole dance.

Chelsea placed the mug in the sink and wandered over to Luke's bedroom door. It was so unlike him to sleep in and, judging by the stillness of his form, without fidgeting. She looked into her room at the alluring bed but decided instead she'd check on the baby.

He was completely covered by the duvet, his shape picked out by the indentations of the cover. She picked up a corner and lifted it slowly and carefully so as not to disturb him.

What she saw caused a sensation like a knife cutting the wires that held her together inside. She threw the duvet back.

In a tide of blood, her little boy's cat, Sparky, lay on the mattress with his throat slashed.

She recoiled and then pulled the duvet away completely.

Luke was gone.

69

7.05 A.M.

Rosen stood at the door of Trent's cell and raised the spy-hole cover. Trent sat on the floor, paper in one hand, pen in the other, head down; a young man at the edge of a void.

He closed the cover and stood with his back against the wall as the custody sergeant unlocked the door with a skeleton key.

Leung and Bellwood stood in the open doorway, just outside the cell, with Trent's solicitor beside them.

'Up you get, Jay,' Bellwood prompted him. But he didn't move a muscle. A closer inspection of his closed eyes revealed a sheen of tears on his long eyelashes.

Bellwood turned to his solicitor.

'Would you please go and take the paper and pen from your client.'

Mrs Cairns walked into the cell and, stooping, took the paper and pen from Trent's unresisting hands. Leaving the cell, she handed them to Bellwood.

'Anything to say, Jay?'

Nothing. The custody sergeant closed the cell door. Catching Rosen's eye, Bellwood handed him the folded paper.

Rosen opened the paper, expecting to see a page of rapidly composed paragraphs, but was instead faced with two words.

He turned to the custody sergeant and the solicitor.

'I want him back in Interview Suite 1 later.'

'What does it say?' asked Bellwood. Rosen turned the page for her to see, showing her the two written words:

Macy Conner.

70

7.10 A.M.

The office at Isaac Street was teeming with life and felt more like the concourse of an inter-city railway station than a murder incident room.

The brief sleep Bellwood had snatched earlier that day had been troubled by something she'd seen when she'd visited Macy Conner's school to pick her up. And in spite of the relentless pace of the day, the insistent itch just beneath her scalp caused her to open up her HOLMES 2 laptop and log on to the national police database of all recorded details of all reported crimes.

The silhouette of Sherlock Holmes's head, deerstalker, caped shoulders and pipe came on screen. The corniness of the introductory image on such a sophisticated criminal database never failed to amaze Bellwood.

She wanted to try out a trio of names; names that had played on her mind as she'd dressed after Rosen's phone call had woken her in the dead of night; names loosely related to events of recent days by death, childhood and geographical location.

She thought back to the gates of Bream Street Primary School, and recalled the names of three sisters: Denise Rainer, six. Jane Rainer, four. Gail Rainer, two.

She typed the three names into the laptop, the relevant dates and 'Lewisham'. Then she speculated. Murder. Home.

Behind her back, she sensed someone approaching her.

'Carol, what's happening?' It was Rosen.

'I'm putting a line on the lottery, a lucky dip. . .'

'Hey?' He crouched behind her to see the screen.

'I'm trying out a long shot, a very long shot. The three sisters on the plaque on the wall of Bream Street Primary.'

'What's your hunch?' asked Rosen.

'I don't know. It's bugging me, though. If I get to go to bed tonight, it's going to keep me awake if I don't check it.' She clicked for a match.

A text box appeared with the girls' names.

Denise Rainer 6 years
Jane Rainer 4 years
Gail Rainer 2 years
Class description: VICTIMS
Force ID: 97
Station ID: IS

'It was our nick,' observed Bellwood. Memory erupted inside Rosen's skull like the arrival of summer thunder.

Class ID: VICT
The first Associated Documents box – witness statement 1:
Father – Donald Rainer.

'It was a house fire,' said Rosen, speaking the memory aloud as it came to him.

Bellwood opened the father's witness statement and read out: "'I was in the front room watching TV. It was afternoon and I must've fallen asleep or something. The girls were upstairs playing. The last time I saw them alive was when I went to the toilet. I was asleep downstairs but woke myself up by my own coughing and there was, like, smoke in the living room and when I jumped up, there were flames all over the stairs and the girls were not downstairs. I could not get through the flames myself. I thought they may have gone into the garden because they were not screaming. So I went to look for them. When they were not in the garden, I called for help and then I ran away. I don't know why I did this. I was in shock."'

Rosen scrolled through the contacts on his phone until he came to Mrs Price, the head teacher of Bream Street Primary. He pressed 'call'.

'Did he get life?' asked Bellwood.

'He didn't go to jail in the end,' said Rosen. 'I want to check. Keep looking through the associated documents, Carol.'

After three rings, a tentative, 'Yes?'

'Mrs Price, it's DCI Rosen.'

'It's Saturday morning.'

'I'm sorry to trouble you, but I need a little background information. How long have you been head teacher at Bream Street?'

'Twelve years.'

'So you remember the Rainer sisters?'

'Denise was in the reception class when she died, Jane was in morning nursery and Gail used to come into the yard with her father to deliver and collect her sisters.'

'And you can remember the details of how they died?'

'Oh, yes, it was awful. A house fire, started by the father, who tried to be clever and make it look like he was escaping from the inferno. But it didn't wash.'

'Why did he kill his children?'

'If you look into your records, I'm sure you'll be able to put two and two together.'

'Help me with the sum, Mrs Price.'

'It transpired after the fire that the father was a convicted rapist.'

'Was his victim a child?'

'An adult female. The girls didn't manifest any of the signs of sexual abuse. The whole thing came out of the blue.'

'What's your view, Mrs Price? Completely between you and me.'

'It's no mystery. Their mother – she had learning difficulties, as did her husband but, unlike him, she was consistent in her story – she went into court and said she'd just discovered he'd been abusing Denise. She'd threatened to expose him and so, when she was out at the shops, he set up the so-called accidental fire. He collapsed two streets away, suffering the effects of smoke inhalation. He was trying to kill his victim, his daughter; the witness to his horrible actions. It was almost the perfect crime.'

'Anything else to add?' asked Rosen.

'That's all, Mr Rosen.'

He thanked her, closed the call down and turned to Bellwood.

'I've just flicked through the lead fire-fighter's statement and I'm on the forensic report. The girls were shut in a bedroom, the bedding was doused in lighter fuel and the fire was started with a Dunhill lighter belonging to the father. He poured fuel on the stairs,' said Bellwood.

'Was anyone else around and about? Go to the mother's witness statement,' said Rosen, his heartbeat rising, his instincts sharp.

Bellwood opened the statement and Rosen skimmed the text.

'"There had been other children there in the house that morning, coming and going. I can't remember their names but they had gone home when I went to the shops. One was called Lucy-Faye Peters. Lucy-Faye Peters lives across the street."'

The unusual combination of first names brought Rosen directly to one child who he'd encountered in recent days.

'Lucy-Faye Peters. Bream Street Primary,' observed Bellwood. 'Macy Conner's friend.'

'Open the witness statement from Lucy-Faye's mother.'

Bellwood scrolled through until she found it: Mrs Marlene Peters. *Click*.

'"Carly Rainer, the girls' mother, dropped Lucy-Faye back at my house just before lunchtime on her way to the shops. Macy Conner was with her. Carly Rainer walked away with Macy and said she'd drop her at Bannerman Square on her way to the high street—"'

Corrigan raced into the incident room.

'David! David!'

Rosen looked across. Corrigan was in a lather.

'David. Listen, boss, bad to worse, I'm afraid. Come down to reception.'

71

7.18 A.M.

As Rosen raced down the stairs leading to the door into reception, he heard a woman crying hysterically. The nearer he got, the louder she became, not because he was closing the distance but because she was increasing in panic and volume.

He threw open the door. It was Chelsea Booth. She almost looked through him, as if he was an apparition.

'Luke?' asked Rosen.

She nodded. 'He's gone, he's gone, he's gone—'

'Did Macy Conner take him in the night?'

She shook her head. 'He was. . . in bed. She left. . . after five—'

'Did you see him in the early hours? Chelsea, come on. . .'

Thoughtfulness invaded the mania in her eyes. 'Looked like. . . shape. . .'

'Did you see him directly, touch him, when you got home?'

Her face collapsed. She shook her head. 'No.'

'Listen to me, Chelsea. I'm going to send Corrigan with you back to your home. I need the most recent photograph you have of Luke, a description of the pyjamas he was wearing or the clothes that are missing from his wardrobe. Photograph. Clothing. I'm sorry, Chelsea.' He held her hands briefly. 'Go and get those things. Quickly.'

As Corrigan walked Chelsea out of the building, Bellwood stepped into reception and followed Rosen outside, into the fresh air.

'Whoever's got Macy and Chester,' said Rosen, 'they've also got a two year old with them: Luke Booth. The child of another witness.'

'Where are we going?'

'Looking for three missing children.'

72

7.45 A.M.

A kindly looking man approached the glass door of Lewisham Library saying, 'I'm sorry, we're not open until nine.' Rosen showed his warrant card. 'OK.'

Having seen the place that Macy called home, Rosen understood immediately why she spent so much time here. It was warm and comfortable; there were books galore and things to do. And if the man who had let them in was an example, the adults were polite and helpful, the readers bound by a collective love of books.

'Where's the children's section?' asked Rosen.

'I'll take you,' said the librarian, leading them up a set of stairs. Rosen clocked his badge. TIM. 'First floor. Lending library, adults and children.'

'We're looking for Macy Conner,' explained Rosen.

'Oh, Macy, yeah, she's a really good kid, bright as a button.' It sounded like he genuinely liked her. 'She's here most days.'

'When was the last time she was in?'

'Macy, yeah, let's see, the day before yesterday. It's not usual for her to miss a day. Comes in, sits on the comfy chairs, book after book after book.'

'Does she ever bring anyone with her?'

'No, she's a loner. But she does talk to the staff. She's one of those kids who's more in tune with adults than her peers. She's not in trouble, is she?' He was deeply concerned.

'No. . . we're trying to help her. . . Does she ever mention other places where she likes to go?'

'No, she just talks about books and computers and her grandmother, of course. She's dying. You can tell it's causing Macy a lot of pain. I've tried to get her to go to a young carer's support group but she says she's too busy. She gets books out from the adult section for her grandmother. With her being so ill, she sent a letter in with Macy asking for special permission—'

As soon as they arrived at the desk, Rosen said, 'Tim, can you pull up two lists?' Rosen quickly eyed the clock on the wall. 'Macy's reading record and her grandmother's.'

'Which one do you want to see first?'

'Macy's.'

Within seconds, Rosen was on the other side of the desk.

Celtic Myths and Legends, Tales of the Norsemen, The Celts: An Introduction, Ancient Lives, Prometheus and other Greek Myths, Coping with Bereavement, Issues: Domestic Violence, Countries of the North: Scotland, Lizzy Borden and other Ghastly Tales, Rodents and other Furry Friends: A Guide to Keeping Pets and *The Druids*.

'Have you got *The Druids* in stock?'

'She brought it back the day before yesterday.'

Rosen recalled the pitiful sight of a bruised girl living below the poverty line with a burden of books on her back.

'Can you get me it but, before you do, can you call up her grandmother's reading record?'

'No problem.'

Rosen took a deep breath. The list appeared on screen, and Tim moved over to a small, wheeled cart of books to be reshelved and started flicking through the titles on it.

Catherine Cookson Omnibus, Flower Arranging Made Simple, The Golden Bough – Rosen's eyes jarred, but then moved on – Katie Flynn's *Strawberry Fields, Helter Skelter,* Josephine Cox's *The Woman Who Left, World's Most Infamous Serial Killers,* Pliny *Natural Philosophy, Recipes for Perfect Picnics, The Gallic Wars* by Julius Caesar, *Her Benny* and *Herod: Portrait of a Serial Killer.*

What's going on, Macy? thought Rosen. The contrast in titles made him deeply uneasy.

'Here's that book you asked for,' said Tim, coming back and handing him *The Druids.*

Rosen opened the book, flicked through and was arrested by a double page of twenty symbols representing twenty English letters and phonic blends: the symbols scratched into the wall on Bannerman Square and written with UV pen on Stevie Jensen's limbs.

See we is many. See I are one. Rosen felt the words as a physical pain in the core of his head.

'When did she take the book out?'

Tim looked at the computer screen. 'A year ago. She's had it out on continual loan since last April. Just kept renewing it. I nearly bought her a copy from AbeBooks last Christmas, but the manager blocked me. I was surprised when she brought it back. She brought everything back, all the books she'd borrowed for herself and her grandmother.'

Rosen flicked back to the index. H. Human Sacrifice. Page 42.

The page was creased and made grey with over-use.

When the Romans came to Britain they were shocked to discover that the Celts practised the rite known as human sacrifice. Writing from the time tells us that the Celts used to burn convicted criminals, sometimes in huge cages called Wicker Men, as a sacrifice to the gods.

There was an illustration of a druid leading a young male towards a stake, where another druid held a burning torch to ignite the wooden logs at the base of the stake. In the sky above, the sun was pictured as an eye, burning, an all-seeing witness to the human acts that honoured the gods. Under this was another illustration of a Wicker Man stuffed with men, cattle and other living beings.

She had underlined one line with pencil and then rubbed it out, but the indentation on the page was clear to see:

> The Celts believed this rite would ensure the fertility of crops and the renewal of life.
>
> Human sacrifice was most common in the Highlands of Scotland in the rite known as Beltaine Fires. Beltaine Night was celebrated on May Day, 1 May, each year.

Beneath the remorseless clock on the wall, Rosen read the day's date: Saturday, 1 May.

Tonight. Half past eight. Tonight. Five to eleven. Tonight.

'Did she ever talk about this book?' asked Rosen now.

'No.'

'I need to take it away with me.'

'Do you have your library card? I'm joking. . .'

Patches of light formed in Rosen's mind, connections. The UV graffiti on Stevie Jensen's leg shot through his memory.

'OK, we're going to plant an officer here today, Tim. Are you here all day?'

'Till we close at five.'

Rosen handed Tim his card. 'If she shows up, call me immediately on this number. If she shows, keep her talking, keep her here.'

*

As ROSEN SAT in the passenger seat of Bellwood's car and she fired up the engine, he said, 'Macy sat where I am?'

280

She pulled away, then answered, 'And we're going to head past Stevie's scene of crime. Just like I did with Macy next to me.'

'Quick 24,' said Rosen. 'Carol, "See we is many. See I are one" – it's an anagram, it must be.'

73

9.15 A.M.

In the incident room, as she began calling round the team on her mobile, notifying them of the 6.45 P.M. meeting, Bellwood received a call on her landline from the front desk downstairs.

'Thomas Glass's mother's in reception and she wants to speak to Rosen,' explained WPC Church.

'He's just gone down to interview Jay Trent. What's happening?'

Church's tone dropped to confidential. 'She's with a guy. It's not her husband. They've got information. Regarding the contacts in her husband's business database.'

Bellwood instructed WPC Church to escort Emily Glass and the man accompanying her to Interview Suite 2.

As she walked down the stairs to meet them, she called up John Glass's business database on her open laptop

She walked into the interview suite and heard the man speaking softly to Emily. She recognized his voice from a phone call they'd had. It was Glass's PA, Julian Parker.

Bellwood placed her laptop on the table between them. 'I'm very, very sorry, Mrs Glass. We all are.'

Emily Glass took it on board and simply answered, 'Yeah.'

Bellwood looked at Julian Parker. Julian turned to Emily and said, 'Ready?'

'On the way over here, we've had a very. . . frank. . . discussion,' said Emily Glass. 'About my husband. I've just found out. . . where he found the artist.'

'The artist?' Bellwood coaxed.

'He should've said, shouldn't he?' replied Emily. Her hands knitted tightly on her lap. 'It was close, wasn't it? It was a link. Did he forget? I don't know.'

Bellwood looked at Emily Glass and the expression *It is the end of the world* ran through her mind.

Emily looked back at Bellwood and said, 'I didn't know exactly where the boy came from? It was just London.'

'London?' Bellwood tried to focus her. 'London's a big place.'

'Lewisham. Where Thomas was found. You'd have thought my husband would have remembered. I mean, it was only months ago that he came and painted the mural on Thomas's bedroom wall. I didn't know which part of London he came from; I didn't even know if it was north or south of the river.'

Bellwood cast her mind back to the phase of the investigation when Thomas Glass was a missing person and she had seen the intricate space paintings on the boy's walls. She resisted now the reflex to take out her phone on which she had photographed the planets suspended around the sun, the rocket, the Milky Way. Jagged panic curved deep within her.

'Who came to paint the mural on Thomas's wall, Mrs Glass?'

'All of a sudden, John, *John*' – she shook her head, articulating her chain of thought rather than answering Bellwood's question – 'who couldn't give a damn whether the rest of the world lived or died, suddenly became this big philanthropist. Started talking about social responsibility, stopping the rot in London's rotten heart.'

Emily Glass covered her face with her hands. Bellwood focused on Parker.

'You have the database on screen,' said Julian. 'Scroll down and you'll find a defunct charity, Outlook. When Thomas asked for his room to be painted with a space mural, rather than commissioning a professional artist' – Julian glanced at Emily whose face and eyes were still covered. He made a quick gesture rubbing his thumb and fingers together, signifying money – 'John decided he'd go socially responsible and support a young people's charity. Outlook. That's where he found his young unemployed artist.'

Emily dropped the mask of her hands.

'Thomas loved him, couldn't keep away from him in the three days he was at the house painting the mural on his wall,' said Emily. 'I think it was the happiest I'd ever seen him.'

The recollection of her son, alive and happy, pressed down on her and fresh tears ran down her face.

'What was the name of the artist who painted the mural on Thomas's wall?'

Through tears, Emily was unable to speak.

'Pee-Cee – I guess that was his street tag, his nickname,' replied Julian. 'I personally handled the payment. His name's Paul Conner.'

As the name tripped into the air, Bellwood formed the name silently on her own lips.

'Does that connect anything?'

'Very much so. Thank you. That figures.'

'Do you think. . . I can't bear to say it. . . do you think. . . Paul seemed so nice, so gentle and kind. . . do you think he might. . . have abducted. . . Thomas. . . and. . .' Words finally failed Emily as she struggled to address such an horrific idea; she covered her face with her hands again and wept into that shield of privacy.

Bellwood held Julian Parker's gaze.

'DS Bellwood, I'm no longer John Glass's PA. If there's anything I can do to assist with your investigation, then I'll happily do just that.'

'I'll be in touch,' said Bellwood.

She touched Emily's arm and spoke gently. 'Do you have anything else to tell me?'

Emily shook her head and leaned forward, as if trying to find a hole in the air to swallow her alive. Julian folded an arm across her back.

Bellwood held a hand up. *Wait.* Parker sat back and Bellwood scrolled up so that the names of two organizations were visible on screen at the same time. Outlook and Fingertips. Bellwood pointed at each name in turn and looked at Parker.

'Not now,' said Parker, barely audibly, indicating Emily.

As Bellwood escorted Emily Glass and Julian Parker to the door of the interview suite, she said, 'I'll escort you to the front door. Can I just ask you one last thing? Did John Glass have direct contact with Paul Conner, face to face?'

'Not that I know of,' said Emily. 'But what do I know about him?'

'No, as I said, I dealt with the payment for the work in Thomas's bedroom,' said Parker. 'I'll be in touch, DS Bellwood.'

74

9.25 A.M.

Rosen sat alone at the table in Interview Suite 1, his phone in hand, listening to Bellwood's account of the meeting with Emily Glass and Julian Parker.

'Tell Corrigan to go and track down John Glass and pick up the little bag of shit for questioning.'

The door opened as he closed the call down. The custody sergeant escorted Trent back from the toilet. His solicitor followed, her frustration barely contained beneath the surface.

Trent sat down opposite Rosen, and the custody sergeant asked, 'Do you want me to wait with you, DCI Rosen?'

'If you'd wait outside, please, Sergeant Morgan,' replied Rosen. 'This isn't going to take a great deal of time because we simply don't have it to spare.'

As the sergeant closed the door, Rosen focussed on Trent. 'Me *again*. Just for your information, we've just made a direct link between Thomas Glass and Paul Conner. As in *he knew his abductor*. Are you shielding Paul Conner?'

'I'm not gay.'

Through almost gritted teeth, Rosen said, 'I'm not interested in your sexuality.' He took a breath. 'There are three children missing now.' He took in both reactions in one glance: Trent deadpan; his solicitor looking away from Rosen. 'Your brother, your *brother*, Jay. And a toddler called Luke Booth, and Macy Conner. You go off to your cell to pour your heart out with the written word and what do you come up with?' Rosen showed Trent the piece of paper and read aloud, '"Macy Conner."'

'She's an evil little bitch and she's not scared of no one.'

'Oh, so you do know her?'

'Yes. I reckon she planted those photographs under my bed when she came calling for Chester.'

'Forget the photographs. Macy Conner? As in she's an evil little bitch and she's not scared of *me*?'

'She'd better be.'

'Scared of you?'

'Scared of me, yeah fucking right.'

'Mr Trent, calm down,' said his solicitor. 'I'd like to request a break for my client.'

'No,' said Rosen, thinking, *She isn't scared of you, Trent,* and asking, 'Why are you scared of a ten-year-old girl?'

Trent stood up, picked up his chair and turned it round. He sat down and faced the wall, his back turned to Rosen. He, who had terrified others – grown men, gang members and hard cases into silence – had met his nemesis in a ten-year-old girl. If the whole situation hadn't been so dangerous, fraught and urgent, the moment would have been sweet and hilarious.

'Well, we're getting there—' said Rosen.

'No comment,' snapped Trent.

'—bit by painful bit.'

'No comment.'

'Let's just hope—' Rosen raised his voice.

'No comment.'

'—we can get there—'

'No comment.'

'—before another person—'

'No comment.'

'—or before people get burned to death.' Rosen looked towards the door. 'Sarge! Sergeant Morgan.' He stood as the door opened. 'Before Mr Trent returns to his cell, I think his solicitor would like an opportunity to talk to her client. And, Mr Trent, I'm coming back for you.'

75

10.20 A.M.

Rosen inspected the hastily assembled missing-persons stand in the north wing of the Lewisham Centre. Blown-up images of Macy, Chester and Luke looked down on passing shoppers but, on their faces, recognition was absent. He thanked the constable and community officers manning the stand and walked away, his spirit dense with fear and the passage of time.

In the ground-floor toilet of the centre, Rosen splashed water onto his face to lighten the heaviness that dogged him. He looked at his reflection in the mirror on the wall and recognized the uneasy cast around his eyes: fear, naked and rampant. Words carouselled around his head. The rhythm of the graffiti, *See we is many. See I are one* gripped Rosen. A warmth erupted in his stomach and a lightness drifted around his being. The words seemed to echo from the walls.

He picked up a plastic bag from the sink next to him, his purchase from Toyland, and headed for the door.

See we is many. See I are one. Each syllable like a fat drop of water in an endless rite of Chinese torture, each sound smacking the bone of his forehead.

'See we is many. See I are one,' whispered Rosen, as he hurried past shoppers walking blithely through the mall.

In his bag there was a box. Scrabble. Plastic letters clattered and clashed inside the box just as the words of the anagram bounced around Rosen's brain.

See, are, I, see, I, see, are, many, we, see, are, is, are, one, see.

As he hurried back to his car, the noise in his head grew louder than the thunder of traffic and the babel of human voices.

76

12 NOON

In Interview Suite 1, there was a new face across the table from Rosen and Bellwood. Instead of Mrs Cairns, Trent had a new solicitor, a young man who introduced himself as Mr McNulty. Trent sat stone-faced, his lips clamped.

Rosen addressed Bellwood. 'Do you know why Mr Trent has a new solicitor?'

'No.'

'In the interests of fair play, Mr Trent, would you like to give your version of this morning's events?'

'No comment.'

'Then I'll explain to you as well, Mr McNulty. Last chance, Jay.'

'No comment.'

Bellwood placed two envelopes on the table, the first with the enhanced CCTV image. CC4U had motored with their work, and the second contained specific close-ups of Trent.

'OK,' said Rosen. 'After our interview with Mr Trent this morning, Mrs Cairns had a discussion with him in which she stated her prerogative to resign from the case if she was of the conviction that her client was not being one hundred per cent truthful with her about his involvement in the crime we're investigating. Mrs Cairns resigned. Because she knows you're lying through your teeth; as do we, as do you.'

'No comment.'

'Where did you pick Thomas Glass up from?'

'No comment.'

Bellwood took out the main CCTV picture, placed it in front of McNulty. McNulty looked from the picture to Trent and back. Trent stared ahead.

'Mr Trent, I suggest you look at the picture.'

Trent leaned into his solicitor, stage-whispered, 'It's a doctored image. They're setting me up. I admit nothing.'

'OK,' said Bellwood, spreading out the close-ups. 'As you can observe, Mr Trent has a dimple in his chin.' She pointed at Trent's chin and the same dimpled chin in a close-up of the lower half of Trent's face. 'You'll also notice if you look at the picture, Mr Trent, that the purple heart-shaped birthmark on your neck is featured in the same image of your chin.'

Silence.

'You admitted you're scared of Macy Conner.' Rosen picked up the baton.

'No comment.'

'This is the situation—'

'No comment.'

'Trent, I'm not talking to you; I'm talking to Mr McNulty. I need to know from where he picked up Thomas Glass. It could well be the three missing children are there. That's all I want. A location.'

'Mr Trent.' McNulty picked up the photograph. 'Mr Trent, we need to talk frankly about this.'

'Indeed you do, Mr McNulty,' agreed Rosen. 'And I'd like to offer one theme for your discussion. Given the nature of his involvement in a violent crime against a child, we're looking at two probable outcomes for your client. One, he's looking at a life sentence, but it won't be served with other high-security prisoners. No, he's looking at a life sentence on a sex offenders' wing.'

Lightning – brief but undeniable – flashed through Trent's eyes.

'Let me know when you're ready to talk, but in the meantime, Jay Trent.' When he had eye contact, Rosen stood up. 'I'm looking to charge you with conspiracy to murder—'

There was an urgent knocking on the door.

'Come in,' said Rosen.

Gold came into the room, walked directly up to Rosen and whispered, 'The footage has come in. A and E, Lewisham Hospital, the night Thomas Glass was admitted. David, you've got to see it.'

'I'll be there in two minutes.'

Trent was slumped forwards, his face downcast. Rosen looked at the top of his head.

'Where did you pick up Thomas Glass?'

'No comment.'

Rosen stood up. The hands of the clock were moving faster and Trent wasn't going to budge.

'Maybe. . .' – Rosen sat – 'you know you're cornered. Sex offenders' unit. Maybe that's what you *want*, Jay. You'd be in your element with those guys. . .'

In reply Trent banged and banged the table. 'Shut your fucking mouth, you fucking mother-fucker!'

'Where'd you pick the kid up from?'

'No comment.'

For the second time, Rosen stood. 'Sex offenders' unit it is then.' He walked to the door. 'Your call, Jay. If you don't believe me, ask your solicitor.'

77

12.23 P.M.

On the screen of Gold's laptop, Rosen orientated the hospital's A & E reception. The door leading in, the seats filled with patients waiting to be seen, the reception desk with the receptionist speaking to a patient, the door leading into the treatment area and resuscitation room.

'Ready?' asked Gold.

'Press play,' said Rosen.

A nurse came through the door of the treatment and resuscitation unit. A woman stood up from the seats and hobbled after her through the door.

A young man came in through the main entrance: Paul Conner was followed in by his younger sister, Macy. Rosen glanced at the time on-screen – 21.45.

It didn't add up to the time given by A & E administrators. It was earlier than the arrival time of Thomas Glass.

Paul Conner headed straight for the reception desk. Macy stopped, not far from the door. He carried on. She turned around and walked out. He approached the desk, and spoke to the receptionist. Macy was gone. The receptionist pointed to the space behind Paul. He turned. And headed back towards the main door.

Gold paused the footage with, 'Here's what happened outside.'

Exterior to A & E. Macy Conner walked calmly towards the ambulance entrance to A & E treatment and resuscitation. An ambulance arrived, the driver jumped out. A doctor and a nurse appeared at the doorway leading in. The driver opened the back door and, with his partner, took a boy on a stretcher from the rear of the ambulance.

The four adults, focusing completely on the boy on the stretcher, didn't notice the little girl drifting towards them. They pushed the wheeled stretcher into the treatment and resuscitation area.

Rosen recalled being told how on the corridor to resus, Thomas had suddenly become emotional and agitated.

Bellwood said, 'The nurse doesn't remember seeing Macy but she did see the door closing, the door leading back into A and E reception.'

'Want me to show you Macy Conner going back into the reception through that door?' asked Gold.

'I'll take your word for it,' said Rosen.

78

1.13 P.M.

Bellwood finished off a cup of coffee that had become cold as she went through the tangle of telephone connections to reach Social Services. As she did so, she watched Rosen across the space of the incident room at Isaac Street. He looked miles away. On and off, since mid-morning, he'd been staring down at his desk, moving small objects around like a soothsayer divining significance in a set of stones.

She noticed the Toyland bag on the floor beside his desk and a rectangular green box alongside it. Scrabble.

'David?' she called.

'The graffiti on Stevie Jensen's body. . .' he replied, without looking up.

He took out a pen and scribbled furiously on a piece of paper, crossed out what he was writing, scrunching the paper angrily and added it to the growing pile in his bin.

'What's your thought?' asked Bellwood.

He shrugged and returned to the objects on his desk. His face had the cast of a blind man staring at a twenty-foot-high canvas: so close to seeing, but so deeply in the dark.

Just as Bellwood was about to go over and see what Rosen was up to, her phone rang. She picked up the receiver.

'DS Bellwood speaking.'

'Hi, it's Sally Emerson, South London Social Services. We spoke earlier.'

'Thanks for getting back to me, Sally. Anything to report on Macy Conner?'

'Yes. She came to our attention about six years ago when she entered the reception class at Bream Street. Her teacher at the time reported she was sometimes a bright child but on several occasions appeared withdrawn and suffering from physical neglect: she spent a week, Monday to Friday, in the same white school shirt. We approached Mum, offered her support. I think the visit from us was enough of a wake-up call – Macy started coming to school clean and tidy, and made excellent academic and social progress throughout that year.'

'So it was a blip with her mum?'

'That's what the notes conclude.'

'And there's absolutely nothing else on her?'

'There is, but it's indirect, as it's related to the case of another family. The Rainer family.'

'The three sisters who died in the house fire.'

'Yes.' Sally Emerson sounded surprised.

'What's the link?' asked Bellwood.

'After the girls died and it became apparent that one of the girls had been abused by the father, there was a logical possibility that the other two girls had been his victims also. And any other children he'd had access to. Macy Conner was in Denise Rainer's circle of friends in reception. There was a police investigation. Macy and some other children who'd been in the house at some point were brought in to speak with a child psychologist. Halfway through the trial, Rainer hung himself.'

'What about Macy?' asked Bellwood.

'Macy was fine – there was no indication whatsoever that Rainer had abused her. She was barely aware of the man's existence. Which was ironic, because Rainer stuck to his story about the cause of the house fire throughout. Tell me, are you aware of the case?'

'Limited. He was asleep downstairs. When he woke up, the stairs and bedroom were blazing. He ran out of the house.'

'Then he elaborated the story,' said the social worker. 'He stated that he'd been drinking in the morning and that had confused him initially but after much thought and soul searching, he remembered. When he woke up, smoke everywhere, he looked out of the window and saw Macy Conner running away from the house. Macy, aged five. That's where the story of Macy, Social Services and the police ends. Absolutely malicious nonsense, but malicious nonsense that he stuck to until the day he died. Don't know why he picked on her, but pick on her he did.'

'Was she aware of this allegation?'

'I don't know, Carol. The best person to ask would be her mother.'

'She has a brother, Paul?' prompted Bellwood now.

'I went digging for you. Paul was placed under the care of the community psychiatric nurse, but he refused all offers of help after he was released from hospital. This is going back three years or so.'

'Why did he need the psychiatric nurse?'

'He tried to kill himself when he was about fourteen or fifteen. He tried twice: once with painkillers, once by slashing his wrists.'

Bellwood sighed heavily, taking the story in.

'What about Chester Adler?'

'We're aware of him because he tortured and killed a cat two years ago, aged eight, but the main therapeutic work with him was done by the RSPCA. Our investigation into his background showed a stable picture, working mother, nice home. He's got pretty big learning difficulties. His IQ came out at seventy-five, five points above the threshold for a statement of special educational needs. Therefore, he doesn't have a case worker.'

'Do me a favour, Sally, and keep talking to any of your colleagues who were around in 2009. If anyone remembers anything at all—'

'That's it!' Rosen announced, his face lighting up with clarity and free-falling as significance bit him.

'—about Macy or Chester, anything you haven't come up with, call me directly.' Bellwood thanked her and closed the call down.

'What is it, David?'

'Over here, Carol.'

Bellwood hurried over. On his desk there were Scrabble squares that spelt out:

SEE WE IS MANY

SEE I ARE ONE.

In Rosen's hands, there were several small pieces of paper.

Rosen isolated two words from the top line. SEE MANY.

Bellwood watched. He withdrew the N from MANY, leaving MA Y, and covered the word SEE with a single piece of paper on which he'd written a single letter C.

'SEE and C sound the same. Replace the word SEE with the letter C.'

C MA Y

He moved the C into the space where he'd removed the N from MANY.

MACY

Bellwood felt something tighten inside her. She looked down at Rosen's desk.

'Look at the second line, Carol.'

SEE I ARE ONE

Rosen covered the word SEE with C on a paper, then a letter R over ARE.

C I R ONE

He moved the remaining letters from the first line next to his construction of the second line, and the N from the original MANY.

C I R ONE WE IS N

He drew the C alongside MACY and quietly invited, 'Go on, Carol.'

MACY C

In five moves she constructed MACY CONNER, leaving:

I WE IS

Rosen moved the remaining letters in front of the name staring up at them.

I WE IS MACY CONNER

'"I we is Macy Conner",' said Rosen. 'In Ogham. On Stevie Jensen's leg in UV marker.'

His phone was out.

Bellwood's face creased. 'She. . . didn't. . .?' They looked at each other. 'She couldn't have,' said Bellwood.

He scrolled through speed dial.

'Carol, you know and I know that there's no such thing as *couldn't have*.'

'Who are you calling?'

'Henshaw,' replied Rosen.

Bellwood examined the anagram, saw the way it played out to its logical conclusion.

'James, it's Rosen. What are you up to?'

'I'm about to go in to deliver a lecture. Additional Saturday class for sixty students sitting their finals next week.'

'Do me a favour, James.'

'Go on.'

'Stand them up and meet me at Isaac Street.'

A moment passed. 'I'll see you at Isaac Street,' said Henshaw.

The door of the incident room opened and Corrigan stormed in.

'He's not at home, he's not at work, he's not answering his phone. It looks like John Glass has fucked off into hiding somewhere.'

79

1.43 P.M.

itting at Rosen's desk, Henshaw scrutinized the anagram Rosen had worked out, and listened to the allegation made against Macy when she was five years old.

'*I we is Macy Conner*,' said Henshaw, thoughtfully.

'What is it, James?' asked Rosen.

'When we were in her flat, in the early hours this morning, I listened to your conversation with her mother.' Henshaw stood up, his face grim with mounting anxiety. 'We have to go back there now. We've got to speak with her mother.'

Bellwood, Henshaw and Rosen walked through the almost deserted incident room. With the exception of one officer acting as anchor in case of incoming calls, everyone was on the streets, searching.

As the door closed behind Rosen, he turned cold and, digging his hands into his pockets, felt his fingers trembling and the blossoming sickness of fear.

He pictured Macy on their first encounter in the MIR, a small girl with a cut lip and blackened eyes, crying for the loss of innocence in the world in which she lived. The UV writing on Stevie's leg and the charred pit of his face. The words *Could it be possible?* haunted Rosen's imagination. It was as if she was sitting inside his head, whispering,

But, Mr Rosen, how could I possibly. . .?

His phone rang.

SARAHMOBILE

His heart flipped. How they loved to use their victims' phones. The breath inside him stilled as he connected.

'Yes?' he snapped.

'David, are you all right?' asked Sarah.

'I'm. . . I'm so pleased to hear you.'

'You don't sound yourself.'

'Are they taking good care of you?'

Her voice dropped. 'There's a cop at the door with a gun. I'm in the middle of suburban nowhere. I'm fine. Stop worrying.'

Time was flying. 'Listen, I'll call you later. Love you.'

He closed the call down. As he caught up with Bellwood and Henshaw, he wished he was with Sarah, and the rack inside him turned another notch.

80

2.05 P.M.

On the journey from Isaac Street to Bannerman Square, Rosen noticed the almost complete absence of children on the streets. The regular Saturday afternoon buzz was flattened, and Rosen read the same story over and over again on the faces of adults being stopped and questioned by uniformed officers. . .

They hadn't seen a thing.

Bellwood pulled up close to Claude House and opened the door for Henshaw, who had spent the journey writing notes in his notebook on the back seat.

As he got out of the car, Rosen looked up at the building.

'Macy's mother is in. She just pulled away from the window when she saw me stepping out.'

*

'Ms CONNER, OPEN up!' Rosen hammered on the door with the flat of his hand.

'What do you want?' she asked, sourly.

He stopped banging.

'To talk.'

'She's not here.'

The bolt slid back and the chain rattled.

She opened the door and, turning away from them, walked back inside the flat. With her back against the window overlooking Bannerman Square, Macy's mother said, 'Yeah?'

Henshaw stepped closer to her. 'I heard you describe Macy as a lying little bitch this morning.'

'I was upset, but she is a liar, you know that now – all that stuff about a grandmother was bullshit. She's a very good liar.'

'You mentioned her putting on little plays behind her bedroom door, putting on funny little voices?'

'What about it?'

'Do you ever listen to what the voices say?'

'No, it's boring, I'm not interested.'

'Have you *ever* listened?'

'I've heard stuff.'

'When?'

'When Macy shouts in those stupid voices.'

'What do they shout?'

'I. . . don't. . . know.' Her temper was fraying fast. Henshaw stepped back, made a gesture to indicate there would be no more questions, but then asked, 'Did you say the voices were women?'

'I didn't say they were women. They're men's voices.'

She turned and looked out of the window. 'It's all Macy, Macy, Macy. No one gives a shit about me. I'm a person. I matter.'

'I agree with you, Ms Conner. You are a person and you do matter,' said Rosen. He stood next to her at the window and for a short while said nothing, just followed her gaze onto Bannerman Square, the mobile incident room, the scorched tarmac, the eye on the wall, the absence of a CCTV camera.

The light from the sky cast a silver sheen on Macy's mother's eyes.

'It must've been hard growing up without your parents,' said Rosen.

'I didn't know any different. Nobody loved me, ever, *ever*. You hear me?'

'I hear.'

'The kids' fathers both fucked off while I was expecting and I thought, the kids, they'll love me, but they didn't, they don't love me. But guess what? I just didn't love them either. That way no one's getting fooled. You see it all the time looking out of this window. Mothers picking up their kids and swinging them and hugging them. I just don't get it, and I don't see the point in pretending.'

'Paul and Macy aware of this?'

'I told them early on: I don't love you. You don't love me. You just want stuff from me. Food. A bed. Clothes. Gimme, gimme, gimme. That's not love.'

'You've always levelled with them?' asked Rosen.

'Yes.' Rain streaked the glass.

'Even about heavy stuff.'

'Such as?'

'Well, when Macy was in reception class, there was a house fire—'

'Oh, God, not that again, please.'

'*Please* tell me.'

She took a pack of cigarettes from the pocket of her Dolce & Gabbana jeans and, lighting a cigarette, took in a huge lungful of smoke, which she blew directly against the glass.

'Some pervert accused Macy of starting the house fire that killed his three kids. One of them was Macy's classmate. He killed himself in custody, swearing blind that Macy was an arsonist and a murderer.'

'You told her this?'

'Every kid on the playground told her.'

'What did you tell her?'

'What I've just told you.'

'That must've been very upsetting for you and Macy?'

'I wasn't bothered. She didn't display any emotion.'

'Do you remember the day of the fire?'

'Yeah, yeah, I do.'

'What happened?'

'She went to play in that house with other kids. Some mother dropped her off here. End of.'

'So she stayed home for the rest of the day?'

'I don't know. She might have gone out again. I was watching telly in my room.'

'With the door closed?'

She nodded.

'When she was five, did she ever go out by herself?'

'Yes, quite a bit.'

The room was profoundly silent. Rosen took in Bellwood and Henshaw and was glad of their company, because he knew he was in the midst of moments he would never forget and would always be sorry he had had to experience.

'We'll leave you now, Ms Conner. If Macy turns up or contacts you, will you let us know immediately?'

'All right.' As she walked back to her room, Macy's mother said, 'Shut the door on your way out.'

'Ms Conner,' said Henshaw. 'How many male voices does Macy use?'

She turned to close her bedroom door and thought briefly. 'Two.'

'Two, definitely two?' asked Henshaw.

'One and one makes two. Are you thick or something?'

She slammed the door of her room shut.

Henshaw looked grim, his face set.

'What is it, James?'

'I want to talk it through with a colleague, Professor Reese.' Henshaw rubbed his eyes as he walked out of the flat, his shoulders slumped as if carrying an immense yet invisible weight. 'I need to look at Macy's medical records. Can you fix that for me, David?'

Rosen took out his phone. 'I'll do it now.'

81

3.39 P.M.

It was as if the three children had not only vanished from the face of the earth but had never existed. The world seemed to be in a state of suspended animation, waiting for darkness to fall and the night to unleash the worst it could muster.

Returning to the incident room at Isaac Street, Rosen asked, 'Carol, did the Charity Commission get back to you on Outlook?'

'No, and it's Saturday so they're shut.' She considered that strand and recalled Julian Parker's words, '*Not now.*'

'What was that, Carol?'

'I'm ringing Parker, John Glass's former PA.' She keyed in his number and put her landline on speakerphone. The ringing tone sounded four times but then his voicemail kicked in. 'Will nothing go right for us to-day?' she said across the recorded message. The recording tone sounded.

'Mr Parker, DS Carol Bellwood. Ring me on this number as soon as you pick up this message. Thank you.' She reeled off the digits and slammed the phone down.

Rosen watched her unblinking.

'What is it, David?'

He decided against saying anything but, in the next moment, changed his mind.

'I haven't told anyone on the team. Sarah knows. No one else. I picked up a call from Stevie Jensen's phone. A death threat. I was told that I was next.'

Bellwood snatched up her bag and car keys. 'Get off the case now. Come on. I'm taking you to Orpington.'

He didn't move. 'They have direct access to me through my phone. They want me here. If I walk away now, there's going to be carnage. If I'm here, we have a chance of salvaging something from this insanity. They're waiting for the dark. They're waiting for me, Carol. I can't walk away from this. The pattern's clear. If they can't get what they want – me – they'll go for the next best thing. It could be Sarah and Joe, but it will be someone connected to me. And they'll succeed. I'm convinced of it. I know you won't. . .'

'I won't breathe a word.' She considered. 'When they thought they hadn't finished Thomas off, that's when they went for Stevie. I think you've got a point.'

She fell into a deep silence and Rosen asked, 'What's on your mind?'

'The same things that are on your mind. Who are *they*? Macy Conner? I we is Macy Conner?'

The second hand on the wall clock seemed to be gliding at twice its given speed.

'Macy Conner. Come on, Carol. Let's get back on the street. We've got to find her.'

82

6.30 P.M.

Sunset was fixed at twenty-four minutes past eight.

Rosen sat at his desk, watching officers arriving for the 6.45 P.M. team meeting: men and women downcast, frustrated after a day of fruitless searching. Any verbal exchanges were hushed and brief and when the phone rang out on Rosen's desk, it drew the attention of most people present.

'DCI Rosen speaking.'

'It's Murphy, custody sergeant.'

Rosen sat up.

'It's Trent. His solicitor says he's got something important to tell you.' Phone down and on his feet, Rosen called, 'Tracey, Carol, Trent's ready to speak.' He headed for the door, followed by Bellwood and Leung. 'Hold fire, everyone else, and wait for further instruction.'

As they left the room, Henshaw arrived, looking like he'd been turned inside out.

On the stairs leading down, Rosen called, 'You got something, James?'

'Yes. Yes, I have, David. She had a brain scan when she was four years old and it's thrown up some disturbing information. I've spent four hours with Tony Reese reviewing her case. She's very sick.'

'James, I've got to go.'

'I understand.'

'Stay put.'

'I'm sorry. It's really bad news.'

'I'll see you soon.'

83

6.35 P.M.

In Interview Suite 1, Trent sat with his forearms on the table. He looked as if he'd aged six years in as many hours. And in that time, it seemed to Rosen, the gravity of his situation had fully dawned on him.

Rosen formally opened the interview and went directly in.

'So, Jay, you have something you want to tell me?' He sounded matter-of-fact but his heart was racing.

'Yes.' Trent looked across the table at Rosen, straight into his eyes. There was something in his voice, bordering on respect.

Rosen held his gaze. Trent wanted his help.

'I'm going to ask you a question, Jay. Ready?'

'Yes,' he said again, as if speaking was a source of great physical and mental anguish.

Rosen felt the weight of his watch on his wrist.

'Have you been thinking about your future?'

'Yes.'

'Are you anxious about your future?'

Trent gave the slightest nod.

Rosen nodded. 'That's understandable. Thomas Glass.'

'Yes.'

'Macy Conner is ten years old and can't drive a car. You're nineteen and can.'

'Correct.'

'Who told you to drive Thomas Glass to Bannerman Square?'

'Macy Conner.'

'Why did you obey her?'

Trent said something, but it was muffled and low. A bead of sweat formed on his lip and he started swallowing fast, the colour draining from his face.

'Do you want a drink of water?' asked Bellwood.

Trent shook his head. His hands shifted and he gripped the edge of the table. Rosen could see the blanched-out colour of the knuckles beneath his skin.

'Why did you do it?'

'Blackmail. She's blackmailed me.' He shut his eyes and his face creased as if he'd swallowed mercury. 'She's blackmailing me!' Trent suddenly leaned forward and to the side and threw up on the floor, wave after wave of bitter-smelling vomit.

Bellwood took out her phone, called the front desk. 'Medicated sawdust, please. Interview Suite 1.'

'What did she ask you to do?'

'Drive the kid to Bannerman Square and leave him there.' He wiped his mouth on the back of his sleeve, tears streaming down his face. 'Oh, fuck, fuck, man. You look at her and you think, so what, just another ten-year-old kid, but she's an evil bitch and it's like she's ancient in the head and. . .'

'Did she ask you to set fire to Thomas?' asked Rosen, his stomach knotting.

Trent shook his head.

'She said something, like she'd get the kid to finish the job off himself. I didn't know what she was on about.'

Bellwood and Rosen exchanged a glance.

'I want to know one thing. The truth. Where did you pick up Thomas?'

'From the lock-up garage at George Grove.'

Bellwood was on her feet. Rosen followed. 'What's it look like?'

'Six units in one block. Silver doors.'

'Which one was he in?' Bellwood was at the door.

Rosen called to her: 'Tracey, Corrigan, Feldman, Gold and you, car park, now! Clue them in on the way down.'

'He was in the second from the left.'

The door of Interview Suite 1 was open.

'Is that where he was held since his abduction?'

'I don't know. I wasn't involved until three days ago.'

Rosen ran for the rear exit of the building, for the car park at the back of Isaac Street.

'Is Paul Conner involved?' Bellwood asked and, with the same breath shouted, 'Sergeant Murphy!'

'I don't know. I wasn't involved until three days ago.'

'Where's Paul Conner?'

'I don't know.'

'Has Macy got your gun?'

'I don't know. Maybe. I gave it to Paul. She ordered him to gun the CCTV. It wasn't me.'

As Sergeant Murphy came running, Bellwood saw Rosen turn the corner. 'Back to his cell, sarge!'

And in a handful of strides, she was round the same corner and on her way out.

The sky outside was thickening with dark clouds. Between the clouds, the form of the moon was made bright by the unseen setting sun.

84

6.44 P.M.

On Lewisham High Street, Rosen hit ninety mph in the thick of traffic. He slowed down to sixty, as cars, taxis and motorcycles crawled onto the pavement and into the central section to allow him through. He clipped the rear of a Fiat Punto and urged, 'Come on, come on, come on!' to a double-decker bus that didn't have room to move. He craned his neck. Red, red and amber, green, amber, red. . .

Slowly, the bus shifted and pulled aside for him to overtake.

Bellwood had the whole team connected to her iPhone on a conference call.

'David, everyone, listen. You're going to have to cut the sound on the siren and hope the other motorists are alert to the flashing blue light. We're on the edge of hearing range of the lock-up. If Macy hears the siren coming, she'll run for it.'

Rosen turned off the siren and weaved sharply into the left-hand lane to take a turning into St Vincent Hill, the road that led directly to the lock-up. The car ahead of him slowed, the driver rattled.

'Climb the bloody pavement but get out of the way!' shouted Rosen, the pulse in his neck banging like a war drum. The car slowed and stalled. Rosen slammed on his brakes and pulled up sharply at the bumper. He shot his window down and, leaning out, waved the car behind him back, back, back.

The driver reversed and Rosen followed, pulling right to overtake the stalled car in front of him and then swerving deftly back into the left-hand lane. He took the corner at forty-five mph and accelerated to ninety again as he coursed up St Vincent Hill. Traffic lights. They dropped down to red. A pedestrian crossing. A woman with a baby in a buggy stepped into the road. 'Get back!' Bellwood yelled from the open window at her side. The woman pulled the buggy back sharply so that she and her baby were on the pavement as Rosen burned the red, touching one hundred.

'Slow down, David.'

He slowed down, asking, 'What's that?' Ahead was a traffic sign diverting vehicles from making the turn towards George Grove. He pulled up at the nearest stretch of pavement and stopped the car.

Bellwood was out and running before his key was out of the ignition. He got out, looked back, saw Leung and Corrigan jumping out of his car, then Gold racing from Feldman's car. He waved them on. Within moments, they streamed past the row of houses just ahead of George Grove towards the lock-up.

Bellwood was almost there. Rosen felt a blossoming of heat in his chest but kept running as fast as he could.

Bellwood was at the lock-up, on her hands and knees and peering under the bottom of the roller-door on the unit second left, near the end of the row.

'It's open,' she said.

She got the fingers of one hand under the door and waved Corrigan, Feldman and Gold back as they arrived. She put her free hand under the door and raised it just as Rosen arrived, breathing deeply, sharply, his nerve-endings on fire.

The door was up by ten centimetres.

'Back off, Carol!' said Rosen. 'They could have Trent's firearm, a petrol bomb even.'

Silence. Bellwood walked backwards, slowly and away. In the middle distance, a baby cried, and the ordinary noise was astonishing. The moon appeared in outline as a bank of cloud fell away.

Gold and Feldman took up position on either side of the garage door. Rosen stood at an angle off-centre of the door but directly in front of it. Bellwood and Corrigan stood on either side of Rosen, the five officers forming a square, a human shield.

'Macy, come out. It's me, Mr Rosen.'

Nothing.

'Do you have Luke?'

The wind rattled an empty Coke can along the rough concrete surface of the ground.

'Is Chester with you?'

Inside the lock-up, a mobile phone rang out.

Rosen walked forward two paces. Gold and Corrigan each took a corner of the door and counted each other in, 'One, two, three!' With a powerful lift they raised the shutter. Bellwood shone her torch into the darkness.

On the back wall inside the lock-up, four sets of symbols from the Celtic oracular alphabet were spray-painted with an aerosol.

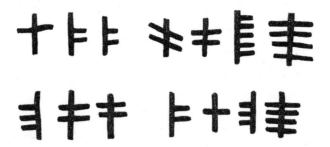

'Keep your light on it, Carol.'

The phone, just by the open doorway, went on ringing.

Corrigan picked it up, connected the call.

316

'Chester, where are you?' It was his mother. 'I'll come and get you. Where are you, son?'

'I'm sorry, it's not Chester. I'm a police officer. DS Corrigan.'

'Have you found him?'

'We're still looking.'

On the other end of the line, she howled.

Rosen studied the symbols and Bellwood asked, 'What does it say?'

He checked the notes he'd made from Macy's borrowed library book and, after a few moments answered, 'It says, *All gone. Too late.*'

85

7 P.M.

At the back of Bream Street Primary School was a field surrounded by the same tall metal railings that bordered the front elevation, playground and the service and delivery yard on the other side of the school.

At the edge of the field, at the base of the railings, was a narrow hole and it was here that Macy stopped with Luke and Chester.

'What we doing back at school?' asked Chester.

'We're going to break in,' she whispered.

'No shit!' He looked amazed and overjoyed, and then fear crept in. 'What. . . what if we get caught?'

'It's the safest place for us. What did the bad guys tell me? Hey?'

'That they were going to come for me and Luke next. Tonight.'

'School's the one place they won't come to. And when this is all over, we'll be able to sell our story to the papers. How much money would you like?'

'A million quid.'

'Why just a million, Chester?'

'Two million? Two million.'

'You get in through that hole and then I'm going to pass little Luke under, so you pull him in, gently, gently, so he doesn't start crying. And then I'll crawl through.'

'We're really going to break in?'

'I've got it all figured out.'

'You know what I'm going to do when I get inside?' asked Chester, as he shuffled through the tight space and under the railings.

Macy looked up at the moon and sighed. Luke grabbed her hand and squeezed her fingers. 'Big boy Chester's going to help you climb under the railings. He'll tug your feet and then I'll come after you. OK.'

'My mum?'

'She's gone to work. You know that. She goes to work. I take care of you.'

'Want home now.'

She reached into her pocket for a cube of chocolate and fed it to him. 'School now. Home later.'

He munched the chocolate and nodded. ''K, Macy.'

She covered his face with her hand to protect it as Chester pulled Luke through and under the railings. She felt a shadow pass over her and looked back, but there was nothing there. *Just the wind*, she thought, *just the cold, cold wind.*

'I'm going to have a shit on Mrs Price's chair in her office. Imagine her face when she sits down on that on Monday morning.'

'There isn't going to be a Monday morning,' said Macy, softly, her eyes drawn upwards to the moon.

'What was that about the morning?'

'Chester, you're going to have to be very quiet from now on and follow everything I say and do. Understand?'

'I understand. I'm not stupid. I walked Luke all the way from Bannerman Square to the lock-up. By myself. No one saw.'

'We're going to hide behind the bins until twenty, twenty-five past eight and then we're going to break into the school.'

'I don't want to hide in the bins. They stink.'

'Where are we not allowed to go?'

'The bins.'

319

'Chester, we're breaking all the rules tonight.'

'We are, aren't we?'

As she dipped down to the ground and squeezed through the hole, she looked up at the face in the moon, but the eyes were covered by a drifting band of cloud.

On Beltaine Night, it appeared the moon was blind.

86

7.10 P.M.

The same blind moon sat silently over Bannerman Square.

Rosen had reconvened the 6.45 P.M. meeting from Isaac Street to the Bannerman Square mobile incident room, central to the area to be searched again.

In a corner of the crowded room, Rosen stood with his back half-turned to the other officers, listening stone-faced to Henshaw's observations about Macy Conner.

'I went over everything – school books, what I've seen and heard about her, her drawing – with Professor Reese. We went away for an hour and independently wrote a diagnosis. Broadly, we came to the same conclusion. Reese is the leading authority on what we both believe Macy Conner suffers from. Your officers need to know.'

Rosen called for order, steeling himself against the sadness he felt for Macy and the unbearable fear of what she was capable of.

The last members of the murder investigation team squeezed into the mobile incident room. Outside, uniformed officers waited, each group of four assigned a detective from Rosen's team. Teenagers milled around behind an invisible cordon, weighing up the police presence, knowing that something was in the wind.

Sombre quiet descended.

'This has got to be quick,' said Rosen. 'The time scale's on your handouts. This is plan A and is based on the information we have to hand. Expect further instructions as we get developments. You've each got an individualized handout. You've each got four uniformed officers to assist you and a geographical location to search. We're looking for the three children whose faces are on the wall behind me: Macy Conner, Chester Adler, Luke Booth. Be careful: Macy Conner is a very dangerous little girl. Approach her as if you're approaching an escaped class-A prisoner. If you find her, contact me ASAP. She could be carrying a Smith & Wesson gun. So far, blunt instruments, petrol and fire are her weapons of choice.'

'Are you certain?' a voice blurted from the room.

'No. But we'll proceed on the basis that Macy Conner is a killer and that she'll kill you if she needs to. James Henshaw has a psychiatric perspective. Please listen very carefully to what he tells you about this child.'

Henshaw stepped forward.

'Quick as you can, please, James,' said Rosen, quietly.

'Macy Conner is a damaged little girl. She's delusional, suffers from intense, one could say almost religious, hallucinations that are not only animated but are sustained over many months. Due to one stream of delusion and hallucination, she's currently in a state of intense grief and mourning, so this already-unbalanced child is deeply destabilized. You're all aware that both DCI Rosen and I came to the conclusion that the murders of Thomas Glass and Stevie Jensen were the work of a collection of individuals, a quasi-religious cult. That is both right and wrong. On top of all her other problems, Macy has a condition called MPD – multiple personality disorder. I suspect, as a conservative estimate, she has two main personalities residing in her consciousness. Based on her account of the night Thomas Glass was burned alive and graffiti left at the scenes, they're both male, complementary psychopathic thugs with religious convictions that exonerate any action they take. If you come across her, you could be in the presence of either of these personalities. Dig deep into your personal experiences of dealing with men such as these. You could well meet up with them tonight. How does this work from Macy's point of view? Imagine living in a house with no front door, with two very sick neighbours who could walk into your home at any hour of the day or night and take over your most personal space. That's what life is like for Macy Conner. She's either in hell or standing at the door of a place we can only imagine in our worst nightmares. She's been neglected and abused, traumatized from a very, very early age. When that's the daily reality, the only place that the child can escape to is inside the mind. One last thing. When she was four, she fell down the staircase of the flats where she lives. She was given a brain scan.'

He held up a colour copy of her brain scan.

'This is it.' He pointed at what looked like a curled orange finger rising up from the base of her brain. 'This is her hippocampus. It should be twice the size of this. It's the area of brain that deals with memory. It's typical of chronically abused children. She won't process what's she's done to her victims as memory but as a bad dream. Is she lethal? I wouldn't treat her as anything less.'

He stepped back.

'Thank you, James. OK. Let's go!' said Rosen, glancing at the clock on the wall, wishing with the vainest hope that the hands would stop.

'Where are you going, David?' asked Carol Bellwood.

'Macy Conner's home.'

87

7.28 P.M.

Rosen listened at Macy Conner's front door, heard the sound of a person moving from one place to another, a TV playing in the background. Fresh cigarette smoke drifted from within the flat. He banged on the door and waited. Nothing.

'Open the door now!' A neighbour appeared at her door, ready to pull him up. He flashed his warrant card at her and she disappeared back behind her own door. 'Get here now, Ms Conner, and open the door. I'm not going away.'

The door flew back sharply. Macy's mother, unperturbed and with a fresh application of make-up, stood in the doorway.

'Rosen, I don't know where she is.' Like she was someone else's problem in a different time and dimension.

He took a deep breath and said, 'Let me in. We need to talk.'

He followed her inside. She closed the door of her room and, in the poverty of the living room, turned her back on Rosen.

'The sooner you talk, Rosen, the sooner you can fuck off out of here.'

'Why?' he asked, enigmatically.

'Why what?' She turned around, breathed a smoke ring through pursed lips.

'Why aren't you pulling your hair out? Why aren't you on the streets looking for your daughter—'

'That's your job.'

'—and pleading with people to help you?'

'If I did that every time she wandered off for hours, I'd look like a real head case.'

'Where else might she have gone to?'

'I don't know.'

'It was you, wasn't it?'

'What was me?'

'You punched her lights out on the night Thomas Glass got burned alive.'

'That's a serious allegation.'

'Why did you beat her up?'

'I ought to report you.'

'What did she do?'

'I am going to report you.'

'I'm all ears.'

'I'm going to make a formal complaint.'

'Just like you threw her down the stairs when she was four.'

She stopped.

'How do you know? She fell!'

'Macy's a lying bitch, is she?'

'What's she been saying to you, Rosen?'

'We've had a few interesting conversations.'

'About her grandmother? You're an idiot.'

Her coldness was complete. She put him in mind of the father of a two-year-old girl who'd been tied to her bed for weeks. Rosen had carried her, a bag of running sores and bones, from filthy squalor back when he was a young PC in north London. There was no point in questioning her further about Macy. To her mother, she was less than nothing.

He changed the subject to one she was interested in: herself.

'Why didn't you give her away when she was born? You'd had Paul, that hadn't worked out for you. Why not give her away? Paul, too?'

She raised the cigarette to her mouth. 'Well.' She looked around. 'No kids, no benefits, no flat.'

'What'll you do if. . . if I find her and bring her back safely?'

'She'll have to be punished. She's caused an awful lot of shit, hasn't she? Yeah, she'll have to be punished, the little bitch. Fuck off, Rosen.'

Rosen walked from the flat, leaving the front door open. She listened as he made his way to the main stairs.

'Bastard.' She cursed the space in which he'd stood and crossed over to close the front door.

As she walked back to her room, there was a knock on the door. 'Oh, what now?' Annoyed, she threw the front door open and greeted the caller, 'You? What do you want?'

88

7.37 P.M.

As Rosen walked downstairs, the door to the fourth floor opened and Chelsea stepped towards him.

'I saw you walking in. I thought you were coming to tell me good news.'

'Chelsea, I—'

'Do you have some news for me? Have you found him yet?'

'We're still looking. There are dozens of detectives and uniformed officers—'

'Come on, Chelsea.' A voice came from around the corner: Sergeant Valerie McGuinness, Victim Liaison.

Rosen touched her on the shoulder, the slightest of contacts, and whispered, 'Chelsea. I'll do everything in my power to bring him back to you.'

'It's my fault, isn't it?'

Valerie McGuinness turned Chelsea to face her. 'This is not your fault. You're a good mother.'

'No. I'm an idiot. And my son's about to pay the price.'

89

8.20 P.M.

The moon was bright now, the sky folding swiftly into night. The North Star appeared.

Tucked behind three huge cylindrical bins, Macy Conner, Chester Adler and Luke Booth watched a car arrive at the side of their school, its headlights dipping and turning off as it stopped. A man got out.

Macy knew him. Corrigan. One of Rosen's men. He was talking on a mobile phone. 'I've checked each side now, David. There's no sign of life and none of the neighbours at the front have seen a thing.'

Macy raised a thumb to Chester. 'Hear that, Chester? No one saw a thing.'

'Yeah, yeah, I'll take the guys back to square one and off we go again!' said DS Corrigan as he got back into his car, turned on the ignition and drove away.

'Give him a minute to get away and then we'll break in to school,' she said.

*

THE SCHOOL HALL was overlooked by a derelict office building. In the door leading to the hall at the back of the school were four panes of glass. It was here that Macy led them. Picking up a jagged rock – one that Macy had concealed the previous day under a pile of leaf litter – she crouched down and set about smashing the lower left-hand glass panel.

'Macy?' said Chester.

'What?' Her patience was paper-thin.

'The gerbil was already dead when I went into the classroom.'

'So?'

'So, who stuck the compass into him?' Chester looked at Macy and she smiled at him.

'Su Li.' She held a finger to her lips. 'Now hush!'

Macy worked on the jagged edges of the glass to create a hole large enough for the three of them to enter the school, one at a time. She reached an arm inside and, tucking her fist into her sleeve, swept the glass on the hall floor aside.

'I'm going in first. When I go inside, the alarm will ring out. Don't worry. Pass the baby in to me and then you climb in, carefully.'

She paused, imagined she heard the sound of steps somewhere behind them, a foot snapping a twig and a shadow shifting across the grass near the hedges. She looked around, unsettled.

'It's my imagination,' she said.

'What is?'

'Nothing.'

As soon as she made it inside, the alarm triggered. Chester lifted Luke through to her, and crawled inside after them.

'The police'll come, the police, when they hear the burglar alarm.' Chester was lost between panic and hilarity.

'No, that's not the way it works. We want the burglar alarm to ring.'

He looked completely confused, as if he'd just been born into the moment in which he existed, with no past, no knowledge, no context to fall back on.

'Why?' he shouted above the painful clatter.

'Because we want Mr Finn to open the school with his keys.'

Luke's lip wobbled and he threw his hands up to protect his ears from the sound.

'Don't start crying, Luke!' said Macy sharply, thinking, *What do I do if Luke gets really upset when I'm in Chelsea's?* Remembering that Prue, the old lady next door to Chelsea's, wasn't there to fall back on, she felt like she was drowning. Luke's crying grew louder.

She picked up the stray rock with which she'd smashed in the glass panel and took Luke by the hand to the PE cupboard.

'Open the door, Chester!'

Chester obeyed.

'Turn on the light.' After some fumbling, he managed it. 'Look, Luke, look at all these balls and hoops and bats and wickets.' Unaided, the toddler marched deeper inside. She shut the door behind the three of them. She turned to Chester. 'Stay in here with Luke – it's quieter than the hall and corridors. Don't come out until I come back, or it won't work out. You want the bad guys to get you, Chester?' He shook his head. 'Then do as I say.'

'I won't come out. Where are you going?'

She took a paper tissue from her pocket and rolled up two balls, which she placed in Luke's ears.

'Can I have some?' asked Chester.

'No, you've got to listen. You've got to stay in here and listen.'

'Where you going?'

'I'm going to meet Mr Finn.'

She left the cupboard, closing the door carefully behind her. Through the skylights in the ceiling of the hall, the moon shone in her eyes and filled the large space with the kind of light she imagined shone in heaven. Softly, she whispered, 'Grandma.' And beneath the harsh alarm, her voice seemed to echo gently from the walls. For a moment, in the corner, in a shimmering light, she saw the old woman. 'Death is here, Macy. And you must say—?'

'Yes.' The living light that was Grandma blossomed and silently exploded.

She was gone.

Macy smiled and spoke calmly to herself: 'When Mr Finn's been, then we'll call the police.'

One hand opened and closed around the rock, the other around a mobile phone. She pictured Mr Finn's huge key ring. She knew where each key fitted. The key to the door in the wall opposite the PE cupboard that led to the stairs onto the roof, that key had a red fob on it, and it was next to the key for the boiler room, with the blue fob.

The sound of the school burglar alarm was textured: some beats painful and others extremely so. Macy rolled up two corners of another paper handkerchief and stuffed them into her own ears.

*

In the PE cupboard, Luke lay down on a small stack of rubber mats and curled himself into a ball. He closed his eyes and whispered, 'Bo-bos, go to bo-bos now.'

'Well, I'll turn off the light,' said Chester, plunging the cupboard into darkness.

Outside, in the hall, he heard a noise, a footstep crunching on glass and then silence. In the sheltering darkness, after thirty-six hours without sleep, tiredness hit him hard.

He lay down on the mats next to Luke and, closing his eyes, heard Macy walking away in the hall beyond the door.

90

8.31 P.M.

Sitting up in bed, next to the empty space where his wife had slept for thirty-two years, Alec Finn sipped a cup of tea and watched his beloved Arsenal get trashed away from home in the second leg of the UEFA Champions' League semi-final.

'And the money they're on,' he said, without any real anger.

Buzz. Buzz. Buzz.

On his bedside table, his mobile phone vibrated against the wooden surface.

'Shall I get it?' he asked the absence next to him. 'What's the option?'

He squinted at the display: MARGE. He connected

'Hi, Marge.' Number 22 Bream Street. One of the clutch of sympathetic residents of Bream Street, the ones who called him when the alarm in school went off, the ones he did odd jobs for in between his daily split work shift, the ones who fed him and plugged the gaps in his loneliness.

'Hi, Alec. Guess what?' The school alarm ringing out registered as a tinkle in the background.

'Sorry, love. I won't be long.'

His feet were on the floor, his eyes on tomorrow's shirt, trousers and underwear folded neatly over the chair next to Alice's side of the bed.

As AC Milan netted their fourth goal, Alec started dressing as quickly as he could to go and deal with the chaos.

91

8.51 P.M.

Four minutes after receiving an urgent call, Rosen arrived at the lock-up. DC Eleanor Willis, Scientific Support, had found a BlackBerry behind a loose brick in the back wall.

He dipped under the scene-of-crime tape. She was waiting for him with the phone in her hand.

'David, it's belongs to Thomas Glass.'

'Anything on it, Eleanor?'

'Check out the video, the most recent.'

Rosen clicked through and pressed 'play'.

Immediately, he recognized Jay Trent's bedroom. The footage was taken from an unusual angle, but the two bodies on the bed were clear to see.

As the sex unfolded on screen, Rosen thought back to Trent's bedroom and worked out that whoever had filmed this had hidden in the built-in wardrobe opposite Trent's bed.

Aggressively, Trent thrust himself in and out of another young man's anus, his hands gripping the subject's back. The young man's head dipped, his face concealed by long auburn hair.

'You're a fucking queer!' growled Trent on screen, stuck somewhere between rage and ecstasy. Trent slapped his back hard and the young man cried out in pain. 'Deserved that. The last. . . time. . . don't make me. . . do this. . . again.'

Trent cried out in vicious ecstasy. Then there was silence and stillness, and from that quiet Rosen heard a subdued snuffling, hidden tears from the closet, and a small voice.

'Oh, Paul. . .'

'Macy,' said Rosen, recognizing the voice in the closet. 'Macy Conner.'

92

8.57 P.M.

As Alec Finn turned the corner into Bream Street, the car he thought was tailing him followed. He pulled up at the main gate of the school and watched in his wing mirror as a man hurried from the car. Alec kept his window up, his instincts twitching.

'DS Corrigan, London Met. Who are you?' The man appeared at his window and flashed a warrant card.

'Alec Finn, site manager. Are you responding to the burglar alarm?'

'Yeah, in a manner of speaking, we are.'

Alec glanced at Corrigan's car and was surprised to see uniformed officers in an unmarked car.

'We're looking for three missing children.'

'Well, they won't be in the school.'

'How can you be so sure, Mr Finn?'

'There'll be no one in the school. The burglar alarm system's rubbish. It's brand new and I've been called out most nights. Cowboy job.' Alec got out of his car. 'I'll show you.'

On the way to the door, he asked, 'Who are the kids?'

'Macy Conner—'

'Macy Conner? No! She's a good kid, my little helper.'

'Chester Adler and a two year old, Luke Booth.'

'Chester's a head case.'

He keyed in the security code on the electronic gate and Corrigan squeezed through. Finn followed him towards the main door of the school and the uniformed officers came after them.

'You've not seen it on TV?' Corrigan asked.

'I only watch the sport these days.' He turned a key in the mortise lock. 'Macy's my little pal.' Finn became visibly upset. He pushed the door open.

Corrigan's mobile rang out and, on the first ring, he picked up.

'Corrigan, it's Gold. Macy Conner's just sent the boss a text. She's scared to death. They're hiding in Brockley Cemetery, just behind Crofton Park. Rosen's ordered half the teams off the streets and you're to get back there now!'

'Are they safe?'

'Chester Adler's caved the baby's head in with a rock.'

Corrigan sprinted back. 'Brockley Cemetery!' he called to the officers running behind him. 'Sirens on.'

'What's happening?' asked Finn. 'Is it bad news?'

But no one replied.

Finn stepped into the school and, approaching the system's control panel, was surprised by what he saw. Instead of the usual chaotic flashing on and off of lights, there were just two lights activated: the school hall and the corridor.

Finn keyed in the code to deactivate the alarm and all went quiet. Even the sounds of the siren vanished.

From the large bunch of keys on his hip, Alec Finn opened the door onto the corridor. *Stay where you are and call the police*, said a voice inside him, but in the next breath the same voice said, *And wait here until after midnight for the police to show up!* It was the useless, lousy security system, nothing more, nothing less.

He stepped into the pitch-black corridor. Monday morning, he'd have sharp words with Mrs Price.

Reaching for the wall light, he felt a heavy blow to the side of his head, a blow that made him spin round as he fell to the floor. A foot connected with his head as he reached the ground, the same foot that then stamped deftly on the back of his skull.

As his senses faded towards unconsciousness, he saw the shape of a human being, a silhouette that belonged to the fabric of the darkness. And then his vision failed as his body shut down. The words, *The eye is the believer. The eye is the deceiver* followed him into the void, a voice neither male nor female, young nor old.

Darkness.

A hand reached down, unbuckled his belt and pulled it from his trousers. The bunch of keys fell to the floor. One hand picked up the keys and the other tossed the blood-stained rock, up and down, in the darkness.

Throwing, catching, throwing, catching.

The rock was wet now, and had hairs stuck to it.

The rock fell onto Mr Finn's inanimate form.

We can always add her flesh to the fire and drive her spirit into the underworld for the rest of time. The voice of Ash.

Do you want that for your grandmother? The voice of Oak.

Macy headed towards the boiler room, sorting through each of the keys until she found the right one.

Don't forget to make your next phone call! Oak's voice was thick and angry.

Call Rosen! Call Rosen! sang Ash, a jolly nursery rhyme.

She unlocked the door to the stairs leading down to the boiler room.

The boiler room door opened. The gentle hum of electricity cables.

She switched on the light and headed for the cupboard where Mr Finn kept his emergency supply of petrol.

93

9.20 P.M.

In Brockley Cemetery, Rosen and Bellwood stood at the crossroads of Blythe Route 1 and stared down the grey path lined with Victorian headstones. On either side of the path, overgrown vegetation and ivy-choked trees surrounded forgotten graves. It was the ideal place in which to get lost at night.

Rosen had sealed off the area around Crofton Park, diverting all incoming traffic and flooding the park and Brockley Cemetery with officers as they arrived.

Within a minute of searching, a voice drifted towards Rosen like a whisper from one of the bodies buried beneath his feet.

'No sign of them, no sign of anything. . .'

An uneasy knowledge dawned on Rosen. She'd manipulated him again and, in turn, he had misled dozens of police officers under his authority. He pictured himself facing the corner of the incident room with a dunce's hat on his head while more competent people got on with their work.

Corrigan walked directly towards him. 'It looks like they're not here, boss.'

'Did you get as far as the school?' asked Rosen.

'I ran into the site manager when we went to check it out. The alarm was ringing. The site manager put it down to a bum system, newly installed. We were about to go in with him. . .' A look of complete sickness spread across Corrigan's face.

The school, a place of security for her.

'She saw you coming, from inside the school,' said Rosen. 'And she sent a text to me to draw you away. Everyone together, together *now*, Corrigan.'

As he ran to his car, Rosen scrolled down his phone for the Pan London Supervisor and was quickly connected.

'DCI Rosen speaking. I need to order out the hostage and crisis negotiation unit. Bream Street Primary School, Lewisham. There are three children in there and one adult.'

'Is the adult holding the children?' asked the operator.

'No, the adult's probably dead by now.'

Rosen got into his car and drew a deep breath as he made his next call, a follow-up call to one he'd made earlier that day.

'It's DCI Rosen.'

'Doug Price. CO19. Central Firearms. Where are the kids, David?'

As Bellwood folded herself into the passenger seat, Rosen said, 'Bream Street Primary.'

'I know it,' replied Price.

Rosen closed down the call and turned the key in the ignition.

'She sent me a text,' said Rosen. He sped around the corner, others already following. 'I should've known better.' He was up to fifty mph. 'She sent me a text because of the alarm ringing out. If she'd called, I'd have heard it. Corrigan was there!'

'David, don't beat yourself up. Focus. Come on.'

On the dashboard, Rosen's phone rang. On the display: Stevie. He took a deep breath and connected the call.

'DCI Rosen speaking.'

'You're in your car.'

'Hello, Macy. It's nice to hear from you.'

'Are you driving fast to catch me?'

'I don't know where you are. I thought you were at the cemetery.'

'Not just yet.'

'Where are you, Macy?'

'I've come to school.'

'School.' Rosen echoed her last word slowly.

'Schoooool,' she echoed back. 'Who's with you?'

'Carol Bellwood.'

'Hello, Carol.'

'Hello,' replied Bellwood. 'You all right, love?'

'Yeah. No. You?'

'I'd be better if I could see you.'

'Well, that's not going to happen, Carol. Sorry.'

'So, I've got Carol here with me,' said Rosen. 'Who's there with you?'

Silence.

'Well. . . quite a few people, but not enough.'

'Quite a few people but not enough? That's a good riddle,' said Rosen.

'Can you work it out, Mr Rosen?'

He repeated the riddle and said, 'Let me think about it. Macy?' He listened to the background in a moment of quiet. She was walking in a large space, her footsteps echoing. He blocked the phone with his hand and whispered to Bellwood, 'Find out where the school hall is in relation to the front of the building.'

'You sent me a text, told me you were in the cemetery?'

'I wasn't lying.'

'You're a girl who sticks to the truth, Macy. Miss Harvey told me that.'

'It's not lying, it's a game.' Rising anxiety filtered through her speech and he heard unshed tears bottled up in a tangled maze of pain and terror.

'I see what you mean, Macy. It's a game, it's not lying.'

At a junction, he slowed for a red light, crawled past it. All clear, he powered back to fourth gear.

'You're driving very quickly, Mr Rosen, I can hear your engine. You're breaking the speed limit. Am I right?'

'You're a clever girl, Macy. Very observant. I'm not breaking the rules. I'm just very keen to see you. I'm joining in the game.'

'I think you're driving at sixty miles an hour, you haven't turned your siren on and your heart is beating very fast.'

'It's as if you're sitting in the passenger seat beside me.'

'I wish I was.'

'Well, why don't we do that?'

'They won't have it.'

'Who won't have it, Macy? Tell me. They're no match for me. I'll tell them.'

'It's not that simple. I wish I was. . .'

'With me, in the car?'

'Yeah. But if I got into your car, you'd have to drive me to the police station and lock me up for a long, long time. But I would love to sit next to you, Mr Rosen.'

'I think we need to get to the bottom of this, don't you, Macy?'

'You're driving too fast, Mr Rosen. Slow down.'

'I can help you.'

'You can't help me. That's not the way this works.' Rosen picked up speed, sixty-five, seventy mph. 'You're the hunter and I am your prey. You are here to hunt me down and you would kill me if it meant saving the life of another human being. Think about it, Mr Rosen.' Her speech shifted and thickened.

'Who am I speaking to?'

'I we is Macy Conner. Have you ever been directly responsible for the death of a child?'

He felt his skin tighten into goose bumps.

'No, I've not done that.'

'How would that play out in your dreams, Rosen? How about the wide-awake hour at two o'clock in the morning? Did you know that's the hour when many people decide to end it all? You want to sit next to me?'

'Sit next to you, yes.'

He slowed down to thirty mph. Rosen and Bellwood, at the head of a convoy, were within striking distance of Bream Street Primary School.

'How about?' said Rosen.

'How about. . .?' she repeated.

'We play I-spy.'

'OK.'

'You first, Macy.'

'I spy. . . with my little eye. . .' Fifteen miles an hour and pulling up to the front elevation of the school. '. . . something beginning with M.'

'Macy?' Rosen tried.

'Yes but no.'

'I can't think,' he pushed.

'Mr Finn, the most important person in the school. Though I can't see him now. He's on the roof. We carried him there. M. I know. Monster. Me. Me monster.'

'You love the truth, Macy. And that's just not true.'

'I spy with my little eye, something beginning with C.'

'Chester,' said Rosen.

'I spy with my little eye, something beginning with L.'

'Luke. Can I talk to them?' he asked.

'No.'

'Can I at least hear their voices?'

'Yes. No. Are they dead or alive? That's what you're thinking, isn't it, Mr Rosen? Well, how about this for a good idea. I can't hear your engine. But I think you're right outside school. Why don't you find out for yourself? Come rescue little Macy from herself. Come into the school. Stop her doing the dreadful things she is about to do.'

In his wing mirror, Rosen saw Gold's car pulling up after him.

'I can't come into the school by myself.'

'Do you want to speak to Chester?'

A door opened and the sound of sobbing hit Rosen, a young child, terrified and begging, 'Mummy, Mummy.'

'Put the towel in his mouth and come here, Chester. I'm sick of the sound of his crying,' Macy screamed.

The sobs and pleas subsided into enforced silence.

'The policeman wants to talk to you. Talk to the policeman, Chester.' Calm now. Polite.

A pause that felt eternal was finally broken when a babyish voice piped, 'Hello?'

'Chester?'

'We've got the little kid. And we've got Mr Finn.'

'Whereabouts in the school are you?'

There was the sound of a struggle, the phone being snatched from Chester's hand.

'Macy?'

'She's not here.'

'Then where is she?'

'She's in grief.'

'For her grandmother?'

'She died in the early hours.'

'Then who am I speaking to?'

'I am Ash and I am Oak, the eye. . . is. . .'

'The eye is the believer? The eye is the deceiver?'

'You've arrived. At the school. And the truth.'

Rosen stepped out of his car and, picking up his phone from the dashboard, under the cast of a sodium streetlight, surveyed the darkened school, the windows obscured by drawn strip-blinds.

'But you're not alone. Eye can see you but you can't see eye.'

The black van of CO19 pulled up, double parking alongside Rosen's car.

'Let me put you completely in the picture, Mr Rosen. Are you listening?'

'I'm listening.'

'Mr Finn's on the roof, half-awake now, cold petrol in face and hair and clothes. Luke is conscious. He's tied to a chair. He's soaked in petrol. One must be sacrificed tonight, or both. If you want to save them, you must come in to the school alone and find me. No one else. Just you, Mr Rosen. The whole building is soaked in petrol, so when you come in don't move too quickly because you might slip and hurt yourself. It's a good game this. You've got ten minutes. Come and get me. Or else!'

The line went dead. Henshaw was at Rosen's side.

'Did you catch that, James?'

Henshaw nodded.

Rosen turned to the growing band of officers.

He addressed Feldman. 'Organize an evacuation of the street. Seal off the entrances and divert traffic at all junctions. Any house with no answer, ram the door and make sure there's no one in there.'

A white van negotiated its way past the CO19 vehicle. Engine running, Susan Clay, head of the Met's hostage and crisis negotiation team, stepped out. Two officers, armed with Heckler & Koch rifles, emerged from the back of the CO19 vehicle. Two extremes: persuasion and the bullet.

Two, then six guns from CO19 appeared with their leader, DCI Price; then Clay and three hostage negotiation officers; his own team: Bellwood, Feldman, Corrigan, Gold and Leung all waiting for him to speak.

Beside him, Henshaw spoke softly. 'Tell them, David.'

Language deserted him. She was delivering on her death threat.

'You can't go in there alone, David,' said Bellwood.

Clay cut in, 'No way, David. Rule number one. Do not put yourself at risk of being taken hostage.'

'We looked at a map of the area round the school on the way over.'

Price sailed across Clay. 'Are these kids armed? Corrigan wasn't one hundred per cent. Do we know where they are in the building?'

'Bellwood texted me,' said Gold. 'I called Mrs Price, the head teacher. If they're in the hall, it's at the back of the building and it's the weakest spot in the school in terms of a point of entry.'

Rosen raised a hand for silence and forced himself to speak. 'We'll assume she's got Trent's gun. She's given me ten minutes to go in there. She has hostages. . .'

'Give me the number she called you from,' said Susan Clay.

Rosen pulled up Stevie's details and reeled off eleven digits to the operative in the telecommunications van. 'Call her now!' she ordered.

'. . . and in nine minutes we're going to find out if she means it.'

'She means it,' said Henshaw. 'She'll do it!'

'Doug!' Rosen turned to Price. 'Get your men into position. She can see out but we can't see in. My guess is all the windows have blinds closed.'

'DCI Price,' Henshaw butted in. 'As your officers move into position' – he addressed the six officers directly – 'conceal your weapons as best you can. If she sees you approaching with guns, she could flip out and torch the hostages.'

Price deployed the men, two to the front, two to the side, and one on either side of the building.

Residents had begun pouring silently from open doors and were directed to either end of the road before being escorted away by uniformed officers.

'Susan!' A hostage negotiator called from the back of the telecommunications van, a phone in his hand. 'She told me she's taken five minutes off the ten because Rosen's not playing the game right. Then she hung up.'

Rosen walked away a small distance, turned his back to try and create a fragile privacy. Three silent fire engines turned the corner. He pressed SARAHMOBILE on speed dial. He looked at his watch as the phone rang out and time poured away. Henshaw was at his shoulder.

'This is a private call, James.'

'I'm sorry. But she's got nothing to lose. Don't do it, David!' Henshaw backed off as Sarah picked up.

He heard Joe cooing, playing at speech.

'He's awake, would you believe,' said Sarah. 'Have you found them?'

'Yes.' He looked at the front door of the school. It would take ten seconds to cross that distance.

'David?'

'Yes, love.'

'What's wrong?'

'I'll see you later, Sarah.'

'Is it a siege?'

'Yes.'

'What are you going to do?'

'Get them out alive.'

A thought cut him to pieces. *This could be the last time we speak.*

'What's happening?' Her anxiety was sudden and complete. 'What's wrong? Tell me.'

'I've got to go.'

'Wait.'

'I love you.' In a moment, he felt his face turn crimson under the sheer weight of terror that mounted inside him.

'And we love you,' she said. They were safe, away from the horror. Tenderness crept through the wall of fear.

Something flared on the flat roof of the school.

Fire.

Fire ran in a line from the back of the building to the front, chasing down a river of petrol, connecting with a target, a bundle of shadows, a form.

'How much danger are you in?'

'If it was Joe, I'd want someone, some stranger, to try and save him.'

A noise. Confusion. Terror. A human being waking into horror. The burning form on the roof moved. Fire engulfed Mr Finn.

'David, I love you so much.' He heard tears in her voice. 'We both do.'

The form was waking into agony, rolling and making an inarticulate sound.

'I love you, Sarah. I love Joe.' *But I have no choice.*

Rosen closed the call down just before the screaming started.

On fire from head to foot, Alec Finn rose up to his knees, his arms outstretched, his screams intensifying.

He fell from the flat roof to the ground below.

She had drawn him to this place, just as she'd drawn him from the Portakabin onto Bannerman Square, and now that he had arrived, she'd used Finn to show him a vision of the children's future – their fate and his. He was no more than a fly that she would pluck the wings off and cast into the flames.

Finn rolled on the ground, sobbing.

He thought of Sarah and her voice sounded inside him: '*Walk away.*'

Rosen wanted to run.

He turned. A sea of faces watched him. Bellwood. Corrigan. Feldman. Gold. Leung. Henshaw. Numbness split the terror inside him and he felt as if he was drifting out of his own body.

'Less than a minute,' said Susan Clay.

Rosen took out his phone, called Bellwood's mobile and added in Gold, Feldman, Corrigan, Price, Leung and Henshaw as a conference call.

Walking towards the front door, he called back, 'You'll all have a soundtrack of what's going on in the building. You can hear me, but I can't hear you. Carol's in charge of operations from outside. I'm going in!'

The smell of burning flesh invaded Rosen's nose and the dying man's agony pounded in his ears. He kept his eyes off the twitching form of Alec Finn.

He glanced at the plaque commemorating the Rainer sisters.

His fear that one day he would come home and his son wouldn't recognize him altered, simplified itself. One day, he simply wouldn't come home, and Joe would have no memory of him at all.

He reached the school's front door and stopped.

'I'm not going in,' he said to himself. Rosen thought of Joe, newborn, naked and helpless, needing everything he could give him.

He made to turn but then a light came on in the corridor. At the far end, he saw Luke Booth tied to a chair, crying, unable to move.

Macy appeared behind Luke and called, 'Mr Rosen, you have seconds or else.'

She dragged Luke out of sight and the light went out.

He turned to the officers behind him and ordered, 'Stay back!'

Rosen turned the handle and, opening the door, stepped into the darkness.

94

9.35 P.M.

The smell of petrol threatened to overwhelm him. Rosen walked towards the internal door connecting reception to the central corridor of the school, opened it and reached for the wall lights. Along the corridor a series of fluorescent strip lights blinked into life and, in the flashes of illumination, Rosen saw a pool of blood on the floor. He followed the trail leading from that pool down the corridor to a jagged rock on which a clump of human hair was glued by blood and tissue.

At the far end of the corridor, Macy reappeared, stepping sideways from a room Rosen guessed was the school hall. She stood perfectly still, the strobe effect of the flickering fluorescents giving her a ghostly aura.

'Turn the light off, Mr Rosen.'

Rosen turned the light off. The corridor was plunged once more into darkness, moonlit through skylights in the ceiling.

In the blue darkness, she looked tiny, small enough to pick up and put in a pocket, a doll. She was perfectly still, and Rosen echoed her stillness.

He sensed a presence near him. A classroom door was open and, in the shadows, the burglar alarm sensor in the corner clicked and the red light winked.

He felt something creep round the edge of his shoe, a subtle but undeniable weight. The pool of blood had seeped towards him, touching his foot.

Macy stepped sideways towards the hall and Rosen took a step towards the classroom door. The windows of the classroom were covered with blinds; he knew he was inside a space invisible to the outside world.

'What are you doing?' she asked.

'I've come to see you. Where are you all, whereabouts in the school?' He hoped for an answer that would benefit Bellwood and the others outside.

'The big hall. Have you got a gun?'

'No. I wouldn't want to hurt you, Macy.'

'Really? If you're lying to me, Mr Rosen. . .' She raised her arm and shook a fist. The rattle of a box of matches. She pointed at him. 'Bad guy!' And then in the direction of the hall. 'Dead baby!'

'I understand. Trust me, Macy—'

'Don't say that name!'

'Trust me, I haven't got a gun. Have you got a gun?'

'Maybe. I am sorry about Mr Finn.'

'What happened to Mr Finn?'

'Someone hit him on the head with a rock and someone asked someone else to drag him down the corridor and through the hall to the stairs behind the door. Then someone opened the skylight on the flat roof and someone and someone else dragged him to the front of the roof. Someone splashed petrol on Mr Finn's face and someone slapped him till his eyes opened. And then someone poured more petrol on him and made a trail of petrol from the skylight all along the roof and someone went back down and then came back and lifted the skylight a teeny-weeny bit and set the petrol on fire. And you know whose fault that was?'

'Whose fault was it?'

'It was your fault, Mr Rosen.'

'How's that?'

'Because we asked you in and you stayed outside. Someone had to show you that you have to do as you are TOLD!' With each word she had grown more irate, and by the end of her explanation, she was screaming.

'I'm very sorry for keeping someone waiting.'

She breathed in and out deeply, sharply, several times. Rosen used the distraction to speak slowly and quietly to Bellwood. 'Skylight on roof. Source of fire. Stairs down into hall.'

'Will you do as you're told now?' Just as she had ascended into rage, so she quickly calmed down.

'Yes, I will do my very best to do as I am told.'

She rattled the box of matches. 'Come down here, Mr Rosen.' She walked into the hall and Rosen followed her down the corridor, each step made sticky with Alec Finn's blood. The smell of petrol intensified and there were splashes of it on the vinyl floor tiles.

He whispered into his phone, 'Carol, I'm walking down to the hall. The place is soaked in petrol. She has a box of matches. I can't hear any voices from the hall but I had the strangest sense there was someone else here. There isn't. There isn't. There can't be.'

From the wall outside a classroom, three doors from the hall, Rosen lifted a mounted fire extinguisher with his right hand. He looked to the left: an open cloakroom. He snatched the nearest of three forgotten coats – anything with which to fight fire.

At the open door of the hall, he dropped the coat and left the fire extinguisher on top of it, careful not to make a sound, to antagonize her in any way.

In the hall, the smell of petrol hit the back of his throat and he had to stifle a cough.

'Stop!' she commanded.

Rosen halted in the doorway. He could see a third of the hall, the central section, but there was no sign of the children. Frosted glass on either side of the door blocked his view. 'Where are you, Mr Rosen?'

'I'm standing in the doorway to the hall.'

'What are you seeing, Mr Rosen?'

'I can see the wall bars for gym on the wall opposite me.'

'What are you seeing near your foot?'

'I can see a green first aid box and an unwrapped length of gauze. . . Oh, Jesus,' he whispered, anticipating what was to come.

'You said you'd do as you're told. Didn't you?'

'I did say I'd do my best to do as I was told.'

'Then pick up the gauze and tie it around your eyes. Your eyes will not deceive. Do it. On Beltaine Night, even the moon is blind.'

He picked up the length of gauze and dug his nails into the fabric, ripping the threads. His heart pounded and his head span. Sweat rolled down his face and spine.

'Hurry up, Mr Rosen.'

On a wall board, outside the hall, was a display called Family. He glanced at the pictures, his eyes drawn to a central image of a plump, kindly looking old lady with silver hair and round-rimmed glasses. *My grandmother by Macy Conner*. He drank in the image with his eyes and the caption: *She smells sweet, like cinnamon.*

He bound the gauze around his head, positioning the narrow slit he had managed to make close to his eyes. It was as if they were almost but not completely closed.

'Ready?'

'Ready,' replied Rosen.

'Walk in five paces.'

He walked the five paces, precisely and with caution, fearing a fall from the petrol splashes he detected beneath his feet. He could make out the wall bars.

'Turn ninety degrees clockwise.'

Slowly, he followed the instruction, catching the form of Luke tied to a chair. The lack of any noise from the child filled him with rising dread.

She was standing to his right. Chester, in the space between Macy and Luke, was motionless, like a living statue.

'Walk forward five steps.'

Five steps later, she was still several steps away from him.

'Can you still hear my voice, Mr Rosen?'

'Yes, I can hear your voice.'

'Is that a phone in your pocket at the front of your jacket?'

'Yes, it is a phone at the front of my jacket.'

'Is it turned on?' Macy sounded anxious and angry.

'No.'

'Take the phone out of your pocket and throw it to the sound of my voice.'

His heartbeat increased. Taking the phone from his pocket, he turned it off and, tossing it towards Macy's voice, threw away his only thread to the outside world.

95

9.45 P.M.

As their link to Rosen died, Bellwood and Corrigan paused at the skylight. The fire on the roof was extinguished and, below, Alec Finn's body had been removed by paramedics.

'Damn! Damn it to hell!' whispered Bellwood fiercely. She put her fire extinguisher down. Gold and Feldman arrived, each with an extinguisher, which they too abandoned.

'The little bitch has taken his phone,' said Gold, quietly. 'That's the end of that plan then.'

'No, it's not,' said Bellwood, picking up her extinguisher again. 'We'll go ahead with it – we just won't have the benefit of sound. We'll take the fire extinguishers down the stairs and wait. We'll improvise. If she starts a fire, Corrigan goes to assist Luke, I go for Chester, Gold, you go to the boss and Feldman to Macy.' She sensed a frisson of resistance to this and waited for someone to say, *Maybe we should just leave her, put her out of her misery*, but no one said a word.

She scanned their faces. They were all good men and their faces were wracked with the same stress and tension that was eating her. Bellwood thought, *In this situation, what would Rosen say?*

'There are four people in there alive at the moment, and our operational objective is to bring four people out alive. Hopefully, uninjured. And if injured. . . with those injuries minimized by us because we were quick and we're good at our jobs. And tomorrow, we'll know we took personal risks to save others. We were fair.'

Gold picked up an extinguisher. 'I'm with you, Carol!'

She pointed at the skylight. 'Quietly! Let's go!'

96

9.46 P.M.

'I've been waiting for you to come back to be with me, so I didn't die alone. I'm going to tell you what is happening because you cannot see, Mr Rosen.'

Rosen stayed motionless, the perfect stillness of the blind. Only his eyes moved. The hall was divided into two halves down the middle, the halves separated by a liquid line. The space reeked of petrol. Behind the line, Macy held a metal can in her hand.

'I'm preparing the human sacrifice.'

She poured a slow stream of petrol on her head and body.

Liquid dripped from Chester, formed a pool at his feet. Luke, tied to a chair, had his head slumped, eyes closed.

She tossed the can across the line in Rosen's direction.

'What do you think about that, Mr Rosen?'

The can bounced from his feet, lines of petrol lacing his clothes.

'I said, what do you think about that?'

'I'm sorry about your grandma.'

'Grandma? *You* couldn't see *her*.'

'Oh, yes, *I* could see *her*,' said Rosen.

'When I went to hospital, she was there, so were you, but you couldn't see her.'

'She has long white hair and a pair of glasses, round-rimmed glasses, and behind the glasses, kind, blue eyes. . .' Rosen said.

'And?'

'She wears a long white gown, a dress maybe, maybe a nightdress because she's been ill in bed since she came to live with you in the summer. But you've been good to her, an angel. I'm touching her hand. It is warm and I can feel the bones and the veins and she smiles at me. She tells me she loves you to read to her and that's why she gave you a letter to take to Tim, the kind man in the library, so that you can take books out of the library for Grandma.'

'She's dead. She died last night.'

'Last night, I went to visit her.'

'You didn't.'

'You were in Chelsea's, minding Luke.'

'She's dead.'

'She told me she loves you.'

'She's dead.'

'She loves you with all her heart.'

'Love is dead.'

'She told me to ask you to come to me.'

'She's dead.'

It was as if the ugly truth was dawning on her. Rosen stretched his arms in her direction.

'Come to me, come to me. . .' urged Rosen.

'I need to bring her back.' She shut her eyes, deep in concentration. 'How?'

Rosen took a step forward.

'How? Come on, come to me, I'll show you how.'

'How, I know how. But I can't remember.' She touched her own head. 'It's here, right in here but I'm blocking it out. . .' Tears of frustration rolled down her face. 'Grandma, how do I get you back?' she screamed. 'Grandma? How?'

358

Rosen's ears rang and his whole being was pierced by the agony in her voice.

He stepped forward, could feel himself shaking.

She looked at Rosen.

'Grandma?' Macy howled and howled.

The sound of her name seemed to remain in the air long after the tormented scream ended.

Silence.

Rosen took a step closer.

'Stop!' She held a hand out, rattled the matches. 'I know how. It's come back to me. Sacrifice. Then she'll return and I'll return and we'll be together, nothing in between us, just us, together. No more Ash. No more Oak. Just me and her. On Beltaine Night, the night of the Beltaine Fires.'

Rosen flicked a glance at Chester. His breathing pattern was shifting, each breath coming faster than the last, and then he made a noise that sounded like a sleeper's helpless cry from the depths of a nightmare.

She shook the box of matches.

'Sacrifice, that's how.'

'Sacrifice, that's not how. When I saw your grandma last night, she told me to tell you.'

'What did she tell you?'

'To tell you it wasn't your fault what happened to the Rainer sisters.'

'But their dad said—'

'Do you believe *him*?'

'—it was. . . me that set the fire. . .'

'Or do you believe your grandma?'

'But everybody said it was me.'

'Everybody except your grandma. And me. I've passed on the message now, from your grandma. And another thing, she asked me to take care of you.'

'She did?'

'Yes, Macy, she did, and she smelled of cinnamon. Sweet and lovely Grandma asked me to take care of you.' He stepped forward and her hand stayed down. Another step towards the petroleum line and she stayed perfectly still. 'And that's exactly what I'm going to do. I'm going to do as I was told by your grandma and she told me to take care of you. You're not going back to the flat, you're not going back to your mother. . .'

'Where. . .?'

'Go on, Macy, where. . .?' prompted Rosen.

'Where am I going?'

Luke lifted his head, the gag fell from his mouth as he opened his eyes and after a moment of perfect stillness and silence, the little boy cried, a sudden cry that built to screaming pitch.

Chester threw his arms out. The boy was in the early stages of an epileptic fit.

Macy looked at the source of the sound. Chester collapsed and flailed his limbs on the floor.

The noise and action acted as a trigger.

'Where am I going?' she screamed.

'You're coming with me.'

'I'm going mad!'

'Come with me.'

'Fucking maaaad, that's where I'm going!'

She pushed the box and lid apart.

'And Death has said *Now* and I have said *Yes*!'

On the floor, Chester slammed his arms closer and closer to the chair on which Luke was tied, his mouth jabbering. Luke shrieked.

She took out a match. Her eyes skimmed from the tip to the side of the box.

Chester's right arm connected with the metal leg of Luke's chair.

Luke's chair turned over and skidded across the floor. He screamed at top volume.

360

She covered her ears and screamed, 'Stop it! Stop it! Stop it! Go away, all of you, go away, leave me alone!'

Rosen took two steps forward.

'Go away!'

Luke's head was in the petroleum line. Chester lay directly in the same line, kicking and grabbing thin air. Rosen ripped the gauze from his eyes. *Go for Macy?*

She placed the tip of the match against the emery. *Human inferno . . .*

'Grandma, I am coming with you. Death. Now. Yes.' *Him and her first . . .*

The rasp of the match on the rough paper. No strike.

Get them out! He threw himself at Luke and Chester, slipped and fell. *Get them out, away, fast!*

'Fire! Fire! Fire! Fire!'

On his knees, Rosen grabbed hold of Luke's leg and dragged. His other hand reached out to Chester but he couldn't make the distance. He held the toddler to himself, turned the child's sobbing face into the bulk of his body.

'Macy!' A voice drifted from the shadows at the back of the hall. Footsteps on broken glass. Macy froze, looked across the ocean that was the hall and Rosen followed her gaze.

Paul Conner stepped from the darkness, a gun in the hand of his outstretched arm.

'Paul?' whispered Macy.

'You want a sacrifice, a human sacrifice?' Paul looked directly at Macy.

Rosen reached out a hand to pull Luke further out of the direct line of petrol.

Paul pointed the gun at him. 'Don't move, Rosen! You want a human sacrifice?' He walked slowly towards his sister.

She dragged the match roughly over the sandpaper. Still it failed to light.

361

'You want a human sacrifice?'

She dropped the match and, hands shaking, took another from the box.

Paul turned the gun away from Rosen and pointed it at Macy.

She jabbed and jabbed at her temple and begged, 'Right here! Right here!'

'I've got one bullet left.' Paul pointed the gun at his own temple.

'Paul? Take the matches off her, Paul!' said Rosen with a calmness that defied the fathomless depths of his terror.

'It's got to stop!' she screamed. And then in a whisper, 'It's got to stop.'

'Do you know why I followed you here, Macy?' asked Paul. Within touching distance of her, he took the gun away from his head.

He leaned forward and kissed her on the cheek, his gun and eyes now on Rosen.

'I listened to you, Macy. I listened to those voices of yours. I listened to your plans. I knew you were coming here tonight, so I followed. Do you know why I followed you here?' The question sounded desperate and sad.

'No,' said Macy.

He stooped and their eyes locked.

'I followed you here because I love you.'

She was frozen.

The gun still on Rosen, he watched Paul's finger on the trigger. The air was thick with petrol fumes. If he pulled the trigger, the whole room would turn into a fire storm.

Paul Conner reached his free hand out and took the matches from his sister.

He threw them way out of her reach.

'This is the last time I'll see you, Macy,' said Paul, his voice marbled with tenderness. 'You don't remember the first time I saw you. I do.'

The harrowed cast of his face softened. 'I was eight years old; you

362

were eight hours old. I came to the hospital to see you. I – I'd waited for you for months. You were in a cot. I looked at you and your eyes were shut and I thought you were asleep. I couldn't take my eyes off you because you were the most beautiful thing I'd ever seen. And then it happened. Slowly, slowly, your eyelids flickered and you opened your eyes. You opened your eyes and I fell in love. It was the first time that I'd known love. So, Macy, whatever happens to you, please believe me, and remember as long as you live, you were the only love I ever knew. You were the love of my life, my one reason for being. You were loved by me and you are my love.'

He kissed his fingertips and touched her face. He turned the gun away from Rosen. Slowly, he walked backwards, away from Macy.

'Macy, we were born in Hell. None of this is your fault. Close your eyes and keep them closed.'

She closed her eyes and replied, 'Yes, Paul, we were born in Hell. Paul? You were loved by me and you are my love. You do know that?'

'I know and I'm happy about that.'

'Can you take me with you, Paul?'

On the edge of the darkness, he paused. 'Death has said?'

'Now,' said Macy.

He smiled. 'And I have said yes, Macy.'

Raising the gun towards his face, Paul Conner edged into the darkness.

Rosen placed Luke down and hurtled across the hall.

'Paul, don't, don't pull that trigger!'

Rosen arrived at the back of the hall. Paul Conner knelt on a bed of glass, his body a diagonal line. With his neck on the jagged window frame and his face and head outside the broken window, he swallowed the barrel of the gun and tilted it towards his brain.

Moonlight. For a moment, his eyes connected with Rosen's.

He pulled the trigger. The gunshot echoed in the night air. Paul's body slumped into death and Rosen felt the weight of the whole world pressing down on him.

Footsteps on the outside hurrying towards the school.

Macy? Rosen turned and hurried back. She was rigid on the spot, her eyes still tightly shut. He picked her up, hands under her arms, a dead weight.

As he lay Macy down on the floor, she opened her eyes and looked at him.

To the right, the door to the skylight staircase opened.

'Paul?' said Macy. A single tear rolled down her face. Rosen sat beside her.

Bellwood, Corrigan, Gold and Feldman came through the doorway. Rosen indicated Chester and Luke with a nod of the head. They moved towards the children.

'I'm, I'm – I am . . . I am . . . in agony, Mr Rosen,' Macy spoke softly. 'That is the thing I forgot to tell you when we first met. I am in agony because I was born in Hell.'

He lifted her shoulders from the floor and wrapped his arms around her. She pressed her face into his chest, her body heaving with sobs.

Bellwood carried Luke past Rosen, their eyes connecting.

'David, there's been another incident on Bannerman Square.'

And with that she took the little boy away.

Paramedics arrived. Rosen watched. Chester, on a stretcher bed, was wheeled from the hall. A second team appeared in the doorway. Rosen held a hand up to stop them entering and shook his head. Too late. They moved back into the corridor.

'Keep your eyes closed, Macy,' said Rosen.

In the unfolding of time, he released her from his embrace and moved her so that her back was turned to the shadows in which her brother's body lay.

'Help me, Mr Rosen.'

'I will help you, Macy. Ready to go?'

He stood up and lifted her by her hands. His left hand held on to

364

her right hand and they walked out of the hall and into the corridor.

Rosen gave DS Eleanor Willis, Scientific Support, the go-ahead to enter and pointed in the direction of Paul Conner's body.

As they walked up the corridor, Macy said, 'Promise me, Mr Rosen, you're not taking me to Bannerman Square.'

'I promise you, Macy, I'm not taking you to Bannerman Square.'

'You're not taking me home?'

'No, you're not going home.'

'The police station?'

'No, you're not going to the police station.'

'Then where are you taking me?'

'I'm taking you to a place where you'll be safe.'

97

10.32 P.M.

Rosen dipped under the scene-of-crime tape at the door of the flat where Macy Conner once lived, thinking, knowing, *She'll never come back here.* The thought comforted him.

He moved aside in the narrow hall to allow two mortuary technicians carrying a grey body-bag to pass. Bellwood was in the living room, looking out of the window where a crowd was gathered and police cars were parked.

Everything in the dismal living room was as it had been, except for one thing.

The walls were splattered with blood.

Bellwood turned. In her hand was a piece of paper in a clear evidence bag.

'You've phoned Sarah?' she checked.

'Soon as I handed Macy over to our child protection officer.' He indicated the bag in her hand. 'Paul Conner's suicide note?' asked Rosen. She nodded. 'What happened?'

'It must've been just after you left. Paul turned up here with Trent's gun and shot his mother in the head. It was Paul, not Trent, who took out the CCTV on Bannerman Square. He used the same silencer when he shot his mother.'

'Did he write much else?' asked Rosen.

'Plenty. He abducted Thomas Glass as a reprisal against John Glass. Glass had ripped him off – he didn't go into the details. Macy tailed him to the lock-up he'd rented where he had Thomas holed up. When Macy found out what Paul had done, she had him over a barrel. She threatened him with the police unless she could have a copy of the key and access to Thomas Glass. Paul was desperately trying to buy time, trying to think of a way out of the hole he'd dug himself into and he agreed to her demands. He was overwhelmed with fear about the consequences of what he'd done, but then guilt kicked in and he couldn't bear to go near Thomas or the lock-up. Macy told her brother she could sort the problem out, she could make Thomas believe anything she wanted him to believe.'

'Where did Trent fit in to this?' asked Rosen.

'Trent knew nothing of any of this at that point. She had regular access to Trent's house because of her *friendship* with Chester. And the front door key that Chester provided for her. She made a secret pornographic film of her brother and Trent. . .'

'I've seen it,' said Rosen, recalling a dismal memory.

'Paul confessed to Trent, who was all for tearing Macy into tiny pieces. At which point Macy sent a copy of the film to Trent's phone using Thomas's BlackBerry, showing him sodomizing her brother. She threatened to post it on the internet, and so had Trent eating out of her hand.'

'He wanted a ransom from John Glass?'

'That was a part of the original idea. Bitter resentment and desperation. He was out of his depth from the word go.'

Rosen looked around at the grim walls of the flat, Paul Conner's reality.

'So, he started one thing,' said Rosen, 'and it turned into something else. Teenage boy. Stupid. Out-manoeuvred by his smarter kid sister. Who messed her face up?'

'Paul. But that was only because she told him to. Where is she?' asked Bellwood.

'She's sedated in hospital. She's going into a secure unit, looks like she's being moved out of London. She'll have care twenty-four-seven.'

Bellwood digested the information and asked, 'Want to know what the last line of his letter said?' Rosen nodded. '"I'd rather kill myself than go to jail but before I do that, I want the satisfaction of taking the bitch out with me and then maybe Macy will stand a chance."'

'You heard back yet from Julian Parker, Glass's PA?' asked Rosen 'No.'

'Call him. Tell him to report to Isaac Street now for an interview.' Rosen glanced at his watch. On the road to eleven o'clock. 'I don't care if he's in bed. I'm not going home until I get to the bottom of this.'

'David, one other thing.' She produced a small transparent evidence bag inside which was a photograph of Rosen. He recognized it immediately as the image that appeared in the central photos from the book, *Herod: Portrait of a Serial Killer*.

He recalled the loans lists he'd seen that morning in Lewisham Library.

'She must've cut it out from a library book,' said Rosen. 'Where did you find it?'

Bellwood looked in the direction of Macy's bedroom. 'On her bed. Under what passed for a pillow.'

Rosen looked and, for a moment, felt himself drowning in sadness.

'OK, Carol.' He pulled himself together. 'Let's hear what Julian Parker has to say.'

98

11.05 P.M.

Julian Parker faced Rosen and Bellwood from the chair occupied earlier by Jay Trent.

'"Not now,"' said Bellwood. 'Those were the words you used when we were with Emily Glass, when I pointed out the contact detail for Fingertips. Can you fill me in on that?'

'It's an escort agency. John Glass has a controlling sixty per cent share in it. Emily knows nothing about it, or knew nothing about it.' He paused. 'How can I put this. . .?'

'Try plainly,' said Rosen.

'John Glass sleeps with prostitutes on a regular basis. So he was mixing business with pleasure, that way he didn't have to pay for the goods in his own company. But that's not the end of it. He took an interest in the charity Outlook because he saw it primarily as a source of cheap labour, all these unemployed kids from south London. He started finding work for them, the girls and some of the boys. As escorts. When the genuine people at Outlook found out, they referred their organization immediately to the Charity Commission.'

'Paul Conner was an escort?' asked Bellwood.

'No, but what happened to him is pretty much typical of the way the escorts were treated by Glass. Paul was a talented artist. When

Thomas wanted his room painted with a mural, Emily got quotes from professional artists. They all ranged in the low four figures. John vetoed it on the grounds of cost and then had the bright idea of using Paul. They agreed a figure. Five hundred pounds. Paul did the work. John said the quality wasn't good enough. He instructed me to issue cash in an envelope because Conner didn't have a bank account.'

'How much did he pay him?'

'Two hundred pounds. I know. Despicable, isn't it? I'm happy to say I no longer work for him.'

'So what was the upshot of all this?' asked Rosen. 'What was Paul Conner's immediate reaction?'

'He phoned me and asked to speak to John. I told him he was unavailable and would he like to leave a message. He said he would.'

'What did he say?'

'He said, "Tell your boss I've got nothing to live for and nothing to lose but what I am going to do is fuck him up for the rest of his life."'

'Did you get a ransom demand?'

'No, not that I know of.' Julian rubbed his fingertips against his thumbs. 'Ultimately, his meanness cost him his son's life. If he hadn't shafted Paul Conner, none of this would have happened. None of it.'

'Thank you for attending. You're free to go now.'

99

11.32 P.M.

In the empty incident room, with nothing more to be done, Bellwood dug her car keys out of her bag but looked up as the main door opened.

'Hi, Carol, have you seen David?' James Henshaw walked into the room.

'He's just gone home, James.'

'It'll wait until morning. Goodnight, Carol.'

As he got to the door, he stopped at Carol's voice.

'Fancy a drink, James?'

He turned and, after a few moments, said, 'No, thank you. I want to go home. I want to see my son, I want to see him sleeping safely in his bed.'

'Understandable,' said Carol, disguising the sting of disappointment and telling herself James was being a good father.

He looked torn: to speak or not to speak? 'He's been through an awful lot for such a young boy,' said James. 'He lost his mother two years ago, when he was five.'

'I'm aware of that and I'm deeply sorry.' It had been in a road traffic accident in the South of France. When she'd attended his lectures, Bellwood had googled him to check out his academic credentials and had learned a whole lot more.

'You know, this whole business. . . it's rattled me. Goodnight, Carol, and thanks for the offer. I appreciate it.'

The door closed and he was gone. With no one to pretend in front of, Carol let out a deep sigh of frustration and felt her tired spirit curl up inside her.

She took a deep breath and waited, not wanting to see James in the car park, not wanting to see anyone at that moment in time.

The door opened and Henshaw stepped back inside.

'I've been meaning to say to you. . .'

'Yes, James,' she chirped, with false lightness.

'September, I'm running a profiling course for Met officers, limited places, there's probably going to be a lot of applications.'

'I'll put my name down and hope for the best.'

'Oh, no,' said James, surprised. 'No, I've been meaning to say to you, if you want to come on the course, just say the word and your place is guaranteed.'

'Thanks, James. Yeah, put me on that list.'

'And would you like to go for lunch on Monday? I can fill you in on the details.'

'Monday?' It was clear as a bell what she was going to say next, but she gave the impression of thinking about it. 'Yes,' she said. 'I think I can do Monday.'

'Great,' said James. 'Call me and let me know where you'd like to go.' He grinned at her and left.

She sat down at her desk and felt a smile break out on her face.

Inside her, two bright sparks connected and the flame of hope erupted into life.

100

11.50 P.M.

Sarah opened the front door. Her face was red, her eyes raw, and her irises seemed drained of their colour. For a series of moments, Rosen was tongue-tied as he read the anguish in her face. Guilt coursed through him as he stepped over the threshold of his home.

'How long have you been back from Orpington?' asked David.

'Not long.'

She closed the door and neither of them moved. Then, she kissed him on the cheek, her fingers brushing lightly on his throat.

In the familiarity of home, he suddenly became aware that he'd dragged the outside world in with him. The stench of petrol, which had dried into his skin and clothes, overpowered the hall.

'Go into the kitchen,' she said. 'I've poured you a Jameson's. It's on the sink. Strip your clothes off. I'll run the bath and bring you your robe down.'

'Thank you.'

She looked directly at him.

'You didn't have to go in there, David.'

He watched as she turned and walked upstairs, and wished she'd slapped him hard on his face rather than kissing him and welcoming him home.

In the kitchen, he downed the drink and slowly started stripping off his clothes. He found a bin liner under the sink and dropped into it his shoes and trousers, and wondered what he could say to Sarah when she came back.

In the bathroom above the kitchen, pipes rumbled as the bath filled with hot water. His shirt and jacket, and underwear, were the last items into the bag. He pulled the drawstring and, opening the back door, tossed it out into the garden.

As he relocked the door, Sarah entered the kitchen.

'I'm sorry for what I've put you through.'

'The news said two lives were lost.'

'One murder, one suicide.'

'How many lives were saved?'

'Including mine?'

She was drifting towards him, an almost imperceptible motion. The kitchen was dark and her face was washed with moonlight.

'Including yours.'

'Four.' He touched his chest and said, 'One adult. Three children.'

'You'll have to throw your clothes away.'

'I knew you'd say that. I already have done.'

'It said on the news about gunshots and an adult male' – silently, tears rolled down her face and they sank into each other – 'I had visions. . .'

Shock caught up with him. The adrenaline that had kept him going ebbed and he felt like he was going to faint. Sarah pushed against him, propping him up between the back door and her own body. 'What would have become of us? Did you think of Joe and me?'

'Of course I did.'

'But you still went in?'

'Sarah, I was lucky tonight. Next time, if there is a next time, I won't tempt fate. I swear to you.'

She weaved her hand into his and, leading him from the kitchen to the stairs, she said softly, 'Come on, you stupid, stupid man.'

In the warm water of the bath, he stared into space.

She massaged shampoo into his scalp. On the surface of the water, there were rainbows of petrol.

'Three children saved?'

'Yes, three.'

She took the shower attachment and rinsed his hair.

'Maybe one day, someone will save Joe's life,' she observed.

'Do you forgive me?'

'I'm working on it. Stand up.'

He stood up and she turned on the shower.

'Rinse yourself down.'

From the bedroom, Joe cried from his Moses basket and Sarah went to be with him.

Hot water coursed down the pathways of Rosen's body and, after a minute of showering, he was wide awake. Dry and in his dressing gown, he went into their bedroom, where Sarah was feeding Joe with a bottle. He sat beside them on the bed.

She took the bottle away and, without a word, David took his baby son and the bottle from his wife. He stared into his son's half-shut eyes. He looked up, and something had shifted in Sarah's face. She looked on her husband and son with complete love. It was the same look he returned to her.

Calm minutes passed and Joe's eyes started closing fully.

Rosen placed the bottle on the bedside table and Sarah took the baby from him. He looked at his son and was grateful to the core of his being that the three of them were together and safe behind the locked doors of their home.

Sarah lay Joe down in his basket. 'He can sleep in here with us tonight. Just tonight, mind.' She turned off the light.

He lay down next to Sarah and she curled herself into the shape of his body. Slowly, he felt himself drifting away. Random light danced in the darkness of his mind's eye. And, between the light and dark,

Macy's face formed, her eyes open, staring directly and without any visible emotion. Then her eyes closed and her face dissolved into the dark. He felt himself sinking, the image of her face fading. Her mouth opened and her voice drifted across Rosen's unfolding consciousness.

'I've got to go now,' she whispered.

Her face dissolved and the light died.

He felt Sarah's shape fitting into his body, two parts of the same unit. From the side of the bed, he heard Joe breathing. Rosen opened his eyes and looked over to the Moses basket. A beam of moonlight strayed through a chink in the curtains and played on his little boy's sleeping face. He reached his hand out and stroked Joe's silky hair.

You're going to be fine, thought Rosen. *Just fine.*

As he settled back on the pillow, he slipped quickly towards sleep, and his last waking thought was amazing. Something unique and beautiful was approaching fast.

Tomorrow. An ordinary day.